Combat Fatigue

MW01593502

I really enjoyed dropping bombs.

Manfred von Richthofen

TABLE OF CONTENTS

HOME IS WHERE THE HEART IS

FEAR OF FLYING

GUILT IS GOOD

IN THE LION'S DEN

THERE IS A LIFE AFTER WAR

MY BIGGEST FANBASE IS IN BOSTON

HOW TO SEDUCE AN NCO IN 213 EASY STEPS

CASE CLOSED

I AM NOT A SOLDIER

June 2010

"Do you want a quick death or would you rather die slowly?"

The boy is leaning casually against the wall and seems to expect an answer from me. He is wearing a Doors T-shirt and looks no older than seventeen.

"Your English is great", I say. I mean it. There's an accent of course, but he pronounced every word the way it's supposed to be.

I'm trying to sweet-talk my jailer. Or my captor. Maybe he is my kidnapper's little brother. He hasn't introduced himself yet.

"You didn't answer my question."

I need to think. I've got to be cautious. It's important that he sees me as a person. He must see the suffering human being in me and not a representative of the enemy occupying his country.

I clear my throat. God, what I would give for a glass of cold, clear water. I can't really think of anything that could awaken his compassion.

"So what kind of rapid death are you offering? Beheading?"

He doesn't seem to know the word 'beheading'. But a proud Arab would never admit to a gap in his knowledge. I lift my right hand to my neck and make a self-explanatory move. Being a right hander, I'm actually quite glad that they chained my left hand to the wall. Things could be worse.

"And do you intend to film the whole thing?" I pretend to ask out of curiosity. I sound so detached, it's as if my potential decapitation had absolutely nothing to do with me.

The boy is visibly shocked. "Are you crazy? We're not Al Qaeda! If we decide on a quick death, then you get a bullet between the eyes. With the kind of ammo that won't make your head explode."

I nod. "Wouldn't be so great for the carpet. Or the wallpaper."

I know I'm not doing this right. Instead of showing him that I am a poor scared shitless little girl, I'm making fun of him. I take a deep breath.

Concentrate, for God's sake. This is as life-or-death as it gets!

The boy, too, has noticed that I'm way too casual. "Are you always this relaxed? It doesn't seem to bother you that you will die soon."

I shrug. Somehow my left shoulder isn't getting any better. There's a throbbing pain that sometimes fades away, only to come back later. "When I was your age, I was very insecure. I was so shy I hardly ever opened my mouth."

He scratches his belly, which makes Jim Morrison's face briefly disappear in a fold of his T-shirt. I focus on the other band members, but none of their names come to mind. I guess they were not as famous as Jim Morrison.

My remark about being shy seems to puzzle the boy. "If you used to be scared of people, how come you're not shitting your pants right now?"

Damn, his English is good! Do they learn this at school?

"I don't know. I'm probably not the girl I used to be. I'm all grown up now, I guess."

Our conversation is taking an absurd turn. What is he going to ask me next? If I had a good childhood?

"Well, I had to grow up when my father died and I became the head of my family", the boy explains to me. "And what turned you into an adult?"

I don't need to think about this. "Bagram Airfield."

"What's that?"

I can't help grinning. "A small American town in the middle of

Afghanistan that smells of waste incineration and kerosene. Nine hundred aircraft movements per day. Everyone has to wear a rifle, no round in the chamber, weapon on 'safe'. During the day, you have to be careful not to get caught with headphones in your ears because the military police will give you a ticket. And at night you have to watch out so you won't get raped on the way to the bathroom. You grow up real fast at Bagram."

The boy shakes his head. "I cannot believe they send women there. In my country, women are protected. How can you send girls into a war zone? Unbelievable."

I look at my left arm. It stopped hurting a couple of days ago, but the cast stinks. I should ask the boy if he's planning to take it off anytime soon, but I feel too weak to ask him for anything. It's tiring enough to answer the boy's questions.

"Tell me how you came up with the idea of becoming a soldier?"

"I'm not a soldier, I'm an Airman. In fact, I used to be a car mechanic. My father has a small workshop. And then I joined the Air Force and learned how to fix planes."

I move my left arm so that it rests on my lap, hoping that the boy will notice the unpleasant smell coming from my cast. "I live in Idaho with my family. I had a school friend who was very ambitious. He wanted to be an actor. So he had to move to the big city. "

"What does that have to do with my question?"

"Ah, the impatience of youth!"

We stare at each other for a while until I lose the duel and blink. "Do you want to hear the rest of the story now? You asked me what made me join the armed forces."

The boy nods.

"All right. Jesse moved to New York to conquer Broadway. One day, I went to see him there. The week in New York cost me two months' salary. I didn't want to be a burden because he only had this tiny room in a shared apartment, so I stayed in a hotel. And then I went back home."

The boy makes a sweeping motion with his arms on either side, as if to say: *So what?*

"It was shortly after 9/11. My flight was leaving from Newark, and I was hanging out in the terminal when I saw them. Two soldiers were guarding the entire airport by themselves. I thought they were Marines, but in hindsight I think they were National Guard. Back then I didn't know jack shit about the military. A man and a woman. They traipsed through the terminal in combat boots, their weapons dangling at their sides. They were very different from the rest of us. They had nothing to do with us civilians, as if they lived in a different world. I wanted to see their name tags, but I had to get closer. So I followed them, and after they spent some time just walking around the gates of Lufthansa and Air France, they turned back. They were heading right in my direction. I never got to decipher their name tags. The man looked at me, scanning my face for I-don't-know-what. As if I were a potential threat. My cheeks must have turned bright red."

I have to laugh for the first time in a week. "The woman walked past me real close. She winked at me."

The boy looks at me as if I had completely lost my mind. "And that's why you joined the military? Because somebody looked at you?"

"My heart was beating so fast, I don't think it slowed down until I was on the plane. And it took another few weeks until I realized that I didn't want my normal life any longer. I wanted to be part of something bigger."

I see a dawning understanding in the boy's face. "You wanted to go on an adventure."

I nod. "Yup. And I guess I got that adventure. Just not the way I had imagined."

And that realization has both of us laughing.

I LOVE BAGRAM

August 2004

To: idahoDad12@gmail.com
From: mars_air@yahoo.com
Re: Greetings from the desert

Dear Mommy, Daddy & Grandma,

Greetings from the first war zone where my country needs me. From here the Soviets tried to conquer and subdue Afghanistan. They didn't succeed. Should this be a warning sign? Of course not.

After all we're doing things differently. Outside the wire, we're trying to convince the Afghans of Western values, and we build roads and schools for them. And inside, we make ourselves super-comfortable with a Popeye's, Green Bean (some kind of military Starbucks), gyms, movie nights and a really nice PX where you can buy everything - TV sets, carpets, bicycles...

The guys in my unit seem to be alright, but they've been here much longer and know each other well, so I've got to admit I still feel like an outsider at the moment. But that's just temporary, I guess. Like I said, I'll stay inside at all times. I will get to see absolutely nothing of Afghanistan except the snow-capped mountains that surround us on three sides. In other words, there's nothing to worry about!

The most exciting thing that happened to me in the last six weeks was the flight from Ramstein. I'm attaching a picture of the monstrous C-17 Globemaster that is so big it can also transport tanks instead of people. When it does, it gets so heavy that it takes forever until it reaches its normal flight level. But that wasn't the case when I was on it. You have to imagine that you board the plane from the back, you walk over the

tailgate and then start looking for a seat. Space
is tight, especially because most people are
sitting in (almost) full battle dress. There are
no windows, no flight attendants, no display for
watching movies. During the flight the light
inside the cabin is kind of dark green. At least
you can't hear the men snore (I only saw one other
woman) because the engine noise is so loud (they
didn't waste much taxpayer's money on insulation).
And another difference between this and a
commercial flight is the way the pilots steer the
plane - it's much rougher. If the plane is
supposed to turn off to the right, then it jerks
to the right like, immediately. WHAM! to the
right. And landing at Bagram felt insanely
reckless, almost like a nosedive...

And that's why I love the military: everything is
different. This is exactly what I wanted. I'm very
happy here and I hope you guys don't worry about
me!

Tons and tons of love,

Marina

I was very proud of this email. Sitting still with my computer in my
lap after a thirteen-hour workday was not that easy. I had to pull
myself together to give my parents and my grandmother an
absolutely positive image of my work whenever I wrote to them. The
truth was more complicated and not as rosy as I painted my new life
at Bagram: as an aircraft mechanic, I probably had the most
thankless job in the Air Force. My colleagues and I slaved away
during long shifts and came back to our bunks exhausted from work
and smelling of hydraulic fluid. Our pay for a sixty-hour work week
was the same as the salary of someone sitting at a desk, and that guy
started his weekend after forty hours. Of course we worked in shifts.
All this was difficult even before Bagram, but here there was a lot
more pressure than what I'd experienced before in Spangdahlem or
in the States. The only consolation was that the pilots had no more
free weekends either.

Being an aircraft mechanic was not sexy - as opposed to actually flying the planes. I also felt inferior to the grunts who did the dirty work outside the wire and risked their lives on a daily basis. They were so tough they could go without sleep for days. These were the warriors everyone looked up to. We, however, were the idiots who kept the whole flight circus going. Without us the entire base wouldn't make any sense and there would be nothing to bomb the enemy with. But aircraft maintenance is like cleaning toilets: you only notice it when it's badly executed. I wasn't close enough to my co-workers to figure out if they were as frustrated as I was.

The worst thing about my misery was that the only one to blame was myself. I never wanted to join the Air Force in the first place. I wanted to fight. I dreamed of combat, picking off enemies from rooftops, kicking in doors, arresting terrorists. But my family had the last word in my career choices. It was three against one, and I never stood a chance. Marine Corps? No way! So they sent me to where they thought nothing could possibly happen to me.

It didn't take much to imagine my mother's horror when I called her from Texas to announce my deployment to Afghanistan, and I made it worse by mentioning it might be for a whole year. Most people in my career field worked stateside, but if they were assigned to a base outside the US, it was usually an exotic location in Europe or Asia. Normally the foreign assignment lasted just a few months but the Global War On Terror constantly needed new manpower, and I was now part of an insatiable war machine, cannon fodder like everyone else.

May the GWOT be with you.

To: jesse1983@hotmail.com
From: mars_air@yahoo.com
Re: Greetings from the desert

Hi Jesse,

Two months have gone by since I arrived on a planet called Bagram Air Field (BAF). Along with many civilians (who earn much more for their work) and soldiers from Poland, South Korea, France, Australia etc. And of course with my people. Long live the Air Force...

The first crazy thing I noticed after finding my quarters - in my case a plywood hut, which is divided into eight bunk-sized cubicles - is the traffic outside. Our main street is called Disney Drive, and crossing that road is no easy task, depending on the time of the day. It's constantly clogged with private cars and military vehicles. MPs are everywhere. You can get reprimanded for not wearing reflective belts (you need to be seen in the dark, otherwise you get run over by the Stryker brigade ;-). You salute officers at all times. Worst of all: I have to carry my rifle everywhere. I'm terrified of forgetting it at the chow hall or somewhere else someday. If I want to leave it at home, I have put on my PT clothes and at least pretend to be jogging or on my way to the gym.

I just wrote an email to my parents and lied to them about how happy I am. They worry too much, which is completely unjustified. I will never set foot on Afghan soil throughout my deployment. I'm a "Fobbit", someone who remains permanently on base.

Unlike smaller outposts that get hammered on a regular basis, we don't get attacked much. When the alarm sounds off, we run to the bunkers and stay there to wait for the big voice that sends us back to work. Since ragheads can't aim for shit, incoming mortars don't do too much damage. There's a guy who told me that he always uses the alarm to go shower. To be alone in the communal showers has got to be the mother of all luxuries here. But we do hear detonations pretty often. Sometimes it's because a goat stepped on a mine and exploded. In addition, our E.O.D. guys are constantly on the move both inside and outside the wire to rid the countryside of land mines that the Soviets placed everywhere when they were here. Then there's the bombs that our enemies buried in the ground for us. If an explosive device is found, it gets blown up in a controlled detonation. The first time I heard a bomb go off, I almost fell off my chair at the chow hall. You would think that nights are less noisy. Unfortunately, that's when our larger aircraft do their take-offs and landings (they're less easy to target in the dark). And 3 AM is usually a good time to test run the engines of the fighter jets.

A lot of people pop sleeping pills but I have no desire to cram even more chemicals into my system in addition to the malaria pills I have to take.

Of course there are things I would never tell my parents and my gran: for example, the ceremony for fallen comrades, during which we all stand on the roadside and salute while the cars drive past with the flag-covered coffins. The surviving comrades sit on the truck bed right next to the coffin. I hate seeing men cry. And I feel bad. I can do my job here in relative safety while others have to face enormous risks for us.

Well anyway, my eyes were swollen and red when I came back to the hangar after the ceremony yesterday, and my boss gave me a funny look.

Most soldiers coming through BAF are on the way to their next deployment or on the flight home. Some of them look roughed up, as if they'd come straight from some wild valleys where they had to live for a year without electricity and plumbing. You can see how they struggle with the FOB lifestyle - they barely make the effort to properly tuck their cammies into their boots, and they look bewildered when they can't get into the chow hall because of that. And they're surprised every time they see a female.

Most of our toilets are Port-A-Johns. You don't even want to know what smell I sometimes wake up to in the morning. Unfortunately I lost some weight because the constant smell of all kinds of things just keeps ruining my appetite. Oh BTW - I'm a Desert 10 (or Bagram 10): that's what they call any decent-looking women who would score maybe like a 5 or 6 in "real life"(that is, outside of any war zones). Needless to say, women are clearly in the minority here. I kind of like that. I like jogging around in PT gear to show off my toned arms. Recently I got on the bus and it was obvious that every soldier who was alone was hoping that I sit down beside him. This gives me a completely new sense of power. I don't know what to do with it - yet.

In other words, everything here is different from Lapwai. Why am I not surprised?

I hope that you're doing well. And I hope that Spielberg finally calls!

Marina - Goddess of War

September 2004

It was the low point of my life. Things could not possibly get any worse. My Staff Sergeant was so mad at me that he attacked me and almost completely lost control. I had managed to turn the golden boy into a brutal macho. My thighs ached, and I was limping home. Once I got to my hooch, I took the mountain bike and started cycling around the base in the midday heat. My rifle was slung across my back. As always it was loaded, and I felt every ounce of it. I shed some tears of self-pity that nobody noticed, but crying didn't really help. I was all alone now. My colleagues couldn't stand me, and I was sure that my boss was waiting for an excuse to send me home. It was extremely rare for anyone to get sent home for screwing up, but I didn't feel too confidant I was going to finish my deployment like everyone else. I just needed to provide my Staff Sergeant with a reason to kick me out of the unit. A single misstep would be sufficient. In our highly regulated work environment, making a mistake would not be too hard.

I started slowing down. I was drenched in sweat. As I was aimlessly cycling around the base, I had not really noticed how the scorching hot afternoon was turning into an unpleasantly hot evening. The sun seemed to be burning holes into my neck. I stopped to drink water. I emptied my bottle and tossed it into a trash can. On the other side of the street, I noticed a bunch of guys sitting on plastic chairs under an ugly brown parasol. They wore civilian clothes, but upon closer inspection I saw two handguns strapped to thigh holsters. That looked cool. They were all barrel-chested and wore beards.

I got back on my bike and rode on. When I turned left on Disney, it occurred to me that I could get ice cream. I felt no appetite at all. I simply needed something to do with my free time.

I spent twenty minutes standing in line, a huge waste of time on my only day off. The chatter of the two soldiers in front of me was getting on my nerves. They were discussing the pros and cons of paying extra money to get a better internet connection. I didn't want to hear any human voices. So I was glad when their conversation was interrupted by an F-15 thundering over our heads.

Finally I got my ice cream. Delicious walnut flavor filled my mouth. I pushed my bike and started into the direction that led me home. I was now on the same side of the road as the group of bearded men sitting in the shade. It seemed as if I was the only person walking around for miles - everybody else was in air-conditioned cars. The sunlight was blinding, but when I was just a few yards from the guys, I pushed up my shades. I slowed down until I was standing right in front of them.

I counted four handguns, one per beard. The men wore T-shirts and khakis with heavy work boots and looked like contractors. But the way they lounged on their plastic chairs and kept a vigilant eye on me led me to a completely different conclusion.

These guys are looking for bin Laden.

Of course there were thousands of guys at Bagram who looked just like that. Some were Army, some were contractors. But I decided that I was looking at ultraviolent operators.

"Hi", I said and licked my ice cream. I looked straight at the brunette's face which somehow reminded me of Andy Garcia (when he was still young). He looked at me with brown eyes and seemed to be thinking.

"Hi. I'm Tim, and what's your name?" he said finally.

"Marina. I'm in the Boy Scouts, and you?"

Two beards chuckled, but Andy Garcia didn't get it. "What do you mean, Boy Scouts?"

"U.S. Air Force. They call us boy scouts because we're not door kickers and all that."

General amusement ensued. The ice was broken. I took on some more of my walnut ice cream which was beginning to melt. I enjoyed the full attention of the men under the umbrella while sweat was trickling down my back. Without looking, I was pretty sure that dark circles were forming under my armpits.

"I really wanted to be a Marine", I said without being asked. "Would've been a perfect fit, with my name. I was crazy ambitious and I trained for six months, running and lifting weights and all that. Of course I didn't tell my parents what I was planning. Well, one day my mom found all the brochures and books on the Marine

Corps that I was hiding under the bed. She went completely apeshit. After a few months I convinced my family that nothing can possibly happen to me in the Air Force. And that's how I ended up in the Boy Scouts."

The dark-skinned beard had tied his hair up in a pony tail and looked really pretty. He laughed about me. "Tell me, do you always do what your mom tells you to do?"

I shrugged. "You don't know my mother. And if you did, believe me, you would do exactly what she says."

I had all four of them giggling. I didn't even know how funny I could be. The sun was melting my ice cream.

I looked Andy Garcia deep in the eyes. "What are you guys doing here then? Are you tourists?"

The blond dude thought that was funny. "You got that right, girl."

"I'm not a girl."

And that's how I steered the conversation into a different direction. While the air around me was getting thinner, I licked the rest of the ice cream until there was only the cone left. I looked at Andy Garcia, who looked back at me with a calm and focused expression. No one spoke. The cars and trucks were rushing past us, and two Hercules flew over our heads in quick succession. Finally I tossed the ice cream cone into a garbage pail that was located right next to the blonde. I could almost smell what was going on in the minds of my audience. From now on, every move I made had a meaning.

"So what's your MOS in the Air Force? Collecting stray golf balls? Filling out spreadsheets?" The man with the least impressive biceps had the most ink. He leaned forward and picked up his can of Coke from the ground. He moved like a panther. I wondered what this gesture would look like if Andy Garcia did it.

"I fix A-10s. The only aircraft that we don't have to share with the Army or the Marines. In fact it's more of a monster-machine gun that they built an airplane around."

I realized I was lecturing my audience about something they knew all too well. Anyone with Iraq or Afghan combat experience would already know all about the A-10. But my new friends didn't seem to mind.

"Cool. The one with the shark face?" the blonde asked.

I shook my head. "The Spang planes don't have shark faces. But they look dangerous enough if you ask me."

"But you do realize that they're called 'Warthogs' for a reason, right?" Andy Garcia said. He had a pleasant voice, a bit scratchy but with lots of bass. And he sounded like he came from the deepest South. He probably grew up in the swamps of Louisiana and hunted crocodiles after school.

I let out a very dramatic sigh. "Dude, these jets are not supposed to look pretty. They're death and destruction dealing machines. Would you expect a professional killer to be attractive?"

They looked convinced. It didn't escape me that my new admirers looked me up and down. But my camouflage uniform kept any existing curves very well hidden (which was kind of the point). So they had no choice but to guess what they'd see if I was standing there in a bikini.

"Well anyway, I do the maintenance on these things. Without me they would crash, and we would lose the war. Which makes me a very important person."

My audience laughed. They got the irony alright. I had to answer the next question. The blonde asked me about my "ethnic background".

"I'm Native American. Full blood. Not watered down. My tribe is the Nez Perce. That's why I'm darker than you and don't need to hide from the sun."

"Well in that case, I'm glad you didn't accidentally end up in the U.S. Cavalry", said the dark-skinned guy. "Would be kinda inappropriate, right?"

"All I know is that they replaced their horses with those monstrous Strykers. I would hate to be locked up all day in that death trap.

Plus, they're even uglier than the A-10", I said.

The sun was almost blinding me. I would have liked to cover my eyes with the sunglasses but I wanted to maintain eye contact with Andy Garcia. I was in control now. I totally owned this group of admirers. Now I just needed to pick one.

"So how are your accommodations? I live in a plywood cabin that smells funny. And you?"

Andy Garcia, whose real name was Tim, seemed to have realized that he was the chosen one. He jumped up (displaying the grace of a gazelle) and said, "Actually, we have a life of luxury here at Bagram. You wanna see my B-hut? "

"Sure, why not?" I pulled my sunglasses down and put my hands on the handle bar of my bike. "Lead the way."

Andy Garcia pointed to the other side of the street, and without saying goodbye to his buddies, we crossed the street together. It was clear that the others were now studying my ass as I walked away. Nice. All those things that usually drove me completely insane (or at least very frustrated), I liked all of a sudden. Even the late afternoon heat stopped bothering me.

I expected that we would walk towards the CONEX buildings. They were fairly new and consisted of a smart container system, with state-of-the-art plumbing and air conditioning. The whole Army seemed to live there. But he led me through a series of huts that looked a lot like my hooch.

"Isn't it strange that the Air Force has to live in this makeshift crap? After all we're the ones who are running the show here. It's called Bagram Airfield and not Bagram Army Field or something." I looked at my companion who was grinning but didn't answer.

"You can take your bike inside", he said as he opened the door of his hooch. I pushed the bike into the room and was surprised. Although the hut had exactly the same floor plan as my home, it was set up differently. The door opened onto a tiny hallway, where I leaned my bike against a plywood wall that looked dangerously thin. We walked into the main (and only) room through a door that was pretty narrow for someone of Tim's build. This room was furnished with four beds, four lockers and in the middle, a table with four chairs. Each bed was standing in one of the four corners of the room, but there was no such thing as privacy here.

"Steve, I have a visitor", my new friend said to a man who was lying on his bunk.

Steve was only wearing briefs and looked up from the magazine he was reading. He stood up and put on a pair of pants. Then he took the magazine and shuffled past us outside without so much as a glance in my direction.

"Which one's yours?" I asked. My host pointed to a bed in the rear right corner. I walked towards it and felt his eyes on my back. It gave me a pleasant tingling sensation. I carefully leaned my weapon against a small shelf, then I sat down on the edge of the bed to take off my boots. I stuffed my smelly socks into the boots. The floor was covered by a fine layer of sand. I looked up at Tim who was standing in front of the bed and looked down at me with the same calm expression he'd had during our entire conversation on the street.

"Shall I take off more?"

He nodded. "Yes please."

I giggled and pulled off the shapeless shirt of my uniform. It felt as wet as my socks. I stood up and pulled off the ugly gray desert camouflage pants that made all women look the same. My legs were toned and freshly shaven. I could almost hear him holding his breath as I was standing in his personal space, my face inches away from his. He reached into my hair and gently pulled the ponytail holder out of my military bun. The hair tie fell to the dust-covered floor while he leaned in to me, slowly, one hand going through my hair, the other hand on my back.

Anyone who has never kissed a beard, has no idea. It was a completely new experience, scratchy, weird, and hot. Finally, he moved away to undress. I watched as he took off his shirt. He had a few hairs on his chest. His whole upper body was sensational. I dropped my bra and underpants on the floor and lay down on his bed. He was on top of me right away.

He was so heavy.

Everything about it felt good. In the beginning he tried to hold back, but he lost control pretty soon. It was over almost immediately.

There wasn't really enough space for both of us on his narrow rack. He lay on the side, and I did the same thing because I wanted to hug my back against his broad chest. I could feel his breath on my neck. His left arm was loosely hugging my hip.

"Tim, do you want me to go now?"

"Are you crazy? We just got started."

I said nothing. I didn't want to outstay my welcome.

It didn't take long until the door opened and Steve ended our short moment of privacy. He didn't go back to his bed because he was headed in our direction instead. He stopped just in front of our bed and took in every detail of my body. No one said anything. Steve seemed to commit to memory what he saw, and eventually he went back to his corner.

Tim kissed some sweat off my neck. That was pretty much all he did, but it was enough. My breathing was heavy, and I tried not to emit a single noise. I turned to lie on my back. Tim had to make way, so he got on top of me and we were immediately entwined again. His movements were slow and controlled. Now I was the one who couldn't hold back, and I heard myself get louder against my will. Steve was probably trying to memorize my moaning so that he had a soundtrack matching the images of my naked body.

"I love you, and you're wonderful, and please don't leave me", I whispered afterwards, and Tim laughed.

"It's been a while since I had such a grateful woman", he said.

I opened my eyes. We were squeezed tight, side by side on the too-small bunk. My head was resting on his upper arm, and I looked up at him. From below, his beard looked even scarier.

"When was your last time?"

He gave it some thought. "I guess about four months ago. I had to endure even longer periods of time without sex."

Suddenly I got scared. "How long are you staying here in Bagram?"

"No idea. We're on call. Could be anytime. But you're not supposed to know that, girl."

"I'm not a girl."

He laughed. "Not anymore. Now that you finally had yourself a real man."

"How do you know that you're the first one?"

He had to move down a little to kiss me on the mouth. It did not stop. It would never end. Sometime later, I heard a blanket rustle. It was probably Steve, pretending to sleep.

At least he didn't take a picture.

BIZARRE LOVE TRIANGLE

The next day nothing felt real. I desperately tried to focus on my job. Sometime in the afternoon I got yelled at because it took me too long to get the laptop for the diagnosis. Dazed as I was, I couldn't move any faster. My brains felt like scrambled eggs, and the aching bruises in my thighs didn't help. I couldn't get the sensations out of my head that nearly overwhelmed me the night before: the creaking sound that Tim's plywood rack made whenever one of us moved, the way he touched me, the scratchy beard. It was just too much. I was a train wreck when I got off my shift but still went to the arranged meeting place.

He picked me up in a beat-up truck in front of the Burger King. We didn't speak in the car. Small talk with a complete stranger is not that easy after all.

We were alone this time, but we only had an hour. That was barely enough for two different workouts, the first one fast, the second one slower and gentler. Just as I was reaching for my shirt, the door opened. Three dudes walked in. Steve I already knew. I kissed my lover on the cheek and left. I walked past his three roommates without looking at them. A little arrogance never hurt anyone.

And then I had to go back.

I'd forgotten my goddamn weapon, and this didn't occur to me until I was almost out the door. The other three were sitting down at the table to play cards. They looked surprised as I came back. But when I walked past them with the rifle slung over my shoulder, holding my head high, they went into hysterics. One of them was laughing so hard he almost fell off his chair.

This time I didn't have my bike with me. It had a flat tire. I had to walk home through the warm summer night, but there wasn't anything romantic about it. I couldn't afford to look at the stars unless I wanted to break a leg. I stumbled more than once. The ankle-twisting gravel on the ground basically makes up the foundation of Bagram. Every time you stumble over one of the bigger stones, it reminds you of the fact that the Afghans really don't want us here. I wondered if I shouldn't have asked Tim to take me home in his car. But maybe it was better not to be seen in male company.

The last thing I needed was a reputation as the mattress of Bagram.

On the third night the inevitable happened. This time we were on foot, with me pushing my bike, because we had met at the Green Bean. Tim wanted to buy me coffee, but I didn't need one. It was just too hot. He tried to drink his Frappuccino while walking, and I looked around discreetly. Nobody was paying us any attention, and still I was sure we weren't going totally unnoticed. In an officially sex-free zone with hardly any women around, people do get curious when a man and a woman are walking down the street together without wearing the same uniform. Especially when the man looks as if he had Taliban for breakfast.

The inevitable was Tim's remark about his best friend.

"You know", he said all of a sudden as we turned onto his street, "my friend Dan and I, we share everything."

"Yeah? Absolutely everything?"

He nodded and took a sip of his coffee, licking the milk foam off his upper lip, which was kind of hot.

"But I'm not an object that you can share with others."

"I didn't say that", he said with a friendly smirk.

"I'm not a horse that your best friend can borrow for a ride."

Tim laughed so hard he folded at the waist and let out a weird guttural sound. "I never heard that one before. Can I tell the others?"

"Yes please", I said sternly. "Can I safely assume that right now, you don't have your twelve best friends waiting for me in your hooch?"

He looked around and found a trash can for his coffee cup. We were almost there, and I started worrying. Tim looked at me, a kind smile spreading on his face.

"You know what you are? You're my girlfriend here at Bagram. You belong to me, and me only. Okay?"

I nodded, and we walked on.

In the B-hut we were alone again, and this time it was better than ever. Maybe because he'd called me his girlfriend. I didn't even know Tim's last name, but I had a strong desire to marry him. He was just perfect.

When we were done, I was lying on top of him. A small fan was blowing hot air in my direction. His little chest hairs were scratching my face. He had his hands clasped behind his head. I enjoyed how his chest was gently moving up and down, and I listened to his breathing which was only occasionally drowned out by a Chinook. The door opened and a new face appeared.

The man looked younger and had no beard. His face was sharp-angled. Unlike his brothers in arms he had a standard military haircut. He was only wearing shorts and flip-flops. Huge Gothic letters on his chest screamed "INFIDEL". The danger that emanated from this man felt very real.

"You're lying on top of my buddy", he said as he stood in front of the rack, looking down on us.

"Man, I'm so sorry."

He laughed along with Tim so that my head wobbled up and down on Tim's chest. I climbed off of my lover and sat on the edge of the bed. Infidel bent down in front of Tim's fridge and took out a can of soda. He opened it and handed it to me. Tim managed to sit up behind me and crawl out of the bed.

"Gotta pee", he said as he dressed. Then he went outside and left me alone with the heathen.

"You are crazy thin", Infidel said and sat down beside me on the bed. He had a cleft chin and surprisingly long eyelashes.

I got up and picked my clothes off the dusty floor. I got dressed as fast as I could. Sexy time was over.

I sat down next to Infidel and drank my soda. "I guess I work out too much, and I definitely don't like the food here."

"I see."

He leaned over to the shelf to switch on the tiny music system. When he turned it on, the room filled up with electronic blubber. Just as he opened his mouth to say something, a C-17 thundered overhead.

I love the Globemaster, I thought suddenly. I visualized it on the flight line, and I could smell the kerosene. A gray monster that took children to Bagram so that they could grow up to be adults.

I cocked my head. "What if I just say no to you? What's gonna happen to me?"

He laughed. "We may look like savages, but we're not rapists."

We just sat there and listened to the music. Finally I put the empty can on the floor and said, "Tim's not coming back so soon, right?"

He nodded. His eyes were green and reminded me of a poisonous snake.

"Why does he want me to sleep with you?"

He shrugged. "I guess he's worried about me. I can't really come down from a high after a mission. I would need drugs to get back to normal."

"What does that mean, you can't come down?"

He put an arm around my shoulder. "It's not like coming down from an adrenaline high. I simply can't get all the pictures and impressions of what happened out of my head, even at night. Especially at night. I can hardly sleep. "

"True, you have dark circles under your eyes. I gotta admit that I can't sleep here either. How many people do you know who live in a fucking airport, honestly?"

Infidel's smile was genuine. It didn't fade away even as he tried to describe his sleeping disorder. "I don't care about the noise. I have the same problems in a hotel in Germany or at home in South Dakota. I can't simply switch off my memories."

It was nice to know that other people couldn't bear their life either. But we were now at a point where a decision was due. The clock was ticking, and sooner or later this cabin would fill with its residents. His arm on my shoulder felt heavier and heavier. He looked at the floor. He seemed to be waiting for something.

"Look", I said. That made him smile again.

The music ended. Outside I could hear voices. Someone laughed, someone else said YO YO YO.

I studied his impressive cheekbones. He had a warrior face. "You and your friends think I'm a slut." He looked at my hands on my knees.

"That's not what I am", I continued. "I'm very lonely right now, and I chose Tim because I was hoping he'd make me feel better."

Infidel had a warm smile.

I felt like explaining everything. "You know, I really like him. I don't think I'll ever see him again once he's gone. That still doesn't make me a slut. It's not my fault I didn't meet him in my hometown. We would have dated, we would have gone to the movies. I would've introduced him to my friends."

Infidel nodded. "I don't think you're a slut. And your little arrangement is working for both of you. Tim is having a good time too, and I'm happy for him."

He leaned over to the shelf again and pressed a button on the stereo. Some more electronic music came out, and I asked: "Is that dance or trance?"

He laughed. We kept sitting side by side on the edge of the bed until eventually the door opened and my lover came in.

"Did you score?" he asked his friend, who shook his head

immediately.

"Maybe tomorrow", Tim said with almost fatherly concern.

He drove me to the nearest bus stop. I almost fell asleep on the bus. I was exhausted but happy.

The next night Tim noticed my thighs and my bruises.

"What the hell is that?"

He was standing in front of me while I was putting my shirt back on. I looked up at him. "Jeez, is that the first time you noticed them? We've been together for four days now!"

Tim knelt before me and inspected my legs at close range. "Who did that?"

"My Staff Sergeant. We had a little altercation. And - no, I don't want you to beat him up for me."

That was a good one. Tim probably figured my statement was a joke.

"How did you get him so angry?" Tim asked.

"Long story. I'll tell you tomorrow. If you're still around." I jumped up and picked up my weapon.

"I'll take you home."

As we walked out into the night, I realized I was going to miss this particular B-hut.

As Tim and I walked towards Disney, we didn't speak for a while, but I wanted to talk. I wanted to tell him about my work troubles and about how lonely I was. And I wanted to tell him that he was my savior. My everything. But I said nothing and kept pushing my bike.

Tim finally broke the silence.

"Listen", he said.

I shot him a curious side-glance. He was wearing a Yankees baseball cap and Oakleys just like a lot of other people, but he looked about a thousand times better than the average guy. It suddenly became painfully clear to me that I'd never in my life be able to have sex with normal dudes.

"Yesterday you met Dan. What did you make of him?" he asked me.

I gave it a thought. "Dangerous. Ticking time bomb. Super-green eyes. If my mother knew what kind of men I hang out with, she'd freak, that's for sure."

"You think you can do him tomorrow?"

Two Marines walked past us. I wondered if they'd heard Tim's question. I stopped. Tim did the same, patiently waiting for a response.

"No, I won't. I'm not your toy."

He shook his head. "Fine. No problem."

I started pushing my bike again and didn't look at him. I wondered if I had disappointed him. "Where do we meet tomorrow?"

"Pizza Hut. Every day a different location. A moving target is harder to hit."

"How about if I join you guys? Can I transfer to your unit? I could do your laundry and your dishes while you're out hunting terrorists. Like Snow White and the Seven Dwarves."

"You mean as a mascot? I'm afraid you'd have to sleep with all of us. And in my unit there's some guys that are definitely not your type."

We giggled. It felt like an exclusive club that consisted of just two members. It was almost like a conspiracy, since what we were doing was more or less illegal. Suddenly I knew what was missing in my life: someone to share a secret with.

The Internet connection was surprisingly fast when I was back in my hooch. I had the laptop on my knees while I went through mails in the hope that someone from Lapwai was sending me love. It was the first time in three days that I checked my inbox. But nobody at home seemed to be worried about me. No news from Spangdahlem and nothing from the States. What I got instead was a warning.

```
To: mars_air@yahoo.com
From: afriend173@gmail.com
Re: Slow the fuck down
```

Marina,

It's not a great idea to turn into a Special Forces groupie just because you don't know what else to do with yourself. These people screw everything they can lay their hands on. The dude you've been seen with picks up a girl every single time he comes through Bagram. I can imagine you don't really care what people are talking behind your back, but maybe you could take a step back and look at the bigger picture? Girls like you are extremely bad for the rep of any female service member. You know from your own experience that women in this war zone have a lot of problems to struggle with. Behaving like a slut doesn't make you look like a reliable and professional person. As I said, it's bad for everyone here who's female. You know all the stereotypes: the pretty girls join the Air Force, the contractors just do it for the money, the SF guys have a license to kill, and women join the military just to find a husband.

By the way, it doesn't go unnoticed that you sometimes forget your weapon in the gun rack. If you ever misplace it, expect to be crucified. They will shut down the entire installation UNTIL THEY FIND IT!

Most of the female service members have the same
ambitions that the men have: they want to do their
job well. They want to be taken seriously. They
want to get ahead in life. Girls like you are just
making this so much more difficult.

You can get laid when you're back in Spang.

Think about it.

I read the message about a hundred times. Then I went to sleep. A couple of hours before my alarm was supposed to go off, I was wide awake. Whoever called himself a friend was someone who worked on my team, there was no doubt about that. Not only had this person seen me with Tim, but he also knew that I was a scatterbrained rifle-forgetting airhead.

I tried not to get angry while I was thinking about the well-meaning advice I'd received from someone who preferred to stay anonymous. I thought he was a coward. He could have told me all this in my face. I wouldn't have started crying. He also kept calling me a girl. I was a fully qualified car mechanic. I was also an aircraft mechanic, working on three different continents. I was not a girl anymore.

I took an early bus and saw a drone as I looked out the window. These were the only aircraft that I thought were kind of creepy. Someone had told me they could operate these drones from a center in the States, which I found hard to believe. And if it was true, it made these weapons even more creepy. How could someone staring at a computer terminal know exactly what was happening on the ground several thousand miles away?

Our workday was unbearable. The heat was driving us all crazy, and I didn't bother with lunch. The way to the chow hall was too far in the mid-day heat, at least for me. My exciting new hobby led me to come home late at night so that I was suffering from even more sleep deprivation. There was a small fridge in the hallway, next to the NCO office. I ate a plain yogurt that I'd stashed there some weeks ago. It still tasted okay. I started rummaging for left-over stuff. I could hear the door open and kept my head inside the fridge, ignoring the Staff Sergeant as he walked past. I decided to open an old Coke can that had been in the fridge for ages. Even if it belonged to someone else, what could possibly happen? They couldn't do much more than yell at me.

Rohrman came back. I was leaning against the refrigerator, holding the chilled can to my forehead. He stopped. I looked past him out the window. Outside the sky had darkened. A huge summer storm was coming.

Rohrman looked at me. Suddenly he leaned forward. His face was only inches from mine, and I counted exactly three freckles on his nose. There was an evil sparkle in his blue eyes.

Deep Sea Blue, I thought.

"Don't let yourself get caught by me, baby", he hissed. "Prostitution is definitely a reason for a dishonorable discharge."

He moved back about half an inch. I felt a strong desire to break his nose with my chilled forehead. Instead I took a deep breath. I leaned my upper body towards him.

"May I whisper something in your ear? It's strictly confidential."

He was surprised. He probably thought that I was too traumatized to speak to him at all, after his thigh-squeezing act of violence a few days ago.

He moved a step forward, put his left hand on the fridge, made another half step towards me – and actually lent me his ear.

"I don't take money for it", I whispered. "I just want to let off steam."

Then I slowly walked back to work. The only sounds in the hallway were the clunk of the soda can in the trash and a distant rumble of thunder from outside.

Throughout the afternoon I was waiting for the storm, but it only started when I was in the shower. The downpour was not yet over when I had to leave for my date. I rode my bike to the Pizza Hut in the pouring rain and locked it to a lamppost. I was early, so I decided to stand in line like everyone else. As usual I wasn't really hungry but I wanted to avoid standing around for no apparent reason, especially not when there was a risk that my boss had his spies in position.

How he knew that I spent my nights in someone else's bed, was beyond me. Someone must have seen me, maybe when I came home at two in the morning. That someone had probably written the Slow the fuck down-mail and at the same time talked to Rohrman.

But seeing me walk down Disney with Tim wouldn't necessarily prove that I had an active sex life. There was a whole lot of things that you could do in Bagram even in the middle of the night, like go to the gym. Could it be that someone saw me leaving Tim's hooch? I knew less than ten people on this base. So for anyone to see me with Tim, there had to be someone spying on me for quite a while. This mystery was totally unsolvable. I decided not to think about it any longer.

I was sitting at a table and biting into my overpriced slice of pizza when my date showed up. I wasn't really surprised that it was Infidel and not Tim. He winked at me and then turned his back to me as he stood in line. His long-sleeved shirt was wet. From where I was sitting I was almost able to read all the tour dates of some death metal band. There were a whole lot of other people with sidearms strapped to thigh holsters, but he was the only one who looked as if he actually needed his weapon once in a while. I ate my pizza. The men at my table tried to flirt with me but I didn't say much because I was going to have to shake them off sooner or later anyway. Eventually they got up and left. I looked around discreetly. Dan was sitting further back, chatting with a soldier and eating his calzone. When he was finished I stood up and walked towards the exit as slowly as possible.

Outside, he joined me up shortly thereafter and asked, "Can I try your bike?"

I gave it to him and watched him as he disappeared around a corner. It took a while until he came back.

"The saddle is too low, but I gotta say a bike is just the right thing here", he said approvingly.

"Where are we going? Do you live somewhere other than Tim?"

He shook his head. "We're going to do some tourism."

On the way to our tourist destination, I told him about my very brief conversation with my supervisor.

"He thinks you're a prostitute? That's bad news. You're going to have to tread lightly." My companion looked seriously worried.

"What's your problem with him anyway?" Dan had a very peculiar way of scanning the surroundings for danger. It looked perfectly normal when he looked to the right or left once in a while, and he managed to turn around to look out for possible spies without raising suspicions.

"So?" I asked. "Do we have company?"

"No, I don't think anyone's following us. But I'll remain vigilant. By the time we get there, I'll be able to know for sure if we're safe or not."

"If you want to, you can give me back my bike now."

He laughed. "Why, do you want to make a run for it? Are you disappointed because I showed up instead of Tim? He told me you don't want me. Totally okay with that. We're just gonna hang out. And then I'll tell Tim that we had bombastic sex, and he's gonna stop bugging me. Now tell me what happened between you and your boss. To me it sounds like he's got a thing for you, if he keeps pushing you into a corner."

"On the contrary", I sighed. "You got it all wrong. He hates me and he'd love to send me back to Spangdahlem today rather than tomorrow."

"What happened? How did this thing start?"

He stopped in order to pretend he was checking the bicycle chain and again scanned the area.

"All right. But I have to go back to the very beginning of my deployment."

Dan stood up, and we walked on. The humidity in the air was just as maddening as before. At least the sun had disappeared behind a grey wall of clouds.

"I jcined a really good team. They told me from the beginning that they all get along great and that there's never any trouble. The Staff Sergeant is a golden boy from the East Coast. College-educated. Very self-confident, very charming, everyone loves him. At first I was into him like everybody else."

The sun came out from behind a dark cloud. It did something nice to the big puddle next to us on the road. The mirror effect of the puddle was almost blinding.

I cleared my throat. "I was pretty nervous at the beginning, and when one of my colleagues cracked a stupid joke about women, I guess I overreacted. I forced him to apologize to me right away. In front of almost the entire crew. Well, and then the atmosphere was basically poisoned. At least when I was in the room."

Dan was fascinated. "Why did you overreact?"

"I was surrounded by men 24/7. At work, at the chow hall, on the whole base. I was clearly a minority, and that made me pretty nervous. I thought that I had to stand my ground right from the start so that nobody would fuck with me. I think I also wanted to make sure people wouldn't harass me with all kinds of flirty stuff."

"And?"

I laughed. "My plan worked without a flaw. No-one tried to hit on me so far."

We stopped in front of the Russian Tower. This was the building where the air traffic controllers had been working back when the Soviets waged their war against the Afghans. Dan walked me around the building and opened the back door. It was made of steel and looked freshly painted. He pushed the bike into a bright hallway.

"Newly renovated", he said and leaned the bike against the wall. "They're finished in about two weeks, and then some POGS from the Air Force are going to move in. But until then, we have the place to ourselves."

"Where did you get the key to the door?" I asked.

"I organized it. Organization is next to godliness, girl."

"Yeah, whatever."

Even in the hallway the air was still humid, but the room temperature was cooler than outside. Dan took my hand and led me up three stories. The actual ATC room was circular and looked as if it had been abandoned a long time ago. It would have been interesting if the ancient Soviet equipment had still been in there, but there were only shelves and desks left, everything made of fake wood. In one of the windows the glass was smashed. A breeze of fresh air was coming in through the hole. We looked out the window for a while. The view was beautiful because the sky was divided into two parts: most of it was a light blue with some hint of orange. To the east, the horizon changed into a dark wall of clouds in the distance. A Blackhawk clattered above the valley. We were enclosed by mountain ranges on three sides. The whole view of the airfield was fantastic.

We toured the entire room. I noticed that there was a sleeping bag on the floor on the west side. Two cans of real beer were standing next to it.

"You found beer? How did you manage that?"

He grinned. "I organized it."

"You're repeating yourself."

He let go of my hand. I sat down on the sleeping bag. He sat down next to me and handed me a can that spelled Zywiec.

"I got it at the PMC", Dan explained.

"Err... well, I thought I knew all the acronyms. I guess I was wrong."

"Polish Military Compound. These guys are allowed to get shitfaced every single day. Unbelievable." Dan shook his head in disapproval as he opened his beer.

I took a sip. The beer was cold and absolutely delicious.

"If my Staff Sergeant finds me here, that's it. I'm done", I said, wondering what Rohrman was doing while I was having a good time with one of my admirers.

Dan nodded. "Except that he wouldn't make it into the tower. One of my buddies is standing watch on the ground floor. I can assure you that no one can get past Gucci."

"Gucci", I giggled.

"Actually, Gutierrez, but that's a secret." Dan finished his beer. I handed him my can.

"You need it more than I do", I said generously.

"Thank you." He closed his eyes and gulped down the rest.

"Dan, why do you want to lie to Tim? I don't really feel comfortable with this. I told him I wasn't gonna sleep with anyone else."

Dan pushed the empty cans away. He gently put a hand on one of my knees. He looked straight ahead as he started talking.

"I don't swing that way."

I gasped. I had no idea.

Dan breathed slowly in and out, his chest heaving as if he was sighing. His voice was calm. "I'm sure you're not planning to tell anyone."

"Hell no", I blurted out. "I would never do that. I'll take the secret into the grave."

"Good."

After that we just sat there. The sleeping bag wasn't too comfortable on the concrete floor. I felt like asking a million questions. I didn't even know where to start. Before I could begin interrogating Dan, he asked me about my job problems. I really wasn't in the mood, but he insisted on hearing the story about my Staff Sergeant.

"I was very insecure when I got here. But I managed to make friends with a woman in my hooch. Her name's Sandy. She was working different shifts. We didn't see each other that often, but sometimes we hung out together. She took me to the gym and showed me how everything works. I'm always going to be grateful for that."

Dan got closer, his thigh brushing mine, and cocked his head, puzzled. "Why? You didn't know how to use the equipment?"

I nodded. "I never went to a gym before. It was great to have someone with me the first time I went. Otherwise I would've made a complete ass of myself. Or maybe I would've broken something, who knows."

"Alright. Go on. I want to know how you made your boss angry." Dan looked out the window. The evening sun was warming the back of his T-shirt. I wondered if his tattoo wouldn't look better if he had it on the back.

"Well, one morning I heard Sandy cry. I went over to her cubicle or her room or whatever you want to call the spaces we live in, and she was lying on the rack, crying into her Hello Kitty pillow. She looked very vulnerable. Then she told me that she was raped by a soldier. The two met at the PX when she was looking at magazines, and he asked her to take a walk with her, just like you and me today. He attacked her somewhere behind a dumpster. I wanted to listen to her and stay with her as long as possible, so I didn't take a shower that morning, and I didn't bother with breakfast. And of course I tried to convince her that she had to report it. But that was completely out of the question. I tried to talk her into this with all the arguments I could think of, but she refused. And I had to get to work."

Dan looked at me thoughtfully. "It's definitely a big fuss when you report a rape. I guess she figured she wasn't strong enough to make it through the whole procedure."

I stared at him. "Tell me, are you as stupid as everyone else?"

Dan was surprised. "What do you mean?"

"You're Special Ops, and they don't take idiots, right?" My voice was too loud. "Do you really not get it? If a rapist gets away with his crime, he'll start looking for his next victim. These are people who need to be fucking court-martialed if you ask me. I want to be protected from such criminals, is that so hard to understand?"

"You're probably right."

"Of course I'm right", I said. I lay down with my hands behind my head. A pillow would have been great. Dan was playing with the empty beer cans.

"Well, it doesn't matter. I tried one more time to talk to her. She told me to let it go. But I had the name and the unit. I tried to find him. And eventually I was lucky - or unlucky, depending on your point of view. Anyway, after a while I knew pretty much at what times he goes to eat. So I took all my courage and approached two people from my team and told them the whole story. I opted for Kyle and Robert because I liked them best. It wasn't easy, I can tell you that much. All the guys on my team were keeping a safe distance from me. I asked them to come with me so that the three of us could at least intimidate this guy."

"And what did they say?"

I sat up again. Dan put his arm around my shoulders, just like when we first met.

"They agreed. To my big surprise. From this point on we always went to chow together." The memories made me smile. The whole thing was anything but funny, but my temporary friendship with Kyle and Robert had been a good thing. "That was actually the best time I had until now, when the three of us were making plans to corner this scumbag. It was a real conspiracy. And then we found him in the North DFAC. He was sitting at a table with a friend and they'd just started eating. So we sat down at his table. My buddies were sitting on either side of the other dude, and I took a chair and positioned myself very, very close to the enemy. That didn't go unnoticed. There's quite a few people who looked over from the other tables. He had zits on his chin, and he wasn't even good-looking. I told him the stuff I had agreed on earlier with Kyle and Robert: that we knew about the rape. That he's a filthy, mean asshole. He and his friend stopped eating. His friend gave him a puzzled look. He clearly didn't know what this was about. But my victim was staring right ahead without making eye contact. I was the only one speaking. I took my time and I was super calm. I was a cold-stone warrior, threatening the enemy. At least that's how I felt back then."

Dan pulled his death metal shirt over his head. I looked at his upper body. The sight nearly took my breath away. His abs looked like they could pull a truck. Whereas Tim looked like a bear, Dan was more like a sleek panther. He was the hottest gay dude on base.

I tried to finish my story. "Basically everything went as planned, except that the guy showed no emotion whatsoever. I was getting angrier all the time. I was totally invading his personal space. We wanted to scare him, you know? The asshole was as rigid as a statue. I needed to get a reaction from him, anything. So I started telling him a few things that popped up in my head, out of nowhere. For example, the fact that I heard of a soldier who shot himself after he'd been raped in the shower. And if I should ever hear that there was an incident like Sandy's rape again, I would personally hang this asshole from the nearest lamppost."

I didn't really expect that Dan would find this amusing. He chuckled. "Very nice. That must've left some impression."

I shrugged. "His friend turned really pale, and there was still nothing from the dude I was threatening. But you should have seen my buddies. They were horrified. Robert made a sign that we were leaving right now. All three of us stood up at the same time. That didn't go unnoticed either, and I felt a lot of eyes on me. I felt like a superhero and I had a fucking warrior swagger while we walked out of the hall. Lara Croft had nothing on me. We didn't talk for a while, but once we were far enough, my colleagues basically ripped my head off."

Dan nodded. "It's somewhat risky to threaten a soldier with hanging him. That might backfire."

"That's what happened. It didn't take long until everyone at work knew about it. I was more isolated than ever. Robert and Kyle kept their distance too..."

It was almost funny. "You know, Dan. I have every reason to believe that people are more or less scared of me."

Dan took off his big boots. The kind of hiking shoes you need to wander through rough valleys and to climb mountains. I wanted to ask him if he was wearing these shoes when he was rappelling from helicopters. But I didn't dare to ask. After all we didn't know each other that long.

I took a deep breath. "Anyway. It didn't take long until my Staff Sergeant heard the story, and one day I found myself sitting in his miniature office and had to listen to his lecture on good judgment and common sense. He made clear how disappointed he was. According to him, there are clear rules for everything that can happen at the airbase, and there's no room for interpretation. I'm one of those people who are so arrogant that they take everything into their own hands instead of first talking to their supervisors. Trust responsibility communication yadda yadda. What made me angry was not what he said, but the fact that he was as cool as usual. As if he was just reeling off his standard teaching program. As if he didn't really care that you can rape people with impunity here."

"But you can't. Rape doesn't go unpunished", Dan said. He had trouble pulling the sweaty socks off his feet. "You can only punish a crime when the victim reports it. Or when a witness saw something. It's not your boss's fault that Sandy wanted to sweep this whole thing under the carpet."

"I know it's not his fault. But he was making me angry, the way he was talking to me. He kept goofing around with all the others in the team, he knew all kinds of personal stuff about them. I was such an outsider already, and now I was sitting there and had to listen. He didn't want to know anything. He didn't ask me why I'd done it in the first place, why I dragged Robert and Kyle into this. Nada. I noticed that my hands were trembling, that's how mad I was. Once he was finished I got up and was almost at the door when he thought of a question all of a sudden."

Dan was wiggling his toes. "Go on."

"Can't you put your shirt back on? I can't really concentrate with what I'm seeing right now."

He laughed. "So you are into me. Figures. Girls always think of gays as a challenge."

"That's bullshit and you know it", I protested. "I'm into Tim. I told you. I'm gonna cry my eyes out when he's gone."

Dan sighed. "Me too. I don't think he's planning to re-enlist when we get back to the States. I will definitely miss him."

All of a sudden there was an elephant in the room. I didn't dare look at my newfound friend.

Dan's smile was mischievous. It seemed that he knew exactly what I was thinking.

"Listen", he said after a minute of very heavy silence. "I worship Tim. He's more than my brother, he's a demi-god in our unit. We all worship him. But I don't fantasize about him. Not my type, okay?"

I nodded.

"You're blushing, Marina. Why don't you tell me about Rohrman and what he said to you."

I cleared my throat for the grand finale of my story. "Okay, well, as I said, I'm on my way out, I've got my hand on the doorknob, and he asks me if it doesn't bother me that all the helicopters here have Indian names. Chinook. Apache. Black Hawk. Kiowa. I turn around and stare at him. He goes around his desk and there he is, standing right in front of me. And he's showing me his elitist sonny boy smile. And then he asks me why there's no Nez Perce attack helicopters."

Dan laughed out loud. "Fuck me! That guy is funny as hell!"

"I kind of tried to hurl myself into him. Maybe I wanted to push him away or something, no idea what was going through my head. And he brought me under control with a simple hand movement. He pinned me against the wall by pressing his knees into both of my thighs. He's taller than me. And he took my wrists and held them very closely to both sides of my hips. If someone had walked in at that very moment, it would've looked like we were just about to kiss. His face was like an inch away from mine. He laughed at me. If it was physiologically possible to burst with anger, I swear to God I would've exploded. I couldn't move, his knees were really hurting me. And he kept laughing. He was clearly enjoying this."

I had to pause. Cold rage was filling my chest.

"And then what? Did he let you go?"

"No, he had to humiliate me a bit more. First he blew his RipIt-breath into my face. Then he said to me, and again, he was super calm when he said it: you have no combat skills whatsoever. A 100-pound Taliban could easily take you on. You don't belong in a war zone, you belong in a garage. Go home and fix cars, girl."

Dan was shaking with laughter and I wanted to slap him.

"I take it I entertained you well?" I asked him, my voice dripping with sarcasm.

"That was better than Halo, Marina. I'm very satisfied."

WATER IS THE BASIS OF ALL LIFE

My kidnapper is speechless. He's probably not used to someone telling him weird stories.

I decide to take a chance. "Tell me, do you think I could get some water? I'm just so incredibly thirsty."

"Why? You can get into the bathroom yourself, the water is right there."

I shake my head. "The chain is just long enough to get to the toilet, but there's a few inches missing for me to get all the way to the sink. Please."

He gets up and goes into the bathroom. I hear water running and almost start crying with joy. He comes back with a tumbler that he presses into my hand. There's a yellow tinge, but I decide that this part of town has decent tap water. While I'm drinking he takes the empty plastic bottle next to my bed and fills it up at the sink.

"Thanks", I say. I'm genuinely grateful.

"We thought the chain would be long enough. But if you really ran out of water, you'd have to drink out of the toilet."

The handcuffs are hanging on a thin metal chain which ends in a hook that they must have drilled into the wall just for me – unless they abduct people on a regular basis. Whenever I move, the handcuff starts scraping against the plaster cast, which is slowly beginning to crumble away.

My prison ward sits down across from me on one of the two old wooden chairs. I carefully put the bottle back on the floor with trembling hands.

"I know, but I was scared of catching a disease if I drink out of a toilet bowl."

My basement has a tiny window which is secured from outside by a steel grid. The sunlight comes in from the street. It's the only light source here, and I'm more than grateful for this. It could be worse. I could be locked up in a windowless room and lose all sense of time. But since I have a normal day and night cycle here I know that I've been in this room for a week.

The boy just said "we". So there must be others. Not really surprising because it simply cannot be that I was kidnapped by one little teenager.

"Tell me, did you guys ever talk about selling me? Not to al-Qaeda, of course. I was thinking of my people? They would be happy to get me back."

The boy shakes his head regretfully. "Your government pays nothing. The US doesn't buy back hostages on principle."

I didn't know that. But then I guess I never really thought about such things before.

"Where d'you snatch me?"

My visitor looks at me with a clueless expression.

My voice doesn't really do what I want. It sounds like it wants to escape my body. "I don't remember how I got here."

The boy shrugs. "Maybe your memories will come back. If they don't, that's not my problem."

I feel helpless and humiliated. Maybe I shouldn't have told him I don't remember anything.

He cocks his head and smiles all of a sudden. "Let's just say we're professionals. We do this all the time. You Americans are easy to catch."

No, not really.

I can't think of any other service members that are MIA, except this one dude who lost his mind and walked out of his FOB. A few years later he showed up in a propaganda video, bearded and unbelievably haggard.

I can't give up so quickly. "You know, I had plenty of time to think. And it occurred to me that there was a case in Libya where the French bought some Eastern European nurses from Gaddafi. I think they paid a lot of money for them. Maybe you could get in touch with them?"

The boy laughs. "I think Gaddafi has other problems at the moment."

"Right." My voice is starting to fail me. The Doors fan sitting across from me is only half listening now. I feel like screaming at him. I don't want to be passed on to the Libyans, for God's sake. I want to be purchased by a wealthy European country.

I guess I'm starting to sound totally desperate. "But here in Baghdad there's all these embassies. You could ask the Brits or the Norwegians, I really don't care."

The boy shrugs. "We still have to determine what we'll do with you. We didn't actually take you to earn money with you."

I pick up my water bottle and cling to it. It's the most precious thing I own at the moment. It's three-quarters full, but I have no idea how long I'm going to have to live with it.

"We're in Baghdad, right?"

The boy laughs and stands up. "Why do you care where you are? You won't get out of here alive anyway."

True, I think. Bury my heart at the bend of the Euphrates. Or the Tigris. Or anywhere else for that matter.

And with this he leaves me. I hear the key turn twice from the outside. It's a fucking steel door of course. I lie back down and cover myself with the smelly fleece blanket. I'm starting to feel cold again, despite the summer heat coming in from the street. This probably has something to do with my weakened circulation. Or the fact that I didn't get anything to eat for a week.

I saw a survival show once. They said that you can go for weeks without food if you don't move too much. So I stay still. Somehow I'm happy. I know why: I had a conversation with another human being for the first time in a week. I told him stories about the wild times I had in my youth. He was interested in me. I had company for an afternoon. There's no doubt he liked my stories. Even though he looked a bit shell-shocked after I was finished with my first Russian tower story.

This makes me smile.

Boy, if you knew what else I've got...

THE BEST TIME OF MY LIFE

I doze off for a while. Ever since I got here, I never manage to get any real sleep. But I can rest. If I think of nothing for a while, I start "dreaming" in a state of total exhaustion from lack of food. And lack of hope. Maybe it's a survival mechanism that my brain has cooked up, but these last few days, my hometown of Lapwai keeps showing up as soon as I close my eyes. Just as I'm dreaming of the rolling hills that I see every time I get out of the front door of my parents' house, I get pulled out of my well-deserved semi-sleep. The prayer chants of two different mosques are competing with each other, it's unclear who wins. The little window is closed; I listen to the faint sound of Arabic voices praising God.

I'm not sure if God is here right now.

But then he's supposed to be everywhere at once.

I sit up and take a sip of water.

If I don't want to lose my mind, I will need some kind of strategy here. Maybe I should systematically try to remember all the happy moments in my life. Every good thing that ever happened to me, starting with the puppy I got for my sixth birthday, and ending with... what?

I don't know what was the last nice thing that happened before I woke up lying on this old metal bed with my arm hurting like crazy. I'm staring at the wall opposite of me, and while I'm studying the Eighties-style brownish wallpaper, my will to remember is fighting my non-cooperating subconscious. It should be possible to retrieve some kind of memory of what I was doing one or two weeks ago. Who I was hanging out with. Who I was working with here in Baghdad. But the only thing that comes to mind is the smell of Humvee exhausts and the sound of laughter from a teenage corporal at the wheel.

I give up. My brain is probably sugar-deficient and should be shutting down any minute now.

On the other hand, while I was talking to my captor I was perfectly able to recall the good times I had in Afghanistan. Maybe I should go back several years.

Back to Bagram.

I had a date every night (or day) after work, either with Dan or Tim. My shift rotation didn't allow me to see them every day though. Tim seemed to think that I was intimate with Dan. I didn't like this, but I knew that I was protecting Dan. It kind of made me proud. Being dishonest to Tim made me feel uneasy, though. Once I went to see Tim after I got off work at six in the morning. He was cleaning his 9-mil, and I sat down at the table to observe him. Maybe I could learn something. He offered me his cleaning equipment, which I thought was really sweet. I blushed, for whatever reason, and then started cleaning my M4. The others were snoring happily in their bunks.

Tim stowed his weapon away and watched me. Surprisingly he had nothing to criticize. When I was done I left the rifle on the table and yawned.

"How was your day?" he whispered.

I looked at him. His open and friendly face was something I would miss in the future. There was no point in asking how much time we had left. Someday I would knock on his door, and he would be gone.

"You mean, how was my night", I said. "Well, I spent the entire time in the weapons back shop. I tried to fix an ammo feeder. The only good thing about that was that Sergeant Lozano was really helpful. Can't complain about the guy. In the end, we finished our task so fast that we could've gone home early tonight. But then we ended up cleaning two Hogs."

"Inside or out?"

"We were all outside, ten of us. Cleaning the bird from the outside basically means wiping it down. I was standing on a ladder when we were taking care of the first one, and I gotta say I don't like that. I'm always afraid someone trips over it. I would hate to break my arm from falling off a ladder, you know? I don't think you get a Purple Heart for that."

Tim laughed. "We had a cherry LT who predicted that some day, in the near future, they're gonna hand out Purple Hearts for PTSD."

I wondered for the first time if Tim was an officer. I had no idea. He looked at the rifle, all shiny and black and totally lethal. Never to be used by me.

"You should put a cute sticker on it", he mused.

"Girly stuff? Something pink? What exactly do you have in mind?"

His smirk was adorable. I couldn't believe I was talking about weapons with him. He started rubbing his neck.

"I didn't think this through yet", he whispered. If he got any closer his beard would scratch my earlobe. I wondered if this was going to be hot or just plain irritating.

"The reason I'm suggesting that you mark your rifle is that you can't afford to have it mixed up with someone else's, you know? I've noticed a lot of people make sure they can always recognize their weapon, especially here at Bagram."

He was right, of course. I'd even seen an M4 slung behind someone's back that had a sticker saying "If found, please contact..."

"What about you?" I asked.

Tim shrugged. "Grunts always have their rifles customized so they can tell the weapons apart just by looking at the modifications. I have an aiming laser mounted on the RAS. Steve has a 203, Gucci has night vision and so on."

"You guys all use an M4?" I was almost disappointed. I'd always thought that special forces had special weapons.

He nodded. "It would be a good weapon in the cities of Europe. We could fight the Russians with it."

"And I guess that's not the case here?" I tried to remember to keep my voice down.

"Not here in the sandbox it ain't. It was okay in the Pech valley, but that's not as dry as other parts of Afghanistan. Once you're in the desert, you're seriously screwed. You'll end up cleaning the damn thing all the time. It's either that, or it will jam at the wrong moment."

I took a deep breath. "Are you in a lot of firefights? I wonder what it's like to get shot at."

"It's good", Tim said with a bold grin. "Especially afterwards. It can take forever to get off that adrenaline high."

I opened my mouth for the next question I had in mind, but he laid one finger on my lips.

"Let's go to bed before you fall asleep at the table", he whispered.

"Are you walking me home later?" I got up and stretched.

"Maybe", he said as he pulled off his shirt. "If I'm satisfied with your performance."

His grin was wide and irresistible.

Our meeting places varied. Once I met up with Tim in front of the Subway. We got on a bus. As I got in, it seemed to me as if all the other passengers were watching us. I was proud and worried at the same time. Proud because unlike everybody else I had an exciting love life, and worried because I suspected Rohrman's spies to be on the bus as well. I was genuinely afraid of getting sent back home, now that I was so happy here.

We had Tim's lovely plywood cabin to ourselves. The place was starting to grow on me. Nothing but happy memories. First we ate our sandwiches at the table.

"Gucci says you're too loud", Tim said abruptly.

I choked. Some of my Coke came out of my nose.

"That's why we're trying a new thing today." He took a bite of his giant tuna sandwich.

"And what is this technique?" I asked. I wasn't sure I wanted to know the answer.

"Don't worry, you won't suffocate. I'll watch out. I'll be super careful."

I felt nauseous all of a sudden, and I had to stop eating. "You're not seriously thinking about gagging me, right? I'm not doing this. What if I have something in my nose and suddenly I can't breathe?"

He looked at me with his friendly Andy Garcia eyes. "Do you really think I won't notice?" He shook his head as if my fears were completely irrational.

I wrapped up the rest of my sandwich and watched as he finished his dinner. He washed down the last bite with club soda.

"Marina", he said. "You trust me, right?"

I nodded.

"You picked me up on the street and you went to my place with me, and you took off all your clothes. Just like that. You trusted me from the start. Why stop now?"

"I just don't want to have an accident", I explained. "I don't want them to write on my headstone: Her sex life was a bit too exciting."

Tim seemed to think that this was outrageously funny. We spent some time thinking up witty headstone inscriptions for me. But when it came to his own grave he didn't want to make jokes about it. At some point we ended up on his bed, and I tried to keep calm while he gently filled my mouth with some soft stuff. He was extremely sweet and tender to prevent me from panicking. It worked. I managed to relax. He was so gentle and adorable that I couldn't imagine sleeping with anyone else.

"Does Dan also think that I'm too loud?" I asked when I was able to speak again.

Tim thought. "Nah, he just said you're really into him."

"But other than that, you guys don't talk about me, right?"

Tim's chest moved up and down while he was giggling in my ear.

"What do you think we talk about all day long, me and my buddies? We're on hold. Waiting for our next assignment. We're getting some limited amount of training done, yeah. But we got plenty of free time."

"Does that mean that you tell the guys who live here stuff about me?"

Say no, I thought.

"Of course I do. They're bored to death. They want to know all the details. Steve asked me if he could take a picture of you, but I said no."

I didn't want to imagine what would happen if someone came up with the idea to place a camera on Tim's bedpost. These guys certainly had access to nano-scale special equipment like in a James Bond movie. I wouldn't even notice if someone was filming me.

"Can you guarantee that I won't see myself on YouPorn someday?"

Tim gave me a chaste peck on the cheek. "I can. And you know why? Because we love you. All of us."

I was totally caught off guard when they introduced me to a new Staff Sergeant in the morning. His name was Flanagan and he had blue eyes that made the air around him chill. He exuded a different coolness than Rohrman. I found a suitable nickname for him: Dead Fish, which I wisely kept to myself. I was the last person to be summoned to the NCO office. As he was talking to me, it became pretty clear that he was forewarned. I asked him what happened to Rohrman.

"He was my replacement here for three months because I've been suffering from glandular fever. It was a chronic infection and it took ages to get rid of it", Flanagan said, his cold eyes boring right into mine. I felt like looking away, but didn't.

"You would know all that – if you'd bothered to go to his farewell party. Or if you talked to the others once in a while."

"I had no idea. Nobody invited me." Direct eye contact with my new supervisor was almost painful. I gave him what I hoped was a feral look.

Staff Sergeant Flanagan wasn't very impressed with my attempt at looking dangerous. "I would suggest that in the future, you spend more of your energy on communicating with the people on your team. Otherwise the next few months of your deployment at Bagram could get very boring."

The moment I began to smile, I knew it was a mistake. But I couldn't help it. The smug expression on my face told Flanagan more than a thousand words. The message was clear: Dude, you have no idea how much I'm enjoying myself here. The last thing I need is the company of other mechanics.

Later I told Dan about my first meeting with my supervisor and he was worried, as always.

"You know, this could get very unpleasant for you."

"I know", I said. "But all this shit that's going down at my workplace – it's like a locomotive that's gaining speed. Like a train that I just can't stop anymore. I feel more and more isolated. Although at least I manage to do my job well. I keep learning new stuff and all that, and I think my job performance doesn't leave anything to be desired."

Dan opened a can of beer and enjoyed the first sip. We sat next to each other on the blue sleeping bag.

"You know, I'd really like to change my AFSC. Sorry, I mean MOS", I said. "I'd love to join the Security Forces. At least that way, I would get outside the wire."

Dan laughed. "Girl, you can't be that naive. Do you really think the Air Force sent you to tech school for like six months, so that afterwards you'll stand around at checkpoints all day – or even worse, prison duty?" He shook his head as if he couldn't believe how stupid I was. "You want a different job, sure. I can understand that. But you should choose something that's worth the trouble."

"I just want to be a trigger-puller like you", I said, sulking. Whenever I talked about my dreams and ambitions, people had a tendency to laugh.

Dan handed me his beer, and I took a sip.

"The rest is for you", I said and handed the beer back to Dan.

Dan gave me a long look, his green eyes reflecting the evening sun. At least he wasn't laughing.

"First of all, there's almost no Airman who ever gets to pull a trigger. Leave that to the grunts. Second, any job in combat arms – please stay away. As long as women can't pee in a plastic bottle, they have no business in the infantry, the cavalry, and all the other badass units. You wouldn't get in anyway, I guess, but a little bird told me that some idiots in Washington are planning to open combat arms for women. And my third point is..." He finished the beer in one go and put the empty can on the floor. He cocked his head to the side and looked at me.

"Yes?" I asked even though I wasn't really interested in his opinion any longer. All that people ever did was discourage me. Don't do this, don't do that, don't go there. It's too dangerous for little girls like you.

"With the right training, almost anyone can be a grunt. Why not choose something special, learn some skill that no-one else has? Aircraft maintenance is kind of specialized, and it's not a bad career field, but you've got a lot more potential."

I tried to think about any special skills that could advance my career. Where was my potential? I got my job because I did well in the aptitude tests. But I prepared for those. I ordered ASVAB for Dummies, and I even studied Electronics for Dummies. Being a car mechanic, I was predestined to get a technical job.

"What kind of rare talent are they looking for in the military?"

He tapped a finger on my forehead as if he suspected a pot of gold inside my skull. "Everything that's hard to learn."

"Hmm." The muffled sound of foreign voices came in through the cracked window. I listened.

"Frogs", Dan suddenly exclaimed, jumping up. "Get dressed!"

We rolled up the sleeping bag and ran down the stairs. On the ground floor I grabbed my bike that was leaning against the wall, and Dan held the door open for me so I could push it out. Gucci was sitting on a ledge, chatting with three Frenchmen. They wore silly berets but one of them was kind of cute. I hoped that we would just walk past them – I really wanted to be alone with Dan. It was the good-looking one who whistled through his teeth as I stepped out of the building, pushing my bike.

I suddenly felt very vulnerable. There was a name tag on my uniform. There were now three additional people who knew where I was spending my time. And who I was spending it with. I tried not to imagine what happened if anyone told Flanagan where he could find me every other night. Dan was now standing next to Gucci. I had no choice but to stand around with one hand on the handlebars on my bike, trying to look casual. The French told us that they wanted to visit the Tower. Gucci immediately offered them a guided tour. The conversation went back and forth for a while. I was under the impression that the French also belonged to some kind of special unit. The tall cute guy had his eyes on me most of the time, and at some point, he offered me a cigarette. I shook my head.

"Do you have ancestors from North Africa", I asked. Not that I cared but he seemed to be really interested in talking to me.

"Algeria. My grandparents." His funny accent was kind of charming.

"Do you speak Arabic?" I asked politely.

He nodded. "That's not very helpful here, unfortunately. In Iraq I would be more useful. I have to admit that I'm not very fond of the Afghans. These are people who manage to marry a ten year old girl to a forty year old man."

"Disgusting", I said.

The Frenchman drew on his cigarette. "Oh, and there's so many other things. This whole gay stuff here is just sickening."

"What gay stuff?" I asked. I was confused. "They're all very much into religion as far as I know."

The Frenchman sighed. "That's what I don't really get. You can't take it up the ass and be religious at the same time. But in this country, people are gayer than a fashion designer in Paris."

We both laughed and the others stopped talking. My new acquaintance told them what we were talking about. One of his buddies groaned in disgust. Gucci interjected that he knew of a British soldier who even lost his life because of those things.

"Why, what happened?" Dan asked.

Gucci began to tell us the story. The way he talked was kind of slow. It seemed to me that he wanted to make sure that the French would understand him. "So there was this SAS unit who were working very closely with an ANA unit. One of the Afghans was a soldier who was constantly being raped by his buddies. And that was kind of common knowledge. Everybody in their platoon knew about it, try to imagine that."

Gucci looked at the French, apparently to make sure that they understood. The Algerian nodded on behalf of the others. Gucci continued.

"The Brits knew about it too, and one of them made the mistake of provoking this poor victim. He kept making fun about the fact that the guy had to bend over all the time. One day, the Afghan drew his weapon and shot the Brit. It was horrible. Just horrible."

It was a depressing story and I wanted to go home and take a shower. But I had to keep standing around in the sweltering evening heat because Dan and Gucci were obviously excited to have foreign visitors. It was another half hour before we left the group. I was glad to be alone with Dan again. There were so many things to talk about.

"Let's discuss my future career", I suggested.

"Good idea", he said. But our conversation didn't really get going. Dan never talked about himself and his own line of work. As a result there was always some kind of invisible wall between us. I didn't ask him about what he did for a living because it was clear that he wasn't allowed to talk about it anyway. Since both of us couldn't think of any special skills I should acquire, Dan chose to change the subject.

"That Arab couldn't take his eyes off you."

"Honestly, it's mutual", I replied.

Dan pretended to be outraged. "Girl, you better keep your hands off this guy. You got a real complicated love triangle going on already."

"I don't think it's that complicated", I said. "I think it's actually a perfectly organized triangle. Couldn't be more triangular."

"Right." We'd arrived in front of his luxurious wooden shack. I wanted to kiss him on the cheek, just for fun. But even though nobody was around, I didn't. You're never really alone on a military compound.

"Take care", he said.

I don't know, I thought. I guess I could try.

I'M ~~SEXY~~ STUPID AND I KNOW IT

When I finally made it home I felt sticky all over. The air was still but that could change any time. With my luck, I was going to get sandblasted after coming out of the shower. But first I had to get there. When I opened the door to my tiny cubbyhole I immediately grabbed my towel that hung on the inside of the door. Then I saw Staff Sergeant Flanagan sitting on my bed.

"Oh fuck", I exclaimed. The towel fell on the floor.

Flanagan laughed.

"Men aren't allowed in here. Do you want to lose your job?" I hissed at my boss, picking up the towel from the floor and shaking the sand out of it.

He pointed to the door. "I may stay here as long as I'm in uniform and the door remains open. You don't even know the basic rules here, but that doesn't surprise me at all."

Rules are made to be broken, I thought. But I was smart enough to keep my mouth shut.

I leaned the M4 against the wall. Then I knelt down to untie my boots, taking all my time. From now on I wouldn't say a word. Unfortunately Flanagan didn't say anything either. After I'd replaced my shoes and socks with neon-green Crocs, I didn't know what to do. I badly needed that shower.

Flanagan cleared his throat. "Special forces? Do you think that the special skills of these people are going to rub off on you?" He was very still as he was watching me slinging my towel around my shoulders.

I leaned against the doorframe. I was tired. I had to get up in less than six hours. Flanagan seemed to seriously expect an answer from me.

"Actually, yeah. You know, I'd like to cut myself just a thin slice of their intelligence. Maybe I wouldn't feel so dumb now."

He looked at me with a puzzled expression.

"I feel stupid standing around here instead of taking a shower just because my boss is sitting on my bed. If I were Delta or SEAL I'm pretty sure I would know what to do."

Flanagan got up and handed me a plain white envelope.

I was too surprised to thank him, and he left.

I opened the envelope and took out a small piece of paper that someone had ripped from a notepad. The note contained a few handwritten lines. Not written with a ball pen, but with ink. I remembered the Mont Blanc fountain pen that Rohrman was toying with when he was giving me hell.

From: Staff Sergeant David M. Rohrman

To: Airman First Class Marina Laroque

Too bad we didn't see each other yesterday. I wish you perseverance. You'll need it.

I felt dizzy. I slipped the little piece of paper back in the envelope and stuffed it between the pages of a magazine that was lying in the shelf next to my bed. I turned off the reading lamp. Instead of going to the showers, I crawled under the covers. I suddenly felt really bad. Flanagan hadn't come to make trouble. He just wanted to get rid of the letter. And he patiently waited for me in my room – a dutiful Staff Sergeant doing his predecessor a favor. And what had I done? Snapped at him.

I was rude to my boss. How could I be so stupid? The whole thing would have been so easy to avoid if I'd just let him talk when I discovered him in my room.

Needless to say that my night was entirely sleepless. Eventually I gave up and switched on my laptop. I got lucky. For once the connection was good enough for a Skype session. I told Jesse about my exciting love life and my work troubles, and he made clear how much he envied me.

"You seem to have more fun in Afghanistan than I'm having here in New York", he sighed.

"I don't know about that, Jesse. There's a lot of things I can think of that are maybe not so great about this place. For example, the toilet paper. It's like sand paper. My mother sends me baby wipes every month. Or the wind, every time it hits you in the face it's like a cosmetic face peeling. Saves me a lot of money, I guess. But the most annoying thing about living here is the noise level. Most of the flight movements take place at night because it's more difficult for the insurgents to shoot down a plane in the dark, obviously. You can't possibly imagine what's going on here at night. I have those industrial-strength ear plugs but I'd prefer to just pour concrete in my ears."

Jesse laughed. "Hearing is overrated anyway. That way, you wouldn't have to listen to your Staff Sergeant. Is it true that you only have Portajohns?"

"In the workshop we have a real toilet that you can flush. I try to use it as often as possible. But in the B-huts there's nothing. So you always have to get out to the nearest row of Portajohns. That is going to be fucking awkward in the cold season. I've heard that the men tend to pee in plastic bottles at night."

"Good for them."

"Yeah."

We were quiet for a while. I couldn't think of anything to say. Someone slammed a door. Then I heard footsteps. Someone walked past my poor excuse for a window towards the showers.

"You know what?" I said to Jesse. "I think I should have a penis. I'm sure you can get one if you're willing to shell out enough money. I could claim that I'm a man trapped in a female body. Then I could get into combat arms, or I would at least see something of the country instead of sitting around here all the time."

Jesse looked worried for a second. "That's out of the question, Marina. No dick for you! I want you to stay right where you are now. What do you need combat for? Life is enough of a struggle."

I had no idea what he was talking about. But it wouldn't be long until I found out.

EVERYONE LOVES BURGER KING

It's the middle of the night when I hear the key in the door. I sit up in my bed. The neon light bulb that I always stare at when I'm lying down comes to life. It's the first time someone has switched it on. My visitor is about my age. Despite the jet-black hair and the brown eyes he reminds me of Flanagan. He exudes the same air of cold self-control. The harsh overhead light shines down on us and emits an unpleasant buzzing sound.

At first I don't understand why he drags the old-fashioned floor lamp to the side of the bed, but then I see the device he's holding in his hand. I get closer and hold out my left arm. Wordlessly he begins to unravel the plaster with a whirring blade, his head bent over my arm. He's so close to me that I could easily knock him in the face with my right.

Break his nose, maybe. Or crush his eye socket if I hit him hard enough.

My visitor carefully places the parts of the plaster cast in a plastic bag. I try to decipher the Arabic writing on the bag, but I'm not fast enough. He puts the lamp back in the corner of the room and then lays a pita bread on the seat of the empty chair. I pick it up and start eating slowly. There's no plate, but I'm keeping the bread firmly in my hand as I have no intention of parting ways with it. It takes forever to eat up; I'm savoring every bite. This might be the best meal of my life. The visitor is sitting at the rear end of my bed, watching me with the cold eyes of a dead fish.

I'd like to go for his throat. I'm too weak. It's hopeless.

Finally I'm done eating. I feel pleasantly tired so I just lie down again as if I were alone. I can't cover myself because my visitor is sitting on my blanket.

Eventually he gets up and leaves just as silently as he came.

The next morning I wake up from the usual street noise. Clattering mopeds, honking cars, human voices and of course the chants of the muezzins. There's something comforting about the noises of life in the city. It's certainly better to be here than to be buried alive in a hole in the desert or a cave in the mountains. Nature is not your friend. It doesn't care if you're starving or dying of thirst. At least here, I know some of the people will be sad or horrified when my dead body is found and when they realize how much I was suffering in their midst while they were going about their day-to-day business.

It would be awesome if I could see the street from the window. But even if I wasn't chained to the wall I wouldn't get to see much because the window is not much more than a ten-inch high slit in the wall right underneath the ceiling. I guess I would see people's shoes on the pavement. But if the window was just a bit bigger I could slip through. I'd be standing on the sidewalk of a street full of shops and cafés, and I would be surrounded by people.

It would be fantastic.

I try to visualize all the equipment that would be useful for blowing a hole into the wall. There's more than one option here, but each one of them would surely lead to considerable collateral damage. Several dead, a lot more injured. The nasty thing about explosives is that they rip off people's limbs. What if a child is walking by my window when the bomb goes off?

But that's all theory. I'm going to die here.

I had a good life. No regrets.

Since I have nothing else to do, I use the toilet, then I drink all the water from the bottle. Instead of lying down again on my smelly bed, I try to do some calisthenics to get my circulation going. The workout is good for me and after what feels like two hours I go to bed feeling more or less satisfied. Too bad I have no water left.

I need to take my mind off the thirst that's building up in me and that will be torturing me later on. I start working on my favorite fantasy, visualizing it in the brightest colors and the minutest details: Dan and Tim and Steve and Gucci storm the basement to set me free. They kick the steel door open (because that's how strong they are) and jump in with their 9-mils at the ready. Tim smashes my chain into little pieces while Dan is securing the exit. Tim pulls me up from my bed and we leave my prison, hand in hand.

On the way out, I stumble upon my kidnappers. They're lying on the floor, covered in blood.

With this beautiful image in mind, I fall asleep.

As always, I wake up in the middle of the night. A couple of dogs are in disagreement right by my window. I'm cold. I won't be able to go back to sleep as long as I hear the dogs' aggressive barking in the street. So I sit down on the floor. It's covered with an ancient gray carpet that emits an unpleasant smell when I get too close. I try a few pushups, groaning in pain and immediately gasping for air.

I remember when I started doing sports – before my mother destroyed my plans for a brilliant career in the United States Marine Corps. It was clear that I had to become much stronger so I decided to train every day. At home, I locked the door to my room whenever I was going to work out. No need to wake a sleeping dog. When I tried my first sit-up nothing happened. I was only a few inches off the ground and couldn't believe it. Just to make sure, I looked up sit-ups on the Internet. Where did these people get the muscles to move their torsos up and down like a seesaw?

At twenty, I wasn't in better shape than my grandmother who'd never worked out in all her life. This shocking revelation almost made me bury my plan to become a warrior. But I decided to give myself a chance. If other people my age were capable of running and sweating and passing PT tests, then this should be possible for me too.

I took up running first, presuming it couldn't be that difficult. After a minute of light jogging there was an unpleasant feeling of pain building up in my calves. Every day. So I had to constantly shift down a gear, something that probably didn't look too good if anyone was watching. I sought out the kind of places where I wouldn't meet another soul. The other workouts I tried weren't any easier. The calisthenics DVDs that I ordered all had the same effect on me: after a few minutes I was drenched in sweat.

The next few weeks were difficult. I had to make time for my new hobby after work. In addition I also had to keep my ambitions secret as I had no desire whatsoever for endless discussions with my parents and my gran. I definitely didn't want to hurt my father's feelings. He'd spent his whole life fixing cars and as far as I could tell, he assumed that I would do the same.

Slowly the pain eased and I started enjoying myself. Outdoors was more fun than indoors. I found some really nice jogging routes, the best ones were along the Clearwater River. I took less breaks and I moved faster as the months went by. Once I came home after dark as my parents were debating whether they should call the police. But the big breakthrough came after about six months, when I finally ran three miles in eighteen minutes: fast enough to keep up with pretty much any male Marine.

But tonight my body is on strike. After a few pushups my upper arms start shaking, so I lie down on the smelly carpet for some stretching exercises. I get dizzy so fast that I give up and go back to bed. The dogs aren't finished arguing, but they've moved down a block.

The boy has to wake me up, that's how deep I slept. I feel more than stiff as I sit up. He puts a paper bag in my lap. It's warm and emits a very familiar smell.

"Oh my God", I shriek. "You got me something at Burger King?"

The boy tries not to smile, scrunching his face to hide the fact that he's just as pleased with his brilliant idea as I am.

I force myself to eat slowly. Even the pickle on the cheeseburger tastes delicious; in my former life I used to get rid of it.

"Listen, you gotta tell me what your name is."

The boy laughs. "You never asked before."

"Yeah, whatever. Until now, I was kinda busy dealing with my own misery. Will you tell me your name now?"

"Khassem."

I drink Coke through a straw. An awesome drink. Why did I never notice that before?

"I know you probably don't care much, but your name sounds real nice."

"Thank you." Is Khassem blushing? It must be his first abduction. He's a cherry kidnapper.

He clears his throat and gives me a stern look. "Now tell me the next story from the Arabian Nights."

"Do you mind if I finish first?" I ask, pointing a greasy finger at the beautiful logo on the paper.

God, I miss my country.

He seems to debate with himself for a while. "Alright. But when you're done eating I want to hear the next thing that happened with your two lovers. And with your new boss."

"Why do you even wanna know?" I ask with too many fries in my mouth.

"Because I want to know what's the next stupid thing you did."

He does have a point.

THE PREDATORS

One week after Flanagan's disastrous visit to my hooch I spent my last evening with Tim and Dan. They didn't tell me where they were going but there was no doubt they wouldn't come back. At first I was alone with Dan. He kissed me goodbye on Tim's bunk. I almost overdosed on his last, passionate kiss. The rest of the night I spent with Tim. I didn't really mind that we were no longer alone after nightfall. In the course of the night his roommates certainly heard some of what was going on. But Bagram is the kind of place where people use earplugs a lot so I figured we had a thin layer of privacy left. Of course I wasn't too happy about their use of the night vision equipment, but I tried not to think of it. It was clear that I would never see any of them again in my life.

Shortly before sunrise it was time for me to go.

"I love you", I whispered in Tim's ear when I kissed him for the last time. We were sitting on the bed side by side, holding hands like teenagers. Steve's excessive snoring was the soundtrack to our romance.

"I love you too", he replied.

"I don't wanna go", I said. One of my tears fell on the sand-covered floor. I fumbled for a tissue in my cammies and blew my nose.

"You have to, otherwise I'm afraid I'll have to kick you out."

"Fine, I'll go now. Please promise me you'll take care of yourself."

I stood up and registered with surprise that he was shaking his head. "Not possible. I'm too busy watching out for my buddies."

We'd travelled by car to get to his home, that's why I didn't have my bike with me. I walked slowly through the night. I was taking all my time because there was no point in going to sleep; I had to be at work in less than two hours. To the east there was a hint of a pink glow over the mountain range. The air was cool, a sign that fall was approaching. Whenever I tripped over a stone I cursed. But it wasn't a stone that made me stumble when I suddenly flew through the air. I was pushed from behind with such force that I couldn't even land on my hands when I hit the floor. My face ended up in the gravel and was immediately pressed down by a boot. That same boot pressed my nose deeper into the ground. Another boot was on my right biceps, and my left hand was under so much pressure from boot number three that I was afraid it would break.

The middle boot wandered down to my neck. One wrong move and the spine would go. Because my face was pushed into the ground I could hardly breathe. The panic made me gag. I began to heave into the gravel. This made my breathing even more difficult. I could feel all my strength leave my body.

I was boneless.

I ran out of oxygen.

But that was only the beginning. The three men in control of my upper body were not alone. A fourth man pulled off the rifle and threw it to his right. I could hear where it landed. He was practiced in the art of unlacing boots and seemed to be in no hurry at all. Fear was racing through me in waves. My attacker pulled down my pants and undies in one go. His calm made me gag even more. I'd emptied the contents of my stomach on the floor. There was nothing more to come.

The silence was absolute. The only sound came from a round being racked into the chamber of the M4. Then there was the soft click of the automatic as it was switched from safe to semi. The fourth man who was kneeling between my legs stopped moving.

"The only reason why I'm not blowing your head off is that I don't want to mess up my girlfriend's fatigues. Blood and brain matter is so hard to wash out." Tim kept his voice down but his message was heard loud and clear. The boot crushing my left hand slowly moved. All of a sudden the pressure was off. Whoever had been standing on me was trying to discreetly move away.

"Yeah, you three can go now. Dismissed."

I whimpered in relief when the middle guy stepped off my neck. Now I was able to turn my head to the side and breathe again.

"You. You get up. To your left. Face to the wall. Keep your hands up, you fucking moron."

With difficulty I sat up. I crawled towards my pants. The underwear I couldn't find in the dark so I didn't bother. The pain in my neck was even worse than in my left hand. With each movement my nerves were firing incendiary signals into my brain. At last I was able to locate both of my boots but I had no strength left. I pulled them on, leaving them unlaced. Finally I stood next to Tim, hands trembling and knees almost giving in.

"Take the flashlight that's on my belt. Here, on the right side", Tim said softly.

I fumbled around. It was surprisingly small.

"Turn around", Tim said to the fourth man who was still facing the wall of a B-hut.

He turned around and I quickly flashed the light to illuminate his face, switching it off immediately.

"Is that the guy you threatened a couple of months ago", Tim asked.

"No", I whispered. "His friend. He was sitting across from him at the table."

"Interesting."

Tim handed the rifle over to me. He twisted the soldier's right arm behind his back and covered his victim's mouth with his free hand. The man groaned in pain.

I moved closer to Tim so he could continue to speak softly. I needed to be close to him anyway. My hope was that the feeling of infinite terror that was raging through me would fade away if I could just stay right next to my man for a while.

"So", Tim whispered. "Now you have to decide what to do with him."

"I can't. I don't have a clear head. "

"You have to, Marina. I can let him go now. He's scared shitless. But then it won't be long till he finds a new victim."

I was standing next to my protector, still weak in the knees, and there was not one clear thought that I could come up with.

"Or we make sure he gets punished. That way, he'll never try to rape a woman or a man again."

From a distance I could hear birds chirping. But most of the others seemed to be still asleep.

"Then there's another option", Tim said, and in one swift and elegant movement he broke his victim's arm. The man screamed into Tim's hand, a muffled sound that no one but us could hear. "We can end him. Here and now. We leave him here. The other three won't say a thing. He will return to the States as a murder victim. He will never again be able to organize a brutal rape. I have no doubt that this was planned well in advance, and that the four of them would take turns."

I hoped that no one could hear me sob. I covered my mouth with both hands. For someone walking by it would certainly be a strange sight: Tim holding up a man who was almost passing out from pain, and my muffled crying.

"I gotta say in all honesty – if they'd managed to gangbang you, I don't think you would've survived that. Your body would have made it through, maybe. But not your soul. They wanted to destroy you."

I started taking deep and slow breaths. The fresh air in my lungs made the fog lift in my head.

A clear thought took shape in my mind.

This has to end. Here and now.

I now knew what to say. "Break his neck."

Tim had turned the attacker away from the wall so that they were now both facing me. I stepped closer and looked at the man's face. It was hard to tell if his eyes were wide with pain or fear of death. Tim seemed to hesitate.

After a while he said: "Well, let's give this ugly story an ugly ending. Sleep well, asshole. See you in hell."

My attacker had lost control of his basic body functions. An unpleasant smell came from his clothes. He'd relieved himself in his pants. A dark puddle was taking shape between his boots.

"On the other hand...", Tim said. "I got a much better idea. I'll walk you home. And this guy, I'm gonna drop him off with the MPs and I'm going to tell them that the rape victim ran away. And I'm gonna say the victim was a dude, that makes things even worse. Then I'll spend the whole day signing tons of paperwork, and our man gets twelve, six and a kick in the ass. Yeah, that's what we're gonna do!" Tim sounded happy and satisfied.

Before I could even begin to insist on the death sentence that I had just delivered, Tim began to shove the guy, making him walk in front of him and all the while supporting the broken arm of his victim.

"Don't forget your rifle, Marina."

When we arrived at my hooch we had to say goodbye again.

"Look", Tim said. "I gotta get going now. I want you to know that there are people who love you. You're a wonderful person, but you have to learn to take care of yourself now. These fucktards are not coming back for you. But you gotta find yourself some friends if you wanna survive Bagram. Do you understand that?" He looked into my eyes as he kept covering the soldier's mouth.

"I promise you that I will take care of myself", I said. My voice was hoarse. I turned around, completely forgetting to thank him for rescuing me. In my room I put down the weapon and took my plastic basket with the shower stuff. While I walked towards the shower barracks I saw Tim and my wannabe-rapist in the distance. Tim was carrying the guy over his shoulder now. My guess was that he'd passed out. He was lucky that Tim wasn't just dragging him to the MPs.

The sun went up behind the Hindu Kush. A new day began.

I spend two very lonely days and nights in my little basement, slowly running out of water and crying a lot. The solitary confinement I'm enduring makes me think of my worst time at Bagram. In addition to my growing thirst, I feel this insane desire to keep talking to Khassem and to tell him what happened after I was rescued by Tim. But he doesn't show. All I can do is keep myself busy with elaborate prison break fantasies where Tim and Dan play the lead roles. But some of those daydreams are variations in which Flanagan and Rohrman come to my rescue. Sometimes the two guys from my unit that I liked the most, Robert and Kyle, get to shed their aircraft mechanic identities and turn into heroes. My imagination gives them the chance to kill my captors in cold blood and then carry me out into the light.

I'm not really sitting in a dungeon here. My prison is a basement room with carpeting and wallpaper. Maybe this is where the owner of the shop on the ground floor lived. I imagine that there's a small hardware store, or a place where they can fix electric devices. Sometimes I picture people repairing stuff, and customers coming to pick up the goods, maybe arguing about the price. My mini-apartment has no kitchen but it has a tiny bathroom with a shower, a toilet and a sink. The toilet will save my life if no one comes back to provide me with water or food. I'll be able to drink water from the toilet water for a few weeks if I'm lucky.

And then I guess I should start praying.

Khassem makes his next entrance sometime in the middle of the night. He hands me a glass filled with water, and as always he fills up my bottle. He's brought along another bottle. I can spot an orange on the label, and the Arabic writing confirms that there used to be juice in it but the bottle is filled with water. Which is of course fine with me. I don't need any luxuries here. But the question that is torturing me is how long I have to make do with my new supplies until I get the next refill. Five days? A week?

"What does that mean: twelve, six and a kick in the ass?"

I stare at him, not bothering to conceal my anger. "I'll tell you that next time you bring me food. Thanks to the fact that I'm not getting anything to eat, I'm now a size zero. I could walk the runway at the Paris fashion shows."

Khassem laughs. "You're funny, even though you know that the end is near."

The water has provided me with a new feeling of strength. I jump up and fling the chair into his direction. Khassem hops to the side and is visibly enjoying himself.

"You're not behaving like someone who's starving", he says.

I feel dizzy and I sit down on the bed. It's not enough, theres's white noise in my ears and I get so nauseous that I have to lie down.

I can hear the sound of a passing car from outside. I'm not under the impression that Khassem brought me something to eat.

"Court-martial. Twelve months military prison, six months loss of benefits, dishonorable discharge from the army."

"Is that the normal sentence for rape?"

"Are you crazy?" I swear if I was able to, I would now strangle him for his stupidity. "Are you really that naive? We sweep rape under the carpet. The only person who gets punished is the victim. Rape victims usually leave the military because their career is destroyed anyway."

"I don't feel sorry for you people at all. You decadent pigs."

Khassem is obviously not in a good mood today. It's contagious.

"Look, Khassem. I got an idea. How about you fuck off now and just let me die here?"

He slams the door before he locks it twice from the outside.

Khassem recovers from our first fight surprisingly fast. He's back at lunch time, and he doesn't come empty-handed. This time he offers me a warm falafel, the scent of which brings me back to life. I had actually spent the rest of the night adjusting to my new reality: that there was no way I was going to survive this. But maybe, now that I'm munching on a fried chick pea burger, I should reconsider. Just as long as I don't get my hopes too high.

I sink back on the pillow, lazy and full. I feel sorry for my digestive system. Whenever my stomach has shrunken to the size of an olive I stuff it to the brink with food.

"Hey – don't go to sleep", Khassem bitches.

"I know you want to hear the sequel. Oh man, I really need some coffee now."

"How would you like a cappuccino?" Khassem's voice is dripping with sarcasm. "Would you like some cinnamon on it or would you prefer cocoa?"

"Nah, I'm good. Any additional intake would make me throw up I guess."

I'm trying to concentrate. It is very important to keep my kidnapper happy.

"Where were we?"

"You told me of your near-disaster. With the four guys who assaulted you. And then you went to take a shower."

"Right, the Bagram showers", I moan and turn so that I can lie sideways. I look at Khassem. He's a really handsome boy. It would be a shame if Special Forces blew his pretty head off. But the price that he'll have to pay for my freedom will be high.
"The communal showers were really awful back then. I don't know if it's any better these days. Nobody went there without flip-flops or Crocs, but you could still get the soap residue or other people's hair spilling into your shoes. The smell of mildew was so gross. It was either that, or the whole shower would stink like a chlorine gas explosion."

Khassem is unhappy with my description of the hygienic conditions I've had to endure. He wants to see action. "You're still whining. Now go ahead and tell me what happened next."

"Fine", I sigh and close my eyes. "But you won't like it very much."

For the first time since my arrival in Afghanistan I used the mascara and the other make-up that I had bought in Germany at the last minute. The foundation I needed to mask the many scratches on my face. I could feel a bruise on my neck and applied some make-up in the hope that I could cover it up. The face powder gave my face this immaculate look, almost like a pale fashion model. Using lipstick was asking for trouble. I was a train wreck. I had the right to look good at least.

The others didn't say anything but it was clear that my new look didn't go unnoticed. On the way to chow I suddenly found myself walking alongside Robert and Kyle, my former co-conspirators against Sandy's rapist.

"Everything okay?" Robert asked me.

"Sure, yeah", I answered, but my voice wasn't quite right.

Don't cry, don't cry, DO NOT START CRYING.

While I was trying to pull myself together my colleagues walked next to me without speaking. Kyle was the stronger of the two and had the broad back of a combat swimmer. His cropped brown hair and the way he was carrying himself made him look like a grunt who was on his way to the next night raid. Which was funny because he was actually a nerd and knew everything about computers, electronics and of course avionics.

Robert used his hair length to test the limits of the grooming standard. He always worked out a lot with Kyle but unlike his friend, Robert remained wiry no matter how much he bench-pressed. He was the boy next door who had no desire to get an education in order to sit behind a desk for the rest of his life. He initially wanted to be a pilot but wasn't willing to spend four years at college for this. But fixing planes instead of flying them was an endless source of frustration for him. He wanted to leave the Air Force as quickly as possible. This was something he had told me when we were on our secret mission. The hunt for Sandy's rapist had taken a few weeks, and during that time I learned a lot about my two colleagues. After our fall-out they refused to have anything to do with me.

It felt good to have company. With Robert and Kyle at my side I didn't feel the usual tension building up in me. I was often so nervous that I didn't feel any appetite. On a military compound people are always moving around in pairs or in groups. As a young woman I was getting noticed anyway. But when I was in the DFAC alone with my tablet and looking for a seat, I felt the eyes of hundreds of people on me. For the same reason I hardly ever mustered up the courage to go to the gym. It was less scary to go running.

We disinfected our hands before getting our food. I wasn't hungry and chose the same meal as Kyle. We found a table and sat down next to two Army females. I managed to eat my lunch, which surprised me. I'd been sure that I would not get anything down today.

"Hey, look at that. Isn't that fantastic?" Robert was waving his plastic fork in the air. "I just hacked into my potato and the fork still has all its teeth! Do you think they changed the cutlery suppliers?"

Kyle grinned. "Rohrman mentioned something yesterday. He said that so many people complained that they had no other choice than to finally get us better cutlery."

"No fucking way." Robert tried to cut a soft piece of meat with his plastic knife. The knife didn't seem to cut anything at all but Robert carefully exerted a limited amount of pressure until he finally had a piece of meat on his fork and triumphantly waved it in the air.

"Even if you got three thousand people complaining, that's not gonna change anything at all", Robert explained. "Nobody gives a shit if our chow is good or not, or if we actually have knives and forks to eat it with. No, I think what happened is that some senator's son ended up in Bagram by mistake and then he complained to Daddy, and Daddy took care of this in Washington. So now we got a different multi-billion dollar company sending us the cutlery. That's how things are done."

That was one of the things I had missed about my friends: Robert's rants against the system and Kyle's dry sense of humor.

"I don't know what you're getting upset about", Kyle said. "Why should anyone care about us at home? We're a tiny minority. People who serve, you know. Less than one percent of the population is in the military. We should consider ourselves lucky that we get cutlery and don't have to eat with our fingers."

Robert subjugated the fork to a stress test by trying to smash a potato. The fork broke in half. It was the first time in a while that all three of us were laughing. Robert left to get a new fork. As he sat down again, he said with mock sadness: "Well, I think minorities like us should be fostered and protected and encouraged to find their place in society."

"We're the 1%, baby", Kyle said.

The two soldiers got up and left.

I took a deep breath, summoning up all my courage because my buddies deserved to hear the truth from me. They looked surprised when I actually started talking. And then I told Kyle and Robert what had happened the night before. My voice was strangely flat. The effort not to burst into tears was killing me. I got a headache that stayed with me all day.

My audience was stunned. Just when Kyle started saying something a group of civilians sat down at our table.

"Let 's go", Robert said, jumping up. He took my plate and put it on his own so he could slide my empty tray under his. That way I had nothing to carry on the way to the exit. This small gesture was something that Kyle also registered, and he shot me a curious side glance. My heart was beating fast. There was nothing I could do about being nervous. I followed the others and waited for what they had to say about my story.

Robert put his arm around my shoulder, and we walked back to work. When the hangar appeared in front of us, he said: "What I really wanna know is if this whole legal procedure will work out the way your friend thought it would."

I didn't know what to say.

Kyle said: "As I understand it, he wants to bend the truth and use his testimony so that they have no choice but to lock the guy up."

I nodded. "I think he's going to add whatever detail he thinks would be handy. He was absolutely determined."

"The way he broke the dude's arm – awesome", Kyle said, which made all three of us giggle like conspirators coming up with some great new ideas. For Staff Sergeant Flanagan who was just now stepping off the bus, this was certainly an unusual sight: Robert's arm around my shoulder, and the three of us laughing together. Robert let go of me when we got to the maintenance hangar. All of a sudden I had two friends. Which was exactly what Tim had asked of me. So I decided to take this one step further and also to inform Sandy.

I only saw her three days later. She'd just come home from her night shift and looked at me with open hostility when I entered her room.

"I'm tired as fuck, Marina. This better be important."

I had to summon up all my courage to tell her about my encounter with the four predators. Her face turned way too pale as I was describing what had happened the night before. An uneasy feeling got hold of me but it was too late to stop now because I still had to tell her about the happy ending. When I was finished she slapped me in the face and began yelling at me. I took flight before she could hit me again.

It was all my fault.

Sandy had swept her rape under the rug. She was in full denial. That was her way of coping. And I was the one who made all of those memories come back. No wonder she freaked. I ended up spending another night tossing and turning. Shortly before sunrise I gave up on trying to sleep. I took the laptop and tried to set up a Skype session. At the last moment I changed my mind. It was just too risky. I was not going to break into tears during a conversation with my parents.

In the next few weeks I did exactly what the other thirty thousand residents of the airbase did: I went to work and to the gym, I surfed the web when the connection was good enough, did some reading in bed, and tried to sleep. That was pretty much it. At night I was terrorized by nightmares. At work I had Robert and Kyle. Robert's special skill was to complain about everything that he saw. At lunch this was highly entertaining.

"Does your laundry also disappear? There's always something missing when I get my laundry back. I swear to God, this Filipino dwarf is secretly wearing my boxers."

Kyle nodded. "I just don't understand why there's no laundromats here. I wanna wash my clothes myself."

"There's a small one that opened up at Fluor village", I mentioned. "But I heard they only have eight washing machines and there's a long waiting list."

"Besides", Robert said thoughtfully, "a laundromat would be a good place to meet women."

"Do you have a girlfriend at home?" I asked Robert. He laughed.

"Is that a joke?"

I was confused. It was kind of normal to have someone waiting for you at home, and not just your family.

Robert looked at me. "You?"

I shook my head. "Neither girlfriend nor boyfriend."

We all laughed. It was so good to have these two with me.

"Do you miss your lover?" Kyle was starting to work on his yogurt. He didn't look at me. Maybe he was trying not to blush. It wasn't working.

"I miss both of them", I said finally. It was important to keep up appearances, even though my friends probably didn't care too much if someone was gay or not.

"Holy mother of fuck!" Robert cursed so loud that other people at our table stopped talking.

Kyle's spoon fell to the ground. My buddies stared at me in awe.

"You slut", Robert whispered but our neighbors heard that too.

I gave him a friendly smirk.

Kyle picked up his spoon from the floor, wiped it off on his napkin and emptied his yogurt. Then he looked at me sideways and said, "I want to know everything. We are now walking back and you're gonna tell us everything. In all details."

Robert nodded. "It's either that, or you're going to chow without us next time."

At first I tried to resist. I didn't really intend to invent the kind of sex I never had with Dan. And I certainly wasn't going to tell them about the roommates in Tim's B-hut who had heard (and maybe seen) so much of the action. And the last thing I wanted to do was talk about my feelings for Tim.

"You have no right to invade my privacy."

Kyle laughed. "What are you talking about? We're not hacking your computer, we're asking you to spill the beans."

"Girl", Robert snorted. "In a war zone there's no such thing as privacy. Most of us here know exactly what the others look like naked. But not necessarily because they want to know."

"It's not fair. I never ask you guys about your love life", I protested.

Kyle laughed. "Because we don't have one. There's nothing to talk about."

"What do I get out of this?"

I could see how they were both struggling to come up with an answer.

Robert suddenly stopped. "Do you realize what your lovers were doing for you when you were together? They protected you. Every time you walked home at night one of them was following you at some distance. Or maybe they were jogging behind you when you were riding your bike."

We were standing on the sidewalk, looking at each other, and I knew that Robert was right. There could only be one reason why Tim was able to rescue me when the predators came. He was always there. He probably took turns with Dan. Maybe even Gucci was tasked to accompany me home discreetly.

"D'you understand what I'm getting at?" Robert was dead serious now. "Everyone needs friends. If nobody cares about you here, you're as good as dead."

He started walking again. We walked along beside him.

"And besides, what's the problem with that? We only want to satisfy our curiosity", Kyle asked.

I shrugged. "I don't want to fill your imagination with images. I don't wanna play the lead role in your movies. With what I have to say, I could satisfy much more than your curiosity."

Apparently that was an incredibly witty remark. Kyle nearly fell over laughing and had to hold on to Robert's shoulder. They both needed a while until they could go on walking back to work. If we got back late Flanagan would definitely notice.

"Is she crazy or what?" Robert looked at Kyle. "She wants to actually control what we're fantasizing about."

Kyle shook his head. His face was serious. "Marina, what do you think we've been doing here for the last three months? And the others? And I don't even want to know what movies were playing in Rohrman's head when he was alone in his bunk. Every time you were busy, he was watching you. You never even noticed."

"In other words", added Robert, "do not worry about our sexual fantasies. There's a lot of other women we think of. You're just one of them."

I sighed. "Oh great. I feel so much better now."

In the workshop we stored our rifles in the gun rack. My new friends looked at me with an expression of hope. They were clearly expecting great things from me.

"Okay", I said. "Tonight. Let's go to the gym first. I really hate going there on my own. And then afterwards we have to find a suitable place to talk."

"Why?" Kyle asked.

"I'm not gonna tell you in a Pizza Hut how to drive an elite warrior crazy."

DISASTER BREEDS DISASTER

I was doing great, enjoying my new friendship with Kyle and Robert. They were more than grateful for the way I entertained them, always hungry for details. There was no doubt they would use my stories as an inspiration for a more fulfilling love life sometime in the future. Our evening walks in the cool autumn air were just what I needed. I had an audience that was actually interested in me. When I went to bed I was exhausted but happy. Robert gave me sleeping pills. The nightmares were less frequent, but when they came I had to leave my reading lamp on for the rest of the night.

Tim was right. If the predators had managed to carry out their attack as planned, nothing would be left of the old Marina Laroque. They would have broken me. I would have come back to the States as damaged goods. Maybe I would have remained functional, still able to go to work. During the day, I would have repaired cars and helped my Dad in the gas station, in the evening I would have dinner with my parents and my grandmother. Maybe hang out with old friends, or maybe not. TV. Internet. Bedtime. But what would my sleep be like?

Unsurprisingly my sex drive disappeared completely, despite the fact that I loved Kyle and Robert so much. It just felt so incredibly good to spend time with them. They were fun to be with. They listened to me. Everyone could see that I now had two protectors. But I never felt any desire to touch them. I had no doubt they would be available in case of need.

They approved of the nickname I had found for Flanagan and started using it on a regular basis.

"Actually, Flanagan's great as a crew chief if you ask me", Kyle said once when we were eating at a Subway. We'd actually managed to occupy three seats and tried to sit there as long as possible. "I've been working under him for over two years now. He's got absolutely no problem with explaining stuff more than once. And he likes to get his hands dirty."

Robert nodded and looked around. The store was packed and the sandwich guys worked frantically behind the counter. A couple of civilians had their eyes on us, probably hoping that we would get up soon.

"Slow down, Rob. You're eating way too fast", I said to Robert.
He grinned. "You know what I was just thinking? Twenty years ago the Russians were sitting here and they were eating blinis and bitching about Afghanistan and what a shithole it is. Now we're doing the exact same thing."

Kyle added: "And twenty years from now the Chinese are gonna be sitting right here, sipping their yucky soups and whining that the Afghans are totally ungrateful."

"And all the graffiti in the Portashitters are going to be painted over by Chinese characters", I said. The whole idea was hilarious. We spent the next half hour trying to make up Chinese Portajohn graffitis.

When we left, two Marines rushed over to take our seats.

Things could have stayed like that. I was absolutely content with my new life style. I had another three months to go. It looked like an eternity but it was at least somewhat manageable. Kyle had fueled my competitive spirit. As a result my upper arms started to take on interesting proportions. We went running together, which had the advantage that we could leave our weapons at home. I looked at my pitch-black M4 now with different eyes. Tim had saved my life with it. Of course he could hold have pointed his handgun at my attacker's head instead. But he had used my rifle.

For technicians like us, rifle training was scheduled only once every six months. I was looking forward to firing my weapon again. It was clear that I would never, ever have the opportunity to shoot at another human being. Just as my mother had wanted. The question was what to do with the "potential" that Dan had seen in me. I told Kyle and Robert about the conversation I had with him.

"This Frenchman said something very interesting when you were hanging out at the Russian Tower", Robert said. "He thought that his knowledge of Arabic would be useful if he was deployed to Iraq instead."

"So what? The French are not with us in Iraq", Kyle said.

"Just sayin'. In Iraq things are just getting worse every day. Sooner or later we're all gonna end up there. Maybe Marina should learn Arabic."

Kyle laughed. "Do you have any idea how long this will take? Must be about as easy as learning Chinese."

I watched my friends as they were discussing my career options. I was proud that I could actually call them my friends. We were sitting on plastic chairs in front of the hangar, eating sandwiches that Robert had organized. It was almost warm still, and we were enjoying the October sun. There was no wind, which meant no sand between our teeth.

"I don't want to go to Iraq", Robert said after a while.

"Why?" I asked. "We'll never get outside the wire anyway. And as long as we stay on base, nothing can really happen. I know there's occasional incoming, but it's not going to be worse than here. The accommodation, the food... I'm pretty sure it will be the exact same thing. "

"Are you sure that nothing can happen to us here?" Robert asked, his lips a thin line all of a sudden. "Then what do we have all the bunkers for?"

One of those "bunkers" was situated to the left of our hangar. It was actually an above-ground concrete tunnel, fortified with sandbags. It was open on both sides so that you would simply run inside. We were used to alarms but it never seemed like anyone ever got hit by a rocket.

"That reminds me of something I wanted to tell you guys", Kyle said, crumpling a napkin in his hand. "Did you hear about Rohrman? I overheard something when Flanagan was talking to the LT."

"What was it?" I asked with my mouth full.

"Rohrman is stationed in Kandahar, and it seems that place gets hammered all the time! So anyway, there was a mortar attack recently. If I heard right, he lost a leg. And his eyesight."

"He's blind?" Robert was horrified. Kyle nodded.

I swallowed down a bite. My appetite was gone, and I wrapped up the rest of the sandwich for later. If I could eat the rest of it in addition to dinner, it would be good for building up muscle mass. Ever since the near-gangbang, I felt the need to become physically stronger. Even though I had no hand-to-hand combat skills, I wanted to at least have more muscle power.

After work I tried to impress Kyle by using more weights but he just laughed. "If you pull a muscle now it's going to set you back several weeks."

A soldier working his biceps with a dumbbell was sitting across from me and making eye contact. His desire was almost palpable and I felt truly sorry for him. His hormone levels were probably driving him crazy every night and every morning, and he didn't have a lot of options to get some relief.
Kyle was reading my thoughts.

"Yo, look at me, girl!" He pointed to his eyes with two fingers and I had to laugh. "You're our property, and we will not loan you out to the Army."

On the way home Robert thought of a few reasons why we should stay in Afghanistan permanently as an occupation force. Our path along a row of B-huts was pitch dark because of some electricity problem, and we tried not to stumble.

Robert cursed as he almost tripped on one of the rocks. "One good reason to make Afghanistan our new colony: the beautifully veiled women. I don't know what makes me more horny – the pretty blue burqas or those black tents."

Kyle had another idea. "I got a better reason. The heroin. We could use it to flood enemy countries with it. Heroin instead of firepower. I read somewhere that there's a huge heroin problem in Iran."

"My guess is the CIA came up with this idea already", Robert replied.

A Chinook was clattering overhead. Through the windows I could see the light on the inside. It looked like a totally misshapen flying bus.

I arrived at my hooch. "See you later."

The two waited until I was inside. We had showered in the gym so that I didn't have to step out anymore. I slipped into my blue pajamas and turned off the reading light. My earplugs were in a small plastic box that I could even find in the dark.

And this is how my first night of absolute horror began. Shortly after falling asleep I experienced a nightmare of a new quality. Staff Sergeant Rohrman was on his way to a dark cave in the mountains of Waziristan. He was alone. While he was making his way inside, I was standing guard in front of the cave, my rifle at the low ready. I looked up into the night sky. And then Rohrman began screaming.

"I can't see anything! I can't see shit! Help me!"

But my job was to pull guard duty. I had absolutely no desire to leave my post. Rohrman's yelling was getting desperate. I could not help him. I didn't want to help him. I didn't care about him at all.

I woke up and found myself shaking with fear.

From now on every night was just like that. A couple of hours of shut-eye, and then a nightmare about Rohrman needing help shook me so hard that I was too scared of going back to sleep. At work I moved like a zombie. The lack of sleep made me weak. There was no way I could keep working out or going for runs with Kyle. Once a day I forced myself to eat. I desperately tried to focus on my work but even that couldn't distract me from the depressing little movies playing in my head.

I saw Rohrman on crutches, awkwardly making his way through what seemed to be a nice mansion. On the outside I could see a portico flanked by gracious white columns and of course there was an American flag. This is where the East Coast elite lived. Inside the house, Rohrman cautiously moved around, his crutches barely making a noise on the dark hardwood floors. It was his parents' house so he didn't need his eyesight to find his way around. He limped into the living room. It had huge French windows giving access to the garden and was furnished with elegant leather sofas. With one hand, Rohrman started feeling around the coffee table to find the remote control. Once he had it he slowly sat down on the couch. He positioned the crutches to his side and turned on the TV.

He just sat there and listened to it.

After three days I stopped eating altogether. Work got even harder. There were dizzy spells I had to hide from the crew, and the smell of hydraulic oil and exhaust gases made me throw up sometimes. Kyle and Robert gave up trying to talk to me. I was pretty sure that they were secretly watching me in the hope that they could at least catch me when I fell over.

But I was hanging tough. My head felt as if it was wrapped in cotton wool. Everything I heard was muffled. I had every reason to worry about understanding the instructions coming from Sergeant Lozano. My body felt no longer like it was a part of me.

On the fifth morning I felt someone gently touching my elbow. I slowly looked up from my ammo feeder and saw Dead Fish silently giving me a nod, pointing towards the office. I followed him. As I was trudging along all the way through the maintenance hangar I felt my colleagues' eyes on me.

Flanagan closed the door behind me and pointed to the old miniature sofa that was big enough for two very slim people. I sat down and looked at the door. Rohrman had pinned me against the wall right next to the door frame. Back when he could still see.

Flanagan was busy doing something at the sink in the corner. I closed my eyes, wishing I could take a nap. The air in the room was stuffy and warm. But my hands and feet felt incredibly cold. As Flanagan sat down next to me I opened my eyes. He handed me a glass of freshly squeezed orange juice. Out of courtesy I drank it all. Since he made no effort to take the glass back, I just put it on the floor.

The Staff Sergeant sat down next to me. He managed to leave about one inch of space between us.

"Marina, talk to me."

I was staring ahead, studying the stains on the plywood wall where someone must have swatted flies in the summer.

"Do you really want to go on psych leave? That would be extremely detrimental to your career."

He could certainly see by the look on my face how much I cared about my career right now.

He sighed. "Fine, then I'm gonna start. Your buddies told me you were attacked. You narrowly escaped being raped. So my guess is what's happening right now is a totally normal post-traumatic stress disorder. Nothing special. It's treatable, right here on BAF."

I shook my head.

"That's not it", I whispered. I wasn't too sure if he had heard me at all.

"Well, what is it then?" He was so close to me that I could smell his deodorant.

"Rohrman." I whispered like a little girl who's afraid of the dark. I barely managed to hide my face in my hands before I started crying uncontrollably. My upper body was increasingly shaken by my sobs and I could hardly breathe. After a while Flanagan stood up and came back with a Kleenex box. But it still took some time before I was even able to reach for tissues.

The tissue box was on my lap while Flanagan's arm was on my shoulder. I had to wipe away tears and blow my nose, but at least I managed to stop crying after some time. I stuffed the used tissues into my pockets because I didn't know where else to put them. I didn't mind that Flanagan was observing my meltdown like a scientist looks at his mice. I didn't really care about anything at all. Finally I gave him a sideways glance. His expression was as cool as ever.

I moved closer, which wasn't difficult given that we didn't have much space, and laid my head on his chest. It felt good. Since I was sitting to his right I could not hear his heart. But I was sure that it stopped beating for a moment.

We sat there for a while without talking. The orange juice had provided me with a bit of energy. I suddenly felt the urge to tell my boss about my nightmares. I kept my head on his chest as if that was where it belonged, and started at the very beginning. I described how unpopular I was after my first week on the job. I told him how I instigated Kyle and Robert to hunt down Sandy's rapist. How lonely I felt afterwards. And how Rohrman provoked me with his Indian attack helicopter question.

Flanagan's voice had more bass than usual as long as I had my head on his chest. "And when did your relationship start with Rohrman?"

"We had a very bad relationship. There was no sexual relationship, if that's what you mean."

Flanagan's arm slipped from my shoulder down to my back.

"I don't understand."

"Me neither", I admitted. I didn't know what was wrong with me.

"Okay, we'll deal with it later. Go on."

I continued with a less complicated version of my great love story, turning my fake sex triangle into a boring "normal" relationship consisting of just Tim and myself. I figured Flanagan didn't need to know of Dan's existence. However, I told him all the details about my encounter with the four predators. I wanted him to feel the horror. It worked. He was cursing under his breath while I was talking about it.

"Kyle and Robert were there for me. They really saved my life afterwards. Without their friendship I would've lost my mind here."

Flanagan said nothing.

"I don't sleep with them. Word of honor."

He laughed. I wasn't sure I'd ever seen him laugh before. It was good. My head was gently moving up and down on his chest.

"Alright, let's go back to the problem", Flanagan said firmly. "You have nightmares because of Rohrman's injuries, is that right?"

"Yeah, and daytime is not much better. I think of him all the time. You know, I keep visualizing how he's always hopping around on one leg. And he has to be extra-careful not to bump into something because he can't see anything. That's what's killing me. I can't deal with the fact that he's blind. I can't deal with it."

I seemed to have endless supplies of tears. They just kept coming, and it didn't look as if I would ever stop crying again. I had to lift my head from Flanagan's chest to pick up the Kleenex box from the floor. Flanagan immediately stood up and went to make more orange juice.

This time he was also handing me a banana.

"Oh God no", I moaned.

"Oh yes", Flanagan said.

I drank my juice. Since I made no attempt to take the fruit he began to peel it and broke off a piece. Without even asking he stuffed a chunk of banana into my mouth. That was so cheeky that I had to laugh against my will, and he just kept going until I had finished the whole banana. Unbelievable.

I punished him by laying my head back on his chest. He let it happen and I wondered for the first time whether he liked it.

"Now. Let's move on to the important part of this interrogation." Flanagan's voice sounded colder than ever. Under normal circumstances, the new, dangerous tone would have made all my alarm bells ring. But right now, I couldn't have cared less about what he was going to do to me.

"What was going on between you and Rohrman if there was no sex? There's gotta be a reason why you're losing it. Can't be just because you feel sorry for him. I'm not buying it."

"Honestly, I have no desire to go through another crying fit", I said. I was exhausted. There was no way I would keep talking about my feelings. "I have no idea why I can only think of Rohrman, and nothing else. It doesn't matter. I'm feeling much better already."

"It does matter", Flanagan replied, raising his voice to an unpleasant level. Which was kind of funny since I was still clinging to him like a scared little girl. "Other people's lives depend on the quality of our work. Not just the pilots. The grunts on the ground who need the close air support. The convoys that get attacked. A mentally unstable crew member is someone I have to send home immediately."

"I'm perfectly stable now. Swear to God." I heard myself speak. It sounded weak.

"Convince me, girl. Otherwise you're going to find yourself in Ramstein tomorrow and back in Idaho by the end of the week."

This was serious. I had to come up with something to placate my crew chief but my mind was blank. I just wanted to lie down and sleep.

"What was in the letter?"

I immediately knew what he was talking about. I reached into a side pocket of my camos and pulled out the crumpled envelope that Flanagan took off me and opened right away, almost as if he'd been waiting for this opportunity all along. He read the note.

"Hmm." Flanagan's cluelessness was almost endearing. He smelled good. We had been sitting in his overheated office for the past two hours, and there was a slightly sweaty scent mingling with his deodorant.

I needed to explain something. "I feel extremely guilty that I didn't go to his farewell thingy. It's so fucked up. I was so disconnected from the crew that I didn't even know Rohrman was leaving. Well, in the last few days I kept pulling out this letter and reading it over and over."

"What do you make of it?" Flanagan wanted to know how I felt about this note.

It was pretty crazy that I should talk about my feelings with my superiors. But it also seemed to be my last chance to keep my job.

"Well, when I read it for the first time I didn't know what to do with it. I kind of forgot about it until five days ago. Once I knew he got hurt in Kandahar, everything was different. By now I'm under the impression that he wanted to tell me something. I didn't miss him at all after he was gone. But now ... "

I started crying. Again. It was simply unbelievable. "Now I miss him so much that it almost physically hurts. He was much nicer than you and a lot funnier. My nickname for him was 'golden boy', but I kept that to myself for obvious reasons."

Flanagan's arm was now wandering up and down on my back, as if to comfort me.

"Rohrman was very professional", he said finally. "He probably had a thing for you but he was smart enough not to do anything about it. And you're a silly girl. You fell in love with him after he left. How stupid is that? And now you don't know what to do with your feelings, and you're fucking shit up for everyone here. Jesus."

I didn't have anything to add to his scathing judgment. I felt like lifting my head off his chest, though. A little bit more distance was probably a good idea but I didn't dare to move. The fatal blow was coming, I could feel it.

Flanagan's voice was now below zero. "An all-male military force is a good thing."

His suppressed anger was clearly audible.

I wondered what was the procedure for kicking me out. Would my boss say: You're fired, just like in a normal company?

"Last chance, girl." Flanagan gently pushed me away. Instead of getting up he took my face in both hands. "What are your feelings for Rohrman? I want an honest answer."

"I love him", I whispered.

"Okay." He looked content as he stuffed the letter in the envelope and gave it back to me. "You're on sick leave today. You go to bed and tonight you're going out with your buddies – eat, work out, play Xbox, I don't care. Tomorrow you come to work as if nothing ever happened. Can you do that?"

I nodded. His hands were surprisingly warm. He let go of my head, stood up and walked to the desk. I disappeared without a word. I ran home and that was where I realised I had forgotten my rifle at work.

Fuck it.

I covered my miniature window with a plastic bag and went to sleep.

Kyle and Robert were my crutches for the remaining time of our deployment. They'd known each other for two years. They were both from the big city, Kyle was East Coast and Robert was from California, and I entertained them with my exotic childhood in the countryside. The questions they asked me were typical of urban hipsters.

"D'you guys really manage to listen to country music all the time?"

"Do you all get an assault rifle for your fifth birthday?"

"Is it dangerous to hang out in Idaho for someone who's black?"

"Do you get cable TV? And Internet?"

I tried to dispel their prejudices and told them about life on the rez.

"What if I want to see you again? Am I allowed into your reservation, you know, being a white man?"

"Are you guys really all alcoholics?"

"Where did you learn to speak English so well?"

"Are you actually allowed to leave the reservation at all?"

They were always making fun of me and my origins. It was their way of showing me their affection. Robert was a rebel who refused to take anything seriously. He liked to turn all aspects of his work life into ridicule. Kyle usually pretended to be shocked about the fact that his friend had zero respect for the whole military universe.

"And besides, you don't bite the hand that feeds your sorry ass, Rob. A little gratitude would be perfectly okay."

Robert nodded. "Right. Gratitude. For the sensational working conditions. And our comfortable homes. And of course the excellent food."

"Don't forget the pay! Your brother must be green with envy, that poor lawyer", Kyle added.

"Oh yeah, absolutely", Robert said.

Kyle gave Robert even more food for thought. "Just think for a minute, how bad it would be to go to college instead. From one party to the next. Bar-hopping. Spring break. From one woman to the next. What a sad life. You don't want that."

Robert nodded. "Kyle, you've just straightened me out. It's only now that I'm starting to realize how great my life is here. Hunting Taliban, ten hours a day of urban warfare, jumping out of helicopters, smoking out Al-Qaeda caves in the Hindu Kush. The great adventure. Oh no, wait, that's what the others are doing. Those who actually get outside the wire instead of being imprisoned on an oversized airport for a year."

I had to laugh. "I didn't know that you're dreaming of combat. I mean, from a physical point of view you should be able to join the grunts. You're in fantastic shape."

Robert shrugged. "Yes, but not mentally. The first firefight, I would shit myself. I think."

I was surprised by so much honesty. "But the soldiers spend months just training for that before they get to the war zone. I'm sure they're not born stone-cold warriors."

Kyle didn't agree with me. "Rob may look like a killer but he's a wimp. He would give every one of his dead enemies a decent burial and put a wreath on the grave."

"And besides, I wanted to be a pilot. That way I don't have to be scared of getting hit if I can be shredding Taliban from a height of a thousand feet. The Gatling is a really nasty weapon."

"Yeah but seriously", I said. "If you really want to be a pilot, go ahead. You can pull this off, even if it takes a few years."

Robert put his arm around my shoulder. He did this pretty much every day, and it felt good.

"Let me think about it. In the meantime, we should go on bitchin' about our employer, alright? Maybe you got something to contribute to our discussion."

"True", Kyle agreed. "You're always just listening and enjoying the show. Try to say something derogatory. Come on. You of all people should be able to find something."

I tried to think very hard. My new friends were watching me. But there was nothing.

Robert sighed. "That girl is a bit thick. My guess is the only thing on her mind is sex."

"Too bad", Kyle said. "But you can't do anything if someone's dumber than a bag of rocks."

I punched Kyle in the abdomen, and he acted as if he would collapse from the blow.

ARABIAN NIGHTS

Khassem does not show up for days. I guess he's trying to punish me for the super-emotional story I tried to entertain him with. He certainly doesn't want to hear about a lovesick little girl crying her heart out for a man she never even touched. It's more likely that he expected something more saucy from me. No wonder he's disappointed. It would be a shame if he no longer came to visit.

After all I still have some very sexy stories in store for him.

But instead of Khassem the other guy shows up in my basement: the broody young man who freed me of my plaster cast and whose name I don't know yet. I'm too proud to ask. Just like he's too proud – or too arrogant – to say "Hello" or "Salam Aleikum". He just walks in and hands me a pita bread. I try not to look too greedy as I'm biting into the delicious bread. He refills my bottles in the bathroom. I would really like to ask him how long I have to make do with my water ration, but I refrain from asking him. Even a hostage has her pride.

He sits down, this time on the other chair at the wall opposite me, and watches me eat my bread. This is where Khassem always sits. I try to eat as slowly as possible but it's hard. I let my thoughts wander – I need to distract myself from the sight of the stranger who is staring at me with an openly hostile look on his face. And he looks tense, too. I wonder how my relationship with my abductors is going to evolve over time. Will I be affected by the Stockholm syndrome? Could it be that I'm going to fall in love with Khassem because he's the only one who goes to Burger King for me?

I'm trying to think of a stupid nickname for my visitor. It doesn't take long until I come up with something perfectly suitable. I call him: Dead Fish (IV). IV stands for: Iraqi Version. Unfortunately this idea makes me grin.

He stands up and slaps me in the face. My head bangs against the metal headboard of the bed. I sit down again, pretending not to care. I feel something warm running down my left cheek. I'll take care of that later. My right ear is buzzing because that's where his hand landed. At least he didn't break my cheekbone.

"You're left-handed. Like Obama." I laugh at him and know exactly what's coming.

He throws himself at me, his face distorted by hate. He beats me with both fists. It takes several minutes and I try not to scream.

Then I'm alone again.

The pita bread flew out of my hand when he slapped me. It is now positioned dangerously far away in the right rear corner of the room. With much difficulty I get off my bed and kneel on the floor. Everything hurts. Slowly I crawl towards the rest of my bread which is lying on the floor in front of a small table. At first glance it looks as if my chain won't be long enough. But appearances are deceiving. I just need to stretch. After a few minutes of intensive yoga I can use two fingers to pick the bread off the ugly gray industrial carpeting (I try not to think of all the micro-organisms that also live here). I sit up and keep my most prized possession in my hands. There is still about half of it left. I decide to wait until tomorrow. That way I'll have it for breakfast. It won't be easy not to touch it till then. But I'm strong.

I sit in front of the little wood-veneer table. From above, a hint of sunlight is shining on my face, and I enjoy it very much. I'm in no hurry to get back on my bed. It started smelling lately. I spent the last twenty days sweating into the sheets and the pillow. I guess the only reason why it's not the whole room that smells of me is that the narrow window is on tilt. There is a constant supply of fresh air. I look at the iron grid on the outside. It's thin and looks rusty in some places. If I wasn't chained to the wall I would first try to destroy the window and then shake the grid until it falls off.

On the table there is a tiny TV that probably stopped working a long time ago. It looks older than me. Interestingly it's plugged into a socket in the wall. But I have no remote for it, so I give up the idea of switching it on.

I'm sitting cross-legged on the carpet with the pita in my lap. The plan is to stay here for a while and enjoy the sunlight. At least that way, I won't get a vitamin D deficiency.

Unsurprisingly, I discover some bruises developing on my right arm.

I think of the predator who attacked me. I brought this onto myself. I didn't show him the proper respect. This is absolutely crucial when dealing with Arab men. And as if that wasn't bad enough, I showed no fear. He must have been more than disappointed, judging by his violent reaction.

I try to look at the situation from his point of view. I'm an American hostage, and I'm female for God's sake. I should be terrified. I should be trembling with fear all day long. I should have a heart attack every time someone walks in. I'm expected to humiliate myself, to be begging for food and water. And of course I'm supposed to cry all the time.

And what have I done? I compared my kidnapper to the President of the United States of America. That's how stupid I am. I shake my head in disbelief.

I don't cease to amaze myself.

My stupidity will get me killed some day, there's no doubt about that.

If I want to survive this, I'll have to come up with a strategy.
I need a plan but I'm tired. I get up and gasp. The beating was short but efficient. I put the piece of bread on the chair and crawl into my bed. This nap I deserve. Some painkillers would be helpful, but you can't have everything.

In the evening I see the beginning of an idea. There is a tactic that I could apply at least to Khassem if he ever shows up again. It's quite simple: from now on I give him what he needs. I invent a crazy fling with Flanagan. The fact that I never had sex with my boss makes it easier to invent all the things we could have done. I make a mental list of things that we would have been able to do – on the sofa, under the desk, in the hangar, the back shop, the ammo storage rooms... Everything I've ever seen on the Internet, is something I'm now using to fuel my imagination. I try to remember anything sexy I've seen in movies and try to tailor whatever I find to myself and Flanagan. All this will make me look like a slut in Khassem's eyes.

No wait. He already thinks I'm a slut.

I realize that if I go through with this he will possibly see me as the greatest whore who ever lived on Afghan soil. I might as well throw in a few more illegal adventures with Kyle and Robert. Keep it interesting.

After a sleepless night I end up with the outline of a story that stretches over several months and involves quite a few consenting adults. I will serve Khassem a spicy hot sex soup.

He wakes me up one morning just before sunrise. From outside I hear none of the usual street noise. Sounds like Baghdad is still asleep.

I get another pita.

Why can't I have orange juice for breakfast?

I pretend to be grateful for the insufficient food supply while I'm munching my bread. At the same time, I'm planning today's tactics. At first I will have to tell Khassem a true story because this is a logical prerequisite for the invented sexual adventures that will follow.

I sit up and tell Khassem of my reunion with Staff Sergeant Rohrman.

Thanks to my friendship with Kyle and Robert I was recovering from my nervous breakdown in record time. The three-hour crying session in Flanagan's office had probably contributed to my recovery. Of course I couldn't completely shake off my thoughts on Rohrman's blindness but very often I was able to file them away, to be dealt with at a later stage. Or possibly never. I really had to concentrate on my work. My ambition was to be the best aircraft mechanic of all time. I read a lot and I was constantly looking for information on the Internet. It was weird that I was the only woman on the team. Technical stuff was not more difficult to learn than, for instance, languages. And repairing a broken part of something had to be a much nicer activity than being a nurse or taking care of old people.

When I came back late one night from the gym, I found a note on my bed. The Staff Sergeant asked me to come to his office at 0245. I wasn't too happy about going there in the middle of the night. I set my alarm clock to 0215 so that I could brush my teeth before going.

I laid out my favorite underwear so I wouldn't lose time when I got up. I had no doubt that Flanagan had taken a liking to me and wanted to take advantage of the whole situation.

We had 24-hour bus service so that I didn't have to walk. Being foot-mobile in the middle of the night and being alone would have been enough to make me panic. I usually managed to block any thoughts of the night I was attacked, but my memories kept getting triggered whenever I say Army uniforms.

I was totally stressed out when I arrived at Flanagan's, which was not a good start for whatever he had in mind. He offered me a mint tea. He was sitting at his desk. I took a seat on a sticky old swivel chair. His desk looked as if he had inherited it from the Soviets. I looked at the steaming cup of tea as Flanagan started his laptop computer.

"Is that your private computer?" I asked mainly because the silence was so annoying. He nodded.

I crossed my legs. That would have looked good if I'd been wearing a fancy costume. But in my desert camouflage uniform and with the stinky boots it just looked ridiculous.

"So", my boss began. "I made some enquiries about Rohrman's state of health. What we heard before were just rumors. Next time I'd rather bite my tongue off than spread any unconfirmed intel that I didn't verify myself."

I felt dizzy. What was he getting at? That Rohrman was dead?

"It turned out that he has lost a foot and an eye. He also suffered third degree burns to the upper body. Those wounds are healing, and for the foot he's got a prosthesis. He's walking around again."

Flanagan looked at me, his face a big question mark.

Are you okay? Feeling better now?

I stared back at him, unable to speak.

"Those are very good news, right?"

I nodded.

"Do you think you will start speaking again anytime soon?"

I looked at him. He could certainly see how clueless I was. I felt mentally exhausted. I wanted to be alone in my rack. I wanted to think about Rohrman's injuries and about the meaning of this whole thing.

"I organized a Skype session for you. Are you gonna be able to talk at all?"

I nodded. He turned the laptop around and gave me a headset. I put it on and looked at the dark screen. Flanagan got up and walked around the desk. He pressed a button and stood by my side, looking down on me.

Rohrman was grinning. "Good morning, Marina."

He was wearing a black eye patch but it didn't make him look like a pirate. Something was wrong with his left ear and the skin around it. His smile went all the way up to his eye, and the image quality was so good that I could see some freckles on his nose. His hair was a little longer than regulation.

"Good morning."

Rohrman's grin widened. "You look good."

"Thank you."

Don't cry, do not cry, do not start crying.

"I heard you're turning into some kinda drama queen. And your boss is a fuckin' trainwreck because of you."

"That's bullshit. I'm no drama queen, and Flanagan's doing great."

This seemed to be just what Rohrman wanted to hear. He looked at me with the kind of curiosity he'd never shown me before. I suddenly realized that I'd forgotten to brush my hair.

"I'm very glad you're not blind", I finally managed to say. My voice was hoarse. Speaking was so difficult all of a sudden. I was mad as hell at Flanagan who really could have given me some kind of advance warning.

"Well, I am now officially disabled. This, of course, is not so great. I wanted to spend my whole life in the Air Force."

"Why? You've got a college education. There's got to be other ways to make a living."

Rohrman looked a little surprised.

Finally he said: "No, I dropped out of college a year before graduating. Now that I'm back in the so-called real world, well... I have to honestly say that I can't stand all these fat and sloppy civilians. They're just so boring, I don't know what to do with them."

We were quiet for a while. Our conversation had reached a dead end because Rohrman was already unhappy about his future. It had just barely begun. And I had no idea how I could possibly cheer him up.

But in the end, Rohrman managed to revive his golden boy routine.

"Did you ever find a replacement for those operators you were banging? Or do you live like a nun now?"

I shook my head. "I play by the rules now. No screwing around. I have become a model Airman. Staff Sergeant Flanagan is standing by to confirm this."

Rohrman laughed. I looked up to my boss who was smiling.

Rohrman said: "Marina, you're no Airman. You're an Airpunk."

I burst into tears, and Rohrman disappeared. He ended our conversation just like that.

Flanagan looked anything but happy as he escorted me to our psychiatric couch.

The moment of truth has arrived. I can see barely concealed anticipation in Khassem's eyes. What happens next? Will Flanagan try to comfort his girl by kissing her? Will she return his kiss passionately? And then – will the whole thing get out of control?

"Come on, keep going", Khassem says and sounds almost like he's whining.

"No", I say coolly.

He looks confused.

"What do you mean – no? You want me to beat you? I have a belt. I know how to use it, believe me. And you really don't want to see what kind of marks that belt will leave on your skin."

Don't laugh.

I focus all my mental strength on keeping up my poker face. I'm not going to laugh at my wannabe-torturer. If I hurt his pride, he's really going to take his belt off. A couple of days ago, I was on the receiving end of the other guy's rage. The bruises he inflicted on me are now purple, yellow and green. I would like them to heal completely before adding anything new to my collection of injuries.

I lean forward and try to look as determined as possible.

"Look. I'm trying to survive here. That's not going to happen if I keep getting a Big Mac with fries once a week and a pita twice a week. Over the next few weeks I will get all kinds of deficiencies that can lead to organ failure. And even if I survive this I'm going to end up with long-term damage."

Khassem is taking his time to process this new piece of information. The lifelong health issues that arise from malnutrition were clearly not on his mind until now.

"I need something to eat every day. And today, I definitely need more than the pita bread I just ate for breakfast. Do you understand that?"

"Why should I do what you want? I can get everything I need from you – I just need to take it."

"Alright, let's say we keep things the way they are. I have to go hungry here every day. And you hit me with a belt on a regular basis so that I have to keep telling you about my exciting time in Bagram."

Khassem nods. "That's how it's going to be, I'm afraid."

I shake my head. "Do you really think that I will always have the energy to describe everything to you in detail? My story is only just getting going. What do you think I did with Flanagan once I had his attention? And with Kyle and Robert? I can tell you in great detail how to find illegal substances even in Bagram. And you know what happens when you get Americans, alcohol and drugs together in one room. Right?"
Khassem nods again.

"No, you don't", I provoke him. "You don't know jack shit about us, Khassem. Reality is much crazier than whatever you saw in the movies. We are the nation that invented rock'n'roll and hip-hop. And the porn industry."

Khassem is struggling to keep still in his chair. He looks uneasy, almost agitated. He probably knows he's onto something big here, but he has not yet fully grasped the meaning of it all.

"Khassem, before long I will simply be too weak to entertain you – physically and mentally. I can hardly concentrate on talking to you right now. The hunger is driving my crazy. Some days I have to cry because I'm so thirsty. I just know that story time will soon be over. No more Arabian Nights for you."

At last Khassem makes the impression that he's thinking about my woes.

Time to bring this one home.

I lean forward and look at him like we're about to engage in a conspiracy together. "We Americans are rotten to the core. Our civilization is beyond saving. And I" – now I'm making a dramatic pause – "I'm the worst of them all."

The next two months are the best time of my captivity. Khassem provides me with so much food that eventually even my period comes back. I get stuff from the drugstore. My hair is beginning to turn into dreadlocks and I need endless amounts of conditioner to disentangle the mess. My chain gets extended. As a result I can wash my underwear and my bed sheets in the sink. Unfortunately the chain isn't long enough for me to get under the shower. But I don't complain.

Dead Fish (IV) makes an appearance about once a week. He usually hands me a pita and I pretend to be happy about it. Not once do I see him and Khassem together. I don't dare to ask Khassem about his relationship with the mysterious stranger.

Once Dead Fish (IV) shows up as I'm standing in front of the sink, washing my underwear by hand. I have no spare underwear. He comes into the bathroom and sees me naked. He's immediately gone.

It turns out I'm a talented storyteller. It's a long Native American tradition. I invent an entirely new depraved universe for Khassem. Although I introduce a lot of sexy details in my tales of my decadent life, I try not to overdo it. I don't want him to suspect anything. I need his full trust. He's the only well-meaning person in my life right now – at least as long as I give him what he needs.

First it's Flanagan's turn. He seduces me in the Skype night because I'm a basketcase after my conversation with Rohrman. He does it very slowly and gently so that I can give Khassem graphic descriptions of how we kiss and touch, and so on. Khassem doesn't seem to notice that I have much more details to offer now than in the stories I had told him earlier about Dan and Tim.

I never stop mentioning how totally forbidden and dangerous my new love is. Then Kyle comes into play. This happens because he eventually catches us in the act and throws a fit. Since both I and Flanagan are now in danger of getting blackmailed, it is my duty to appease Kyle and stop him from ratting on us. For obvious reasons, I do this with the help of my well-toned female body. On this occasion, I try to find out what makes Khassem particularly horny. I gradually develop a sense of what he secretly dreams of. I describe my reluctance towards making Kyle my lover. Kyle takes advantage of the situation and subjects me to some pretty rough treatment. One night he even uses a belt. Khassem's eyes shine when I go into detail here.

You sadistic little rat, I think, hiding my amusement behind a stoic story-teller face. I feel sorry for your future wife.

Robert initially doesn't make an appearance in these stories but I give him a role in the drama after a few weeks. One day, in a moment of weakness, I tell my friend everything. This is a good opportunity to again go through all the highlights of my soap opera. Khassem doesn't complain as I describe how I confess my sins to my last remaining buddy. Robert's first reaction is to show sympathy and understanding. He provides me with drugs so that it gests easier for me to make it through the tough sessions with Kyle.

But things change. After a while, Robert wants a piece of the pie. The thrill he gets off on is danger. He insists on doing it in the communal showers in Bagram. There's an enormous risk that someone comes in at the wrong moment – that makes the whole thing so exciting for Robert. He's magically attracted to everything that's prohibited. We hang out with Marines to smoke weed, go to a USO country music concert drugged up to our eyeballs, and we coerce a naive blonde into a mini-orgy in a Portajohn.

During all that time Khassem not once asks me how to repair a jet.

It's a shame that Khassem's interests are so one-sided. I could tell him a lot of things about me that would actually surprise him – if he cared. There's the fact, for example, that my grandmother and my mother taught me the dying language of our ancestors. I learned it when I was a toddler. There are about a hundred native speakers of Nimipuu on this planet. I'm one of them.

The fact that I grew up bilingual helped me a lot when I was studying the Arabic language.

I forgot Robert's idea for a while. But in the course of our deployment, as time began to stretch, I started mulling over his suggestion. Despite twelve-hour work days everyday life at Bagram was getting increasingly boring. There were only so many places you could go. The gym, the PX, the salsa nights or whatever else USO was organizing for our entertainment. After my very special friends had left I was now just as frustrated as everyone else. Kyle and Robert took me weightlifting, but that was it. They spent most of their free time in front of the PlayStation, so I needed something that would keep my mind busy. I ordered a language course in Arabic, and it turned out to be even more difficult than I expected. It was the first time I had to learn writing in a different alphabet. I was all alone with my new hobby.

At the beginning the only fun part was writing. It was the first time in a while that I needed pen and paper instead of typing into my computer. It felt like studying a secret code. I scribbled letters and words into a notebook. The next day I couldn't read them anymore. I looked up lectures on YouTube. It was like first grade, except this time no-one was telling me what to do. Of course I made sure to wear earphones while listening to the language course. Nobody was supposed to find out what I was doing. There was no doubt I was going to fail completely at learning this language, but it didn't really seem to matter because I was doing something new and intriguing, taking my mind off all the problems I had. Whenever I didn't have my thoughts under control I was either sad because I'd lost Dan and Tim, or depressed because of the way Rohrman had laughed at me last time we spoke. There was no doubt that I would never see him again. For some strange reason, that made me just as sad as thinking of Tim and Dan.

I didn't really like the way Arabic words sounded, but speaking was much easier for me than writing, probably a direct result of my Nimipuu upbringing. I practiced saying Merhaba Habibi. It meant something like Hey babe, how you doin'. I had to be extra-careful not to be heard through our paper-thin plywood walls, so I whispered all kinds of exotic sounds into my pillow, trying to woo the non-existing Arab men in my life.

All this, however, is of no interest to Khassem so I keep it to myself. Especially the fact that I was eventually completely obsessed with the Arabic language. Everywhere I lived, I found myself some native speakers who were able to share their wisdom. They were more than willing to talk to me. Any man or woman that I approached was basically delighted I was trying to learn their mother language, and they went out of their way to help me. Without the Moroccans in Spangdahlem and the Egyptian students in Texas I would have given up sooner or later. You simply can't learn a language on your own. With a lot of discipline it's possible to work out the basics. But at some point you need help.

When I woke up in Baghdad, chained to the wall, I initially thought that my knowledge of Arabic would be an asset, something I could use against the men who took me. I was hoping that someday they'd talk to each other and say something important. That they let slip a crucial piece of information that would help me break out of my prison. But Khassem and his dangerous counterpart are never here at the same time. Not once do I get the opportunity to spy on anyone.

At least now I get to recover in record time as Khassem brings me all the food I need. Sometimes I get treats like chocolate or fresh fruit. I'm under the impression that Khassem and his family are doing okay financially. He wears nice jeans and name brand T-shirts. But I'm afraid to ask him about his family background. It's too risky. I don't know how his father died. Maybe it was one of us. We may have dropped a bomb on him by mistake. There are so many ways that civilians can meet their death in a war zone. I feel no need to wake a sleeping dog.

But I'm still alone most of the time. To fight the boredom that sets in whenever I'm not busy eating, I impose an extensive training program on myself. In the morning I'll do whatever callisthenics and pilates exercises I can think of, and at night I try to strengthen my muscles with push-ups. I try running on the spot because my cardio fitness is important, too. It feels stupid though. I definitely wouldn't do this if there was a camera in the room. The chain limits my radius but it doesn't interfere too much. More and more often I catch myself in a good mood. My situation has become somewhat bearable.

Because I feel so much better than at the beginning of my imprisonment I develop all kinds of ideas. Most of them revolve around smashing the unreachable window and kicking in the unreachable door. And my chain inspires me to think of a thousand ways I could destroy it, the most obvious being a non-existent chainsaw. And then one day I have a really good idea. I pick up the chair that's always on my bedside. I hold it in the air and point it at the TV set in the corner. One of the chair's legs is almost touching the front of the TV. I've been stretching and working out so much lately that I am now a very elastic person. One more deep breath. My right arm moves another inch towards the object of my desire. The end of the wooden leg touches the round button. And the old brown plastic device comes alive.

Hallelujah.

It's like Christmas, Fourth of July, and the Super Bowl all rolled into one: the TV gives me an Egyptian soap in black and white, and I jump up and down in ecstasy and shriek like a Justin Bieber fan. All these people! The voices!

My days of loneliness are over. I turn into a television freak and absorb the moving pictures in shades of gray as if I'd never seen a show on TV before. My happiness knows no bounds at six PM, when the evening news are on. The outside world is back.

If at some point during my imprsionment I get affected by the Stockholm Syndrome, I won't fall in love with Khassem.

I'll fall in love with my TV.

But Khassem disappears without saying goodbye. He just doesn't show up anymore. I spend three days and nights without any food intake and no visits from anyone at all. Of course the old fears come back to terrorize me. If it wasn't for the TV, I would have nothing to distract me from the horror scenario I keep thinking of since I got here: what happens if Khassem and the other dude are in a car accident together and die? Or if they both end up in a hospital for a very long time? Who else knows that someone is being held captive in this room?

Probably no-one.

Every time this thought comes up, I use all my willpower to push it away.

On the fourth day I beam at Dead Fish because I'm so unbelievably happy to see him walk into my basement. There is still hope. I will not die.

He does what he always does: lays a pita on the chair and sits down at the end of my bed to watch me eat. So far this has been our only form of communication. I can hardly enjoy my meal because I can't shake off the fear that he, too will soon disappear from my life.

"What's your name?" It takes all my courage to ask him.

He stands up and turns off the TV. It's going to be really difficult to switch it back on, but I don't tell him that. He sits down on the other chair and leans his head back against the wall.

"Saad."

"That's a nice name", I say, and I burst into tears. "Sorry, I was just so afraid when you guys left me here all alone."

"You should be", he replies.

He has that typical, hard Arabic accent but his English is impeccable. He speaks softly and sounds completely relaxed. If wolves could talk, they'd sound like Saad. I'm trying to get my crying fit under control. What do you call this thing that Saad obviously doesn't have? I think it's called "empathy". Someone who's not able to even feel the slightest compassion for other people, is classified as a psychopath. Not all of these people are violent or dangerous. Some lead a very ordinary life. They just don't give a shit about other human beings.

I hope that Saad is one of those harmless psychopaths. He watches as I struggle with a hysterical outburst in my chest. I manage to take deeper breaths. My hands stop trembling. Cool autumn air is coming in from the street. As always I'm sitting on the bed in underwear. Soon this will be uncomfortable, especially since there's no radiator in my room. I wonder if I should ask him for clothes.

"What happened to my uniform?" I ask.

Saad seems to think this question is stupid. His contempt is obvious. As if that wasn't bad enough, he looks bored. If I can't find a way to entertain him he won't come back anytime soon. I have to get my act together. If I panic now, there's all sorts of unpleasant things that can happen to me.

I reach under my bed and fumble for a yellowed postcard that I found a while ago. It shows the Baghdad skyline. On the back it says that it's from the year 1989. It was pinned to the wall. I stared at it for a while until one day I decided to take it off and have a look at the back. It took another few weeks until I decided to do something about it.

Because I had no pen, I used the eyeliner that Khassem had bought me. Not that I would ever use that kind of thing. Razors would have been much more useful. It wasn't easy. I had to sharpen the eyeliner again and again, to avoid making a mess. But I'm proud of the result of hours of painstaking attention to detail now.

Dear Mommy, Daddy and Grandma!
Please don't cry and DO NOT WORRY. I am strong and I'm alive.
My love for
you is endless.
Marina

I had toyed with the idea of testing Khassem. What would be the worst thing to happen if I asked him to send it to Lapwai? But I was always too afraid to ask. Saad reaches for the postcard. He reads it and then looks at me.

It takes all my courage to say, "If you give me an envelope and a pen, I'll write the address on it. I'd be so incredibly grateful if you could send the card. I think of my family all the time. All the time."

He looks at me. He's a wolf thinking about his prey.

"We'll see", he says and gets up.

He leaves me two bottles of water. It's better than nothing.

He's back the next day and gives me the usual pita bread. I eat the whole thing, and while I'm munching my food I'm totally aware of the fact that I'll regret this later.

But things are taking a different turn now.

"Your last meal", Saad says, and I almost choke on the last bite. He pulls the postcard from his hoodie and slowly, carefully tears it up – into exactly sixteen pieces. As if he was carefully following instructions on how to destroy every last bit of hope I had. The little shreds of paper lie on the floor, between his Adidas. On one of the pieces I can decipher the word "Mommy".

Now would be a good time to start crying, but I feel paralysed. I stare into his cold, brown eyes. I know a predator when I see one.

"You're a really smart girl", he says, and I want to scream.

I'm not a girl.

"But you can't manipulate me. What an incredible waste. If only you'd stayed with Mom, Dad and Grandma."

He's holding my 9-mil in his right hand and the way he points it at me is much too casual. My old shooting instructor would rip his head off. I get up and for the first time in four months, he unlocks the handcuffs. He nods towards the TV in the corner. He follows me into the corner and takes out zip ties. He ties my right hand to an old pipe that runs along the wall from floor to ceiling. Then things get painful: he pulls my left arm toward the window and uses the handcuffs again. My left hand is now hanging on the metal handle that serves to open the window. I had to stretch to get there. The zip tie is immediately starting to cut into my skin but it won't be long until I will feel much greater pain. Every muscle in my upper body is tensing up. I'm standing with my arms spread wide under the window that Saad has now closed and covered up with an old towel.

The window handle has an unusual closed form, which means I would never be able to free myself later on. But then, there will be no "later".

Time has stopped. There's only now.

There are only these infinite minutes of preparation. Saad is working with quiet concentration. His calm movements bring back memories that I had successfully repressed for five years. I vomit so hard that I don't even mess up my undershirt. Everything lands on the carpet.

There's no more sound coming in from outside, now that the window is closed. The silence is just as scary as it was at Bagram, when the soldier calmly unlaced my boots and threw away my rifle. I gag, but there's nothing more to come.

The gun is no longer needed now. Saad sits down on the bed next to a fairly new looking issue of *Playboy*.

"What do you need that for if you can have me?" I croak like a very old frog. It would be better if my voice didn't let me down in this last-minute attempt to prostitute myself.

"You're not my type. I need the magazine in order to get in the mood. I want the forensics team to find out that you were raped before your death."

"Well that's good to know." The horror is so overpowering that I feel like I'm rocked by waves of anxiety. It probably looks strange. Cramps are seizing my body. My breathing is unelievably fast. It's like I've just run a marathon.

Saad unwraps a packet of cigarettes and a lighter. "After that I'll have to torture you, but that's going to be short. Unlike other people, this shit doesn't turn me on at all. I just need it for the pictures."

Of course you do.

He holds a phone in his hand.

"Who's going to get the photos?" I'm pretending to be seriously interested in an answer.

"Everyone." Saad is inserting new batteries into the camera. He must have bought it just for this occasion. He looks at me.

"Tell me, Marina. What do you think I've been doing these last four months? Twiddling my thumbs while you tried to put a spell on Khassem?"

I don't know which is worse: Saad's air of composure while he's preparing my violent death, or his perfect English. Without the accent he would be one of us.

"Tell me, Saad. What have you been doing all this time?" I sob.

Finally. Crying is always good. Not that it's going to make any difference.

"I collected email addresses. It's not enough for me to upload you somewhere. This shit gets censored so fast that people won't find it anymore after a couple of days. I want to send the pictures directly to the people who are supposed to see them. I want them to have a heart attack the moment they open the file. Those images – they'll never, ever forget them. It took me so long because it's not enough for me to shock the media. I'm talking about your brothers in arms around the world. I have over twelve hundred addresses of US service members."

"Can you briefly explain to me why you're doing this? That way at least I'll know what I'm dying for", I whisper. My voice is gone. A strange weakness takes possession of me as if I was about to pass out.

"You will die for your country, Marina, for what else?" Saad looks at me like I'm stupid. "You swore an oath. You're representing the hostile army that occupied and destroyed my country. And now you will suffer martyrdom on behalf of your countrymen."

He opens the *Playboy*. Outside the muezzin calls to prayer. Through the closed window I hear him sing. The beautiful Arabic chant fills my chest.

Suddenly I can breathe.

I clear my throat. There's a disgusting taste of vomit in my mouth. I spit on the carpet.

The muezzin has finished his call. I clear my throat a second time and say in pristine high-Arabic: "Everything you do, do it for God."

Saad is so surprised he drops his magazine. He stares at me in shock, and before he can stand up and beat the crap out of me, I start yelling. I know my stuff. I shout like an angry Iraqi woman:

"EVERYTHING – EVERYTHING YOU DO, DO IT FOR GOD!"

Saad flees in panic, slamming the door behind him. He doesn't bother locking it. I keep hanging in the corner of the room like Jesus on the cross, staring at my handgun. It's lying on the dirty sheet I've been sleeping on. If I could untie myself now, I would take the weapon and point it at myself.

I'm done.

All I've been doing these last few months is hone my survival skills. All I tried to do is keep myself alive. I used up all my strength and every brain cell I have to analyze my dangerous environment, listen and watch out for any signs of imminent danger. Trying to control everything that was in any way controllable. I successfully manipulated one of my captors. I had Khassem under control but I had zero influence on Saad. He only wanted one thing: use me for an exemplary execution. If you can't beat them, kill at least one of them.

You can have your example right here, right now. Come back and just shoot me.

The tension in my upper body is slowly getting unbearable. My back muscles are doing their best to outbalance the constant pull that my arms have to endure. By the time I hear the next call of the muezzin I'm not sure if it's my muscles that are killing me or my bones. My neck is cramping. The pain makes me cry, but the crying doesn't bring relief.

I wonder how long it will take. There was a time in the history of our species when crucifixion was a normal method of execution. It would take people up to three days until they died. Jesus went faster because his father took pity on him. I suppose that I could still die of thirst here. What I can't imagine is what happens when my strength is all used up and I can no longer stand. If I get completely exhausted my body cannot slump. But if I'm going to faint, the pressure on my wrists will get so unbearable that I'll wake up from the pain. And then what?

Evening comes. The air in the room is cooler. I'm covered with goosebumps from head to toe. Just when my legs start trembling, I hear the key in the door.

Saad first opens the handcuffs and then begins to laboriously cut the zip ties with a small pair of scissors. It's difficult because the scissors are made for kids. His fidgety movements are not exactly helpful. As he's standing close to me I can smell his body odor for the first time. Saad's shirt is soaking wet, his hair is dripping with sweat. He looks as if he'd been away for the last two or three hours because he wanted to go for a ten-mile run.

Finally I'm free. I push him out of the way because I have to go to the bathroom before my bladder explodes. It seems he didn't expect that. Maybe he thought I would collapse right away. As I'm sitting on the toilet seat I look over to the shower. This is the first time since my abduction that I'm free to move as I please. I have not showered in months.

Before Saad can come up with the idea to visit me in the bathroom, I grab the soap and hair products that are lined up under the sink. The shower faucet is firmly installed in the ceiling, so I decide to wait outside while I turn on the water. At first there's a blast of brown, cold water. I spend a couple of minutes fumbling with the tap. And then the miracle happens. I spend an eternity under the lukewarm water, trying to give my bruised body what it needs most: relaxation. I use tons of soap, shampoo, hair conditioner. As if there was no tomorrow.

It's not clear yet if there is a tomorrow.

After I dried myself with my smelly towel I go back into the room. It's not like I have anywhere else to go. Saad sits on his favorite chair and doesn't look at me. He definitely hates nudity. I notice that my bed is freshly made and there are brand new pajamas waiting for me. Someone thought that a pattern of pink roses would be suitable for tonight. The smelly old fleece blanket is gone and instead I now have a proper duvet, the kind that you find in European hotel rooms. The design of the cover is something I recognize: I know it from the latest IKEA catalog. On the chair where he usually puts the flatbread, I see two hot dogs, a pack of chocolate chip cookies and a bag of salty chips.

I sure as hell am not hallucinating. He was at IKEA. He bought me IKEA food. I should be falling over with laughter. And where's the almond cake?

Saad has the naughty magazine in his lap and pretends to study the cover. He tries to wipe some sweat from his forehead. His expression is the same as always, but his body language is totally betraying him. He's not able to sit still, fidgeting on his chair like a first grader.

The window is still closed, but it's not covered any longer. Night has fallen. I can't make out the light coming in from the street lamp because Saad has turned on the ghastly neon light that's hanging from the ceiling. We never used it before. I'd like to switch it off and go to sleep. Instead I decide to annoy Saad. I can still break down from exhaustion later. I sit down on my bed and ignore the pajamas. The two hotdogs are nice, but too much. I force myself to finish my dinner. Then I wash the last bite down with water and wonder why I'm not getting a coke from IKEA. I imagine Saad standing in line in the food department they always have near the entrance. I'm sure the Baghdad IKEA has exactly the same design as the one in Koblenz, Germany. I close my eyes and see Saad standing in front of the cash register, his palms sweaty, the package with bed linen under his right arm as he's fumbling for small change in his purse.

Everything you do, you better be doing it for the Almighty.

I go back to the bathroom to brush my teeth. Oral hygiene is very important even if you don't know how long you have left to live. Finally I can't think of any more ways to get on Saad's nerves. So I slip into my nice new pajamas. I'd love to know where he got them. But I have no desire whatsoever to start another conversation with this psychopath. I lie down in my completely non-smelly bed and pull the covers over my head.

The end may be near, but first I need some sleep.

THE DEAD FISH COMES ALIVE

The next morning I get cornflakes with fresh milk, served in a small porcelain bowl. And a plain yogurt and a banana. As if this wasn't luxurious enough, there's also coffee in a thermos.

In order to stifle any kind of conversation I switch on the TV. It's nice to walk around freely, but I can feel every single muscle, tendon and bone in my body. Saad is sitting opposite me while I'm enjoying my breakfast. I pretend to be totally interested in the 1950s Tunisian film they're showing. Later Saad picks up my dishes while I'm in the bathroom, and disappears. He comes back for lunch and dinner. And this is his routine for the next few days. We don't talk. I start exercising again, which is a lot more fun since now I can take a shower when I'm done. Eventually Saad brings me bath towels and also some clothes. For the first time in months I get to wear a pair of jeans. Because they're a little too wide Saad gets me a belt the next day.

"Aren't you worried I could use it to hang myself?"

Saad is too shocked to give me an answer. I guess he can't wrap his head around the fact that I speak his language. It's also the first time since my aborted execution that I actually talk to him, and this is clearly too much. He leaves my basement right away and comes back only for the next meal.

The next day I don't switch on the TV in the morning. I look Saad in the eyes while I'm having breakfast. He hates that. There's a newspaper lying next to me on the bed. I keep looking at the headlines. I'm about to finally read something again. I can't wait to be alone with the paper but at the same time I'd like to have a nice conversation with another human being. It's been a while.

"So what's up with my execution?" I ask with my mouth full. Saad startles and nearly falls off his chair.

God, I love my new power.

"Is it canceled or just postponed?"

Saad leans forward and hides his head in his hands. He moves back and forth a bit, as if to pray. But it doesn't look like I'll get an answer from him.

"I can beat you up to make you talk", I announce and take a bite off some kind of pastry that looks almost like a croissant. The service in Hotel Baghdad is quite good these days.

He takes his hands off his face and puts them in his lap. He's managed to put on his stoic *you-can't-touch me*-face.

"I learned some hand to hand combat", I'm bragging.

Saad clears his throat. "Khassem told me you fix fighter jets."

I laugh. "Khassem is an idiot. I never got to tell him about the way my career developed because he didn't care. I found a much more rewarding occupation. They wanted to use my Arabic language skills. As you know, we want to conquer the hearts and minds of the Iraqi people. They had to make sure I could go on patrols with soldiers. So they prepared me for all kinds of combat ops. In theory I can even defend myself with a knife. But I'd rather not give it a try."

I can't believe how easy it is to talk to Saad in his mother language. My Arabic is almost fluent. I guess it was a good idea to binge on Arabian TV shows. It helped me to learn even more vocabulary. I hope that my accent is not too strong. Hassan from Spangdahlem once told me that it always sounds so cute when Americans try to speak foreign languages.

"Of course I didn't get exactly what I wanted. I wanted to join the guys who jump out of helicopters and who evacuate our wounded from the battle zone. That was my dream. I didn't have to re-enlist. But I negotiated until I got what I wanted."

Saad is visibly confused. "You jumped out of a helicopter in the middle of Baghdad? What for?"

"No, they didn't grant me that wish. You have to be male to join the P.Js. And I'm not, as you may have noticed. But I got to join an organization that was never even on my radar. I belong to the Office of Special Investigations. We're like the FBI for the Air Force. Yeah. And because of my language skills they sent me to your beautiful country."

I disappear in the bathroom. It interferes with my privacy a bit that someone removed the bathroom door. Maybe there never was a door in the first place. I hope Saad leaves soon. I really want to go to bed and read my newspaper.

But Saad is still sitting there. I pull off my jeans and he looks away, embarrassed as always. I cover myself with the warm blanket.

"Saad." This is the first time that I pronounce his name. "How did I end up here?"

Saad gets up and goes to the window. "I can tell you that. You scared me to death that day." He looks up at the ceiling. "In the summer I help my uncle in one of his stores. We sell women's clothing upstairs. Everything from sneakers to the hijab to underwear. There weren't any customers the day you stormed in."

I wish I could remember this fateful day. But no matter how hard I try, nothing comes back to me.

Saad is now pacing the room. His voice sounds strained. I guess it was a big day for him too. "So I'm busy re-arranging sweaters on a shelf. Suddenly a soldier, armed to the teeth, is standing in front of me. A woman in full battle dress, yelling some incoherent stuff, totally hysterical. Your uniform was splattered with blood. Your rifle strap got stuck in a clothes rack. You fell on the floor and broke your arm. You were screaming in pain when I dragged you down the stairs. Then I called my father, and he gave you the cast."

I hold my breath. His father?

"My parents are doctors. So he gave you painkillers. Later, I told my father that I handed you over to the Americans. He just looked at me, and I think he knew I was lying, but he didn't seem to care much."

Too much information. I look up at the ceiling and try to process all this. Now at least I know why Saad is as well dressed as Khassem. The families of physicians belong to the rather thin Iraqi middle class.

"How do you get into the Green Zone?" I ask. "And Khassem?"

He shrugs and sits back on the chair. "My mother works there. And Khassem sometimes picks up a friend with his car."

That's why they have access to Burger King and IKEA. I'm just about to ask if there's an Iraqi version of KFC but Saad is done with talking for today. He leaves without saying goodbye.

Now that we've established some kind of fragile relationship, we talk to each other every day. Saad's new role is to entertain me. I ask him two million things about life in Baghdad. I find out that Khassem emigrated to Scotland with his family. His stepfather is an engineer and his mother a nurse, so they will be able to earn a living there.

"What's your connection to him? Are you related?"

Saad shakes his head. "Our parents know each other. Khassem is three years younger than me, and when we were in elementary school our parents absolutely wanted us to make friends. We don't have that much in common, but what do you want to do? We just spent a lot of time together when we were growing up. We played football a lot. I mean soccer. And we did a lot of computer stuff."

I can't get used to Saad giving me so much insight into his life. Especially when I think of how he treated me before. Before my aborted crucifixion.

Something happened to him when I yelled at him about God. But I prefer not to ask. I feel that our new relationship is not yet stable.

"Well, my parents never told me who I should hang out with", I say.

Saad looks tired. The wooden chair that he's sitting on can't be too comfortable. He's avoided sitting on my bed lately.

"But our parents belong to a minority. For people like us it's important to be friends with like-minded families. Khassem has a sister. And I know for sure they were hoping that I would marry her someday."

"What minority?" Khassem and Saad are normal Iraqi names to my knowledge, maybe more Sunni than Shiite. But here I'm treading on shaky ground. I'm not as familiar as I probably should be with the different ethnicities in this country.

"We're Assyrians."

"Oh shit." I spill coffee on my duvet cover. "You gotta be joking!"

Saad says nothing. He turns his head to the side to look out the window. Not that he can see anything there.

I'm stunned. For months I thought I was in the hands of freedom-hating Muslims. I braced myself for all kinds of crazy religious shit. I was afraid they would maybe suspect me of being Jewish. I kind of expected that they would force me to forsake my religion. That's what I would have done. It's perfectly fine to convert to a different creed in order to save your own life. Even Chuck Norris would do that.

But Christians?

Saad decides to take a leave of absence. So I have almost twenty-four hours to think about what it means that both he and Khassem are Christians. I try to remember all the things I've learned about this country. I'm afraid there are some dangerous gaps in my knowledge. It would have been better to read more books on this whole mess called Middle East. Too late. I think that the Christian minority in Iraq was doing okay until we showed up. Soon after the invasion, a civil war broke out. It took a huge effort to bring that under control. It actually took several years and several thousand American casualties. Basically, the Shiites and Sunnis were trying to kill each other. The Kurds took advantage of the fact that nobody worried too much about them, and started their own nation building. Unfortunately there were a lot of different parties now who tried to influence the outcome of this conflict: Iran, Al Qaeda, the Gulf states... There was a permanent influx of money, weapons and fighters. More and more people got radicalized. And suddenly, the Christian minority became a target. Things got ugly: churches were burned down. Bombs went off in Christian neighborhoods. Then there were abductions and murder. Some of the victims were priests and bishops. The Christians realized that they were no longer safe in their own country.

No wonder that Khassem's family has fled to Scotland.

On his next visit, Saad brings me two oranges that are so beautiful and so perfectly shaped that I'd like to keep them. Maybe put them on top of the TV set for decoration. But I can't resist the temptation in the end. I wonder how expensive fresh oranges are in Baghdad. I peel one of them with my hand and urge Saad to take a piece. He refuses. So I go over to his chair and try to stuff it into his mouth, just like Flanagan did with the banana when I was having my meltdown in his office. Saad is horrified and escapes into the left corner of the room, the exact spot where I was supposed to die a week ago. It's clear that physical closeness is pure horror for him.

Interesting.

I wash my sticky hands and go back to my bed. Where else should I go?

"Tell me Saad, do you and your family want to stay in Iraq?"

Saad is still standing in the corner.

"Look, you can sit down on your chair again. Or on my bed. I'm not going to start a new attack. At least not today."

I can't help giggling. This is so crazy. We have now gotten to the point where I have to convince my captor that he's safe from me. The balance of power between the two of us has tilted upside down. This whole arrangement cannot possibly get any weirder.

Saad sits back in his chair. "My father completed his medical studies in Germany. Once we have the visa, we're gone."

I'm amazed. I didn't expect such a precise answer. "And what's gonna happen to me?"

Saad shrugs. "The best thing to do is to drive you to your embassy in the Green Zone. And then we pretend that I freed you. Or helped you escape. That would work for you, right?"

That's shocking news. My time here is coming to an end. I will soon be free. Is this really happening or am I hallucinating?

Saad is watching me. I can't say a word. There are too many emotions crashing down on me. I stare against the wall with my mouth half-open, trying to put some order into my thoughts. Finally I get up and turn on the TV. I find a music channel with super-sweet Iraqi lovesongs, and I turn up the volume. There's a man yearning for his *Habiiibi*.

I go to bed.

This is all too much.

A few days later, Saad has a surprise for me. He hands over my iPod, freshly charged. I'd love to switch it on right away but that would be kind of rude, I guess.

As Saad is putting fresh food on my chair I remember something that I was planning to ask him.

"Did you keep other stuff that belongs to me?"

He nods. For the first time in weeks, he sits down on my bed, keeping the maximum possible distance from me. "Everything. Your uniform, the boots... Everything you were carrying."

"The M4?" I ask.

"No, that one I sold."

"You have got to be shitting me!" I'm suddenly angry. "That means that at some point an American will get shot with my rifle. You stupid asshole! Jesusfuck!"

Saad looks so indifferent that I feel like kicking him in the face. "I sold it on an Iraqi version of eBay. And then later I realized how insanely risky that was. If anyone had noticed... Your folks would have showed up at my door."

"No Saad, they would have blasted away your fuckin' door, you stupid son of a bitch."

I try to imagine how a bunch of badass Marines break into my prison and set me free. That used to be my favorite daydream for a very long time.

"What would happen to you if you got caught?" I ask. "Would you end up in Gitmo or would they just throw you in jail here?"

"I'm pretty sure they would pass me on to the Iraqi judiciary. And that's worse than anything that the Americans have in store for prisoners. They would probably torture me to death. Your government wanted to bring freedom and democracy to Iraq. Didn't work. You exchanged one dictator with another. And now it's the others who are sitting in jail."

Of course he's right. Before my trip to Iraq I was briefed on the political situation and the new balance of power. The justice system here is the same as in most Arab countries: corrupt and ultraviolent. You do not want to spend time in an Iraqi prison. You simply may not survive it.

There are a whole lot of Iraqis who are anything but happy about our imminent departure. In some parts of the country, people are more afraid of their own security forces than of us.

I'm not going to argue with Saad. It's better to change the subject. "Listen. Do you think you could bring back my uniform and my boots? I kinda miss them."

Saad is more than bewildered by my request. He looks at me as if I was delusional.

"You want to wear your uniform again? There's blood on it."

I start crying.

I don't know whose blood it is.

REDEPLOYMENT

I don't sleep well. I keep waking up from noises that come in from the street. I go back to sleep and end up dreaming weird stuff.

In one of these dreams I see David's beautiful face. He's laughing at me for some foolish thing I must have said. Small lines are forming around his good eye and his laugh is totally contagious. I wake up with a strange feeling of happiness, just in time for the first call of the muezzin.

It's still early. Saad won't show up in the next couple of hours. I listen to music, the iPod being the only object of my past that I'm in possession of. Soon the battery will be empty. I sincerely hope that Saad is bringing a charger. I choose an old Spangdahlem-period playlist and think of the past.

March 2006

Coming home straight from Bagram was such a weird experience. I saw my country through the eyes of an adult. At least I thought I was now a grown-up. My hometown looked different. I saw it with the eyes of a service member who's disciplined and in perfect physical shape. Of course I had this problem every time I was home on leave, whether I came from Texas or Germany or elsewhere. This time it was just worse. I'd become accustomed to six- or seven-day weeks and long work days. On an Indian reservation there are a lot of young and healthy people who are perfectly happy to do nothing all day. In Bagram there were a lot of civilians but few of them were fat. On my first visit to a mall I saw so many overweight people that I was actually depressed when I came home. They didn't seem to mind being out of shape. It didn't seem to bother them that they couldn't even run for the bus. When you're obese, you're handicapped. No matter how young you still are. How they could give up on their body like this was beyond me. From that day on I ordered everything I wanted on the Internet.

My friends were glad to have me back but asked surprisingly few questions. Their curiosity was limited. The only thing that was giving me real satisfaction was spending time with my parents and my grandmother. It's only during the last month of my deployment that I remembered to take pictures. I showed them the Russian Tower and other stuff left over from the Soviet occupation. Grandma was fascinated by the fish-shaped balloon that was floating over us at all times, monitoring everything that happened on and around the base. But my family mainly wanted to see people: my crew, my boss, Afghans (luckily there were a few truck drivers who didn't mind getting their pictures taken). And of course they wanted to see me with the Hog. Kyle and I had taken turns posing in front of our beloved monster. With the photos of our sanitary facilities I was able to shock my parents a little.

When Grandma saw a photo of Flanagan, she said: "Oh, he looks mean."

I had to laugh. "He did that on purpose when I told him who the picture is for. That's his kind of humor. He was a great boss. Without his help it would've been very difficult for me there."

"Is he still available?" my mother asked.

"Mom, please! I'm twenty-three. Let me experiment for a while before I settle down."

That was a mistake. An awkward silence filled our living room. Only the fan of my laptop was audible. Love and sex were not really topics we discussed in our family. And from what I'd just said, it was also clear that I wasn't a virgin anymore.

But other than that, my family was more than happy to have me back, and they were doting on me as if they had nothing else to do. One day I took up all my courage and told my father about Staff Sergeant Rohrman. First I wanted to censor the story in the right places. I didn't want him to know about Sandy's rape and how I threatened the two soldiers. But that wasn't feasible. If I left those crucial parts of the story out, I would have had to invent a reason why Rohrman almost ripped my head off in his office. That was too complicated, so I told my father everything.

His reaction was unexpected.

"Where is he now?"

That was the first thing he asked.

"I don't know", I said. "I guess he's home. Recovering. He's probably getting used to his prosthesis. I always imagine how he's trying to run along the Hudson River. And then he's gonna need to think about his career options."

"Hmm." Dad studied his beer can. He had muted the TV when I started talking about Rohrman.

"And he never got in touch with you?"

"No, why should he?"

Dad took a sip. "Well, you're somehow bound to each other."

I didn't want to laugh about him, but my father sometimes had a funny way of expressing himself. Like an immigrant who came to America decades ago, but still uses phrases from his mother language.

"What do you mean by that? Bound to each other?"

"It's very simple. You have some unfinished things between you. Your story is not over yet. You don't know what happened to him at home and he doesn't know if you ever managed to smooth things out in Afghanistan."

I shook my head. "I'm pretty sure he was still in touch with Flanagan. And that my boss told him that, well, that everything's fine and all that."

"But Marina, you have to admit that you can't get him out of your head. He's still present. You still think of him."

If my father wasn't running a gas station, he would have to be a therapist. A shrink who billed 200 dollars an hour in uptown Manhattan. He had the irritating talent that allowed him to take a straight look into other people's souls. With the result that sometimes he said things that people really didn't want to hear.

I took the remote and turned the sound back on. We watched the

Simpsons together. My father knew for sure what was going on in my head while Bart Simpson was blowing up a nuclear power plant by mistake.

It took weeks before I knew David Rohrman's whereabouts. I had to ask Kyle and Robert for help because they still had a better relationship with the other guys in our team than I did. I was stationed in Texas again. It was a bit of a surprise when the mail came with Rohrman's current address: he was in Denver. That didn't quite match his elitist East Coast accent. Maybe he lived there with his girlfriend. Kyle said that he had mentioned some woman in the past. Robert thought he'd heard that Rohrman was planning to get married, at least before he was wounded.

I imagined a beautiful woman who was at least as blond and blue-eyed as he was. I visualized how she opened the door and looked at me. And how I told her that I wanted to see her husband because we were deployed together last year. And I imagined how his wife was too polite to slam the door in my face, and how she would invite me into the house and make me a cup of coffee.

And then what?

Then my former boss would come in and look more than surprised because I was sitting on his sofa. And I would have to explain to him what I actually wanted.

I was having lunch with a bunch of colleagues while all these thoughts were circulating in my head. Fortunately, they were talking about the NFL. Nobody was expecting me to contribute to the discussion.

I couldn't just show up at Rohrman's place without advance warning. That would be rude. I had his phone number, but there was no way I could call him. Our short Skype session had been so disastrous that a phone call was definitely out of the question. It would have been ideal to send him a quick email, but I had no address. I didn't want to pester Kyle and Robert again. I was lucky enough they hadn't asked me what I wanted from Rohrman anyway.

I didn't want anything.

That was the problem.

Two months went by without me doing anything. Spring came and with it the barbecue season. The first rednecks began to show up at work with second-degree burns (especially after weekends). Suddenly I was told to take a six day-holiday in order to reduce overtime. It came unexpected and my family knew nothing about this.

I still needed some time to convince myself it was a good idea to do what my dad had told me. Finally I booked a non-refundable flight. I could still change the date of the return flight, but I'd have to pay a hefty surcharge. That way I was forced to spend five days in Denver, no matter what happened.

I was more scared of this trip than of anything else I'd done so far.

WELCOME TO DENVER (OR NOT)

May 2007

I took a red-eye from San Antonio, pretending to be a businesswoman on a duty trip. Except that my clothes gave me away as a tourist. I had a printout of Rohrman's neighborhood and a timetable for public transport. From the airport I first took a bus, then I had to walk about fifteen minutes. The area was quite nice but definitely not the upscale suburb I had envisioned. I walked past a lot of detached single-family homes. Two-storey terraced houses dominated, many flags, towel-sized front yards. A few bungalows from the Seventies. This was where the plumbers lived and the police officers and nurses. The air was humid and too warm. I took off my rain jacket and carried it under my arm. Then I had to cross a busy four-lane road and ended up in a trailer park.

Oh. Who would've thought?

It was actually not bad at all, definitely in a much better category than the kind of place I would imagine whenever I heard the word "trailer trash". Some of the mobile homes were huge. One of them looked like a Canadian log cabin. The lawns were well maintained. Two unattended children were running around on a modest playground. Small trees lined a gravel foot path, and here and there I saw a few accurately trimmed hedges.

I looked at my printout again. Maybe Denver had two streets of the same name, and I was in the wrong part of town. Could it be that I made a mistake with the zip code? I couldn't imagine that Sonny Boy and his wife lived here.

The number I was looking for was made of wood and attached to the metal frame of a modest white trailer. It was certainly in good shape but it didn't look large enough to provide enough room for two people. White shutters were covering the windows inside, and the door was open. The air probably got real stuffy real fast when your house was made of steel.

I walked up to the open door and didn't like the sound my heart was making in my ears. It was loud and unpleasant: I could hear every single heartbeat. I stopped just a few yards from the door and listened. Ideally someone would come out now so that I could ask. And then it would turn out that my hike through Denver's less-privileged suburbs was a mistake, and I would go back to the bus stop. But nothing happened. I couldn't make out a single sound from inside. It was morning. The neighborhood was quiet. All I heard was traffic from the nearby road, and some birds chirping.

I stood around for a long time, unable to decide on my next move. There was no-one I could have asked. Either everyone here was unemployed and slept until noon, or they were all at work. There were more than enough jobs that were so badly remunerated that people couldn't afford to live in a normal apartment.

I pulled off my backpack and put it down on the lawn. I knelt down and stated rummaging around, checking if I really had everything. It didn't make sense, but I was stalling. Anyone who walked by or who looked out the window of the adjacent trailers had to notice that some stranger was standing around and didn't go away. I stood up and looked around in case I could spot another human being. But nothing happened except that a cat decided to flirt with me. It wrapped itself around my legs and when I knelt down, it jumped enthusiastically into my lap. It was purring so loud that it almost drowned out the sound of the traffic.

Eventually the cat had enough and decided to move on. I felt a bit stiff when I got up again. There was now a stain on my jeans from the freshly mown grass. I picked up the backpack, walked over to the door and knocked a few times.

"Hello? Anyone home?"

There was no answer. When I was about to knock a second time, I heard Rohrman's voice from inside.

"You just spent a solid hour hanging around outside. How about you just come in, for Chrissake?"

He sounded fed up. He was not exactly happy that I was here.

The best thing to do now was to turn around and run away: just forget about the whole trip, along with the $ 280 fee for moving up the return flight. Pathetic but feasible. The one thing I wanted to do even less was to enter this home.

He was sitting at the dining table, reading a newspaper. I walked past a tiny kitchenette and sat down opposite him. The pads on the bench were dark blue and new. The blinds also looked as if he had recently bought them. Now that I was inside I saw that the blinds were transparent. From where he was sitting, he could see exactly what was going on outside. He had been watching me killing time on his lawn instead of just walking back into his life.

He took all his time studying the business section of the paper. Outside I saw the cat again. It was probably looking for me. Finally, he folded the paper carefully and looked at me, raising his eyebrows.

"What can I do for you?"

I cleared my throat. "I just wanted to say hi. Just to see how you been holding up."

"I'm good", he said. "Real good."

It was my turn to speak. I couldn't think of anything intelligent. So I said something stupid.

"You look really dangerous with that eye patch."

"Exactly what you're into."

We could have laughed now, and the ice would have been broken. But his tone was so cold it was chilling the air around us.

"Are you in pain?"

He shrugged. "The burns were driving me nuts for a while. Especially on my upper body. But you wanna know about my stump, right? Wanna have a look?"

Before I could answer he laid his left leg on the table. He was wearing sweatpants. The stump didn't look scary at all, just unusual. Little blond hairs were covering his calves. The amputation had taken place just above the ankle. Everything looked healed.

"It doesn't look too bad", I said. "How do you come to terms with the prosthesis? Is it difficult to walk in it?"

He shrugged again. "At the moment people can still see that I'm limping a little. But it's getting better. I miss running. My doctor says it won't be long now."

"Is someone taking care of you? Or do you live here alone?" I was amazed at my own courage. My question could be translated as: Are you single?

"I don't need anyone. I'm a big boy." He was sitting completely motionless with his back against the hard wood of the bench, hands folded in his lap, the cut-off leg on the table. He looked at me with an expression that was neither friendly nor hostile.

I stared back. The longer he looked at me, the stronger was my impression that his eyes were drilling into my brain and started reading all my secrets, especially the dark ones, like a hacker siphoning off his victim's data. His expression remained blank. Eventually I couldn't take it any longer and dropped my gaze. The table was made of the same plastic material as the countertop around the sink. It had an interesting white-gray granite pattern that I was studying. That was better than looking into David's eyes.

He looked out the window, his boredom more than obvious. Someone walked by with a big dog. I started racking my brain for other questions to ask.

"Hey David." The dog owner stuck his head through the door. "You wanna go grocery shopping? Susie left me the car."

David jumped up. "Good idea. I got absolutely no meat for the barbecue tonight."

He disappeared into the bedroom and left me baffled. I gave the dog owner a friendly nod. He was fat and looked like he'd retired early, possibly for health reasons. If Denzel Washington hadn't become a movie star, he could have looked like this. He managed to engage me in a friendly chat until David came back, wearing sneakers and socks so that I couldn't see his prosthesis. But that didn't really matter anyway because my visit with David was now officially over. I didn't want to give him an opportunity to kick me out, so I grabbed my backpack and got out.

I petted the dog. David took the three stairs down without a struggle.

I said, "Take care".

I turned around and walked calmly back to my bus stop.

I took the bus back downtown and treated myself to a huge lunch at a steak restaurant. After that I was tired and had no clue where to go. I found a small park. There wasn't much going on. I wandered around for a while and found a park bench. I put the backpack in my lap so that no one could steal it. Then I dropped my head in my hands and cried.

David was not alright. He lived alone. He was in pain. His prosthesis prevented him from doing the sports he liked. And he didn't want my help.

It had taken him five minutes to fuck me up.

It almost felt like mourning. I was mourning the lighthearted Staff Sergeant whose good mood filled our hangar as soon as he walked in. The others would have risked their lives for him. I had a serious flashback to the good old times at Bagram. The short time we had worked together was now something I was actually longing for. I spent the afternoon trying to remember everything I ever heard him say. Stuff that I'd forgotten suddenly came back to me. Like the day he had comforted Kyle when he learned that his dog had died. I felt a hot pang of jealousy as Rohrman put his arm around Kyle's shoulder. Suddenly I remembered one morning when we were in the bunker during a rocket attack, waiting for the all clear. He entertained us all with a story about a stubborn donkey who narrowly avoided getting shot by a patrol in Iraq. The story itself was trivial, but the way he told it, we were hanging on his every word. And when the punch line came we all fell over laughing.

Shit, I miss that.

Of course my sorrow was totally inappropriate. In the past I'd had almost nothing to do with the man who was now causing me so much grief. I wasn't a part of his life. He'd never showed me any interest. How was it possible for this guy to throw me completely off track? And worse, it was the second time he managed to do that. I shuddered when I thought of how miserable I was after our Skype session.

I had some addresses of cheap hotels but I just couldn't bring myself to pick one of them. The prospect of sitting alone in a tiny room with a smelly carpet and shit-brown curtains was too depressing. So I wandered aimlessly around, pretending to be interested in the city. The people I encountered all looked very busy. Everyone knew where they would spend the evening. Those who were walking alone were talking into their phones. I felt lonely and this, too, reminded me of my time at Bagram Airfield. It was almost like riding my bike along Disney with nowhere to go and no-one to hang out with.

I found a bookstore, the perfect refuge for someone with nothing to do. I looked through military books. But they talked about war and combat and weapons, and in fact those books had nothing to do with my job. The books on Special Forces were not interesting because they were written by people who were not operators themselves. Nevertheless I went through the picture sections on the off chance I might find photos of Tim and Dan. It was crazy: I didn't know their last names, and I had no clue to what unit they belonged to back then. There was no way of knowing whether they were still alive.

That was another depressing thought.

I knew every inch of Tim's body but I knew nothing about him. The burn scar on his right forearm was vivid in my memory, but I had no idea how he got it. And I would never get the opportunity to find out.

I didn't want to burst into tears in the store, so I turned my back to that section and went to find the self-help literature. Other people had the same idea. This section was more popular than the rest of the store. In order to make people stay and choose as many books as possible, the owners of the place provided their customers with some comfortable chairs and a coffee machine. I flipped through some of the books. They all said the same thing: you have to like yourself first. Before you do anything else. But I didn't like myself at all because I was an idiot who had flown to Denver to make a complete ass of myself.

All that well-meant advice couldn't possibly repair my self-esteem. There was one obnoxiously simple book whose essential message was so easy that I wondered how it was possible to make money with something so self-evident: What you want from life, will not be served to you on a silver platter. You have to take what you want!

I was sitting on an orange chair, across from a graying gentleman who was completely fascinated by a book that explained the difference between men and women. I thought really hard about what I wanted from life. I had no idea. I decided to ask myself simpler questions.

What did I want from life – right now?

Staff Sergeant David M. Rohrman.

I wanted the one-eyed, one-footed grumpy asshole who had not exactly welcomed me to his home.

I wanted to see his scars. All of them. I wanted to lay my head on his pillow. I wanted to know where he grew up, who his parents were, why he had dropped out of college. Why he lived in a trailer. I wanted to hug him and hold him.

But what did Staff Sergeant David M. Rohrman want?

I put the book back on the shelf and sat back on the chair. I closed my eyes to concentrate. How could I find out what someone I hardly knew actually wanted? Just as I had to work through a checklist while doing the maintenance of an aircraft, I had to make a list of all the things I knew. These were the facts I knew about:

- right from the beginning I was the only one in our crew that David was never goofing around with;
- Kyle and Robert both had mentioned more than once that David would secretly check me out when no one was looking;
- according to what Dan once said to me, the thigh-squeezing incident was a sure sign that David had a thing for me, and Flanagan had expressed the same suspicion;
- David warned me that he would get me sacked for "prostitution";
- he wrote me a cryptic farewell note;
- during our Skype session he asked me about my love life;

- in the trailer he admitted to being single;
- and he claimed that I was into men who look dangerous – men like him.

"Goddamn", I hissed.

The gray-haired man dropped his book.

"Sorry, didn't mean to scare you", I said as I took my backpack and stood up. I laughed as I squeezed my way through a group of customers. I needed to leave. Because all of a sudden, I knew what I was going to do. One of the salesclerks looked at me as if I was something to worry about. But I wasn't crazy. I just happened to be the victim of a very violent mood swing.

The mood was good.

Outside, the afternoon heat was like a wall. Luckily there was a Nordstrom across the street. I entered the wonderfully air-conditioned department store and started looking for new clothes. I was completely overwhelmed by the sheer amount of outfits until a saleswoman approached me and asked if she could help me.

"I'm going to a barbecue", I said. The girl looked as if she'd just graduated high school.

"Tonight? It's going to be hot, so you need something light", said the saleswoman.

"There's a guy whose head I need to turn."

The clerk giggled, "Need to?"

I nodded. The girl jumped for joy and then dragged me off to the lingerie department. Underwear was something I hadn't even thought of.

I didn't choose a hotel because I would spend the night in David's bed. If all else failed I would gain entry by force because I now understood fully what I had to do to help myself: *You have to take what you want.*

Shelley the sales clerk found the perfect outfit for the evening and accompanied me into the cosmetics department where I got a professional make up that made me look like a movie star. She and her co-worker didn't release me until I promised to go to the address of a waxing studio. After about an hour of torture I was totally traumatized. I looked fantastic in my new clothes. But to have a complete stranger fumble around with the most intimate parts of my body had definitely been a mistake. I couldn't imagine that other women were undergoing this ordeal every six weeks.

I bought a bottle of whiskey with an unpronounceable Irish name in the hope that the friends I was planning to make at the barbecue would appreciate it. The bus ride was a problem. I felt dizzy all of a sudden, and I remembered that I hadn't eaten in seven hours. I got off at my bus stop. The bus driver winked at me. That was a good sign. Just like the construction worker that I passed downtown. His cigarette almost dropped from his mouth when he saw me. My hair was still tied in a pony tail although Shelley and her colleague had pressured me to wear it open. But I had a tendency to constantly fiddle with my hair. And I was nervous enough already.

I was able to stuff my old clothes into the backpack. I didn't buy new shoes for lack of space. I didn't want to show up at David's place with shopping bags.

I ate an ice cream at a gas station.

A paved road led into the trailer park and branched off into a narrow gravel path when I got closer to the area where David was living. I looked around and wondered where people parked their cars. I stood very straight and took a deep breath. There was absolutely no reason to be nervous. Crashing a party was no big deal. At least it shouldn't be for someone who is accustomed to the sound of exploding landmines and knows how to use an assault rifle. It was only nine PM. I had calculated that at this time people were done eating, and that the drinking was under way. Since alcohol on a full stomach had a calming effect I was hoping that David wouldn't be too upset if I was suddenly standing in front of him.

I walked past David's home. His door was closed, and I followed the smell of grilled meat. Soon I heard voices and laughter.

You can do this.

Behind the mobile home that resembled a log cabin there was a barbecue with a few wooden benches and tables. About a dozen people were sitting around and two of them saw me coming, two young men who both had a weakness for forearm tattoos. I winked at them and got a friendly smile back. I stopped at a table that served as the buffet. There were half-empty salad bowls and clean dishes. A cooler full of beer cans and soft drinks was next to it. The working class version of Denzel Washington was standing behind the buffet. He was totally pleased to see me.

"Hey, I know you! Now that's gonna be a nice surprise for David. Susie, come on over!"

I put my backpack on the lawn. Denzel's wife Susie had some trouble getting out of her camping chair.

"A new face", she said, and I smiled at her.

"My name is Marina. I do not come empty-handed", I said and pulled the whiskey out of the backpack. I put it on the table and took out a Kahlua bottle as well.

"Wow", Susie exclaimed. "You're gonna get us all drunk and then rob our homes while we're passed out on the lawn?"

"Yeah, that's the idea. I need a new flat screen."

Susie laughed. "I like her."

Her husband came out from behind the buffet and took the bottles on the table that Susie had been sitting at.

"David went to the bathroom", he said. "Did you eat yet? We still have a lot of food left."

I felt that I had no more reason to be nervous. I had met just the right people. I filled a plate with meat and salad and sat down next to Susie. She told me about her pets while I was eating. I mentioned the cat I'd met in the morning, but it wasn't hers. I was sitting with my back to the gravel path. The two young men joined us at our table, whether because of me or because of the whiskey, I didn't know. It didn't matter. The important thing was that I had people to talk to.

I grinned at David when he came back and sat down next to Denzel, across from me.

"Where did this super-expensive whiskey come from?" he asked the others.

Susie pointed at me. I kept eating. There was just nothing better than a big fat American barbecue. Denzel, whose real name I still didn't know, got up to fetch glasses and ice cubes. David took the bottle and tried to pronounce the name of the whiskey. That was the signal for the two other guys to start a fundamental discussion about whiskey, and they stuck to the subject until the bottle was almost empty. It was getting dark. Now and then a mosquito landed on one of my arms. The evening air didn't cool down much. I felt really good in my strapless black top. I was hot.

Hey David, look at me. I'm hot!

Unlike the others, I was only drinking beer. I needed to be in control because I had plans tonight. I looked at David and hoped he noticed my impressive eye make-up. He took another sip of whiskey before he started talking about basketball. I wondered if Susie had also noticed that David avoided looking at me. Since he'd sat down at the table we had not exchanged a single word.

Eventually he got up and went to sit somewhere else. Of course he was entitled to do that. I used the toilet in Susie's trailer. I had no plan except to find a way into David's home. I had to stay at the party as long as David was staying, but once he took off, it was going to get difficult. Since he'd so far completely ignored my presence it was unlikely he would ask me to come along. As a worst-case scenario I imagined that he could sneak out and that I would end up standing in front of his closed door.

I remembered how Dan had laughed about my ambitions, and how he told me I shouldn't try to be a doorkicker. "You leave that to the grunts", he'd said. I imagined how I kicked in David's door with my sneakers. It was going to be an interesting night.

When I returned, I saw the bottle of whiskey next to the Kahlua bottle on David's table. The people sitting around him were pretty loud. The only two women I saw were middle-aged and out of shape. At least I didn't have any competition. I sat down on the bench, grateful for the fact that Susie and her husband kept entertaining me. We couldn't agree on which pets were better: cats or dogs. Susie had both a cat and a dog, a constant source of annoyance to Denzel. He liked to sleep in and hated to be woken up in the morning.

At some point the party broke up. I insisted on helping Susie clean up. The barbecue area looked clean and tidy in no time at all. David was still sitting at his table and had an argument with an elderly man who could barely keep his eyes open.

David was genuinely angry.

"One hundred thousand boots on the ground we got there! It's not exactly a small country, you know. How's that supposed to work?" He shook his head and drank from his beer can. There was no whiskey left.

The other man asked, "What do you mean? Not enough or what?"

"Of course it's not enough. Do you know how many soldiers were stationed in Germany in 1945?"

The other one shook his head.

"Me neither", David said, pounding his fist on the table. "But there were several million, that much I know. And they were needed. The Germans fought to the end. They didn't give up, just like the fucking Taliban. Eisenhower was going insane. Anyone trying to desert the German army was found hanging from a lamppost."

The party mood was now over. David's dialog partner seemed to have no desire in hearing stories about the cruelty of war. He thanked me for the good whiskey and struggled to his feet.
As he walked away I positioned myself next to David. He looked up at me and grinned.

"I'm epically shit-faced", he explained. "And you're the one to blame."

"I'm really sorry, man. Shall I take you home?"

David tried to get up. It wasn't only the prosthesis that was making things difficult. His sense of balance didn't seem to work.

"Are you my nurse?" He put an arm around my shoulder.

Denzel was on the other side and held him more or less stable. We slowly started walking, and I hoped that we wouldn't stumble over something in the dark.

"If that's what you want, I'll be your nurse."

He laughed. "But what if I don't want that?"

"You want something else? I can be anything you want. You just need to say it."

It didn't bother me that Denzel was listening. I could imagine that he would later entertain Susie with this.

We were now standing in front of the trailer. David fished his keys out of his pocket. He managed to unlock the door surprisingly fast. We somehow managed to shove him up the stairs and inside. Denzel handed me my backpack. I thanked him and wished him a good night.

Then I was inside. I heard David pee, and I stood in front of the bathroom door to makes sure he didn't have an accident between the bathroom and the bedroom. When he came out I followed him into the bedroom where he crawled onto the unmade bed. I kneeled beside him and asked him to turn around. He let out some kind of grunt and turned onto his back. First I took off his shoes and socks. Then I had to turn on the overhead light to look at the prosthesis.

"Oh man, turn it off", he whined.

I found the click mechanism to open the prosthesis and carefully pulled it off. I turned the light off. A streetlamp was giving me enough light to unzip his jeans. I managed to take them off. David had his eyes closed while I was struggling with his clothes. I decided to leave his T-shirt on.

I pulled the blanket from under his legs. I covered him up and went to the bathroom to brush my teeth. At the dinner table I unpacked the backpack to find my pajamas. Unfortunately there weren't any. Why would a scatterbrained person like me pack a pajama? I felt a bit silly when I went into the bedroom in my brand new sexy lingerie.

David was snoring a little. I crawled under the covers and rested my head on his arm so that I could have a good look at his face. He was what some people called "All-American". He wasn't as square-jawed at the average movie star, but other than that he fit the beauty ideal for white guys.

I leaned over and kissed him softly on the mouth. I stroked his hair. I told him that I loved him.

I was as happy as I could ever be.

The next morning I woke up to birdsong and sunrays shining on my face. I looked out the window and saw that the bedroom was bathed in bright daylight. David was still asleep. I stood up and pulled the blinds, something I'd forgotten in the night. The birds were so loud that I closed the window too.

I spent some time in the miniature bathroom. I found some hairs in the shower and made them disappear. David was probably taking care of the cleaning himself. Who would get a cleaning lady for a trailer?

In the fridge I found everything I needed for breakfast. I had scrambled eggs with toast and bacon. What I didn't find in the kitchen was any kind of food for lunch or dinner. Maybe he always ate out or ordered Chinese. I tried to imagine what else kept him busy all day except reading newspapers. There was no PlayStation but some books and magazines. He probably had his laptop in the bedroom.

After breakfast I sat outside on the stoop and waited for the cat, but it didn't show. A woman I didn't know walked by and looked surprised when she saw me. Eventually I went back in and started reading one of the magazines. As usual, when reading political stuff, I noticed how completely clueless I was. I had to rack my brains to remember the name of our Defense secretary. At least I knew who our Commander-in-chief was.

That wasn't good enough. If I wanted to conquer David, I had to be equal. I had to be on the same level intellectually and not the silly girl who only knows how to repair planes (and cars). But where should I start? There was a whole world of knowledge out there. I decided to deal with this matter as soon as I was back in Texas.

Shortly before noon David traipsed into the bathroom. I went out and sat back down on the stairs. I wanted to let him have breakfast in peace before he had to make conversation with me.

To my surprise he sat down next to me with a sandwich and handed me a glass of orange juice.

"That's for me", he said. "I just need you to hold it."

He was still wearing the shorts and the T-shirt he'd slept in. The stairs were a bit small for two people. It was nice to be so close to him. I noticed burns, and for the first time I saw shrapnel wounds to the amputated leg.

David noticed that I was studying his wounds. He smirked like a little boy who's got mischief on his mind.

"My upper body looks much worse."

I nodded.

"But then you know that. We had sex last night, right?"

"Of course we did, but it was dark", I lied. "And all I did was pull down your jockeys. It wasn't necessary to take all your clothes off."

He laughed and took the juice back.

"Was it good? I was too drunk. Don't remember a thing. Not even how I got home."

"Yeah, it was nice. You were grunting like a pig though. I hope you do that only when you're drunk."

"Nah, I always do that", David laughed. "Why? D'you really want to do it again?"

I nodded. "I'm flying back on Sunday."

David gulped down the last of his sandwich.

"And until Sunday, I'm supposed to take care of all your needs?"

"Yup."

He stood up, still laughing as he cleaned his glass in the sink. Then he went to take a shower.

The sun shone through the leaves of a birch and warmed me. I felt as light as a feather.

What a beautiful morning.

The cat showed up and seemed to be very pleased to see me again. We played and cuddled for a while. When I was alone again, I got up and went inside. David was sitting at the dining table, reading something.

This time he put the newspaper aside faster than when we first met.

"Let me take you downtown", he said. He was fully dressed. His hair was still wet.

"It looks good when your hair's longer", I said outside while he was locking up.

He turned around and took the stairs down. This time he was having difficulties.

"I have to blend in with the normal population. I don't want to be called a baby-killer."

"That would be unfair", I said. We started walking towards the bus stop. "It's drones that kill babies, not us."

"You know what someone said to me in Kandahar? We may have drones but the enemy has calendars."

I laughed. "I heard a different version. We have the fancy watches, the Taliban have the time."

"They do. They know full well that we're not gonna be able to stay forever. And if we pull out, this whole shit starts again. Northern Alliance against Pashtuns. As if we'd never been there."

I had nothing to add. I suddenly recalled the snowy mountains of the Hindu Kush.

"You know what? Somehow I miss Bagram."

David laughed. "You are one crazy chick."

"Thank you. It's a compliment, right?"

"Oh God", David groaned. "I don't know how I'll survive the next four days."

We spent a beautiful summer day in Denver pretending to be tourists. David took pictures of me in front of monuments and buildings whose names and meaning I forgot immediately. I was just too distracted by his voice and the excellent mood he was in. He was charming as hell, performing his Sonny Boy show just for me, not like in Bagram when he was goofing around with everyone but me. Sometime in the afternoon I felt the urge to ask him about it. There had to be a reason why he totally ignored me at work. But I kept my mouth shut and enjoyed the show.

But David didn't want to be photographed with me. When we were standing in front of an ultramodern museum building, I spotted a trustworthy-looking couple, and I asked David to hand them the camera. I wanted at least one picture of the both of us.

"Nah, don't bother", he said and took a picture of my disappointed face.

He treated me to lunch and I paid for our dinner. His decision to drag me to the movies underscored my suspicion that David was stalling. Apparently he wanted to spend as much time with me as possible in the company of other people, away from his place. He didn't seem eager to be alone in the bedroom with me. And here too, I didn't dare to ask.

We watched a very good action movie. The bad guys were working for the CIA and tried to kill a very pretty woman. They didn't succeed, of course. But it was a close call. They blew up her house instead.

"I wonder what it would feel like for us if we watched a movie where the bad guys are in the Air Force?" I asked David on the bus ride home.

He was looking out the window. "What do you mean?"

"Well, in all these movies, the CIA agents are always the bad guys. The only good agents are the ones going rogue, those who disobey orders. Just think what it would mean if they gave the role of the evil organization to the Air Force in the future. That wouldn't be good for our image, right?"

David shrugged. "I don't know. I know quite a few service members who would love to be recruited into that organization."

I decided to keep my strange thoughts to myself in the future. We got up when our stop was in sight.

"You know", David said suddenly, "maybe the dark stuff you hear about the CIA actually attracts a certain type of people. It's like the world of finance. Some people want to work at Wall Street. They want to be sharks among other sharks. I'm not sure if that's a good thing or a bad thing."

"Right."

Traffic had died down on the large road that separated the trailer park from the adjacent neighborhood. We crossed it and walked towards the gravel path. I would have liked to keep our conversation going. Sometimes I had the impression that David took me seriously when I came up with ideas of my own. Unfortunately this didn't happen too often.

In the trailer I went straight to the bathroom. After a quick shower I came out and noticed that David was in the bedroom. I rummaged in my backpack in the event that I had simply overseen my pajama the night before. Maybe it was hiding at the bottom of the backpack. But there was nothing. So I went to bed in underwear. The blinds were down, and David was lying on the side, facing away from me. That way I couldn't see his face.

I crept quietly into bed and covered myself with a blanket that he'd laid out for me. The night before we'd shared a blanket. I listened. His breathing was regular, he really seemed to be asleep.

I lay on my back and stared at the ceiling. With every minute that went by I felt a greater urge to touch David. I still hadn't seen the scars on his chest. He was still wearing the eye patch. Certainly because of me.

David slept, I lay awake. He didn't need me. I needed him more than ever.

Maybe it wasn't need. Maybe it was desire. An unhealthy crush on someone who possibly never wanted me.

It was a restless night. I woke up and looked around. The air was stuffy, so I opened the door to the living room. David was now lying on the other side so that I could look him in the face. He was even more beautiful in his sleep. After a while I couldn't stand it any longer. I stroked his hair.

"I love you", I whispered.

The next morning David made breakfast and then we went to buy a pair of pajamas. I wanted to do this quickly but David insisted on searching for the perfect pajamas in several different department stores. By the time we found one that David was happy with, it was time for lunch.

Killing time again, I thought. But I said nothing. I felt vulnerable because I was his guest. He could kick me out anytime, and then I would have the choice between finding a hotel in Denver or flying home. It was safer to just let David do whatever he wanted without questioning him.

We took the bus home. David wanted to take a nap. I read the newspaper.

Then we went bowling with Susie and Denzel. It was a fun evening. There was absolutely no indication that he was in touch with anyone he'd served with. I wondered if he'd deliberately cut all ties to his former life. Susie was our designated driver. The men were anything but sober when we got home around midnight. The same game began: David disappeared straight into bed, and I took a shower before I followed him. The pajama was light blue.

I stayed awake as long as possible, watching David's peaceful sleep. There was nothing I could do to solve this problem. If he didn't want me then I had to simply accept it.

On the morning of the third day I decided to say something.

"You still haven't shown me your upper body."

David took a sip of orange juice. "Yeah. It's my body, you know? I don't have to show you anything at all."

So even that wasn't going to happen. I was too proud to ask David why he always kept me at a distance. I took a computer magazine and pretended to read.

David brushed his teeth at the kitchen sink. I guessed that he didn't enjoy locking himself into the tiny bathroom. He sat down at the table, and I tried to get a new conversation going.
"Are you from around here? I always thought you were from New England."

"I'm from Denver. My mother's from here, and we lived nearby. Her sister married a lawyer from Connecticut. And when my mum was having all kinds of trouble, I moved in with my aunt and uncle. I lived in New Haven from the age of fourteen. My aunt and uncle took pretty good care of me. I guess because they had no children. I went to a really good school."

I put the magazine aside. "And then you went off to college?"

He nodded. "I was going to be an engineer. My relatives wanted me to have a really good education."

"What happened to your mother?"

David shrugged. "She's doing better. She was suffering from this huge depression for like, her whole life. But now she met someone. I think she finally got over the fact that my father left."

I was always fascinated by dysfunctional families. Because I grew up in a normal family where nobody leaves anyone ever.
"How old were you when he left?"

"Seven."

I didn't ask how bad it was for a little boy to be abandoned by his father. He started studying the sports section again.

"Do you want me to fly home earlier", I asked softly. I didn't want to go anywhere. I wanted to stay here forever.

"No, why? We can do something fun today and tomorrow. And then I'm going to enroll in college. Try to find me a suitable girlfriend. And you'll do the same in Texas. Find someone whose hair you can ruffle every night."

We had two more beautiful days with perfect weather and David being the perfect host. We hiked through a forest and I had a picnic for the first time in my life. There was another barbecue, this time in my honor. David only drank beer and was almost sober when we went to sleep. On Sunday morning we borrowed Susie's car. He dropped me off right outside the terminal. Parking was strongly discouraged. I had my backpack on my lap. All I had to do was open the passenger door and be on my way.

David kept the engine running. The moment he opened his mouth to say goodbye I suddenly remembered something I'd wanted to ask him: "Are you sending me a picture of your burns? I'll keep it to myself, of course."

David shook his head. I saw pity in his eyes.

"Marina, I will not send you any messages, pictures or whatever. We're now going our separate ways. Don't start crying now, okay? I'm proud to have known you. You're my favorite Airpunk!"

He leaned over and gave me a kiss on the cheek. I couldn't hold back my tears and got out of the car, slamming the door with all the force I could muster.

I ran into the terminal with tears streaming down my face. I had not been that angry in a long, long time.

Saad's sudden appearance puts an abrupt end to my daydreams. For a second or two, I'm confused. Making the mental transition from David Rohrman to Saad Whatever-his-last-name-is is a bit difficult, and for a moment I resent him for pulling me out of my memories. He comes in like it's the most normal thing in the world. He might as well say: "Hi honey, I'm home." I can't believe his visits are routine now, both for him and for myself.

This time he's brought a microwave. He puts it on top of the TV and plugs it in. I watch him place a plastic container inside. It looks like I'm going to have home-cooked food today. I can't wait to see what kind of breakfast he's planned for me.

"Why were you crying?" He sits down on his chair.

"I miss someone. Shouldn't come as a surprise. I've been here for five months now. When are you getting your visa?"

He shrugs. "Don't know. I wish I could tell you that. My family can't wait to get the hell out of here. But it's not so simple. The Europeans are not in a hurry. I can imagine that they're not too keen on immigrants from Arab countries."

"Shouldn't it matter that you're Christians?"

"We're not officially an oppressed minority. In that case we could ask for political asylum. The problem is, we're just unofficially being oppressed."

I'd like to ask Saad if he's really going to drop me off in the Green Zone when the time comes. In order to do this, he would have to put a lot of trust in me. I could easily rat on him. Even though I don't know his last name, there's a whole lot of intel I have on Saad. He's a math student. His parents are doctors. All this info would be passed on to the German authorities. They would easily find Saad among the recently immigrated families. But the Germans wouldn't want to get their hands dirty. The CIA can move around freely in Germany. They would intercept Saad in the morning, when he's on his way to the university. And they would put him in an orange jumpsuit before he ever has the opportunity to visit the *Oktoberfest*.

"Do you happen to have a charger for the iPod?"

Saad shakes his head. "I forgot it at home. I'll get it tomorrow."
"What about the food?" I point at the microwave. "Did you get that
at home?"

Saad looks almost embarrassed. "My mother cooked it for me."

"So we're going to eat it together?"

"No, it's for you."

I get up and put on my sweater. It's getting a little cooler every day
now. Maybe I should ask Saad to join me in my bed and to warm me
up a little. Now that I get so much to eat, I'm almost back to my
normal weight. I get to work out a lot. I'm in good shape. And that
means my sex drive is back.

I sit on the edge of the bed.

"Listen. I've got to ask you something. Why did you want my body to
be found here? Doesn't make any sense at all. They would've caught
you. Because your uncle is the owner of the shop, and also because
you wanted to leave some DNA in me."

I'm embarrassed to bring this up. But there's just so much I don't
understand about Saad's erratic behavior. I look at the chair next to
my bed. My breakfast for today consists of cornflakes with milk,
coffee from the thermos, and a banana. I start eating.

Saad clears his throat after a while. "I wanted to escape to Jordan
the very same day. With a friend. As you certainly noticed, I've
changed my mind."

I wonder how much of a logistical effort it is for Saad to bring me
food every day, and sometimes several times a day. Especially
because he has to keep it secret from his family. And how much the
whole thing costs him. I finish my breakfast. I put the dishes on the
floor. I want them out of the way so they don't fly across the room if
Saad freaks out.

"Saad, are you gay?"

He looks at me. He's surprised, but not angry. Not yet.

"What makes you think that?"

I laugh. "Because you don't think I'm sexy. Most young men would shamelessly take advantage of the situation."

"Most young men are stupid", Saad replies. Now he's angry. "Can you even imagine how thoroughly fucked we would be if I got you pregnant?"

He's absolutely right. Of course. That doesn't change anything about the fact that he certainly has the same needs as me. I sit back down on the bed.

Saad is still mad at me. As if he couldn't believe the stupid questions I'm asking.

"If you were pregnant, I would have no more options. I couldn't get you back to your people because that would mean that my child would grow up in enemy territory. Or even worse, because you would have an abortion. And just killing you would be out of the question because that way I would also kill my own flesh and blood."

I nod. "That's one hell of a predicament, what with all those Christian values."

"So the only solution remaining would be to marry you. But that somehow exceeds my imagination."

I laugh. "Mine too. Does the bride wear white here, too?"

Saad is looking over to the window. He always does that when he's trying to avoid me.

I think of a funny question. "Are you trying to keep your virginity until you get married? That's what a lot of people try to do around where I live. Not exactly a resounding success."

Saad doesn't seem to care that I'm trying to provoke him. "I'm not going to discuss my love life with you. Even in this country it's not illegal to have a girlfriend. And to be alone with her sometimes. Do me a favor and don't confuse us Iraqis with the Taliban. You don't know shit about our culture anyway."

His English is so good. I can't really get used to it.

"Saad, your English is so incredible. Why choose Germany if you could go to England?"

Saad sighs. "I told you, didn't I? My dad knows Germany, he was there when he was young. He told me the language is basically like English. It will take me a year to learn it. That's what he says. I guess he knows what he's talking about."

It's not like English at all, you idiot. If it was, I'd be fucking fluent.

I feel like starting a fight. "Yeah well, I think you'd be better off in England."

Saad shakes his head. "I was in Ireland for a year, in Cork. It was the year of the world cup. We watched all the matches, almost every single one of them. Best summer of my life. It's a beautiful country, but I'm not interested in islands. I think Germany is more suitable for me."

"I lived there. It was nice. I had a BMW. Nobody looked at me funny. They don't seem to care if someone looks exotic. And it doesn't matter if you live in a big city or somewhere in the countryside. There's so many immigrants from all over the world, you're going to fit right in."

This must be the very first time that Saad is seriously interested in what I have to say. His eyes look bigger.

He looks at me with absolute concentration, as if trying to remember something very important.

"My dad had a BMW for a long time. He kept it until it literally fell to pieces, after almost half a million kilometres. Did you live in Bavaria?"

I shake my head. "I went there once. The cops were driving BMWs. The driving schools had them too. I even saw a BMW ambulance. I gotta admit that was kind of impressive."

It feels so incredibly nice to discuss something that Saad actually cares about. I want to keep this going. Outside, a truck with a broken exhaust is drowning out all other noises from the street.

"Which team did you root for during the world cup?"

Saad shrugs. "All the Arab teams, of course. They didn't last long. And after that, it didn't matter. It was just a fun thing to share with others for those four weeks. Do you know if it's expensive to watch a match? I mean, in a stadium?"

"Definitely. I never went, because I don't give a rat's ass about soccer, but as far as I know it's not just expensive. It's almost impossible to get tickets. At least for the big teams."

"Yeah, that's what I thought", Saad says, looking disappointed. "It would be the perfect present for my father. A ticket to watch Bayern München."

I laugh. "You could afford the very best seats in the VIP lodge if you sold me to Al Qaeda."

Saad nods. "Great idea. I'll look them up in the Yellow Pages. I'm sure they will make me a nice offer. And then I'll finally get rid of you."

We really shouldn't be joking about this. It's not funny. It takes a while until we both stop giggling.

Suddenly I remember something I've wanted to ask him for some time now.

"What's going to happen with your girlfriend when you leave Iraq?"

That was a mistake. His facial expression is back to that *I-don't-give-a-shit*-look that I really hate about him.

"Seriously, Saad. Is she coming with you?"

"No, I'm going to find myself a new one in Germany. There's got to be a lot of pretty women in the science departments."

Saad really knows how to kill a good moment.

"You know, I once had a friend who was hoping to do exactly the same thing: he tried to find a woman at the University of Denver. Didn't work out, though."

"And why not?" Saad looks bored. He obviously couldn't care less about my friend.

"Nobody wanted him. He was disabled, and all those stupid cows were too embarrassed to be seen with a guy who has a glass eye and a limp."

It was not a good idea to talk about David. I go to bed and pull the covers over my head.

Today is a good day to cry.

Saad keeps pampering me. He's the perfect host. He brings me a charger and my uniform. It's nicely folded, waiting for me on the chair. He puts my desert boots on the ground. I can't take my eyes off the relics from my past. But I feel nothing. No sadness, and still no memory of the day that I was wearing them for the last time.

I'd like to make fun of him. I could ask for a BluRay player and a better TV, but I don't know the Arabic word for "flatscreen".

"Saad, this isn't your real name, right?" I've finished an excellent falafel and I need to lie down on the bed. My stomach is so full that I can barely keep my eyes open. I totally need a nap.

"What do you mean?"

I sit up. "I believe that you and also Khassem have given me wrong names."

Saad says nothing. Today is the first time in a while that he's sitting on my bed. I move closer to him and gently move my foot against his lower leg. It's just a light brush. Contrary to my expectations, he doesn't jump up and freak out.

"Saad, why d'you change your mind?" I don't need to explain what I mean. We both know what I'm talking about.

Saad once again looks tired. He's brooding.

"All right, let's start at the beginning", I say. "You and Khassem have a whole lot of hatred for us Americans. Tell me why."

This may be a silly question after nearly ten years of war and more than a million dead. But I like the idea of pretending to be naive. Besides, I've got nothing else to do. And I'm not really scared of Saad anyway. I make myself comfortable on my blanket with my legs drawn up. Saad just sits there, staring at the wall.

"Look", I start again. "I don't want to offend you. Everybody has a sense of pride when it comes to their own country, and the last thing I want to do is to hurt your feelings. But you gotta admit that there's this incredibly level of poverty here and half of the people are illiterate. When we invaded, we opened a door for you guys. Whether you go through it was your choice. And I think many of you were quite happy to see Saddam hang, right?"

Saad nods. "The execution was fine by me."

"And?"

"But everything else was not. In the decade before the invasion, you and all your allies completely destroyed our economy with your sanctions. My parents are doctors, you know. They came home from work and they were so miserable. There wasn't enough of anything. Total despair. Medication was scarce, equipment, specialists, anesthetics for surgery, all those things that you need to keep patients alive. People came to the hospital with small children who were dying of malnutrition. You guys finished us off – long before the invasion. Why do you think your people took Baghdad after just three weeks? There was almost no resistance!"

He's right. The invasion was easy. The aftermath was difficult.

"I'm not going to spend the next hours listing all the strategic mistakes you made." Saad is done lecturing me. He looks straight ahead.

"Well, the rest is easy to sum up", I interject. "After we pulled Saddam out of his hole in the ground, we should've packed our stuff and we should've gone home. And then you would've spent the next few years killing each other, and then Iraq would have broken into three parts, and that would have been your problem, not ours. We could have saved a lot of money, and thousands of our troops would still be alive. And tens of thousands of our service members would have no disfiguring injuries and no trauma and so on, and so forth."

Outside a car is racing past. That car badly needs to be fixed. The squeaking of the fan belt is so loud I could probably still hear it in the shower. I get up and go to the window. The chilly December air cools my room down so much that I need the blanket whenever I'm not moving around. I close the window and go back to my bed where I make sure to sit down even closer to Saad. He doesn't seem to mind.

I wonder whether I should just simply turn the Stockholm syndrome upside down. Saad wasn't receptive to my charms so far, but he seems to have fewer reservations lately. And I don't think that he has a girlfriend at the moment because he has no time: he's studying, he helps out at the store and he seems to spend every free minute with me. The girlfriend he's just invented.

So what are the pros and cons of seducing my abductor? It would be a hedge against his next mood change. He may have promised to set me free. But if he really wants to immigrate to Europe with his family, he can hardly afford to let me live. The risk would be enormous. But if he's had a sexual relationship with me for a while, I figure he won't be able to put a bullet in my head. There seem to be some moral limitations to what Saad can and can't do. I'm sure that's also the reason why he didn't go through with my execution.

On the other hand, I can feel how I'm getting stronger every day. I can see some new opportunities on the horizon. I could knock out Saad and run. I'm in acceptable physical shape. I've learned in my training how to quickly subdue an enemy, and lately Saad seems to be taking no precautions against me whatsoever. Right now the key is inside the door, and he's sitting right next to me like a buddy who came by for a visit.

But maybe he can read my mind. He stands up and picks up my iPod from the chair. He checks whether the charging cable fits.

"Saad, did you ever google me?" I ask.

I could jump him right now. At least in theory. I'm definitely out of practice at the moment.

"No, why?"

"I'd like to know if I'm officially dead."

He plugs out the TV so that he can charge the iPod. I wonder what kind of music he likes.

"Did you ever listen to it?" I ask him while he's on his way to the door.

He removes the key and turns around to face me. "What I liked was this weird out-of-space playlist. I ran it on my stereo when I was preparing for a statistics exam."

"Did you pass the exam? And what grade did you get?"

He shakes his head. "The professor was killed on his way home. He wanted to buy groceries from the market. That day, someone set off a car bomb. Fourteen dead."

He slams the door, and I listen to the key in the lock twice.
I'm alone again. Maybe it's better this way.

At night I dream of Khassem and Saad. They come see me in Texas and can't stop bickering. They complain about everything, behaving like spoiled brats and driving me nuts. Nothing in the US is good enough for them. Sometime during the course of the dream, they turn into Robert and Kyle. We go see a NFL game in Austin. They treat me like a retard because I'm clueless when it comes to football. By the time the match is over, I'm completely frustrated because my friends can't take me seriously. Eventually Kyle says to me: "Go back to Idaho and fix cars, girl."

I wake up in a bad mood and discover that I only have some chocolate cookies for breakfast. I eat them all while I watch a Kuwaiti morning show.

I lost touch with Robert and Kyle years ago. I hope that Robert is a pilot now, and I wouldn't be surprised to find out that Kyle is making a fortune in Silicon Valley. But I don't know.

I have no idea what has become of the two friends who saved me. For years, they were my support in a difficult environment. They took care of me while we lived in a war zone. And in a world full of guys who were suspicious of me at the very least, if not hostile.

Infinite sadness washes over me. A tsunami of regret takes full possession of me. Robert and Kyle disappeared out of my life. Just like someone who sits beside me on a bus and gets out at the next stop. How could I let this happen?

I see Kyle sitting opposite me at lunch, an old PT shirt covering his broad chest while he was enjoying his pasta. It was his last month in the Air Force. Robert was in for another two years, and he was far from happy about Kyle's impending departure.

"Dude, we worked together on three different continents, you realize that?" Robert watched Kyle, visibly waiting for some kind of reaction. "We were practically married to each other."

Kyle grinned. "What did you like best, Rob?"

"Don't know", Robert replied. "Actually, the best time was here in Texas."

"You have got to be shitting me", Kyle protested. "What about the shit we got away with in Germany?"

Robert laughed. "Yup, I almost forgot. We were young back then."

At Spang, Robert and Kyle had spent some time and considerable amounts of money in the club scene. They traveled throughout Germany to attend concerts and all kinds of music events.

"What was best in Germany?" I asked. "The parties? The food? The people?"

Robert was faster than Kyle, who still had a full mouth and needed to swallow down his pasta.

"The women. Open-minded. Easy-going. Those Europeans have loose values. That's the way I like it."

I giggled. I'd heard some stories from the past, stories of wild parties and of designer drugs that don't appear in any test.

Kyle emptied his glass of water, wiped his mouth and looked around. "I have a theory."

"Oh, wow. I think I'm getting excited", Robert said. "D'you hear that, Marina? He's got a theory."

Kyle nodded. "Pay attention, my friends."

He made a dramatic pause.

"Basically it's like this: it's always the first time that's the best. I don't mean sex. For that you need some practice. But my theory applies to everything else you do. For example, the first time abroad. Spang was about a thousand times more fun than Bagram."

"That's it?" I asked, not bothering to hide my disappointment. "That's your theory?"

Unlike me, Robert seemed to like Kyle's idea.

"My first uniform. The first time that I saw the Gatling. My first flight in a Herc. The first night club in Germany. Yeah, your theory has something to it. Maybe it's not quite waterproof."

"And the great thing is", Kyle added, "you can apply this rule to other areas. The first *Matrix* movie. The first *Rage Against The Machine* album. And so on and so forth."

All three of us were deep in thought, trying to validate Kyle's theory. Robert pushed his empty plate aside to start drumming on the tabletop with his fingers. He always did that when he was thinking hard. Finally, he thought of something.

"The first Gulf War", he said triumphantly. "A sweeping success!"

"True", I said. I envied him because this idea had not occurred to me. "I guess the second one we shouldn't have bothered with."

I LOST MY HEART IN HEIDELBERG

I wake up in the middle of the night. I keep my eyes open in the dark. There's always a little light coming in from the street. A vivid dream of David is on my mind, and I'm trying to remember how it started. This time he's shown up in his pre-Kandahar version, with all limbs and eyes intact. As usual, I can't recall the beginning of the dream. What I know for sure is that David is hiding behind something. He secretly watches me as I get dressed for my wedding with Saad, and I pretend not to see him. The wedding ceremony takes place in a very nice garden. As I walk down the aisle, David jumps up from behind a hedge, brandishing an AK-47. He mows me and all the wedding guests down. As I'm slowly bleeding out on the lawn, I feel really guilty about David. I have a bad conscience even though I never promised to marry him.

June 2010

To: mars_air@yahoo.com
From: one-eyed-dude@gmail.com
Re: Guess who remembers you

Marina,
do you still love me? Or have you found someone suitable at last?

Of course I'm hoping for the latter. But it's hard to imagine. Your buddy Robert told me recently that you don't like to commit yourself to just one lover. And that you've learned to be much more discreet about your love life, thank God.

I got my engineering degree and am now stationed in Mannheim, where I have the kind of tasks I'm not supposed to talk about. I'm wearing a uniform again, and isn't that what really matters at the end of the day: to be able to look in the mirror and say to yourself: you are one good-looking motherfucker.

Do you happen to be free next Saturday? We could

meet and talk about old times. Since Mannheim is kind of unromantic, I suggest Heidelberg.

3 PM at the main train station, in the entrance hall?

In case you forgot what I look like: still wearing the sexy eye patch.

I'm sending you hot kisses,

David

I got the message on a Wednesday and spent two sleepless nights going over every word he'd written and everything he didn't mention and of course all the stuff he could have written. To come forward after five years of total silence was more than cheeky. Especially since he was the one who had demanded that silence. When he dropped me off at the airport in Denver, David had kicked me out of his life.

After the initial shock of reading the email, I immediately knew that I would accept David's invitation. I simply had to see him again. But I was too proud to send him an answer.

His message made me downright sick. On Friday I felt completely unable to attend the training session and debated whether I should call in sick. But I couldn't afford to miss classes now because they were thoroughly preparing us for our deployment. I would hardly have the opportunity to catch up.

So I went to work with dark circles under my eyes. The entire afternoon was reserved for MMA training, something I really didn't think I would need in Baghdad. It was more than exhausting. I fell into bed without dinner and woke up on Saturday late in the morning.

I raced down the autobahn in my vintage BMW with the stereo at full blast. I hadn't bothered with eye-make up or anything else for that matter, wearing the same casual clothes that I always wore. I wasn't going to make a fuss about looking good for David.

Finding a parking spot in Heidelberg was hard. I ended up leaving the car on a supermarket parking lot. My heart wasn't beating faster than usual as I crossed the street in front of the station. David was standing in the middle of the entrance hall, beaming at me as I walked towards him. We hugged.

"You didn't answer my email", he said.

"I didn't deem that necessary, David", I said coolly. "I'm an Airpunk, did you forget that?"

He laughed and grabbed my hand. "Come on!"

Outside a chilly wind blew open my jacket. It was too cool for the season. I pointed in the direction where I'd parked the car, but he pulled me toward the tram. We found two seats and sat down next to each other. The tram looked like it was half a century old. Our seats were made of hard, dark brown wood.

"Did we pay our fare?" I asked.

"Nope, but we're getting out in five minutes."

He looked out the window. I searched his face for changes, anything new that wasn't there last time I saw him, and found none. He looked the same as in Denver.

"David, you're still holding my hand", I said.

He turned his face to me, still beaming. His enthusiasm made me speechless. The tram stopped in a curve with a screeching metal-on-metal sound. The tram driver got out, fumbled around on the tracks with an iron rod and climbed back into his seat. Two Japanese tourists watched the procedure with endless fascination and took at least a hundred pictures.

"Do you remember how you used to ruffle my hair every night?" David smiled as if he was talking about fond memories of our wonderful past.

I groaned. "Jeez, David, we didn't see each other for years, and the first thing you come up with is that!"

David laughed. "Getting off at the next stop. We're going for a hike today."

"Sure, whatever", I said.

We wandered along the river, with a view of the old town. Even with dark clouds overhead it was a pleasant and touristy thing to do. I suddenly realized it was the last fun thing I was doing before boarding a plane to the Middle East. David's timing was perfect. I didn't mind that a strong wind was blowing. A few raindrops came down. We found a café where we ate cake and talked about our careers. I was relieved that we were discussing normal things. The last thing I wanted was to talk about our nights together in his trailer. There was no need to remind me of how much he had humiliated me in Denver.

David bought two large bottles of water and stowed them in a backpack that looked heavy.

"What else you got in there?" I asked. The backpack was quite large.

"Oh, you'll see", David said in a suspiciously cheerful tone. He grabbed my hand again and led me into a side street. It went uphill, and the steep incline took all the breath I had.

The road led to a wide, paved footpath that was closed to car traffic. After a short time we stood on a hill and looked down into the Neckar valley and onto the old town. It was safe to assume that this was one of the most popular places from which to take pictures of the city. The ruins of the castle were on the other side of the river and looked pretty spectacular. I wondered if the castle would be as famous as it was if it was still intact.

We weren't the only tourists, despite the unfriendly weather.

"This road is called *Philosophenweg*", David said after a while.

"Tell me something philosophical", I said.

"Hmm, difficult."

"Alright. And where are we going now?"

He kept holding my hand. Which was a clever move. That way, I wasn't able to feel anything but unbridled affection for him. While driving towards Heidelberg, I had imagined in great detail how I would yell at him. I'd even wondered if I should use my newly acquired combat skills to beat him up a bit.

But all my aggressive feelings toward David had evaporated. I wanted to just stand next to him and feel his warmth.

"D'you remember how you used to whisper in my ear every night?"

I rolled my eyes. He pulled me further down the path, past a park bench that was occupied by an old couple.

"Look, that's what we're gonna be doing in fifty years", David said.

It was all very strange, but David's excellent mood was contagious. We didn't talk much. Whenever we did, the conversation was about trivial stuff. Eventually we turned left and wandered into the forest. A wide footpath led us uphill. We stopped in one of those little half-open wooden huts that hikers used for breaks. Someone had left their trash in it. Empty soda cans and wrapping paper were littering the floor.

I only drank half of the water because I had no clue how much more hiking David was planning to do for today. The cabin was round and almost completely closed. The only light source consisted of the narrow entrance, and some more light came through the hole in the center of the roof. That hole was also meant to be an exhaust for the fire pit in the middle of the room.

"Almost like a teepee", David said. "I don't know anything about Indians, though."

"Well, there's usually no benches in a teepee."

David moved closer, his thigh touching mine. He put his arm around my shoulder.

I started crying. David sighed and said: "I'm sorry, Marina. I never wanted to hurt you."

"But you did", I answered, looking for a tissue in my jeans pocket.

David moved even closer. He kissed me on the cheek like I was his long-lost sister. He had his left arm on my back and started ruffling my hair with the other hand.

"I'm sorry."

"You were definitely not sorry back then", I said. I wanted to hide my face in my hands. I couldn't do that as long as David was holding me with both arms.

"Yes, I was sorry. Even back then. But I couldn't help it. I was depressed."

He was caressing my cheek now. I felt like screaming at him.

"Why did you never touch me like that before?"

David shook his head. "You're not listening. I was depressed. What I'm trying to tell you is that I had a real, clinical depression and I thought of killing myself every day."

"Why?" I was almost yelling. "What kept you from seeking help? You could've talked to me, you know."

"Right. I know." He was now going through my hair with both hands. It felt kind of nice. Maybe he wanted to give me a punk rock hairstyle.

"I was miserable, but of course I didn't want to take it out on you. You were just standing in my trailer. That was kinda shocking, when you showed up."

"You had five days to get used to it", I said angrily. "You didn't even show me your scars."

"I'll show you tonight."

I had to blow my nose, so I got up, and David had to let go of me. I walked around a bit, hoping that I wouldn't start crying again anytime soon. Not putting on any eye make-up today had been a very wise decision. In the meantime, David started rummaging in his backpack. He laid out a blanket on the dirty floor. I looked out the door. A red squirrel was hopping straight up a tree trunk. It jumped onto the next tree and disappeared in the dark. The forest air was noticeably cooler.

David was now sitting on the blanket, and I sat down beside him. In the fireplace I saw crumpled bits of newspaper burning bright, and the firewood that was carefully stacked around it was slowly catching fire. We were close enough to feel the warmth of the fire. The warm glow gave us enough light to unwrap our sandwiches.

"Is this some kind of romantic, Indian-theme get-together?" I asked.

David laughed and took a bite of his bread.

"Tell me, how long in advance did you plan this? And the firewood? Did you bring that in your ruck?"

He nodded, visibly pleased with the flawless execution of his plan. "The only thing I forgot was to bring a trash bag. If I'd been able to clean up this place, it would be even more romantic."

I drank some water. When I screwed the cap back on, something crawled across my hand.

"Are we staying here all night?"

"Nah, it's getting too cold."

The walk back to the Philosopher's path was even more romantic. We stumbled over tree roots in the dark. My right foot was wet because I'd stepped into a puddle. David's flashlight was useful, but after a while I asked him to switch it off.

"Why d'you want me to turn it off? Are you afraid of attracting wolves?" David switched off the light. The forest road immediately became invisible.

"We're playing spooks. We're field agents, and they dropped us behind the front lines. Now we have to make our way to the meeting point with our contact person. I hope your gun is loaded."

"Oh crap, I forgot the ammo."

I giggled. "That's just great, David. If we get attacked, we only have our fists to defend ourselves."

David sighed. "You mean to say I have my fists. You, in the meantime, can hide behind my back."

"You're wrong", I protested. "I've acquired some new skills, you know. I don't do aircraft anymore. You know that, right?"

"Yeah, I found out a couple of things about you. You're much smarter than I thought. I couldn't believe it at first when I heard you actually speak Arabic now."

The cloud cover tore up a little. Moonlight shone on the trees. Something rustled in the undergrowth, maybe a little mouse that woke up from hearing our voices.

"Marina, did you miss me?" He stopped. His hand was in mine.

I hesitated. "You go first. Tell me if you missed me."

He let go of my hand. He was standing in front of me now, slowly placing his hands around my hips. "Yes, but I tried to push you to the back of my mind. But once I got my new assignment, and it was in Germany of all places, well... I didn't try to suppress all those memories any longer."

I placed a chaste kiss on his mouth and then pulled back. We looked at each other. Even through the darkness I could see that his golden-boy smile was gone. I kissed him again. This time he leaned in, pulling me closer with both hands on my butt until we sank to the floor. The ground felt cold and damp, not that it mattered. David took off my sneakers as I opened the zipper of my pants. He helped me out of my jeans, and then we were together.

We took our time. There was no hurry. We had the whole night. I wasn't cold, despite the fact that my naked butt was lying on the wet forest floor. David had his hands all over me. My hips he liked best. But he also liked ruffling my hair, which was getting wetter. His hands were dirty from the forest floor, and I could feel how damp earth ended up pretty much everywhere, on my neck, on my legs, in my hands. I dug my nails into his skin, hoping to leave some bruises on his shoulders and his neck.

David's breathing sounded like he was trying to control himself. He was holding back to make it last as long as possible. Sometimes he just plain stopped, not moving at all for what seemed to be several minutes. Whenever we were motionless, the sounds of the night got through to us, and at the end I saw a small creature scurrying past us.

"Oh. My. God." David whispered almost inaudibly in my ear when it was over. He stood up, looking for my pants. I sat up.

"The flashlight would be handy now", I said.

"True." I couldn't see David anymore, but I heard him fumbling for the flashlight. He switched it on. "So I found your jeans, but what did we do with your panties?"

"Well, they're black. I don't think we're gonna find them before dawn."

We gave up the search for my underwear. I got dressed. David shouldered his backpack. We wandered through the forest. I felt like I got transported into a fairy tale. If we'd never found our way back to the Philosopher's Walk that night, it would have been okay.

It was my lucky night. Nobody had towed my car. We drove to Mannheim and stayed there. Sunday was spent almost exclusively in his bed. In the evening I had to leave.

I was quietly freaking out and didn't know what to do about it. The last farewell at Denver airport had been a medium-scale disaster. I'd never really recovered from that event, and I was positively terrified of what was going to happen this time.

"I have to go now", I said in the kitchen, rattling my key chain.

David was sitting at the kitchen table. He looked up from his paper. Yesterday's ease was gone. He stood up and hugged me.

"You picked a strange time", I said suddenly. "On Wednesday I'm flying to Balad Airbase."

"I know", David said, squeezing me tighter. "I hope you have a good time in the sandbox. Does that sound stupid?"

I nodded. "More than stupid. Which is not surprising. Intelligence is not evenly distributed, I would say. We'll have to accept that I'm the smart one and you're the one with the combat skills."

David laughed. "Your big mouth will keep getting you into trouble. You know that, right? Don't fuck up in Iraq, okay?"

"I'll try."

He squeezed me tighter. "That's not good enough, Airman. You have to do more than just try."

"Okay, okay. I'll do my very best."

I drove home through the pouring rain. There was almost no traffic on the A6. I didn't turn on the music. Instead I tried to memorize everything that had happened this weekend. Once I was home I would write it all down. Only shortly before Kaiserslautern did I realize that David had chosen this weekend deliberately.

He knew these were my last few days in Spang. He'd heard about my imminent deployment.

I drove onto the emergency lane and stopped. The other cars rushed past me. I searched my phone. I wanted to call David and ask how long he'd been planning to meet with me. Why he'd chosen this particular weekend. Whether he wanted to see me just one last time. Maybe all he wanted from me was closure.

I stared at my phone. A bright picture that I had taken of the bird tree in Bagram was staring back at me. I didn't have David's number. He never gave it to me. A twelve-ton truck sped past me, maybe just inches away. I realized that today was the last time I'd heard David's voice.

Saad's computer is made in China and designed in California. I didn't expect that from a math student; I would have thought he'd prefer a more elitist operating system. I'm so excited that I almost drop my water bottle. Last time I had an Internet connection, it was summer and I was free as a bird. Finally I'm going to find out what's actually happened to me and how I ended up here. I must be officially MIA, so there's got to be something in the media about me. All of a sudden I feel incredibly grateful towards Saad. Apparently he's decided to help me. As if that wasn't exciting enough, I feel a growing confidence that once I read about myself on the Internet, I'll remember everything that happened.

But as always I'm wrong when it comes to guessing Saad's intentions.

"We're going to watch a movie", he announces as he takes a hot plate out of the microwave.

Fuck fuck fuck.

I try to hide my disappointment. I can watch movies on my TV set all day long. Dinner is great, though. There are chickpeas mixed in with the rice. The braised lamb is spicy and just plain delicious. I wonder what it would be like to sit at Saad's mother's kitchen table. We could have a nice conversation in her language. I'm sure she would like me. And she would certainly let me use her Internet.

I decide to enjoy my food. It's not like I have lots of other options here. Maybe later I can convince Saad that it would be interesting to google me. I don't see why he should have a problem with that.

While I'm eating, Saad is sitting on his chair with the notebook on his lap. The longer I watch him typing, the stronger the fear gets. It's the thought I've been trying to ignore for as long as I've been here, but of course it keeps coming back: the fear that I won't get out of here alive. It's like a manic depression. One minute I'm optimistic and looking forward to seeing my parents again, the next moment I fall into the abyss of despair. I can't estimate how concrete Saad's plans to emigrate really are. He's changed his mind before. If the

Germans deny Saad's family the visa, he'll keep watering and feeding me for a while and then, well, he'll have to take a decision. The only people who know of my whereabouts are Saad and Khassem. So far no one else has tried to enter this room. But I won't be able to hide here forever. With every day that goes by, the danger of some hostile force finding me here is increasing.

The easiest thing for Saad to do is to sell me to some fanatics. Or to some criminals who are free of any ideology. Anyone who wants to make a quick buck. My market value has to be enormous: I'm part of the the much-hated occupation force, in fact the greatest war machine ever in the history of mankind, and I'm a woman. The things people could do to me in HD would be enough to shock my fellow countrymen and possibly the rest of the world. Saad could use the money to leave the country with his family. It would provide him the means for a fresh start.

What could possibly prevent my kidnapper from selling me? Pity? A Christian sense of responsibility? I'm not sure how deep those values are rooted in someone who grew up here. This country has been at war for decades. Saad and his friends have never known peace. I think it's significant that he never asked me about my religion or my political beliefs, and he certainly never wanted to know anything about my family. He doesn't care about me, even if he's been treating me well lately.

I know only too well that things can change very quickly. At least since I arrived in Baghdad.

I do my dishes in the bathroom. I look at my face in the mirror and I see an exhausted woman who's way too pale. I've been locked up for half a year now. A college semester. A football season. If I stay much longer, I'll never get out of here.

Something needs to happen. Today. I go through all my options while I'm taking all my time washing my hands. I want Saad to think I still have things to do in the bathroom.

1 - Knock out Saad and escape.

2 - Kill Saad and escape.

The latter option has the advantage that I'd have all the time in the world to prepare my prison break. I wouldn't have to worry that he could regain consciousness. I need the laptop to find the best way to the Green Zone. I would be in no rush to find out how to get through the city unnoticed.

Of course I'd be sad about his death. And I'm sure I'd feel guilty about killing him, possibly for the rest of my life. But right now, what I want is to get the fuck out of here.

I don't want to watch a movie - I want to go home.

Saad is sitting on my bed. He rolled up the blanket and squeezed it between his back and the wall. My half of the blanket has the pillow on top of it.

This dude is incredible. It's like he wants to make everything as comfortable for me as possible. In order to see anything on the 17-inch screen, I have to sit right next to him. Saad puts an arm around my shoulder, and my heart starts beating as if I'm a teenager who's about to be touched for the first time.

All right, I think. *First the movie, then some steamy sex, and then I'm going to break your neck.*

The film's title is "TAXI TO THE DARK SIDE". That sounds like an action movie or a thriller, and much more importantly, like a movie in English. After my extensive tour of the Arab world of television, there's some tingling anticipation in me, and I look at Saad's profile, watching him looking at the display. He does have nice features. His expression is neutral as always, and his left arm is resting loosely on my shoulders.

My excitement doesn't last beyond the opening credits. We're not watching the latest blockbuster starring Matt Damon, but a documentary. It's about a taxi driver who was mistakenly arrested and tortured to death. This is not a popcorn movie, and it's not going to be a cozy movie night. I'm trying to emotionally brace myself at the last minute. I make a mental effort to remain completely unmoved while they show the torture methods commonly applied when dealing with suspected terrorists, and when the people who later got charged with these crimes calmly explain exactly how to sexually humiliate prisoners. This has nothing to do with me.

Of course we get to see the world-famous photographs from Abu Ghraib. Back when the scandal broke out, I always wondered how anyone could be so stupid to take pictures of their own crimes. How retarded do you have to be to document this for the rest of the world? But the film is not just about torture in Iraq. It keeps going back to the story of a young Afghan named Dilawar. He endured five days in a prison in Bagram until he died from his internal injuries. The fact that he was innocent played no role in the way he was treated.

Whoever made this film has no mercy for his viewers. And certainly no consideration for people who have fond memories of Bagram. I get to see the autopsied corpse of the victim, followed by footage of Black Hawks flying into the sunset, always with the Hindu Kush in the background. With the result that I suddenly feel this completely insane nostalgia for Bagram, while I have to listen to a soldier describing how he beat a prisoner to pulp - in all details.

You miserable son of a bitch, I think without looking at Saad.

Now I understand how Saad came up with the idea to tie me to the ceiling with my arms stretched wide: this is how Dilawar died.

Infinite humiliation. Excruciating pain. And a prisoner who didn't stop imploring his God for mercy in his last hours. That's what you call a crucifixion. I know what my nightmares will be like tonight.

"Thank you for a great movie night", I hiss as the credits roll. I really don't want to sit so close to Saad, but his grip on my shoulders is harder now. If I try to move away from him we're going to have a fight.

"I figured you would enjoy the movie", Saad says smugly. He shuts down the computer without letting go of me.

"You know perfectly well that I've got nothing to do with this. I was a mechanic, for fuck's sake. And later I changed my career path and became a Special Agent. And I never even touched anyone!" I don't think I sound angry.

"Oh please. Stop pretending you're a naive little girl. You're too old for that. I can't stand all those stupid excuses."

The screen is now black, and Saad closes the laptop. He leans his head against the wall and closes his eyes.

"You guys always have an excuse. *Those were only a few bad apples. We didn't want this. It's war, and you can't make an omelet without breaking eggs. The torturers all went to jail. We're trying to build schools for your children, and you guys try to blow us up. We're here to bring you freedom!*"

What can I say? I didn't even know there was a prison in Bagram. It's not the first time that I feel infinitely stupid. This keeps happening to me again and again. Someone confronts me with things that I should have known. My ignorance is the thread running through my life, as if God himself wanted to make sure that I always end up looking like an idiot.

I remember when Dan explained this *Habeas Corpus* idea to me: that anyone who gets himself arrested has the right to a hearing. I wonder if Dan knew of the prison at Bagram? He must have. After all, it's operators who are usually tasked with finding terrorists and turning them over to the authorities.

I'm starting to feel cold. The little hairs on my arms and neck are standing up while Saad keeps holding me tight. How many men were dragged to Bagram prison by Tim and Dan? And how many of them were actual insurgents? If only half of the claims in the film are true, then we locked up as many people as possible. And the question whether they were guilty of anything at all wasn't really important.

"Saad, why did you show me this movie? You wanna teach me a lesson or what? So that I come back to the US and tell people what I learned here? You want to turn me into a peace activist?"

Saad opens his eyes. "What for?"

He doesn't bother looking at me. "You're leaving. You set the course for us. You designed our political system. The Shiites have all the power now. They established brand new torture prisons, this time with the active support of your people."

"What do you mean when you say 'my people'?" I can't hide my anger any longer. I shouldn't ask him what he means. I have absolutely no desire to hear a lecture on how evil we Americans are.

"With 'your people' I mean the military. Whenever something particularly hideous happens, you guys are always hiding behind the spies. That was in the movie we just saw: the CIA invented it. But the military advisers who are teaching the Shiites how to torture their enemies, these are your people."

"Dude, I'm in the Air Force", I yell. "We may drop bombs on your homes, but we have nothing to do with this shit! "

Saad laughs. I'm going to strangle him with my bare hands as soon as I get a chance.

"You know what you're doing?"

Saad's smile is infuriating.

I'm going to attack as soon as he lets go of me. I'm going to kick him until he's lying on the floor in a fetal position. I'll break his nose with my right fist, and I'll smear his blood on his shitty Abercrombie & Fitch shirt. Then I'm going to pull off his jeans and underpants to humiliate him just like I've seen it in the movie. When I'm done with him, I'm going to smash his skull with his computer.

"You're lying to yourself. You're neatly separating things that belong together." He looks at me like a psychiatrist looking at his patient.

"You repair aircraft, the others throw bombs on innocent people. You're in the Air Force, the Marines are committing crimes against humanity in Guantánamo. You're in the military, but it's the evil intelligence community who's invented torture. You serve your country, but the politicians are pulling the strings."

I don't want to listen to Saad any longer. I lean forward. This is a test, but Saad passes it by gripping my shoulder and pulling me back against the wall. He's pretty strong for a nerd.

"You're part of a giant killing machine, and for that you're going to burn in hell." Saad sounds very pleased with himself.

"No I won't. I'm an atheist." I can't think of something better to say, because right now is the time for action rather than words. I'm only three seconds away from starting a brawl.

"And you know who established the torture program in our prisons? Someone who reports directly to Petraeus. The rock star of the Iraq war. Your superhero who's going to turn your Afghanistan quagmire into a triumph. Petraeus' special guys also helped organize the death squads. You know? They kidnap people straight out of their homes and..."

"I know what death squads are", I shout. Saad's iron grip on my shoulder makes me even more furious. "Leave me alone! Shut. The. Fuck. Up. And let go of me!"

Saad jumps up so fast that I'm too surprised to react. He forgets the laptop that's lying next to me. He slams the door behind him and locks from the outside.

I'm alone with my anger. There is no one that I could beat up now.

It would be great if I had a punch bag. I need more than an hour of push-ups and sit-ups to get rid of all that excess energy. I turn my attention to the Macbook and discover that it's basically empty: it's got all the usual software, but no files and of course, no WiFi connection. The only thing I could do with that thing would be to write texts and make spreadsheets. I could watch that awful film again because the DVD is still in the drive.

Instead of smashing the computer to little pieces, I put it on the floor under the TV table.

I'm still keyed up and if anyone else were here, I would definitely start a fight.

I wish I had access to mind-altering drugs. I go to bed and try to take my mind off Saad and all the nasty stuff he threw in my face.

Instead, I think of my work in Baghdad.

If I ever get out of here again, I'd like to see the soldiers that I served with in Baghdad. They'll hardly remember me, I guess. People move on. If my memory is not completely screwed up, I must have started my new assignment about two weeks before I was abducted. I can vaguely recall a few rides through the outskirts of Baghdad. Tall palm trees in front of impressive homes. Residential buildings with gardens. Wide boulevards lined with T-walls to fend off suicide bombers and car bombs. The same merciless sun as in Afghanistan. Blue sky every day, as if the Arabs had not yet invented the cloud. Some parts of town where the new Shiite elite had established itself had a suburban feel. We drank tea with a dignified elderly gentleman who told us about the decades of suffering his family endured under Saddam. I acted as an interpreter and got a headache.

In the Humvee on the way back to the firebase, Captain Gillespie gave me a pill to chew. His long arm reached all the way back, and he gently dropped the pill in my hand. He was a six-foot-four marathon runner. He spoke too softly for a grunt, and yet I had the impression that his men adored him. My guess was that he'd already proven himself in numerous combat missions. He was on his third deployment to Iraq.

I let out an exasperated sigh. This is so frustrating. All I remember of the time immediately before my abduction is bits and pieces. I hear a dog barking outside, and I wonder who feeds it. Maybe I should just position myself underneath the window and shriek hysterically until someone shows up. I've run this scenario in my head about a hundred thousand times. All sorts of things could happen - I could fall into the hands of bad guys. Or I could be rescued by a man who simply feels sorry for me.

What I can't imagine is a woman saving me.

It's strange that I went through the trouble of learning the language of a country where women are basically doormats. The more I think about my motives, the more it seems to me as though learning Arabic was compensation: since I'll never be in combat arms, I'll at least be smarter than everyone else.

I'll never forget reading my deployment orders for the first time. They assigned me to an army unit that I was going to accompany outside the wire. I imagined how my boots would touch Iraqi soil. And how I would roam the streets of Baghdad with soldiers armed to the teeth.

Suddenly I have a vivid picture in my head of myself and some guys in a Humvee. There were three of us and two Iraqi policemen. Somehow we were supposed to teach the Iraqi authorities how to maintain law and order after our withdrawal. Even though all American forces were supposed to withdraw from the cities, my unit was still patrolling Baghdad because we were training the local police authorities. In the evenings we had to drive back to base, far out of town.

I was in the back between the two Iraqis. Sergeant Miller was driving, and the passenger seat was occupied by Captain Gillespie. Miller was from Brooklyn and didn't talk much. Once I listened to some colleagues in the mess hall gossip about him.

"Miller can't make up his mind if he wants to be an Irishman from New York or a gangster rapper."

The soldier sitting across from me had zits like a teenager.

He shrugged. "Them New Yorkers are full of shit anyway, if you ask me."

I sit up in bed. It's crazy that I get to remember so many different fragments of my past. Why today? Is that a diversion tactic that my brain has come up with so that I can forget how mad I am at Saad? To prevent myself from bursting with rage?

Maybe it was the movie. The footage from Afghanistan revives a period of my life that was, well... special. My Bagram phase was intense. It was there that I established some impossible-to-define bond with David Rohrman that will never really go away.

It's been half a year since we hiked through a dark forest together. I wonder if he knows that I went missing. It may well be that he never heard a thing about it. I doubt that the media made a big deal about my disappearance. In the States people don't seem to worry too much about us and the wars we're fighting. In the news broadcasts and on the Internet it's all about celebrity meltdowns and the eternal power struggle between Republicans and Democrats. One of Kyle's high school buddies was genuinely surprised that Kyle had been deployed to Afghanistan.

"I didn't know we're still fighting there."

Even if David has recently tried to contact me, it doesn't mean that he'll get worried because he's not getting any reply. He might conclude from my silence that I'm just not interested. Maybe he found himself a girlfriend.

This idea reminds me of something he told me as we were lying in his big futon bed, exhausted but happy. He told me that he couldn't remember the last time he was on the make. He couldn't bring himself to hit on a woman. He was just too uncomfortable about his injuries.

"Is it the eye or the foot?" I studied his back. It was free of tattoos and scars. Just a strong, male back.

"I don't know. Both, I guess. The face they obviously see right away, and I don't take off the prosthesis before I get to the bedroom. I just can't face any embarrassing situations."

I looked at him and was overwhelmed by pity. David was thirty, and he deserved to have a relationship as much as anyone else.

"Then you should simply take me", I suggested. "That way, you'll never need to play the field anymore."

He laughed as if I was just joking.

"Right now, I'm going to be away for six months", I continued. "While I'm deployed, you can go see some hookers, I don't care. But after that you're mine."

Instead of answering, he buried his head between my breasts. A Mannheim tram rattled past our building. It sounded like a souvenir from a previous century.

"I wonder what our babies would look like", David said abruptly and laid back down next to me. We both stared at the ceiling.

"Well, our first child is a girl", I said after a while. "She will have my black hair and your blue eyes. She'll be light-skinned and incredibly beautiful."

David agreed. "And her name will be Snow White."

"Of course. Our second child is a boy. He's got dark hair and he gets my eyes. People will ask him where his parents are from because they can't figure out his ethnicity."

"I like that", David says. "Every time someone asks him he can tell a different story. Hispanic, Native American, Israeli."

"And because he looks a bit nondescript, he could work as a spy."

David sat up. "Anyone ever tell you that you're a bit obsessed with the topic? Sometimes I get the impression you dream of being a spook yourself."

I laughed. David knew me very well, which was strange since we were never together.

"But seriously", David said, rearranging the pillow behind his back. "With your language skills they would even take you."

I yawned. "I don't know. It probably takes much more than just that. Let's see how things work out in Baghdad. I think that it's going to be a big adventure. And besides, I still have to come back safe and sound."

David turned towards me. "You take care, don't do anything stupid. Stay safe. In the meantime I'm gonna keep my bed warm for you."

It's good to cry. I pull the blanket over my head. This is the first time

I've been wide awake all night long. Maybe I'll fall asleep when the sun rises and the competing chants of the muezzins fill the streets of the city. Finally I get up and close the window.

FREEDOM IS NOT FREE

I wake up in the dark. The street lamp near my basement stopped working a couple of days ago, so there's no light coming in. I open the window to get some fresh air. I eat some cookies and watch the news on Al-Jazeera.

I try very hard not to think about Tim or Dan or Dilawar.

In the shower I wash my hair. I don't like doing this too often because afterwards it takes hours to dry, and my scalp feels unpleasantly cold. I wonder if everyone here has to live without heating. But then there's supposed to be entire neighborhoods in Baghdad where there's no sewers and no trash collection whatsoever. When I was young I had no idea that there are people who've never taken a shower in their life. But I was a different person back then.

I've certainly learned to be grateful for what I have. It's amazing that I'm imprisoned in this luxurious basement and not in a dark dungeon. I'm a lucky gal, and I know it.

A deafening explosion yanks me back to the here and now. It's like a pressure wave going right through my body. The concussion throws me against the wall. I hear myself letting out a gasp of surprise.

Breathe.

The floor of the bathroom is covered by debris. The shower tap has dried up. I take very cautious steps as I walk over the rubble that instantly sticks to my wet feet.

My room is still standing. It's just covered with dust and dirt. The window is gone. Acrid black smoke wafts in, along with cold winter air. Outside I can hear something sizzling. There's the crack and pop of burning plastic. I can't make out any human voices, no shouting. I stand under the hole in the wall and look up. The black smoke is subsiding. I take the chair and step on it to see more.

Dawn has come. A small car has blown up on the other side of the street. The hood is open, with blue flames coming from the engine block. On the driver's seat I see a corpse burning. At first I see no one else on the street, but then suddenly my view is obstructed by someone who is crawling by my destroyed window. His bare legs are visible because his pants were shred to pieces, and I can smell his blood. The smell evokes a memory that completely distracts me from the drama that's going on out there.

I've smelled blood before.

I had blood on my lips.

It was the Captain's blood, and it came from his throat. I used my fingers to cover the open wound on his neck. My hand was steady. He looked up at me and couldn't speak.

I sit down on my bed, and the rubble digs into my wet skin. I stare at my hands. I tried to keep this man alive. He must have had a piece of shrapnel in his neck. But I don't remember any explosion. Was there a gunfight? An ambush? Maybe someone shot him in the neck.

He had green eyes. He didn't look scared. What I saw in his eyes was sadness. His life was coming to an end. Perhaps he was thinking of his wife and his children.

I keep wondering what went through the Captain's head as he lay dying on the street. It's only when the screaming starts, that I snap back to reality.

I inspect the door. It's still sitting in its frame and doesn't look any different. I guess I'll have to take the alternative exit, through the hole in the wall.

In the bathroom I use a damp towel to scrape the dirt off my skin. I want to be clean when I put on my uniform. It fell off the microwave when the bomb went off. I pick it up and put on clean underwear before getting dressed. The uniform feels oversized, but it's still a good feeling. I discover a few specks of blood around my nametag. The small flag on my right shoulder is still spotless. When you put on a uniform, you become part of something bigger. I put on brand new socks. The laces of my boots are dusty. I get up, and suddenly I know who I am again.

The bed needs to be moved to the wall below the hole. It's not heavy, and I lean the thin mattress against the wall. I will not spend another night on it. Then things get difficult. This bed basically consisted of a worn-out metal grid on a frame. No wonder the middle of the mattress always felt hollow. To use the grid as a ladder is probably not a good idea. I'll end up crashing through the grate when I climb on it.

So the bed is useless. Maybe I can use the frame as a stepping stone though. I put the TV and the microwave on the floor and pull the table over so that it's sitting under the hole. I carefully position the chair on the table. There are only a few inches between the chair's legs and the edge of the table, but it should work. It has to.

Most accidents occur at home.

I step onto the frame of the bed and then onto the table. Then I climb up on the chair. The cold winter air helps me breathe. I reach outside with my right arm, groping for whatever is out there. It might be best to use both arms. Outside there still seems to be a remnant of the grid that used to cover the window, just enough steel on both sides of the hole for two hands to grab it. Pull-ups were the only thing I couldn't do well in basic training, but this is more like a dip. If I can't do this here I'm as good as dead.

The first attempt fails miserably, but I'm in high spirits. Today's the day. I turn around. Now I have my back to the wall. This is much more like a pull-up, and it should work. I try. My body doesn't move up an inch. The angle isn't right. I feel tears of rage welling up, but I'm not going to start sobbing like the little girl I used to be. Since I have to reach outside as well as upwards, my arms don't have the leverage that I would need to pull myself up out of this hole.

So I have to find another way. I turn around again, carefully touching everything I can get hold of on the outside wall. I want to find out if I can do it with a lateral arm movement, like a butterfly swimmer.

It's hopeless. The hole is clearly large enough to squeeze myself through, but I won't be able to pull myself out. I suppress hot tears of frustration and let out a helpless yell of anger. Never in my life have I felt so lonely.

Finally I go to the bathroom and brush my teeth. At least I have something to do. I brush my wet hair. I use hand cream to smooth out the little scratches I just inflicted on the palms of my hands. I try to kill as much time as possible until I have to go out and face my problem.

The metal bed is upright against the wall at the exact same spot that Khassem was standing on my first day here, when he asked me if I'd rather have a fast or a slow death. It used to be brown, but most of the varnish has gone. On closer inspection, I realize that the grate is mounted on the sides of the bed frame. I take it off. It's easy because it wasn't welded to the frame, it was just lying on top of it. On each of the long sides of the grate there are two thin metal latches, their sole function to stabilize the whole thing. Just to make sure, I press one of them, and it doesn't give in.

I take the grate to the door. I push the handle in case Saad forgot to lock up, something I've never done before. Unsurprisingly, the door is locked. I won't be able to pick the lock because it's totally old-fashioned, the kind of lock you can use as a peephole. I look through it, but there's only darkness on the other side. There's less than half an inch of space between the steel door and its wooden frame. I stand on the side of the door and try to squeeze one of the metal latches between the door and the door frame. It works. Now I slowly pull down the grate until the latch is at the height of the door lock. The idea is to somehow break the locking mechanism.

Nothing happens, which means I have to try something else. I position the grate at a ninety-degree angle to the door. Again I try to squeeze the side of the grate into the doorframe, but this time I'm pushing both latches in to get more leverage.

Nope.

I will not give up.

I'm alone. There's no one out there who gives a shit. All my loved ones think I'm dead. The only person who can get me out of here is me. Simple as that.

Sweat is covering my back.

I'm doing it wrong. Instead of trying to move the steel door, I should destroy the doorframe since it's made of wood.

All I need to do is carve some of the wood out of the frame so that I have better access to the lock. I spend what seems to be an eternity searching the floor for a sharp object. If the metal grid in front of the window was blown away from the car bomb, parts of it must have landed in my basement.

As I crawl around on the floor, searching the rubble and cursing myself and the universe, I can feel my breath getting heavier. White noise is filling my ears. There's a panic attack on the horizon – just what I needed.

Just as I'm about to give up I see a little black object near the TV set. I dust it off. I can't tell if it's part of the window grate, but it doesn't matter. It's sharp enough.

Now comes the tedious part of my task. I attack the doorframe by taking thin layers off the wood. After about ten minutes I'm dripping with sweat. I've managed to take about an inch off.

I take a break and drink an entire bottle of water.

I move the grate back to the door and slip one latch into the gap that I've just widened. This time, it goes in deeper. I can feel that I have more leverage.

On the third try I hear a distinct crunch in the door. For the fourth attempt, I lower the grate just a couple of inches. For the fifth attempt, I move back up. I feel giddy. I see that the door gap is now two inches wide.

I lean the grate against the wall and pull the bed frame towards the door. The legs of the bed are made from thin steel tubes, and I'm positive I can squeeze one of them into the gap. They're about three times longer than the latches. The pressure must be enough to destroy the lock.

My arms are shaking as I'm pushing one of the legs into the door gap, trying to position it right where the goddamn lock is.

I will never forget the sound of the breaking lock. The modest little click I hear makes me so happy that I have to laugh out loud.

The door is just slightly ajar, and all I have to do is walk through.

I'm not ready yet. I fill my water bottle. For the last time I look around my semi-destroyed bathroom.

I take the lipstick that Khassem bought and that I've never used. I write something on the mirror:
FREEDOM IS NOT FREE.

The hallway is dark and smells musty. A narrow flight of stairs leads to the ground floor. I should leave the building, but I can't resist the temptation of checking out what was above me all the time. I open the unlocked door to my right and walk into the sales room that must belong to Saad's uncle. There once was a showcase, but the explosion shattered the glass front into millions of pieces. The floor is littered with tiny shards and the same debris that I found downstairs. All shelves and clothes racks were overturned. An old-fashioned sales counter has survived the blast unscathed. I walk over to the far end of the room where the massive wooden construct is still standing. The cash register looks like a prop from an old movie, and behind it I find Saad lying on the floor, curled up in a fetal position. His face and upper body were hit. An incredible amount of tiny shards found their way into his skin, and he's sweating from the pain. He's bleeding from an infinite number of micro-wounds. But there's no pool of blood forming underneath him. He'll survive, I guess. I have to carefully climb over his body to get to the cash machine.

Saad is awake and alert. He looks up to observe me as I take all the cash from the till. I stuff the money into a side pocket of my pants. The sales counter has a dozen drawers, and I open all of them. Within half a minute I manage to find my beloved 9-mil along with the holster. I take all the time in the world to reattach it to my thigh.

A padded laptop bag is leaning against the counter, and I fill it with a tablet that's in sleep mode. I wonder where Saad's phone is.

Saad is still lying on the side, so I first browse the left side of his jacket and pants pockets. Then I have to gently turn him over. I don't want to hurt him after all. His face is as white as a T-shirt. Once he's lying on his back, he extends his legs as if to make himself comfortable, still panting as if he had trouble breathing. In the right pocket of his shirt I find a very nice smartphone. I can only hope that I'll remember how to use it after all this time. There's a wallet in his jeans, and I stuff it into the laptop bag.

Saad looks exhausted. I discover a wound I hadn't seen before, on the right side of his neck. There's not much blood coming out, but when it does, I detect a pulse rhythm and I suppose that this piece of glass sits dangerously close to his carotid artery.

He looks at me as I kneel down next to him, and keeps his eyes open as I kiss him on the mouth.

"I've always wanted to do that", I say instead of a farewell.

Now things will get difficult. For the first time in a while I'm fully and completely responsible for my actions. I'm going to have to take a lot of decisions today. If I make any major mistake I might not live to the next morning. This is a war zone even if the politicians are claiming the war is over. To make matters worse, I'm foot-mobile in a country where women don't really walk around alone. Armed women in cammies and desert boots are not a common sight in Baghdad. I will need a disguise.

So far no one has come up with the idea of checking if anyone's hurt in here. Saad's phone didn't ring, nobody is popping their head in. In the middle of the room I put the laptop bag on the floor and start looking for clothes. I find one of these full-body coats that cover a woman's hair and go all the way down to the feet. It's called *Abaya*, it's pitch-black and it's perfect.

I'd also like a pair of sunglasses. I scan the rubble and the upturned shelves for anything resembling any kind of eye pro until it occurs to me that I'd seen a pair of shades in a drawer. I go back to the counter, the only sound in the room being the crunching of glass underneath my boots. I can hear some people yelling outside, but no sirens or alarms going off.

Saad has closed his eyes. Maybe he's not going to make it after all. I can't believe there's still no ambulance, no signs of firefighters or cops.

In one of the top drawers there's a large selection of sunglasses, and at first I can't make up my mind between movie star and pilot. Decisions, decisions. Finally I opt for the latter, put the glasses on and leave the store.

And I'm still not leaving the building. I spontaneously decide to go upstairs instead of out into the street. The building is in good condition, and someone keps the staircase clean. It has six floors. There's a fire escape to the roof. I push the steel door and o out into the open.

I stand under an immense blue sky.

It's almost too much. I look around and take in the Baghdad skyline. What an incredibly ugly place. Most buildings look like the architects never got around to finish them. Electrical wires everywhere. Twelve foot blast walls line long boulevards, as if concrete could stop the lunacy of a suicide bomber. The only nice features of this city are the mosques and the palm trees. I can't make out any churches but I know there are some. No cranes are dotting the skyline, no trucks are rumpling through the city on their way to a construction site. Nobody is building anything in this town.

It takes a while until I know what I have to do. First I find out on the tablet how far away I'm from the Green Zone, trying to visualize how to get there by foot. It would be best to completely memorize the itinerary. Otherwise I'd have to take out the tablet midway, which may not be a good idea. Same thing for the phone. These luxury items are crime magnets in a town where most people are dirt poor.

When the muezzins call to prayer all at the same time, I take a short break to enjoy the music. The sun warms the few parts of me that are not veiled. It's nice to be free. I can now do what I want. I can throw myself off the roof. Or I can jump from roof to roof like they do in action movies.

I suddenly realize that the Green Zone is not an option. I would have to make my way through an infinite number of checkpoints, most of them not even manned by Americans. Now that I'm thinking about it, I'm not even sure whether there's anything at all that we're still in control of in Iraq. The official transition of power to the Iraqis is scheduled for this month. But there are about thirty thousand of our troops still in country. Are some of them here in Baghdad?

Damn.

My intel about the current situation is completely out of date. Suddenly I feel pressure inside my chest.

I don't know where I'm supposed to go. Everything American needs to be fully protected in this country. If it wasn't for the extensive security measures we're taking every day, the Iraqis would have killed us all. And this means that I have no point of contact. I can't just walk into the nearest Hilton and ask them to call me a cab.

Of course I could use the phone. I could call the American Red Cross and tell them where I am. But that would mean I would have to wait here until someone comes to pick me up.

I try to imagine how this would work. How long does it take to get hold of some quick reaction force that could speed through the streets of Baghdad until they get here? There are certainly some people in the embassy who are qualified to do this. But I can't figure out how long I'd have to wait.

If it's too long, I'll panic and get moving. I just don't trust myself at the moment.

I begin to search for other embassies. The tablet gives me plenty of addresses, but I don't see how I can get close enough to Australians or Europeans without having to deal with the enemy first.

I need to come up with a solution, but the harder I think, the blanker my mind gets.

From below I finally hear the familiar sirens of an ambulance. It would be interesting to know if they find Saad in time. And what this whole thing looks like on Al Jazeera.

Al Jazeera. They have an office in Baghdad.

I find the address of their Baghdad bureau and this is it. I now know where I have to go.

I'm in high spirits again, and if I can't immediately find someone to share my newfound happiness with, I will explode. I type my home phone number, giddy with excitement, and almost drop the phone because my hands are trembling.

The phone rings twice. My mother picks up. She sounds tired.

"Mom, don't freak out. Do. Not. Panic. Okay?"

Nothing happens at the other end of the line.

"Mom, it's me. I'm free. I freed myself. I'm coming home now."

"Marina." She's crying: Normally this is very contagious. But I'm too happy right now. And besides, there's going to be a huge cryfest when I get back.

"Mom, please tell only Dad and Grandma and no one else. Okay? I'll be home real soon."

She sobs into the phone, and I strongly suspect that later on, she'll think of all the things she could have said to me, for example, 'I love you' or something. But I have to go now.

And yet, I still can't get going. There's one more thing I need to do, one message I need to send. It takes a few minutes until I find out how I can send an email from my private account. I don't want David to think that someone has hacked into my *.mil*-account.

```
To: one-eyed-dude@gmail.com

From: mars_air@yahoo.com

Re: Guess who


David ,


You can't keep running away from me. Once I've
finally left Iraq, you belong to me.


Your Airpunk
```

Downstairs I decide to check up on Saad. He's gone, and I hope they take good care of him at the hospital. Not that the hospitals in Iraq have a good reputation. I heard they're not well equipped because the funds allocated to them are siphoned off by corrupt government officials. If Saad survives, who knows, maybe we'll meet again in Germany. It would be more than weird to run into him in Mannheim or Frankfurt.

I know it's stupid, but I cross the street in order to look at the charred corpse in the burnt-out car. About a dozen people are standing around the smoldering wreck. The man who died here still has one of his wrists cuffed to the steering wheel.

He didn't even want to die.

I start walking west on the half-destroyed pavement. Two veiled women are trying to make a pool of blood disappear. They pour buckets of water on the blood, but instead of dissoving, the blood mixes with the water to form a larger, pink puddle. A teenage boy is sitting on the curb, watching the two women. He's wearing sandals over naked feet. I don't think he has a grandmother who could knit him a warm pair of socks, but he doesn't look like he's cold.

I can't help anyone here.

I have never been in a position to help anyone in Iraq. My flight to Balad Air Base was a waste of American tax dollars. It's time to leave.

I turn right, away from the chaos and the destruction. This is the first time in my life that I'm traveling alone in Iraq, and it feels good. Nobody cares about me. No one is interested in my laptop bag. It's a chilly winter day and there are not many people on the streets.

An elderly man is smoking in front of a hardware store and looks up as I jump over a puddle. For a brief moment, my boots show up under the abaya, but I'm not too worried. I'm invincible.

Superwoman on the move. I'm on a freedom-induced high that doesn't even go away when I make a wrong turn somewhere and find myself in a side street where I meet a couple of stray dogs. They're not sure what to make of me, so they start growling. I decide to ignore them and walk past them into a courtyard.

There's a mountain of discarded old tires in one corner, and a boy who climbs the mountain, climbs down again and then repeats the whole thing. I ask him for directions. He is delighted that he can be of help. He's brimming with energy and points his fingers in about a hundred different directions. I could have asked my smartphone, but it's so much more fun to listen to the small Iraqi as he tries to explain to me how to get to my destination.

His shoes look as if they had been passed down from one generation to the next. I wouldn't be surprised to find out that one of his relatives was wearing these shoes during the first Gulf War. It's a bit awkward to reach into my right pocket. This veiling cloak is not as convenient as I thought it would be. While I'm rummaging in my pocket for some bills, the boy gets to have a quick look at my uniform. He can't hide his surprise. I thank him and give him some cash in the hope that he'll buy himself new shoes.

I walk past giant T-shaped concrete walls. If you have the privilege of living behind one of those, good for you. This kind of wall basically tells the suicide bombers to go somewhere else to blow shit up. I try to visualize how I walk into Al Jazeera's premises and take the veil off, showing myself in all my uniformed glory. They're going to fall off their chairs when they realize who I am. I will give them a long interview, in their language of course. I will become a rock star in the entire Arabic-speaking world. Who knows, maybe my presence will inspire the Arab women to rebel against their oppression.

I can barely concentrate on where I'm going because I want to look at everything. The architecture, the funny car brands, the people on the street. Just seeing other human beings makes me happy. Despite my elation I try to pull myself together. I have to prepare for all eventualities. What happens if there's a metal detector at the entrance to Al Jazeera? Should I go away first and dispose of the weapon? I don't really see how I could possibly stuff my beautiful Sig Sauer into a garbage can. And I don't think I should. It's going to be bad enough to explain to my superiors what happened to the rifle.

Marina Laroque, the woman who always loses her panties and her rifle.

Once again I have to giggle. I feel so ecstatic, so free and so wild that I could start dancing in the streets right the fuck now. I need to come down from this high before the journalists stuff a microphone in my face, unless I want to make a completely ridiculous first impression.

As always, things don't turn out the way I planned.

I come to an abrupt halt when I see two Humvees turning a corner. Are they Iraqis? Did we leave our equipment behind?

I hop in front of the first vehicle. I'm in the middle of a very busy street, moving my arms up and down like a madwoman. Or like someone who's directing an airplane towards the gate.

Then I realize that I'm scaring the folks in the Humvee. So I put my bag on the floor - a risky move. Now it looks like I'm planting a bomb in front of their vehicle. Humvee #1 comes to a screeching halt. A Gunner swings the SAW in position, and my heart skips a beat: he's one of us.

It takes several precious seconds to pull the veil off. I stand in front of the hood of the vehicle in my dusty and bloodstained uniform, beaming like I'm the happiest gal on earth.

No one moves. Somebody starts honking. I cautiously pick up the bag.

Better not to make any hectic moves.

I step to the driver's door. The window is rolled down.

"I'm Special Agent Marina Laroque. I need a ride."

The officer next to the driver says, "Omar, give up your seat and run back to the other vehicle!"

The driver looks at me through his sunglasses and says, "You heard him. Hop in on the other side."

I walk around the car and see an Iraqi soldier jump out. I climb in and sit in the back.

I'm safe.

I laugh as I look out the window. I could embrace the whole world. Instead I cling to my bag. I hope nothing bad happens now. If we hit an IED and die, then everything was in vain. Then Saad might as well have killed me the day I stormed into his shop.

"Are you crying or laughing", asks someone to my left. There's a lot of bass in that voice. A lot of Texas, too. I'm too afraid to look at my neighbor. Maybe my mind is playing tricks on me.

Maybe I'm in a vehicle that was stolen by a death squad. Just because the guy sounds like an American, he doesn't have to be one.

I feel a light tap on my left shoulder. I keep looking straight ahead, ignoring whoever wants to make contact.

The man clears his throat. "Special Agent Marina Laroque. Welcome back."

I grin. What else should I do. I feel so relieved. I want to kiss everyone. I want to kiss the Humvee. The lieutenant sitting in front of me is listening to a voice crackling on the radio. He's communicating with the troops in the other vehicle. Then he gets through to the base. Suddenly he turns to us and asks me, "What was the name again?"

I can't speak. My neighbor repeats my name loud and clear. The LT announces our arrival at the base and asks for instructions. Finally, he turns around and says: "They have no idea who you are. Who are you?"

HOME IS WHERE THE HEART IS

Two MPs are waiting for me at the FOB. I look around. This isn't the base where I was stationed. It looks pretty much the same though. I'm familiar with the shape of the buildings, the uniforms, the way we do things.

This is my world.

They make me answer what feels like thousands of questions in a stuffy, windowless room. Of course they immediately confiscate my sidearm, something that annoys me because I'd just recovered it. An Army Colonel keeps asking all kinds of questions. I feel cold sweat forming on my forehead and this heavy feeling in my chest that I've experienced more than once today. If they don't believe me, they'll think I'm a defector.

But the interrogation doesn't take too long. I think I can detect pity in the eyes of the Colonel. He tells the MPs to take me to the chow hall. The place is packed. It feels unreal to stand in line with everyone else, waiting for my turn. The MPs don't eat. They watch me as I enjoy my mashed potatoes. There are more and more people who shoot us curious looks. I'm still wearing my blood-spattered uniform. If it weren't for the MPs, they wouldn't have let me into the DFAC. I finish my dinner, and someone takes my tray. On the way out I wonder why no one has confiscated my bag yet.

Then I spend an hour in a waiting room before I get examined by an unfriendly doctor. She takes some blood. She looks into my ears. She measures my blood pressure. The questions I have to answer are idiotic. Who are my parents? Who is the current president?

I feel like yelling at this woman. While I politely answer the nonsense questions, my inner self is screaming: BITCH, I'M ALIVE! I'M BACK! I FREED MYSELF! I'M A SUPERHERO!

She looks completely indifferent when she asks me whether I suffered any sexual violence. I can tell that she doesn't believe me. But I couldn't care less right now.

I use the bathroom next to the doctor's office and then disinfect my hands thoroughly. Crystal clear water comes out of the faucet. I think of home and using my own bathroom, with my favorite bath towel, the blue one that's emblazoned with a giraffe.

My parents and my grandmother must be freaking out by now. I don't think my mother complied with my instructions and immediately called someone at the Air Force Office of Special Investigations. I wonder if they'll take me to Landstuhl to check my health status more thoroughly.

What is the standard procedure when a kidnapping victim surprisingly reappears? Maybe there are no clear rules because such a thing never happens. When someone disappears they usually just recover the body, if at all.

A nurse makes me sign a document I don't bother reading.

And then the two MPs take over, still silent, and lead me to a tent where I'm supposed to spend the night with a dozen other women. There are only three women present as we walk in. They stop talking and stare at me. To be accompanied by MPs usually means that you're in big trouble. I sit down on my bunk and look up at the soldiers. They seem to be waiting for something.

"C'mon guys, say something!" One of them blushes. "It's been so long that I heard American voices."

The non-blushing guy laughs. But before he can say anything, someone shows up behind them and shoves them apart. My Captain stares at me in disbelief and then drops to his knees. He grabs both my hands.

"Hey", I say. I'm too stunned to say anything else.

He buries his face in my hands. Weird.

"Captain Gillespie", I say.

He kisses my hands.

"I thought you were dead", I whisper. He has such a tight grasp on my hands, as if he was planning to never let go.

"That's what I thought as well. I thought I was dying while you had your finger on my carotid artery. I thought you're the last person I get to see in this life."

"What a depressing thought", I say, but Gillespie is not in a joking mood. He raises his head and lets go of my hands.

I pat the mattress. "Want to sit down?"

He shakes his head. "Are you very tired?"

"Nope, not at all. I'd really like to go outside. And see the sky. And everything else."

He looks up at me and then to the soldiers. I don't really have the nerve for long discussions. The fact that I'm back in an enclosed space is starting to make me nervous. I want to get out of here.

"I was locked up for six months", I say, looking directly into the brown eyes of the white soldier. "I need be out in the open for a while."

Gillespie stands up and is suddenly six foot four again. He looks even thinner than I remembered. He turns to the young guys. "I'll take over now. I'm her CO, and I'm taking her back here afterwards."

Strangely enough, the MPs don't argue. Which is weird because the Colonel gave me into their care. I grab my bag and follow my lanky boss outside. It's early evening. We stop briefly to let three Humvees pass by that just rolled in through the main gate. The vehicles stop in front of a square concrete building. The drivers are struggling to squeeze the Humvees between some trucks. Exhausted soldiers climb out and start gathering the equipment that's not supposed to stay in the vehicle overnight. One of them opens the hood of a Humvee, others stand around smoking. A lieutenant with dark circles under his eyes looks at me with open curiosity as I walk by with Gillespie.

I'm cold. That's okay. I'm grateful that I can see the blue sky. Gillespie doesn't talk, not yet. We walk past numbered barracks. Under the cold December sun we take a walk around the entire post. We pass by soldiers playing basketball right next to a stinking landfill. I notice two of them are shirtless, a rare sight. This was always prohibited, whether at Bagram or elsewhere. We turn into a different street and see a line forming in front of a Popeye's.

The sky starts turning red. The air is getting colder. Gillespie treats me to a hamburger. The burger joint is packed. I'm surrounded by Americans, their voices and laughter filling my heart. I know I will remember this forever. I will never again be as happy as I am tonight. For the first time in my life I turn heads anywhere I go, and I enjoy it. No one has bothered giving me a new uniform yet. I wear Gillespie's dried blood on my shirt like a medal.

We continue our walk under the darkening sky. There are no stars yet. I can't wait for them to come out.

"What's in your bag?" Gillespie yanks me out of my thoughts. I stumble over a pothole. He laughs.

"Are you really okay?"

I beam at him.

"Captain, I don't want to go back to this stupid tent", I say all of a sudden. "I want to stay with you."

"Tonight? In our barracks?" Gillespie looks surprised.

I nod. "You guys were my unit. I used to belong to you, even if only for a short time. But we belong together. We're a team."

Gillespie hands me a tissue. Only now do I realize that I'm crying.

"Okay", he says. "Not sure how to pull this off, but I'm going to find a way I guess. Tomorrow I'm sure they're going to ship you out. So why shouldn't you spend your last night in Iraq with us?"

"And my first night in freedom", I add.

He looks worried though. A woman bunking with men would be a novelty. I hope that he'll manage to make it happen.

Then we march on through the endless expanses of the base. What a luxury to have so much space. Maybe the open Idaho landscape is going to freak me out when I get home. I'm just not used to being outside anymore.

Gillespie tells me that my timing is perfect: end of this month, we're officially handing over power to the Iraqi people. This FOB will be completely vacated in the next two weeks. The Army unit I was assigned to is going back to Georgia by New Year's Eve.

"Damn", I swear. Gillespie seems to think this is funny.

"Where am I going then? I want to stay with you."

"But you must have known that we'd go our separate ways again after six months."

I stop and stare at Gillespie. "Sure I did. The one thing I didn't know was that I would spend those six months locked up in a crappy basement. I totally wasted my time in Baghdad. The only thing I know about this country I learned from Iraqi TV!"

Gillespie is embarrassed. Or maybe he feels sorry for me. "You want to talk about it?"

I shake my head.

"You had a TV?"

I start walking again. I don't want to stand around in the cold. The sky is orange. A group of overweight civilians stroll past us. One of them is carrying a Persian rug slung over his shoulder.

I decide to answer Gillespie's question. "I had a TV. I'd like to add that I wasn't tortured or raped, apart from one or two events that were a bit unpleasant."

Gillespie nods. "I guess that's why you're so normal. Well, I mean, your behavior since I found you. I'm so incredibly glad that you're okay, Marina. And I'm eternally grateful to God that he let you live. Unbelievable."

"Actually, that wasn't God", I object while we walk around the gym and take a right turn onto the main road. "It was the two guys who had me. They couldn't make up their mind what they wanted to do with me. The fact that I'm still alive, that's really more or less a coincidence."

Gillespie stops again. I wish we could just keep walking. Once I stop moving, the December chill gets to me. But the Captain puts his hands on my shoulders. He looks as if he's about to burst into tears.

Please don't, I think.

"Marina", he says so softly that I move closer to hear him. "You can't imagine how much I suffered. I no longer wanted to live. I thought the whole time that it's my fault. That you're gone. We had no idea if you were alive or dead. And what those scumbags could possibly do to you in case you're still alive. Everyone in our unit had to get counseling. Carson almost drank himself to death because of you."

I can't remember Carson right now. "Does he know that I'm back?"

Gillespie nods. "I called him in the States just before I ran over to you. It was the middle of the night and I had to tell him everything three times. He couldn't believe it at first. But at least now he can go into rehab."

I laugh, which of course is totally inappropriate. "Do you think I should go see him there when I'm stateside?"

"Sure, why not."

"Can we go to your place now? I think I'm getting tired", I say. Gillespie finally lets go of my shoulders and grabs my hand. We look like two lovers as we walk back holding hands. A bunch of Marines look pretty shocked when they pass by.

"In four months' time I'm a civilian again", Gillespie says. "I'm no longer interested in what others think."

"It's hard to conceive that we're completely gone soon, and this post is still swarming with people", I remark.

"Could be. But there are signs of disintegration. Folks don't take the rules so seriously anymore and the MPs are less of a pain in the neck. We're all on our way out. Who cares if some dudes want to grow a mustache."

We arrive in front of a two-story CONEX box and take an external staircase to the second floor. Gillespie's hooch is bigger than I expected. He leads the way through a dark corridor, past other rooms, and we descend a spiral staircase into a common room with two sofas and a large table in the middle. There's no more daylight from outside, and the two soldiers at the XBox have turned on a small floor lamp in the corner. I sit down on the other couch, and Gillespie leaves again to get some clean clothes for me.

I watch the soldiers playing *Fallout: New Vegas*. The sounds they make remind me of Robert and Kyle. One of the two young men looks over to me, then turns his gaze right back to the events on the screen. Suddenly he drops his controller and stares at me, his mouth open.

"Whoa, what are you doin'?" His friend is angry.

Soldier #1 answers without turning his eyes away from me.

"This is the missing girl from Gillespie's team."

Soldier #2 interrupts the game and looks me up and down. "Are you sure?"

The other one nods. "Gillespie has her picture on his locker. Unfuckingbelievable."

Before they can ask me any questions, Gillespie is back and asks me to follow me upstairs. I wink at my two observers as I get up. Lara Croft is back.

Gillespie has a package under his arm and hands it to me in his room. It contains a clean uniform.

"You know what", I say. "I'm gonna put it on tomorrow. Otherwise I have to sleep in it. I need to be neat and crisp and orderly tomorrow."

"Makes sense. You want to take a shower? I can give you a towel and soap and stuff. I even have hair products." Gillespie looks a little frazzled at the moment. This is all probably a bit too much for him.

I nod.

"Captain, what happened to me? And what happened to you on that day? I remember you were bleeding from the neck, but that's it." My sudden outburst doesn't stop Gillespie from rummaging a drawer for things I will need in the shower. He turns around with a pair of flip-flops in his hand. He looks at me with an expression of helplessness that reminds me of a school child who can't answer the teacher's question.

"Captain, I can't remember. I really need to know what happened."

Gillespie hesitates. He takes a deep breath. "We were in Sadr City. We had intel that someone had set up a weapons cache in a residential building. And from what we knew the insurgents were getting their ammo supplies from there, among other things. In hindsight I think it was a ruse. They were waiting for us. When we dismounted someone shot me in the neck. The bullet kinda grazed me, otherwise it would've been over right away. The carotid artery was partly torn though, and I ended up lying on the floor bleeding out real slow. And then you sat down on top of me and put a finger on my wound."

Gillespie stands there, the neon green flip-flops in his hand.

"I can remember this crazy panic that was gripping my whole body. I'll never forget that. You just can't imagine what it's like when the fear of death takes over. As if the devil himself is taking possession of you."

I don't need to imagine that, I think. *I know how that feels.*

Gillespie puts the plastic shoes on the floor and hands me a towel. He sits down on his bunk. I sit down next to him.

"So we're in the middle of this firefight, completely exposed, and you're sitting on top of me and singing songs."

I laugh in disbelief. "I did what?"

Gillespie doesn't feel like laughing. "Songs in a foreign language. I later learned from your mother that those were Nez Perce songs that your grandma taught you. Your Indian songs saved my life."

Gillespie's explanations are not very helpful. I'm more confused than before. At the same time I can feel my heart beat faster. I still don't recall what happened, but I know that I'm just moments away from finding out. And once I know I'll remember, and everything will come crashing down on me. There's a tsunami of memories looming on the horizon.

I have to ask to make sure that I understand him correctly. "I've stopped the bleeding. By putting my finger on your neck, yeah?"

Gillespie nods. "It's more complicated than that. If you'd applied too much pressure, then I would've died real fast. The physician in Landstuhl told me that later. You've instinctively exerted just the right kind of pressure. But you did something else too: you defeated my panic attack. If I'd freaked out, I would have been thrashing around like a lunatic, and that would have been the end."

"I see."

"You get it, right? You stayed calm. I wouldn't be sitting here if you'd lost it. That was an incredible achievement. Even if you don't get a medal for it - what you've done, nobody can take that away from you. My wife and my kids will be grateful to you. Forever."

I will have to think about this for a while, but I should wait until I'm on the plane home. Right now I have no desire to think at all.

We sit next to each other for a while without speaking. Finally I get up to take a shower. The shower room is big enough for six people, and I'm alone at first. I enjoy the water pressure very much. The Captain's body wash smells masculine and sexy. A soldier in undies suffers the shock of his life when he opens the door and sees me in my full naked glory. I laugh like a madwoman and shampoo my hair like there's no tomorrow.

The towel is the fluffy white hotel type. I dry myself properly. I put on my old uniform and the boots, but not the underwear. I wash the panties and the undershirt in a sink in the room next to the shower. The shocked soldier has been waiting there all the time. Now he speeds past me and slams the door behind him. I spread out the socks and the underwear put on the radiator. I'm not sure if the stuff is still going to be here tomorrow, but why should I care?

Gillespie is lying on his rack. He sits up as I enter the room.

"Where are the others?" I would love to see my team again, even though I worked with them only for a short time.

Gillespie shrugs. "Carson was sent back to the States because he wasn't functional any longer. The other two, Donnell and Schwartz, are still here. Yesterday we were up most of the night and we had another patrol all morning, so they had the rest of the day off."

I sit down next to him. My hair is wet, and the back of my uniform is getting wet.

"Do you think we could do something together tonight? With the other two? Play cards or something, that would be great."

"Sure, why not?"

I feel that I need to explain this. "I just wanna belong, you know? I always wanted to be one of the guys. But no matter where I went, I was always the girl or the bitch or the butch lesbian or whatever."

Gillespie giggles. "I don't know about the other insults, but there's nothing butch about you."

I grab a towel from the shelf beside his bed.

"This one I used", Gillespie warns me.

"That's all right", I reply, wrapping it around my hair.

"John", I say. It feels more than weird to pronounce his first name. "Look. People who join the military expect this whole camaraderie thing. I had a lot of time to think about it. When I was dreaming of the Marines, I had very clear ideas. I think I've always wanted to be in a combat unit because that's where people bond more than anywhere else."

Gillespie smiles. "The others become your brothers. And you wouldn't hesitate to give your life for them. I was an LT in Fallujah, and that was so insanely dangerous. We had big losses. Sometimes we were five people in the Humvee when we rolled out, and we'd come back twelve hours later, with only four people. The guys who suffered with you, you will never forget them in your life."

I let out a long and persistent yawn. I don't think I've ever been so relaxed before. The hot water in the shower has destroyed all the tension in my body. Sitting close to Gillespie makes me feel safe and pleasantly tired.

"I had these totally romantic notions of my time in the Air Force, but I was just a technician, and the others didn't know what to make of me. I think I managed to miss out on everything that makes the military so special. "

"Is that why you wanted to be an agent?"

Gillespie uses the word "agent" with a mocking undertone, but I couldn't care less about that. For someone like him, an AFOSI agent is a bit ridiculous. If I wanted to be taken seriously by a grunt, I should at least fly an attack helicopter.

"I just wanted to get out of the hangar. And it was clear that I would have more interactions with other people if I had to use my language skills. And I'd have to go to crime scenes or investigate stuff or whatever."

"Marina hunting criminals." Gillespie seems to find this idea amusing. "But in fact we just used your skills as a translator."

I shrug. "That was okay. I managed to get outside the wire and see something of the country and meet Iraqis. What I liked most was driving around the city. The fact that I was attached to an army unit made me really proud. It's just too bad I didn't get to spend much time with you and the team."

Gillespie's face has darkened again.

"What?" I ask.

He sighs and leans back, as if he had to brace himself for what he's planning to say. "I think I should tell you what happened after that. After you saved my life."

I take the towel off my head. I want my ears to be free.

Gillespie folds his long, slender hands in his lap. "So. You kept me alive. All around us - total chaos. Bullets flying like in a movie. The medic didn't come through to us at first. But he couldn't have done any better than you. Carson and Donnell went to hunt down the sniper and when they had him, they took him out. Then eventually the medic came through but he didn't dare to pull you away from me. And when the ambulance came, you didn't want to let the doctor anywhere near me. So the others had to use force to yank you away from me and you completely freaked out."

Blood. My whole right hand was red with blood. Even the smell is back.

"You were screaming your brains out. You were so loud. And you were thrashing around like crazy. I think someone slapped you in the face to get you under control. But they were sloppy. They didn't manage to hold on to you. And then you ran away."

That explains everything.

"I know from one of my captors that I stormed into his shop and I was hysterical. But the store was downtown, not too far from the Green Zone."

Gillespie contemplates what I just told him. "That's far away from Sadr City. You must've been running for miles. And it was hot. By the time you arrived at the store you must have been completely dehydrated."

"I'm almost glad I can't remember this shit", I say. Maybe it really is better that I know nothing.

"Are you going to tell me now what's in this bag?"

I'm stunned. "You didn't have a peek while I was in the shower?"

He laughs. "I'd never do that."

"A tablet PC, a phone. Used to belong to my captors."

Gillespie is aghast. "And you're telling me that now? That's evidence! You gotta hand this in, Marina. It could be used to find them."

He gets up and looks as if he wanted to call someone immediately.

"John, sit back down", I say.

Gillespie looks anything but happy, but he does as told.

"Listen. One hijacker is in Europe. The other, the one whose stuff I've stolen, is either in the hospital or dead. Of course I'm aware of the fact that I'm hiding evidence here. But I wasn't abducted by dangerous terrorists. Or criminals. This whole thing was a case of bad luck, not just for me. The guys ended up taking care of me, feeding me for six months, buying me stuff. Of course they should've released me right away. Well, they didn't. But can you imagine what happens after our people have evaluated all the data on the tablet and the phone?"

"Of course I can imagine." Gillespie has his hands folded in his lap. "They'll catch those fuckers. The one who escaped to Europe, and the guy who got injured. If he's still alive."

I agree with him. "The guy in Europe is going to end up in Gitmo. And the other one will spend a very unpleasant time in an Iraqi torture cell."

Gillespie nods.

I'm not mad at him. But I need to explain. "I know what you're thinking. Stockholm Syndrome."

The Captain looks at me and he visibly feels very sorry for me. "Marina, you were in the hands of two men for half a year, right? No one will accuse you of anything. People will understand that you want to leave these criminals alone now. But these two things in your bag, they're evidence in a criminal case, and we have to hand them in. Now."

I shake my head. "We won't. You wouldn't dare to take my stuff. And you know why? Because I won't let you."

I can't hear any noise from outside. It's as if we were completely isolated from the rest of the world. In Bagram there was always something going on. Traffic. People talking outside. Occasional incoming. Flight movements.

Being alone with Gillespie makes me happy. I think it's the first time. I feel good sitting next to him, surrounded by his private stuff. There's a Boston University T-shirt hanging over the only chair in the room. I wonder when he gets to wear it. Now all I have to do is end our disagreement in the nicest way possible. This is a power struggle I definitely have to win, because Saad's and possibly Khassem's fate depend on it. Somehow I presume Saad is still alive. Maybe that's wishful thinking.

"I saved your life", I say. "You owe me. I'm asking you for one favor, that's it. I want you to stuff the contents of this bag into your duffel, and to take it home when the time comes. When you're back stateside, I'm going to pick up the stuff."

Gillespie is speechless.

"I know that I'm asking too much from you. But you're the only one I can ask to smuggle these things out of the country."

"You're not asking me for a favor, you're demanding that I do this for you", Gillespie answers, his voice vibrating with anger. "You want me to break the law."

"Yeah. You're right. Because everyone else is doing it too", I say softly. "As far as I know it's against our laws to torture someone to death or to make someone disappear forever in a prison without ever charging them with a crime. As long as my government does whatever they want, I don't need to abide by our laws."

"Jesusfuck, Marina. You're an anarchist now? If our people find him, then we'll keep him, and I don't think we'll hand him over to the Iraqi authorities."

"Awesome. He's going to have such a great time in Guantánamo."

My sarcasm is too much for Gillespie. He buries his head in his hands.

I start wondering where I'm going to sleep tonight. Gillespie has every reason to return me to the women's tent, now that I'm getting rebellious. He's still my boss.

"You know, Gitmo still has a horrible reputation, but it's not like that anymore", he says. "Of course I don't know how his chances are to get out of there alive. I guess once you're in it..."

Gillespie suddenly sits up straight.

"Marina, I was at the TOC and I told them you're staying here for the night. They're going to pick you up tomorrow. You will be debriefed. That's just a nice word for an interrogation."

I say nothing. At the moment I don't really care what's happening tomorrow.

Gillespie lays a hand on my shoulder. This reminds me of Robert who used to put his arm around my shoulder pretty much all the time.

"Listen. No matter what has happened between you and these two thugs: don't try to conceal anything. D'you understand that? They'll debrief you more than once. You'll need to tell your story several times, and they'll go through every detail with you, again and again. Do not lie to them, they'll find out."

Gillespie looks really worried. I'm the one who should be scared. It feels great to sit on his bed, and to see how afraid he is of what's going to happen to me.

"I have nothing to hide", I say. "I've done nothing wrong. I didn't give out classified information, I didn't change my religion and I didn't spit on the flag."

Gillespie nods. "I want you to get this over and done with as fast as you can. They won't trust you, Marina."

"Captain."

He looks at me. He looks tense, as if he was trying to protect me from something.

"I'm totally in control", I say. "I had plenty of time to think about this. About how I get home afterwards. And about how they take me apart to find out if I was brainwashed."

"Good. How are you going to hide the fact that you gave me the things that belonged to your captor? You might have to take a lie detector test. Or they give you a drug and then go through the whole story for the fifth time. If they find that stuff here, I'm dead."

"No, you're not." I'm so terribly tired that I can't sit upright. So I crawl onto the bunk and lay my head on Gillespie's pillow. Everything smells like him. I would love to share this space with him tonight.

"Marina, as much as I admire you for your life-saving skills, I'm not going to jail for you. You're suffering from impaired judgment right now. Not surprising after what you've been through. I would suggest you don't take any decisions in the next few weeks. You know what? I would strongly suggest you totally stop thinking and worrying about anything at all."

Gillespie looks down at me. He doesn't seem to mind that I'm lying on his blanket with my dirty uniform. I struggle with the desire to just close my eyes. He seriously wants me to stop thinking.

"You're not going to jail", I say. "You know why? They won't ask about Saad's electronic devices."

"Yeah? Why not?"

"Because they'll never come up with the idea that he owns stuff like that. And even if they did, they won't think that I found any of his possessions in the rubble."

"What rubble?"

I close my eyes and feel how every single cell in my body goes into chillout mode. I've never felt this safe before... I realize that the Captain doesn't know how I managed to escape. That's a story worth telling. I quickly sum up my weird relationship with my kidnappers before I tell him how I got out. I tell him about the car bomb explosion in all details, including the handcuffed victim inside the car.

"Good God", is the only thing he says when I'm finished.

Someone walks past our room, his boots going *clunk* on the metal floor with each step.

"Marina, even if they don't ask you about Saad's phone or tablet, they're gonna ask you about the bag."

I like it when he says my name. We are, as my father would say, "bound to each other". We were together when he was dying. The songs from my childhood have kept him alive. I felt his pulse - and his fear of death.

"Nah, I don't think so", I say with my eyes closed. "How would they know I had a bag?"

"Because the Colonel saw it. The MPs. About a hundred other people who looked at you today."

Shit.

Gillespie is right. I open my eyes and see his long, slender back. I wonder how fast he can run. Somehow I envy his wife and children.

"All right", I say. "Then I guess I should fill the bag with something else now. That way they won't come up with the idea that anything else was inside. It's gotta be plausible, you know. The kind of stuff women like to carry around with them."

Gillespie stands up and begins to rummage around for things that he could possibly put in my bag.

"No, no books", I say as he inspects his little book shelf. "I haven't read them."

Gillespie puts a paperback back on the shelf. He works in silence, opens drawers, goes through a backpack.

Finally he takes Saad's equipment out of the bag and places it in a drawer. He fills the bag with a towel, anti-dandruff shampoo and a large folding map of Baghdad.

"You probably had one like that, right?"

"Nope", I say and have to yawn. "But I could've found the map the day I escaped. They will ask me about the M4, which is really really embarrassing."

Gillespie sits down on the chair. He looks like he could use some sleep, too. "Why? You didn't have it on you."

I sit up. "Course I had. My captors took it off me when I was unconscious. They took the M9 too, but I found it before I checked out of Hotel Baghdad."

"Checked out?" Gillespie bursts out in a hysterical fit of laughter. "You checked out of your hotel? Oh God, Marina, they're going you tear you apart tomorrow. They're going to expose everything. Oh God, oh God."

He buries his head in his hands again. It's such an adorable habit. Why did I never notice that before? I almost start stroking his hair. He has this ultra-short Marine haircut that makes his face look even softer. I lay down again. This Spartanic rack is the most comfortable bed I've ever lied on.

"What did you just mean when you said I didn't have the rifle when I ran?" I ask.

Gillespie lets his hands fall back into his lap and looks down at me like a father who tells his child a bedtime story. "Someone picked it up from the floor after you left, and you definitely didn't have it with you when you started running through Baghdad."

Well, that's interesting. The rifle never landed in Saad's shop. Saad lied to me when he told me that he'd sold it on the internet. Maybe I shouldn't care about this at all. There's a sense of foreboding creeping up inside of me. What else did he lie about? Maybe his parents aren't doctors and they never intended to flee to Germany. When it comes to his religion I can absolutely not imagine that he made that up, too. Anything else I'm suddenly not so sure about.

I close my eyes and fall asleep.

As usual I wake up in the middle of the night. Someone is running through the corridor. A door slams and it's quiet again. Gillespie is sleeping on the floor, wrapped in a sleeping bag. He breathes quietly through his nose. I lie down next to him and cover both of us with his blanket. It's nice not to be alone.

I wake up because Gillespie has to shake me off to go to the bathroom. If my sense of time is still intact, then the sun should rise in a couple of hours. Whoever will take me away from here, they're probably on their way now. The military is a 5 AM-type of organization. Sleeping is regarded as a luxury. While I slip into my fresh uniform, our container comes to life. I sit down on the chair and look around one last time. Behind me I can hear water running through pipes. Finally my eyes adjust used to the darkness and find Gillespie's alarm clock. It's 5:20 AM.

Welcome back.

The MPs enter the room along with Gillespie. I barely manage to shake his hand, then I'm gone. My heart is beating too loud. There's white noise in my ear as we jog past the rooms of other officers. We reach the end of the hallway, and one of the MPs takes my bag. The harsh neon lights burn my eyes as we take the stairs to get to the ground floor. We meet one of the soldiers I saw sitting in front of the XBox yesterday. He approaches us wearing nothing but jockeys. There's an octopus above his right nipple.

"Goodbye, Marina", he shouts at us. "Get home safely."

One thing will never change in the military: the mindless waiting for something that is scheduled to happen, but won't happen anytime soon. We run to the helipad, and then time freezes. I sit down on an empty wooden pallet while the MPs are standing around looking more than bored. I didn't have breakfast and I didn't drink anything because my departure was imminent and urgent, and here we are, breathing in the cold air of a winter morning in Baghdad. After sitting around for a while and watching the sunrise, I have no other choice but to get up and walk around a bit. My two guards are not letting me out of their sight. It's an unnecessary precaution. Where would I possibly want to go?

After a couple of hours I force my minders to accompany me to the next Portajohn.

Then we're back at the helipad. I decide to make the most of it by thinking up a workout that I can do right here in the open air. I use the pallet for step aerobics, which probably looks stupid. I do all sorts of stretching exercises. I'd love to hop around a bit, but I would need music for that. My iPod comes to mind. I must have left it in my prison. I can't remember taking it with me when I left my destroyed home, and I curse myself.

Since I don't want to get any stains on my clean uniform, I refrain from doing sit-ups. Push-ups help me stay warm. I don't really care about the soldiers who are walking by on their way to the showers or the DFAC. They watch me work out in front of the MPs. They probably think I'm on my way to a mental institution. It doesn't matter what other people think. I really have no desire to freeze my ass off me on my last morning in Iraq.

I try not to overdo it, though. I don't want to be soaking wet when they finally come to get me. As time goes by, I start getting nervous. How many people will take me apart? What kind of embarrassing questions am I going to have to answer? There are some other concerns I have. Things I haven't even asked myself yet because I was busy trying to survive.

What's gong to happen to my career?

Am I finished as a Special Agent because I ran away? Did they stop my salary?

Who knows if I'll ever get to set foot on Arab soil again.

My darker thoughts are almost under control. I push away the memory of Saad lying on the floor and bleeding out of a thousand tiny wounds. It's difficult to concentrate on my leg stretches as I think of the man who was crawling past my window yesterday. Just when I start thinking of the charred corpse in the smoldering car, I hear the noise of mighty rotors.

I get up and rub my hands to get the sand off. A fantastic Black Hawk flies in from the East and lands on the helipad with elegance and style.

This bird came for me.

A handsome man in civilian clothes jumps out and ducks under the rotors. He says something to the MPs, takes my bag and then pulls me by the elbow towards the helo - without even once looking at me. I climb in and someone else grabs me and pushes me onto a seat. He straps me in while the door gets closed.

The bird takes off immediately. I sit in a row with four seats and look to the left. Through the window I can see the base disappear unbelievably fast. Then we make a sharp right left. The streets of Baghdad are underneath me. This is the last time in my life that I get to look at the weird architecture of an Iraqi city. I don't feel anything.

The noise of the rotors is deafening. Behind the two pilots there's a guy with a machine gun, scanning the surroundings. The flight engineer next to him is talking into his headset.

This is my first helo flight. The bird is packed to the max with uniformed men, some of them Brits. I sit between the man who picked me up and the one who fastened my seat belt. We have no headsets, which is a bit of a disappointment. Radio chatter always sounds fascinating even if nothing interesting is going on. Communication with the other passengers is impossible because of the noise level. I shoot my two companions discreet side glances. I wonder if they're the ones who will interrogate me.

The guy who buckled me up has the same green eyes as Dan. His hair is a bit longer, but his face has the same sharp features. High cheekbones, square jaw and not one unnecessary ounce of body fat. He makes a completely impassive impression as he starts looking me up and down, taking in my brand new boots and my cammies without any patches that would identify my unit or my rank. Then his gaze goes up to my face. With direct eye contact comes the shock.

Dan looks at me with an expression of absolute indifference. Like a stranger on the New York subway.

I breathe in the cold air, and I breathe out slowly.

I stare at Dan as thirty thousand different memories storm into my mind. We are no longer flying over the streets of Baghdad. We're back in Bagram and the Hindu Kush is the backdrop for everything that has ever happened between us. The blue sky that I can see outside could just as well be the sky over Afghanistan.

But something is different. It takes a while until I realize that he has aged. He no longer has those dark circles under his eyes that always worried me in Bagram. But his face is thinner and harder. He leans casually against the seat and radiates the weariness of someone who has seen too many bad things.

I would love to ask him about Tim, right here and now.

But of course I refrain from saying anything. We land on Balad Airfield and transfer onto a small jet. I feel like a character in a TV show where the FBI agents fly form one murder case to the next.

I count eight seats. On the left there are two groups of four with a table in the middle, and the right side only has room for a narrow corridor. Soft voices are audible from the cockpit. Dan pushes me gently onto a window seat and sits down next to me. The other man takes a seat opposite Dan. I get to stretch my legs out. The unknown man stows my bag under his seat. It doesn't look like they're carrying any luggage at all, not even a purse. Dan closes my belt. I lean my head against a chic blue pillow and close my eyes. If the two want something from me, I'm sure they'll let me know.

Of course I open my eyes again immediately. We're flying south, and my guess is we'll change planes in Kuwait. But then we turn west.

First to Ramstein, I think. *Good.*

There's no flight attendant. Dan organizes breakfast from a pantry behind the cockpit. I get orange juice and nice European pastry wrapped in plastic. The other guy gets up to fetch us some coffee, and suddenly I'm alone with Dan.

As soon as the other man turns his back on us, we stop tearing up the plastic wrap. I can see from the corner of my eye that Dan is turning his head to me. My gaze wanders slowly to the right. We look at each other. We have a time window of no more than twenty seconds.

"Dan", I say.

Dan is silent. He looks so much more mature.

We eat breakfast in silence. I don't see why I should be the one to do the small talk here. I spread soft butter on a bun filled with raisins. Maybe they stole some Lufthansa food. After a while Dan gathers our leftovers and takes them to the front.

When he comes back it's time for introductions. The man sitting across from Dan says, "I'm Thomas Johnson, and this is my colleague John Dreyer. Welcome back."

"Thanks", I say coolly. I'd love to know if Dan's name really is John. It's very unlikely. Somehow I'm pretty sure that Dan and Tim told me their real names at Bagram.

Anyone who deals with spooks knows that it's hard to use a fake name to begin with. The danger of giving yourself away is too great. *Hi, I'm Da- ...erm, I mean John.* That would be awkward. And when I met Dan and Tim they weren't spooks. There was no reason for the two to make up fake names because I knew nothing else about them.

I could easily screw up this attempt at lying at me. All I need to do is ask Dan if he still has the "Infidel" tattoo. But that would be stupid. My knowledge might be useful later on.

"My name is Marina Laroque, I'm sure you know that. May I ask who you're working for?"

"We have the same employer", Johnson replies. "Air Force Office of Special Investigations."

I need to process this piece of information. There are some complicated calculations that my brain is undertaking while I'm looking out the window. My life experience. My instincts. All the things that Dan ever told me – they're all pointing in the same direction.

Johnson is lying. He's not an AFOSI colleague.

I smile at him. He probably thinks that I'm pleased to be among peers. Relieved that I won't be interrogated by some other dark powers. Luckily he can't read minds. Because the reason I'm beaming at him is that I've caught him with a big, fat lie even though our conversation is just one minute old.

A long time ago, in another life, I had a drowsy conversation with Dan in the Russian Tower. We'd shared four beers. I was basically drunk. It was just before dawn. Dan was complaining about sand. About sand in his food, in his hair, everywhere. If it was windy, you'd get sandblasted. If it was hot, your sweat mixed with the fine grains between your toes, in your buttcrack, everwhere. The sand reminded him of his basic training, and he used the words *Parris Island* without realizing he was giving away an important piece of intel. My eyes were closed, but I was wide awake.

Dan is a Marine.

Dan kept whining about the harsh climatic conditions in Iraq and Afghanistan. "I can't take it anymore. The sand storms that screw up our equipment. These monster spiders. D'you ever find a camel spider in your duffel? Freak you the fuck out. 100 degrees in the summer."

He stubbed out his cigarette. "You know what? I'm going to write a letter of complaint to the Joint Chiefs of Staff."

"And what are you going to write?" I asked.

"That we should stop these wars immediately. We should get out of these shitholes. The next invasion? I want it in a country that has a decent climate."

I laughed. "Ireland would be nice."

Dan nodded. "How about Sweden. They're supposed to be very open-minded over there. Tap me some seven-foot Vikings."

Johnson looks at me as if he's expecting me to start talking. I think of Dan's Parris Island remark. The problem is that Marines think they're better than the rest. And Dan always made it clear that by joining the Air Force I had chosen the biggest loser.

"The Air Force should be abolished. The combat missions can be taken care of by the Marines and the Army. The Navy gets the Hog. And for the heavy stuff that needs to be flown from one place to the next we use FedEx cargo planes."

Of course I had to protest. "You can't abolish us. We played a glorious role in every single war these last hundred years."

Dan chuckled. "Yeah? When was the last time you guys were glorious? Battle of Britain?"

My history knowledge was not good enough to immediately come up with a smart answer, but I felt I had to defend the honor of my employer. "What about the troops? How do they get in and out of the country?"

He shrugged. "We just put them on commercial airlines. No one needs the Air Force."

These days I could easily find arguments to disprove Dan's silly ideas, but at that time I was too unsure to argue with Dan. But I didn't forget his rant, and now, five years later, it's giving me food for thought.

I look out of the window again. I need to think.

Johnson is lying. Dan would rather chop off his right arm than to join the Air Force. For people with his special skills, the doors are wide open to all sorts of institutions, not to mention the private security companies. That's where the money is. He could make a fortune working as a contractor.

But if Dan is not at AFOSI, then Johnson isn't either. Why they find it necessary to conceal who they're really working for, is completely unclear to me. What difference does it make whether I'm going to be debriefed by the armed forces or the FBI?

The unusual breakfast makes me want to doze off again. Unfortunately Johnson wants to start with the "debriefing". I'd much rather enjoy the flight. In fact it would be quite awesome if Johnson simply vanished into thin air now. That way I could talk to Dan instead of answering a thousand questions about the last six months. I have to tell Johnson The Liar every detail of my adventure in Baghdad.

The ambush and Gillespie's injury are things that I know from hearsay. I can only retell them as I've heard them from Gillespie. My memories are still too vague. Whenever I try to remember that day I think of blood. I remember its distinctive sweet smell and my wet fingers. And Gillespie's sad eyes, the way he looked at me as if he wanted to say farewell. I can tell Johnson about my arrival in Saad's shop only in Saad's version.

Dan keeps his mouth shut all the time. He's clearly not in charge. Maybe he's a trainee.

I talk about the ambush and what happened afterwards for at least an hour. Which means that talking about the other one hundred and eighty days of my captivity will certainly keep us busy until we touch down in Ramstein. Finally, we get to the point where I can start talking about the first time I woke up in my basement. I have to explain precisely how my chain was fastened to the wall - screwed? Nailed? Was there a hook in the wall? Old or new? I try not to sound exasperated.

In between I also get to ask a few questions. I'd like to know more about our luxurious jet.

"Who's paying for this super sexy Falcon?"

Johnson shrugs. "The American taxpayer."

I stay on the topic because I have no desire for even more boring questions. "We have money for three engines made in France but not for a flight attendant?"

Next to me I perceive an almost inaudible chuckle, but maybe Dan was just clearing his throat.

Before Johnson can come back to the drilling techniques that are needed to chain me to a Baghdad wall, I say: "A brand new Dassault Falcon costs about forty million. Or did you get it on the cheap? Bought it from one of our Saudi friends?"

"No idea where we got the bird from", mutters Johnson. "If you use it often enough, it's like taking the bus. It's all about getting from point A to point B".

I giggle. *It's like taking the bus, my ass.*

"Where are we going, by the way?"

"Home", Johnson says and holds my gaze for a while as if to convince me that he's now telling the truth for a change.

I look out of the window a lot during this debriefing. Direct eye contact with Johnson is unpleasant. He has steely blue eyes, the kind of look that is reserved for Nazis or evil East Europeans in the movies. I wouldn't say that he has a piercing gaze but it's definitely more pleasant to look at the blue sky over the Middle East. After what feels like a thousand other intermediate questions we come to the point where I have to talk about my relationship with Khassem. Suddenly I find myself in a completely idiotic situation, something I couldn't have anticipated. If I don't want to lie, then that means that I have to tell Johnson how I kept Khassem happy. The problem is that I entertained my captor with lots of stories about Dan and Tim.

I feel hot and cold. My face must be a nice shade of red. Johnson does precisely what Gillespie has warned me about. He asks a lot of follow-up questions and just like before, insists that I describe all the details. There's no doubt that I will have to tell the whole story again tomorrow, and who knows how many other times. They're perfectly entitled to hook me up to a polygraph if they distrust me. I have no other choice than to do what I wanted to avoid at all costs.

I change an important aspect of my story. I give Tim and Dan new names. They are now Troy and Danny. While I'm talking to Johnson I keep reminding myself to stick to those names, no matter how tired and unfocused I might be at a later stage.

I don't see any recording device, but these things nowadays are so tiny that there's no point in looking for one. I change no other details of my story, and Johnson can soon no longer hide his astonishment.

"You manipulated those boys with real sex stories and then with stuff that you just made up? And it worked?"

I nod. "I was very, very lucky with Khassem. He never touched me although he was keen on getting to hear new stories. Maybe he was gay."

"Or maybe he was not that into you", Dan says so suddenly that I startle. Johnson looks at him with a puzzled expression.

I have to laugh for the first time today.

You arrogant piece of shit, I think. *I'm hot. The only reason you didn't try anything is that you prefer men.*

We refuel in Turkey. At least I think we are at Incirlik. I'm not sure my sense of time is still working. Dan pulls down the blinds just before we land. He does this on all windows, something that really annoys me. Why am I not supposed to see where we are? We're in a country where it's late afternoon. I'm hungry.

Johnson has left the plane, and I sincerely hope that he'll get run over by a truck. I'd like to spend the rest of the flight alone with my ex-fake-lover.

"Today is Monday, so this must be Hong Kong", I say to Dan. "I feel like a rock star."

"You *are* a rock star. Don't let it go to your head."

"Who do you really work for?"

I see Dan smile for the first time. "Does that matter?"

"Frankly, I don't give a damn. I just want to talk to you. Actually, I want to hear your voice. It's been a long time."

Dan looks at me thoughtfully. Before he can say anything, Johnson comes back and runs past us with several pizza boxes. I can hear him turn on the oven and putting our food in. My mouth starts watering. The pizza smell starts filling up the entire plane.

The pilots get out of the cockpit. They pick up their slices in the pantry and sit down at the other table. They wear no single piece of clothing that makes them recognizable as pilots.

"Okay", Johnson says as he wipes his mouth with a napkin. "Need a break." He yawns, collects our trash and gets rid of it in the pantry.

The pilots leave the aircraft. One of them nods goodbye to Dan. They get replaced by two young men who are also wearing civilian clothes. I hear them go through the checklist in the cockpit. Pilots have always fascinated me, especially fighter pilots of course. In Spang it was my biggest dream to make friends with one of the A-10 pilots. It never happened.

What kind of organization lets its pilots wear whatever they want?

Johnson chooses a seat in the front row and reclines it. He covers himself with a blanket.

Dan turns to me and asks: "Do you want to get some sleep?"

"Sure, why not." It takes a while until I've figured out how to recline my seat. I lean back and try to relax. Dan is more knowledgeable. He finds a part of the seat that can be drawn out to accommodate my legs. He reaches back and gets hold of a blanket that he covers me with. This isn't the first time he's using this plane, that much is clear. I'd like to kiss him for his kindness. Even though he is no longer as beautiful as he used to be. But I leave him alone.

I forget to ask where we are going. Maybe I shouldn't really care. As long as the small town of Lapwai appears at the end of the road, I do not care how exactly I get there.

The cabin lights are off, and it's almost completely dark. I doze with my eyes open. I'd love to watch a movie. I missed out on all the new stuff that came out in recent months. The only English-language movie I was allowed to see was the nightmarish *Taxi to the dark side*, an experience I won't forget so soon. I wonder how many people were at Bagram, like me, and know of this movie. Probably a grand total of zero.

We're jetting through the European airspace and the flight is as quiet as a slow drive on a freeway in an old Mercedes. I can't see Johnson's face because he's sitting one row ahead, but his snoring sounds like he passed out. Dan has closed his eyes. I try to do the same. While I'm dozing away my subconscious is looking for films that are comparable to the situation that I'm in right now. In the dream these films slowly transform into other stories. I always play the lead role. Everything that happens is accompanied by a perceived threat. There's some kind of danger looming ahead. I prepare for the worst. I run through the jungles of Borneo together with Jason Bourne, the CIA hot on our heels. Faces and places change as the dream develops into a full-blown nightmare until at some point I find myself in a huge corn field, staring upwards. A small jet is moving through the endless sky. Suddenly a door opens and a man falls from the plane. He crashes into the corn field. It takes much too long to find him. His body has burst like a watermelon, and the sweet smell of blood that I know so well fills the air.

"What?" Dan asks sleepily. He sits up and looks at me. "Nightmare?"

I nod. Dan gets up and fetches me a bottle of water.

I don't feel any thirst, just panic. I need to get out of this airplane.

"Hey, hey", Dan tries to calm me down while I hold the little Evian bottle to my mouth with trembling hands. I swallow and start coughing.

Johnson is awake now. He sticks his head in the space between the two seats, looking tired and surly. "Are you guys okay on the cheap seats?"

Dan raises his thumb. Johnson goes back to sleep. Dan pulls our seats back to their original position. I put the empty bottle on the table and open the gray plastic blinds to see the night sky. A three-quarter moon shines silver light on to the clouds below. The sight is so heartbreakingly beautiful that I want to take a picture of it. I would send it to all those I love: my family, Jesse, David, Robert and Kyle, Tim even.

Dan switches on a small reading lamp above his head. I turn to him in the hope that I can calm down just by looking at him. I should be feeling safe sitting next to him. He's leafing through a magazine. He doesn't move when my mouth comes close to his ear.

"Just tell me who you're working for. I know that Johnson is lying." Whispering in his ear feels good. It's like we're involved in a very big conspiracy. "If you don't tell me, then I'll tell Johnson all the stuff I found out about you at Bagram."

Dan looks unimpressed.

"The problem is, our organization is so new that it still has no name."

"Then why don't you call yourself OPSEC", I say, unable to conceal my frustration. I don't care if Johnson notices that we're arguing.

I look out the window. The dark sky is even more beautiful than before. Thousands of stars have joined the moon. I know that we're not on our way to Ramstein because we've been in the air for too long now. If I'm not mistaken, we refueled at Incirlik for our transatlantic flight.

I don't believe Dan. I'm no expert on national security, but I know one thing: there are so many different agencies that our authorities are struggling to coordinate their work and not completely lose track of who's doing what. Why would someone in the government come up with the idea to establish another service?

It's more likely that Dan now belongs to a subunit that prefers to operate under the radar. That kind of thing has always existed: field agents whose names don't show up in any files. Guys that are allowed to play by special rules. For once I didn't get this knowledge from Hollywood movies, but from a book that Kyle loaned me in Texas.

If even half the allegations in this book are true, then those agents are free to do as they please as long as they deliver results. Torture was never a problem for the CIA or even for military advisers to foreign governments. These days, it's also legit to terminate someone.

What would happen if someone managed to open the door in mid-flight?

With all the effort I can muster I push those thoughts aside. The last thing I need is an acute case of paranoia. Nobody wants to kill me. I'm sitting in this comfortable jet on my way to my home country where I will fall into my family's arms.

They can't make me disappear. After all I met and interacted with a lot of people at the FOB. The Humvee guys, the Colonel who took my 9-mil, the MPs who walked me to the chow hall, and then there were also people who noticed me. If I were to disappear, then Gillespie would one day start wondering why I never came to pick up my stuff.

I hear soft voices though, they're telling me to distrust my own reasoning. They're almost like children's voices, casting doubts on the way I'm trying to reassure myself. I try not to listen.

Can I trust Gillespie?

Maybe he dutifully handed over my stuff to the Colonel because he wants nothing to do with this matter. Actually it's more likely that he simply destroyed the equipment. Nobody would ask him what happened to the stuff because after all, nobody knows of its existence. Gillespie would go home to his family and begin a new chapter in his life. And if I don't show up, he will certainly not make any inquiries.

Of course there are quite a few other people who saw me yesterday. There's a question that gives me an unpleasant feeling in my stomach. How many of these people would notice if they never heard from me ever again? If my name was never mentioned in the media?

I wasn't a celebrity while I was missing. Even though I didn't manage to google myself yet, I'm pretty sure that only people from my unit knew, that there is a Marina Laroque who disappeared in Baghdad without a trace.

The only people expecting my return are my family and David. Because they know from me personally that I'm coming back.

Everything will be fine. I should stop worrying.

I do some breathing exercises to get my pulse down. Johnson has now woken up and is stretching all his limbs.

I reach for the magazine that Dan put on the table. His eyes are closed again.

The magazine cover displays the latest mobile phone models. I wonder how they manage to fill an entire magazine with reports on smartphones. Somewhere in the middle I come across the model that Saad owned. I can't concentrate on the text myself, but anyway it's almost too dark to decipher anything.

My mother started crying when she heard my voice. I hope she's doing okay now.

My stomach feels heavy and cramped. I feel the blood tingling through my veins. My hands can barely hold the magazine, and I lay it back on the table.

If I disappear my family would move heaven and hell to find out where I ended up. If the government tried to cover up, the press would remain as a last resort.

But who would believe my mum if she said that she heard my voice on the phone?

I let down the blinds again. The moon is no longer visible. The sight of the pitch black night sky is like a threat. We're so high up that we're almost in space.

There is written proof that I am still alive. The message I sent to David.

He would eventually start investigating. But how hard is it to make an email disappear? For someone like me it's impossible, but the hackers of the NSA will have no problems with that.

Drenched in sweat, I stare at the empty seat across from me. My gaze wanders to the small plastic bottle wobbling on the table. Dan is quietly breathing beside me. He's asleep. He doesn't worry about me and my nightmares. He never cared about me. At Bagram I helped him keep up his straight cover. He got from me what he needed. And that's it.

Now I'm just something that has to dealt with discreetly.

The magazine is still open on the last page I tried to read. Saad's iPhone looks at me reproachfully as if to say: *why did you leave me behind*?

Johnson gets up and walks past us to the bathroom.

Dude, you just made the biggest mistake of your life.

As soon as the bathroom door closes, I jump out of my seat. Dan wakes up and gives me a confused look.

I've had to do some MMA before being deployed to Iraq. I know how to strangle Dan so that he loses consciousness right away. What we didn't learn is how to get a man out of his airplane seat before putting him in a stranglehold. I can hardly position myself directly in front of him because the table is kind of in the way. Since a frontal attack is not possible, I punch him in the right side of his face. He collapses right away.

The pilots did not hear the blow. Through the open cockpit door I can see the tiny lights flashing on the dashboard. The Dassault

Falcon can be flown by a monkey. My guess is that the autopilot is on, and the two are taking a nap.

I turn my attention back to Dan. He's wearing a casual brown linen jacket that I search to find his cell phone. That's the plan: call someone and make sure that Johnson will notice. Then they won't dare to make me disappear.

I don't find a phone, and cursing softly under my breath I feel the cool metal handle of a small handgun under Dan's left armpit. I look around. The pilots are doing their jobs or playing something on their laptops or sleeping. The toilet door is still closed.

Carefully I pull the gun from the holster, a nice little Beretta. It's loaded. I release the safety and jump forward to where Johnson was sleeping before he got up. His jacket is on the other seat. Under the carefully folded jacket I find his weapon, the same model as the one that was taken from me in Baghdad.

And that is the second biggest mistake of your life, you stupid fuck.

I sit down on the seat across from Dan. In order to feel his pulse I have to reach over the table and even get up. His torso is slumped to the side, and I have to make some contorted movements with the weapon in my hand until I can put a finger to his neck. He is actually still alive.

The toilet door opens softly. Johnson approaches and looks a little surprised because I changed seats. His gaze wanders to my right hand. I'm pointing the gun at his midsection. He stops abruptly.

"Sit down next to Dan", I say quietly, pointing to seat at the window.

Johnson hesitates. With my left I pull the gun that I had been hiding behind my back. "Safety's off on the Beretta but not yet on the Sig", I say coolly.

Johnson's face has an unhealthy green color now, but maybe that's from the greenish emergency lights above us. He can certainly see his career going down the drain. He stiffly squeezes himself past Dan to get to the window seat.

"I don't care about your real name", I say. "And I don't give a shit anymore who you work for. But I want to know where we're going."

"DC." His voice is hoarse.

"Where did we refuel?"

Johnson hesitates again.

"Lie to me, and I'll knock you out just like Dan."

"It was not my idea to lie to you and to use fake names", Johnson says, struggling to maintain his composure. This is probably the first time that someone is threatening him with his own weapon.

The first time is always the best. This is what Robert once said. Or Kyle. I start laughing and before I know it, I go off into hysterics. I laugh so hard there are actually tears running down my face. The Beretta is shaking in my right hand, and when I lean forward, my left hand almost drops the Sig. I get a hold of myself before Johnson or whatever his name is can take advantage of the situation.

Never in my life have I felt so good. Everything and everyone is under my control. The world is at my feet.

"Where - did - we – refuel?" I ask now for the second time, this time I speak extra loud as if Johnson had a hearing problem.

"Lakenheath."

"What? Then we're almost there?" I have totally underestimated how fast we are. We even left Ireland behind us. We can be in Canadian airspace pretty soon. I need to think fast now.

DC is out of the question. I have the right to see my family now, not after Johnson and his colleagues debriefed me for three days and after I've described for the hundredth time which type of cordless drill my kidnappers used to chain me to the wall.

I want to go home.

If we filled up completely in England, the kerosene might last all the way to Idaho.

"Listen", I say to Johnson.

"You go to the cockpit, and I follow you. You're talking loud and clear, so that I can hear everything."

Before I can explain what I want, Johnson snorts. "You're not seriously about to hijack this plane?"

The problem is that my opponent doesn't take me seriously. Why should he? He thinks that I'm a confused little girl.

He's not going to follow my orders just like that.

I have to think of something, but I'm too tense to develop new ideas. Maybe alcohol will relax me. I always have great ideas when I'm chilling.

"Fetch us three beers. On this occasion you close the door to the cockpit. If I see that you're talking to the pilot I'm going to shoot you in the back of your head."

It's as if I could read minds: Johnson still doesn't believe me. At an altitude of thirty thousand feet a single shot can crash the aircraft. I guess I don't look suicidal enough for that.

I try one more time to convince him of how dangerous I am. "I'd rather take a dive in the Atlantic with this jet than fly to Washington."

It's not working. Scare the crap out of him, Marina.

My head is empty. Maybe I would need to beat Johnson up in order to impress him. That would be too difficult because I would have to lay down the guns somewhere. And the pilots would hear us. These are the people that I don't want to involve in this. They're just supposed to change the destination on our orders. It's not my intention to land in Lewiston and go to jail.

Dan moans. He struggles to get his upper body in an upright position. His right cheek is swollen.

I gaze at him in the same friendly way that a flight attendant would. "A-Salam Aleikum."

Dan stares at me with his mouth open. "Wa - Aleikum - Asalam."

For the first time, I put my finger on the trigger. The others are watching this little move with nothing less than fascination.

"Time to pray", I say. Then I recite an Arabic poem. It was written a few years ago by Tunisian resistance fighters. It's about injustice and peaceful revolution and what not. And it's definitely not a prayer. I'm confident that the two will not notice the difference. I speak very softly so as not to scare the pilots.

Despite the emergency lighting, I can see that Johnson is as pale as a ghost. He's sharing a plane with a jihadist who has not only stolen his gun, but is also certainly speaking the death prayer.

"Shall I bring beer?" Johnson jumps up, and Dan is watching him in horror. To Dan it must look as Johnson has lost his mind, too.

"Good idea", I say. I follow every movement he makes. Johnson slams the refrigerator door, making one of the pilots flinch. He rushes back to our table with three bottles and then abruptly returns because he forgot to close the door to the cockpit. This, too, he does in the most hectic way possible, but I decide not to worry too much about what the pilots will think.

"Aircraft from France, beer from Ireland. We're living the international jet-set lifestyle", I say after the first sip. I guess right now I look as satisfied and calm as if we were sitting in a bar somewhere.

Dan finishes the beer in under a minute whereas Johnson hasn't even opened his can yet. The cabin begins to smell like cold sweat, and that's a good thing.

"We're running out of time here", I explain. "I need some information from the pilot. In principle this jet has enough range so that you can drop me off right outside the front door of my home in Lapwai, Idaho. But the question is whether we need to fill up again. These are things I need to know before I can take a decision."

Johnson has listened closely. He looks very focused. He contradicts me immediately.

"We definitely have enough fuel only for the flight to DC. Idaho, that's well over 2000 miles extra. No flight captain would fill up completely if it's not necessary. Why should we increase our flight weight if there's no need for it?"

Johnson looks very happy. His objection is legit.

I show him a friendly nod. "In a commercial airliner it's clear that we would only have as much fuel as we need. They have to be cost efficient and all that. But if the American taxpayer is footing the bill, not so much."

"Nevertheless. We definitely need to refuel if we want to make it to the Northwest."

"Maybe", I say. "That wouldn't be the end of the world. I gotta admit that I don't like the idea of a stopover. But we'll find out when you ask the captain."

Johnson is visibly trying to think up something, anything to stop me. He won't give up so fast.

"You get to the cockpit and I'm right behind you, and if the captain says that it's enough to get to Idaho, then that's what we do", I say. "The airport is called Lewiston- Nez Perce County Regional Airport. LWS. It's that simple."

"Not possible!" Johnson's eyes are shining as if he was celebrating his greatest triumph. "We gave up our flight plan hours ago. If we suddenly change it, all alarm systems are go."

He laughs happily. "I'd like to see your face when you look out the window and see the F-16 at close range."

"He's right, Marina", Dan says softly. Although he's sitting straight across from me he manages to look past me.

"If you want to see your parents and your grandmother again, you should come with us to DC. It's just a few days. You can do this. Don't be afraid. There's no reason to be afraid."

Dan actually dares to mention my grandmother. I feel cold fury crawl up my back until it makes my scalp tingle. This asshole can still remember what I told him about my grandmother. And he really thinks he can use that knowledge against me.

"Look at me", I say. Dan obviously has a hard time to look me in the eyes. "You know better than that. We are not some Delta Airlines flight. This is a government plane. The normal rules don't apply to a flight that's classified as "STATE". All we have to do is file a diversion. No air traffic controller will raise the alarms. If we request diversion, ATC is going to ask for a reason. The captain says that we received a changed mission status, and that's it. I know this, you know this, Johnson - or whatever his real name is - knows it too."

Slam Dunk.

Knowledge is power. It pays off now that I've always been interested in international aviation and its procedures. Hell, I even used to hang out with plane spotters. I often talked about such things with my co-workers. Dan and Johnson are certainly racking their heads for counterarguments.

"Dan, switch the cabin light on. I don't want to stumble on my way to the cockpit. At least not with a cocked gun in his hand."

Dan stands up. He finds a switch. It's uncomfortably bright in the cabin, and he sits back down, looking completely exhausted.

"Johnson, tie him up."

Johnson pretends to be surprised. "With what? I got nothing here."

If looks could kill, Johnson's body would be slumping in his seat, lifeless. After a tense moment of silence, Dan digs out zip ties from his jacket pocket and hands them over to Johnson. I watch Johnson cuff Dan's hands behind his back and for the first time, I wonder how much jail time you get for threatening a federal agent with a gun. And if you get twice that for threatening two federal agents. Of course then there's also the question if it makes a difference whether I threatened CIA or FBI or DoD employees. In fact I have not only threatened, but also kidnapped these people. I try to push these thoughts aside immediately.

Johnson proceeds to have a conversation with the pilots - I don't need to press the Beretta into his back; he knows it's there. We don't have enough fuel for a direct flight to Lewiston. The Captain suggests refueling in Chicago. Johnson turns to me to get my approval. I nod. With a calm voice Johnson asks the Captain to file a diversion message.

Dan gets relieved of the cuffs. I'd like to take a nap but that's obviously out of the question. For my own safety it's better to leave the lights on, even though my eyes hurt. I keep focusing on my surrounding. I won't allow my weariness to take over. I send Johnson to the pantry for supplies. Water for me, whiskey for my guests.

"At last something Made in the US", I say as Johnson slams a bottle of Jack Daniels on the table.

I ask Dan to get some ice - because I can. I don't care if they drink their whiskey on the rocks. This is just a matter of wielding power, as long as I'm the one in charge.

I enjoy the frustrated looks of my prisoners. I think I would be a terribly power-hungry dictator. Who knows, maybe I would be bloodthirsty as well.

"We don't drink alcohol on duty", Johnson complains.

"And I don't really like whiskey", Dan bitches. "Can I have another beer instead?"

I point the gun at the tumblers and say to Johnson: "Pour. Drink. Shut up."

We land at Midway, not O'Hare. I try to ignore my heart palpitations as we touch down. This time the blinds stay up. I want to see what's outside, even if it's just the runway lights and the illuminated terminals in the distance. This is my country. This is where I belong, and just as I start feeling safe again, the pilots come out of the cockpit and ask us to step off the plane.

Oh fuck no.

My victims are watching me. I can see hope gleaming in Johnson's eyes. But I focus on my breathing.

"Why do we need to get off the plane?" I ask, my voice sounding perfectly calm.
"That's a safety precaution during refueling. If we had some really strong reasons to stay inside, they would have to send a fire truck just in case."

Don't fuck this up, Marina. It's all good. They're just doing their jobs. Standard procedure.

I'm wearing Dan's jacket, a gun in each pocket. Of course Dan and Johnson hesitate. It would be so great for them if I went out first. All they would have to do is give me a push, and I would fall down the stairs. I motion with my head to ensure they go first.

I step onto American soil, making sure there's enough distance between me and the others. We stand on the tarmac, and I breathe in American air. I can't believe I'm back.

The fuel truck is silver. The deafening noise level of the truck pumping kerosene into our wings makes it impossible to have a conversation. We just watch while the pilots take a tour around the plane.

All the tension falls off as the three engines push us into the night sky. The last time I saw daylight was shortly before we landed in England. My sense of time is completely screwed up. Sometimes when I look out the window and dream with my eyes open, it seems to me as if I'd been in the air for days.

I'm so tired. I can only hope I'll still be able to step down the gangway when I arrive.

"Oh shit", I curse. Dan, who was dozing a little, is wide awake again. Johnson gives me a sullen look.

I haven't prepared anything for my return. My parents have no idea that I'm almost there.

"Your phone", I say to Johnson. "And don't tell me you don't have a

SAT phone."

Johnson sighs. "Encrypted, password-secured. Forget it, girl. And you don't need to threaten me with that gun because you're not going to shoot in the next couple of hours. You're almost home."

Of course he's right. It's infuriating. Incensed, I get up and knock the Beretta into his nose. Johnson doesn't even moan. He visibly clenches his teeth as he tries to wipe the blood from his face.

A tough guy, I think.

I draw another zip tie from Dan's linen jacket. Dan understands immediately. He looks more than weary as he turns to the side and ties Johnson's hands.

Then I aim the gun at a point between Dan's eyes and say quietly: "I do not think that you want to follow me into the cockpit."

I open the door carefully. The Captain smiles at me. He doesn't look as tired as he must be after more than ten hours in the cockpit. I tell him that my colleague's satellite phone is discharged. The copilot lends me his phone without asking. There's nothing normal about these two dudes. Not only do they not bother wearing uniforms, they actually carry sat phones with them. Maybe that's why they're not really curious about their somewhat unusual passengers.

It must be about nine PM, everyone should be home. My father picks up the phone. I take a deep breath so that he almost hangs up, and I announce my imminent arrival. Twice I have to confirm that I am very, very well. I'm just about to finish the conversation as I have a brilliant idea. I ask my father to get in touch with the mayor, the airport management, the chief editor of the local TV station (whose name I have completely forgotten), and also the tribal police.

He probably thinks I've lost my mind. But I don't have the nerve to explain to him that all these precautions will ensure that I can actually reunite with my family. If nobody is present at our landing, I'll get arrested on the plane, and I'll disappear in a county jail. But if there's a TV crew filming the return of a freed hostage, they won't be able to do anything. I'm some kind of war hero, more or less. Anything else would be embarrassing.

I give the copilot the phone back and thank him profusely. I know I'm radiating total happiness right now. I softly close the cockpit door. The last thing I want to do is to sit with my victims, but the last hour of this drama is something that I simply must endure now.

"Well, how's it going?" I ask, my voice cheerful and my mind fresh. I sit down next to Dan, who, unlike me, looks like he's about to pass out.

"Can I remove Johnson's handcuffs?"

"Nope."

Dan is confused. "Why not?"

I shrug. "Just because."

A grim silence fills the cabin. I scrutinize Dan's face. I wonder what made him age so fast. Did he spend all his time in a war zone?

"You know what?" I ask. "Johnson has to be tied up because he lied to me. As punishment. There was no reason to make up fake names. Or was there a reason?"

"Yes, there was." Dan sits up and puts his hands in his lap. "It was my idea. I wanted to unsettle you, because I knew that you know my real name. I wanted to make sure you don't feel too safe."

I'm not sure I really understand this. "You wanted to intimidate me by confusing me?"

Dan nods. "This is the best prerequisite for a successful interrogation. If you have the impression of not really being able to trust us, you won't dare lie to us."

"That's bullshit." I've never heard such nonsense. "Is that the newest interrogation doctrine? You get the best results from someone if the suspect likes you and trusts you. You gotta make him *want* to spill the beans. Oh and by the way. Who do you really work for?"

Johnson clears his throat. "We told you that. We're colleagues. Why do you not believe us, Marina?"

"Because Dan always used to laugh about the Air Force, that's why."

Dan laughs. "Good God, that was years ago. I just said those derogatory things to annoy you. And you took that seriously?"

A familiar sensation rises up: I feel like a complete idiot. Again. They gave me wrong names and I came up with the crazy idea that everything else they say is a lie. That they won't take me home. That they will throw me into the Atlantic Ocean.

Paranoia at its finest.

"Do you still have the ink?" Time to change the subject.

Dan nods. Johnson stares at Dan but doesn't dare to ask for details. In this couple, Dan is the war-weary badass motherfucker. Johnson is the neat government representative with gleaming white teeth and a republican haircut.

It's hardly noticeable. But there is no doubt: our cruising altitude is decreasing.

"Where is Tim?"

I want to look Dan in the eyes so that he can't lie to me.

Dan whispers, "You don't want to know."

I need to know it though.

"Tell me now." My lips briefly touch Dan's ear. Johnson sighs and closes his eyes to take a well-deserved nap.

Dan points his arm out the window.

"In heaven", he whispers and smiles.

I lean back in my seat and close my eyes. I wish I could get drunk now.

For years I've kept up the illusion that I would see him again someday. Maybe from a distance while he's traveling with his family. Or in one of those GoPro movies that troops make and then put on the Internet.

You always meet twice.

Sometimes I was sad because I knew that my hopes were unrealistic.

I feel Dan's eyes on me. As long as Johnson is dozing, I should try to find out as much as possible.

"How did he die?"

Dan shakes his head. "You don't want to know."

"Look, Dan. I just have to know what happened, okay? Even if it's something terrible. I've been worried about you guys for years. You gave me nothing back then, nothing. A simple mail address would have been enough. Just to check on you once a year - to verify that you're still alive. Last summer, a Chinook was shot down with thirty people on board, do you have any idea who terrifying that was? I didn't know if you or any of your buddies was on board."

"Fine", says Dan, sounding resigned. "I'm too tired to argue with you. He killed himself, and it was not so long ago. There was a huge funeral in Baton Rouge. His wife and his three children came, his mistress was there and a dozen ex-girlfriends. And all of us. Half the Marine Corps showed up. He left a horrific suicide note, and we had a hard time dissuading his father from reading it at the funeral. Worst day of my life."

Johnson is awake. He holds an ice cube to his bloody nose and looks out the window.

After a while I ask the question that I really don't want to be asking: "Why?"

"He felt he wasn't able to protect us. There were too many losses. We always had to work with the locals. Most were decent people. But some of them worked for the other side. They all had cell phones. There was no-one stopping them from calling their Taliban cousins."

Dan makes a lot of sense. And yet.

It's appalling. I cannot comprehend how someone like Tim could put an end to his life. He knew how the loss of a loved one feels - how could he do that to his children?

We fly through the clouds. The plane vibrates, fighting the resistance in the air surrounding it. The clouds do not agree with our five hundred miles an hour push through tiny drops of water.

"I want to see the suicide note."

Dan looks at me as if I'd lost my mind. But this is what he must have been thinking for a while now. Ever since he came to with the right side of his face swelling up and hurting.

"I need to understand", I say. "I know I'm not entitled to anything here. But I loved him. I want to at least try to understand it."

I see some lights below us. I have no idea what town is underneath us. Spokane? It looks lovely.

"Dan, how come you're here? I almost got a heart attack when I recognized you."

Dan opens his eyes. "Actually, Johnson was supposed to get you together with someone else. But I heard about your miraculous return when I was on an aircraft carrier in the Gulf. I moved heaven and earth so I could be there."

Johnson takes another ice cube out of his tumbler. "How did you convince your boss?"

"I don't remember exactly." Dan thinks. "I think I told him that I could get more out of you than anyone else."

"But you didn't interrogate me, Johnson did."

Dan nods. "At first, it was Johnson's turn. Then it was my job to take you completely apart. We were pretty sure that you wouldn't tell us the whole story right away."

How incredibly complicated, I think.

If Johnson had shown up with someone else, the two would have just done their job. They would have started debriefing me properly. Everything would have gone smoothly. This whole hijacking would never have happened.

We have a soft landing, and I can feel the power of the engines now working in full reverse thrust. We quickly roll toward the terminal.

"Give Johnson back his freedom", I say to Dan. He cuts through the cuffs with a pocket knife.

Johnson shoots me an angry gaze, massaging his wrists.

Solemnly I hand the weapons back to their owners. I really shouldn't be grinning.

"Who's going to open the door if we have no flight attendant on board?" I ask. Outside I see a few cars on the runway, including a patrol car with flashing lights.

A small gangway rolls toward us. The copilot runs past us to the door and opens it for us.

I'd have to jump out of my seat now. I should be sprinting down the stairs like a lunatic. I should run across the tarmac and jump straight into the arms of my parents. Instead I'm paralyzed in my leather seat, waiting for something to happen.

"Oh God", Johnson whispers, looking intently out the window. "Hernandez was faster than us."

"What", Dan asks. He sounds horrified. "Hernandez is here?"

Johnson nods, turns away from the window and leans back. "Our boss", he tells me.

"Not true", says Dan. "The boss of the boss of our boss."

"This is the end", Johnson says with his eyes closed.

Dan looks at me with an expression of resignation. "Thank you, Marina. You have opened the gate to hell."

"Why?" I ask, although I can imagine the answer.

Johnson leaves his eyes closed. "Hernandez is the four horsemen of the apocalypse all rolled into one."

That's not good. Not that I care. A distinguished man with graying hair bounces up the gangway and swiftly enters the cabin, followed by a young man. They wear very nice suits. They stand in front of our seats and look down on us.

The older man doesn't look at me while the other one can't hide his curiosity. He's almost smiling.

"You let this little Indian girl take control of an entire plane", Hernandez says softly. "If I'm not mistaken you let her beat you up. This girl who just recently joined our agency."

It's true that Johnson and Dan don't look too good, Johnson with his bloody nose and Dan with the swollen cheek that's started taking on an interesting color.

"We're not a taxi company, you know", Hernandez continues. "We're not social services either. It's not our job to return runaways to their parents. We're a law enforcement agency. We interrogate suspects as long as it takes. Even if it's our own people."

Dan and his colleague are listening closely. Hernandez is not the slightest bit agitated, and his anger is barely audible.

"So there I was, having dinner with some brass in a really great place in Nevada. When all of a sudden the manager of the restaurant comes in and slips me a phone number to call urgently. Someone in the DC office tells me there was a flight diversion. And what's the new destination, I ask. No idea. So that was the end of my nice dinner."

I can hear the pilots doing their final checks. I guess they're preparing to leave. There's no noise from the outside, but I feel some humid Idaho air coming through the open door.

Hernandez is far from done. "Do you have any idea how difficult it is to locate the right person at the FAA? The one dispatcher who can look up the new flight destination filed by the pilots after you refueled in Chicago? Must've been a dozen phone calls while the others were enjoying their dessert. Incredibly, I managed to organize a jet that took me from Vegas to this shithole."

Okay, now he's angry. But it's not the boiling rage that makes people do stupid things. It's the cold and controlled disappointment of someone who won't let his frustrations impair his judgment.

"I'll have to sweep this thing under the rug in order to keep you in the service. Not that I want to keep you. Of course you should get fired. But I don't have the patience to get all the paperwork done just to get rid of you two idiots."

I can almost feel a spark of hope igniting the air. Dan and Johnson are still frozen, waiting for Hernandez' speech to come to an end.

Hernandez' sharp suit is a little shiny, as if someone had woven a silver thread into the fabric. I wouldn't be surprised if he'd paid a few months' salary for it. He exudes the kind of self-confidence that fills the whole room.

"What happened here will have to stay here", Hernandez continues. "It's an incredible embarrassment that would otherwise fall back on all of us. Our reputation is more important than anything else. And I have no desire to see the Pentagon cut our budget in half just because my people are incapable of transporting a clueless little aircraft mechanic from one airport to another."

I like the way he keeps insulting me without making the effort to look at me – not even once. And the way he lays into his subordinates without even raising his voice. He has an attitude. And he has something else.

Power. Knowledge. Experience.

I imagine what it would be like if I could display as much confidence in twenty years as Hernandez does now. If I could hop into a business jet with the same gusto and if I could fill a designer suit with the same ease. I have good reasons to believe that his clothes are concealing a body steeled by many marathons.

It would be nice if I could just get up and go now. But I guess I'm supposed to act as a mute spectator until Hernandez' great show of intimidation is over. So I make the best of it by trying to memorize every detail of this historic moment. Maybe I can learn something here.

"The pilots are allowed to get back to work in twelve hours from now, and I couldn't get a last-minute replacement", Hernandez says and studies the magazine on the table. "Which means that all of us - except the girl - need to check into a hotel. In other words, it's due to your utter incompetence that I am forced to spend a night in Idaho."

Again Hernandez just stated the facts, again without showing any emotions, but now I think I can distinguish cold fury in his voice. He pronounces the word "Idaho" as if it's a particularly nasty sexually transmitted disease. I have never felt so much electrical charge in a room. I hope I can get out of here before he explodes.

Johnson stares straight ahead, but Dan is braver. He dares to look our top boss in the eyes. I don't know how many dangerous missions Dan was on. In Afghanistan. And probably in Iraq, too. Certainly he was in a situation more than once where he had to use his weapon. He put his life on the line, suffered from constant sleep deprivation and had to take split-second decisions. There must have been some close calls. Dan is pretty much as hard as it gets. But he has to let Hernandez humiliate him right in front of me.

After what seems like an eternity of strained silence, Hernandez' assistant is allowed to say something. The young man gives me a friendly nod.

"You can go now. Meet your family."

My heart makes a huge leap as if it wanted to jump out of my chest and get out of this damn plane even before I do.

For the first time since he walked into our lives, Hernandez makes direct eye contact with me.

"You say two or three sentences to the journalists. You give no interviews. Go home. In a few days someone will pick you up. In the meantime, you maintain absolute silence about the events of the last twenty-four hours."

I nod. Cautiously I get up. I'm incredibly stiff and awkwardly take a step forward. Hernandez and his assistant move back a little so that

I can squeeze past them towards the exit.

Dan gets up, and Hernandez looks at him in surprise. I stop, waiting for Dan, who is rummaging for something in the left pocket of his pants. He has trouble digging out a piece of paper from the depths of his chinos. He presses it into my hand and closes my hand into a fist, as if he were afraid that I would otherwise lose the paper.

"Tim's farewell letter", he says flatly. "I don't want it anymore. You deal with it."

I feel the hand of Hernandez' minion on my back, gently trying to push me towards the exit.

I need to say something to Dan. But my mind is blank. The hand on my back is getting more insistent. Dan's green eyes bore into mine.

I only need a half turn. My right desert boot crashes into the leg of the young man. He lets out a groan and jumps to the side to evade my next kick. He collides with his boss and I really couldn't care less.

I put the letter in my pocket, and then I hug Dan so hard that he almost tips backwards. I bury my head between his neck and his shoulder. He gently pushes me back and kisses me on the forehead.

"I'm sorry for destroying your career", I say. What else could I possibly tell him.

"It's okay", he mutters. "I'll be fine."

For the last time I look at Dan. I turn around.

The next steps are easy. Cool night air comes my way. It smells like kerosene and rain. There are three figures in front of the patrol car of the tribal police...

I'm home.

GUILT IS GOOD

It takes five days until they come for me, and in this short week I have to convince my family that I'm not a hallucination. They can't believe I'm back. They have to touch me again and again just to make sure, and even my grandmother looks like she expects me to vanish into thin air anytime. Dad keeps asking me to pinch him.

"Ouch, that really hurt", he says every time with an expression of utmost satisfaction.

At night my mom sneaks into my room to check if my blanket is still covering me. She does this several times, every night.

I tell them about Gillespie and Saad and Khassem. I make it clear to them that my imprisonment was a walk in the park in comparison to the horrors that you'd normally expect in captivity. They nod and pretend to understand, but they're afraid to dig a little deeper. I don't think they believe a word I'm saying.

My mom wants to take me to a gynecologist, and I tell her for the hundredth time that nothing happened. As a result she starts crying. I have to comfort her for hours even though I'd much rather go running before the sun sets.

I spend as much time as possible in the open, taking long walks through the rez, jogging along the river and taking the old Ford along the highway. This new freedom is so overwhelming that I forget time and get back home completely exhausted and famished.

My own car is no longer available. My father sold it just weeks before my miraculous return. He's ashamed.

"I thought you wouldn't come back", he says in this small voice that he reserves for very bad events. He speaks so softly I have to ask him to repeat what he just said.

"That's okay", I try to cheer him up, but he's inconsolable. Because he gave up hope.

"You really couldn't know that I was alive", I say. "Not after all this time. I had a class on abduction last year. They told us that people don't come back after such a long time."

My father stares intently at the kitchen floor. "Except they do, Marina. You did. I could've waited. Your mum freaked out when she found out that I sold the Polo."

I don't know what to say and open the door of the dishwasher. I close it again and play with the buttons.

"Dad, you wanted to put an end to the waiting", I say. "That was justifiable. There was no reason to believe that I'd ever show up again."

He leans against the fridge and still doesn't look at me.

"At some point you have to be honest to yourself. Bury your illusions. I mean, look. There was no single sign of life of me after I disappeared. No terror organization claimed to have me. You wanted to start your new Marina-free life."

This last sentence was a mistake. The glass that my father was holding in his hand, ends up on the kitchen floor in a thousand pieces, and I spend the next two hours trying to convince him that everything is okay now.

Of course that's not entirely true. The suffering that I have brought upon my family can never be undone. It's a miracle that my grandmother didn't die of a broken heart and that my mother didn't lose her mind. I try to convince her that she no longer needs her happy pills, but she's afraid of what might happen if she goes off the drugs.

My bad conscience is something I can push aside at daytime, but it comes back with a vengeance at night. Ever since Gillespie told me how I got lost in Baghdad, I know that everything is my fault. I could have just stood around with the others while Gillespie was being medevaced. I would have returned to base with everybody else. I would have gotten a medal because I stayed calm in a combat situation and didn't let my Captain down.

What I did instead was run through the streets of Baghdad like a headless chicken, scaring the bejesus out of passers-by. I still had my sidearm. I don't even want to imagine what damage I could have done if I'd pulled the gun in my state of panic. I could have shot innocent Iraqis and ended up getting lynched by an angry mob.

I'm ashamed of my meltdown. But nobody gets it. The first thing I said on the tarmac of Lewiston airport was, "I'm sorry. I'm so sorry."

I said it over and over again when we were in the car. At home I asked for forgiveness again, but they had no idea what I was talking about.

"Sorry for what?" my mother asked. "For coming back?"

"I'm sorry that I did that to you", I kept explaining again and again. "I lost it and ran away. There was no reason for that. And there's no excuse for it."

Of course my family tries to convince me that it's not my fault. But I googled this. There seems to be no other case in which a soldier completely lost it during a firefight and just ran away. At least not in Afghanistan or Iraq.

Jesse seems to understand me though. We meet at the stables that belong to his brother, and while he's mucking horse stalls, he confirms my suspicion: I'm a wimp, and I'm totally unsuitable for combat ops.

"You freaked and then you lost your memory", Jesse says disapprovingly and rolls a wheelbarrow past me.

I follow him outside, towards the overpowering smell of manure coming from the muck hill.

"I know", I say. "The fact that I couldn't remember what happened at all, even months later, that's really killing me. How am I ever supposed to trust my brain again?"

"Don't", Jesse says. I want to strangle him. It's not really what I wanted to hear from him.

"That kind of shit happens when people are traumatized", Jesse says and tilts the wheelbarrow. A combination of straw and horse manure lands on the muck hill. We walk back to the stable. "But if just one single event has that effect on you, then you're not really made for this. I mean war and all that."

He pushes a lazy horse away and works through the straw with a pitchfork. The wet straw he shovels into the wheelbarrow, which fills up real fast. "But I don't really see why women should be part of a fighting force. These wars are completely unattractive anyway - even for all those guys who wanna go prove themselves."

"Unattractive", I repeat.

Jesse rolls the wheelbarrow out of the stall and closes the door behind him. He throws some fresh straw in and then moves on to the next stall.

"All these warriors dream of is firefights, picking insurgents off of trees like in *Generation Kill* and so on. Looking the enemy in the eye before you shoot him. Just like in the movies."

We make our way back to the muck hill. This time the wheelbarrow is so full that some dirty straw falls on the floor.

Jesse stops and wipes the sweat from his forehead. "What the guys get instead is sitting in uncomfortable vehicles all day and knowing they can be blown up any minute. They never get to see the enemy 'cause the enemy looks like all the other locals and hides among the population. And even when they manage to flatten a building with insurgents in it, they can never find out if maybe there were women and children inside. It's not like *Call of Duty*. It's just messy and frustrating."

I'm in awe. Jesse's psychoanalysis is spot on. I'm actually kind of proud to have such a smart friend.

"No wonder they all go crazy when they come back." Jesse is using a shovel to pile the manure up high. He needs to create more space for the muck that is yet to come.

"That's not true", I say. "We don't all get PTSD when we're back, not even all the people who were in combat arms. And all the others who experienced horrible things, like mortuary staff. Just because you went to war doesn't mean you lose your mind later."

"Oh yeah?" Jesse is leaning against the barn wall as he pulls his phone out of his pocket. He checks it and puts it back into his pants.

"Jesse, the mainstream media makes veterans look bad, as if every one of us was damaged goods when we redeploy. That's nonsense. Most of us find it hard to adapt at the beginning, and that's it."

"What about you?" Jesse puts his work gloves on and starts pushing the wheelbarrow back into the stable.

"Me? I have nothing. Some sleep problems, but I had those before."

"So I don't need to worry that you're going to kill yourself?"

Jesse asks this in a casual tone, as if we're talking about the weather.

"No, I'm fine. I'm just happy to be here again. And I'm enjoying my new freedom."

He grins at me, looking more than pleased. "I believe you", he says, and goes back to work.

Of course I haven't told him about Tim. And I don't tell him about the suicide note that scares me every night even though I haven't read it. The day will come when I have to read this letter.

"What are you doing here in Lapwai? There's no work in New York for you?"

With sweeping movements Jesse shovels new straw into a stall.

"Strangely enough, the work has moved here. I'm involved in a film project that's going to be produced here in Lapwai."

"A movie they're making here?" I ask. "Is that gonna be a documentary about us poor Indians? Alcoholism on the rez and stuff?"

Jesse takes off his work gloves. He shakes his head. "You're not going to believe this. Here in Lapwai, they're making a Western. With me, with my brothers, with our horses. It's going to be epic. Huge. Gigantic. To be honest I still can't believe it."

Jesse is leaning over a sink, washing his hands. He lets cold water run over his forearms to cool off. I dig out my car keys.

"So you mean, like a really old-fashioned Western with cowboys and cavalry and so on?" I ask.

Jesse nods. He walks me to the car. "What happened to your Volkswagen?"

"My dad sold it. But I'd like it back. I can't really make compromises when it comes to cars, you know", I explain.

Jesse laughs. "If this movie is a success, I'll buy you a new car. I'm so glad you're not dead."

We hug. It feels great. "You know what, Jesse? I'm also glad I'm not dead."

IN THE LION'S DEN

They pick me up at six AM, a man and a woman that I've never seen before. We fly to Washington in a beautiful Cessna Citation, and they set me up in a guesthouse in Quantico. This is a lifestyle I could get used to.

They debrief me in a sunlit room in one of the upper floors of an office building. It has a breathtaking view on the Potomac. I tell them in all detail what I've been up to in the last six months. I try hard to take the whole procedure seriously and attempt to leave the best possible impression of myself. Marina the pro. The reliable witness. The woman who was in control at all times. I rack my head in order to describe everything that happened as precisely as possible. Details include the color of the carpet, the brand of the TV set and absolutely any discernible sound that came in from the street. After three days of endless recollections and repetitions, I get restless. The frustration of telling people the same story over and over again is building up in me but I have no outlet. Spending every waking minute in closed spaces does not really help.

I try to loosen up the monotonous interrogations by cracking little jokes here and there. The agents are far from impressed and ignore everything that diverges from the questions they asked. I'm very suspicious of my colleagues. It seems to me that they're trying to starve me emotionally. They have very reserved reactions to my stories. I can't detect any signs of empathy, just professional curiosity. With all the crazy stories I have to tell I would expect to make someone laugh at least. But the only emotion that I see in the eyes of my audience from time to time, is astonishment.

After three days my interrogators are replaced by two robotic women who ask me exactly the same questions as their predecessors. We move into a neon-lit room in the basement of the building, and I get the feeling that this windowless room with its harsh light shining from above has a purpose. They're trying to get me out of my comfort zone.

The women begin to dig deeper. They want to know if I felt attracted to Saad and if I tried to seduce him. How I feel about his religion. Whether I would have been treated differently if I were held captive by Muslims. My motivation for learning Arabic.

Unsurprisingly they're interested in my Arab contacts in Germany and Texas. These are questions I had to answer before when I applied for a job with the AFOSI. In the mind of a federal agent, an American who befriends Moroccans or Egyptians is suspicious. I tell them about my Spangdahlem time, about Hassan's restaurant and his North African friends.

While I'm reliving my past again I try to look at the bright side of it. Maybe it's good for me to talk about everything I've done in the last decade. A therapy I don't even have to pay for. Get some closure. But for this I would need a sympathetic audience. That's not the case here. The women are always waiting for clues that they can use to dig deeper. It seems to me they're looking for my dark secrets.

But the only thing I keep secret is something they won't find. They ask me about the laptop bag more than once, and I keep the same expression on my face. My voice doesn't change. I don't start to fidget. I think I left the bag on the plane. It doesn't matter because the contents were not important. When I finally take the polygraph they ask about the contents of the bag again. I answer correctly by listing all the items that Gillespie put in.

They ride the same pony to death over and over again. They seem to think that I taught myself the Arabic language. I try to explain to them that this isn't really possible. The students I met in Texas gave me lessons in modern Egyptian Arabic at least twice a week for a period of more than one year. I took an intensive course for advanced students at a summer school in Minnesota. It ruined me financially but it was worth every penny. The Moroccans I knew in Germany even gave me homework to do, and they were serious about it. I read zillions of children's books and I searched the Internet for Arabic sound bites. An effort that kept me busy for half a decade. No pain, no gain.

My friends warned me about the various dialects spoken in the Arabic world. The Egyptians made it clear that their variant of the language was something that people outside of Egypt would understand, but not really speak. I figured if I ever needed the language it would be in Iraq. So I had to find Iraqi shows and TV series. At the beginning, I only managed to grasp a fraction of what was said in these shows. I'd been learning the language for years now. The more time I spent searching the web, the less confident I felt. My ambitions were fading away with every new obstacle I had to overcome. I was very close to giving up. Eventually I found a Kurdish family in Killeen who was willing to help. I went there every other weekend. The mother still spoke a Northern Iraqi dialect.

It's the lie detector test that shows me what they're really interested in. There's an astonishing amount of questions about my relationship with Dan. In previous sessions, I spoke frankly about everything that happened within my love triangle at Bagram. At the beginning I felt like a traitor when I told them about Dan's sexual orientation. But it was safe to assume that they already knew that. While the polygraph is scribbling lines on endless supply of printer paper, they suddenly want to know whether Dan and I were in touch between Bagram and the present time.

They distrust both of us, apparently. At least now I find out his last name. Since they never ask for Tim's suicide note, I guess neither Hernandez nor his assistant mentioned anything about it. I can imagine that those two didn't describe my flight back to the States in detail. They will definitely have censored the last minute before I got off the plane. The fact that I almost broke a federal agent's shin is not something to be proud of. I'm glad that nobody seems to know about this.

After ten days and several changes in my team of interrogators I'm done, physically and mentally. Twelve-hour sessions of sitting on my butt have ruined my circulation and of course my sleep; they don't even allow me to go for a run in the evenings. I feel like a prisoner. I believe that's what I am. I feel emotionally starved because no one ever says anything nice to me. I get so needy for human warmth that the friendly smiles of the cafeteria staff become the highlight of my day.

On day twelve we move back up. In the elevator I'm accompanied by a man who didn't bother introducing himself to me. He takes me to Hernandez' office and leaves.

"You don't look too good." Hernandez is sitting on a 1500-dollar chair that would easily accommodate two of him. He closes the laptop that's sitting on a shiny black desk and points to the chair I'm supposed to sit down on.

I'm done sitting. I walk over to the glass front. I get to see the Potomac again. It's named after the tribe of Patawomeck Indians, of which there are still a few hundred around. Survival is everything.

"Make yourself at home." That's Hernandez being sarcastic, I guess. I ignore him.

It's going to be a beautiful spring day. Two rowboats are moving on the river, full of young white men. They fearlessly glide through the water.

"Special Agent Laroque", says Hernandez.

I turn around to face him. "How much longer are you keeping me here?"

He doesn't smile. He exerts the same indifference that my interrogators did. "You're done. We took you apart and found nothing. Seems to me that you're nothing but a rebellious punk. And a particularly disrespectful member of our agency. If it were up to me, your time with the Air Force Office of Special Investigations would be over."

I sit down. The faster we finish this conversation, the sooner I get to go home.

"Did I pass the polygraph test?"

Hernandez nods.

"That means you'll have to get me back to work soon. I can't sit on my ass in Lapwai and continue to receive my salary without doing anything in return."

He's visibly irritated to hear me say "ass". I guess his minions don't really talk to him like that.

"Don't worry, we'll get in touch to give you a new assignment. Right now we want you to recover. You have a few months, and you should use them wisely. For self-reflection maybe. By the way, you don't solve problems by kicking colleagues when they're in your way."

I have no desire to talk about his assistant's bruised shin at the moment. I'm sure he survived.

"What's going to happen to Dan Navalny?" I ask. "You're not kicking him out, right?"

Hernandez' contempt for me is quite clear. He sounds as if it's beneath him to talk to me at all. "Your friend has moved to a very uninteresting department. We want to give him the opportunity to think about professional conduct at the workplace."

I look past him out the window. This situation is so incredibly unusual. I'm not sure why I'm sitting in Hernandez' office at all. Why should the head of an agency department take the time to say goodbye to someone as unimportant as me?

"I think I deserve a medal", I say abruptly. "I saved Captain Gillespie's life."

Hernandez nods. "They put you in for something but that's being handled by the Army. Might take a while."

We have nothing more to discuss. Hernandez' silence fills the room. I'm trying to count the crow's feet around his intelligent eyes. I'm sure they're much more pronounced when he laughs. But Hernandez doesn't look like someone who laughs a lot.

"You said earlier that you would kick me out if it were up to you."

Hernandez shrugs. "My personal opinion doesn't really matter here. People see some potential in you."

I'm confused. What people is he talking about? "Potential to do what?"

"Even more than what you've already accomplished."

"Accomplished", I blurt out. I must pull myself together. I will not jump up from my seat and freak out. "I can describe the hydraulics of the A-10 Thunderbolt in all details, but that's about it. Most of the things I learned in my training as a Special Agent, I couldn't even apply so far. So what accomplishments are we talking about?"

A miracle happens: Hernandez smiles. He shakes his head as if I'd just said something particularly stupid.

"You managed to fend off two confused wannabe hijackers. You survived long months in captivity without losing your mind or your fighting spirit. You hijacked a plane in such a discreet way that you're actually getting away with it."

True, I think. *He has pretty much summed up the achievements of the last half year of my career.*

"Besides", Hernandez continues and plays with his computer mouse without looking at me. "I have a lot of folks working under me who are bursting with ambition. Some of them with the finest university degrees this country has to offer. But few of them would have the stamina to acquire a very difficult language."

I shrug. "I was bilingual even before I started studying Arabic. My grandma taught me Nimipuu when I was a toddler. Long before I started school. So I guess my brain was already prepared for a new foreign language."

For the first time I see something like interest flicker in Hernandez' eyes.

"Maybe, but your command of this exotic language was the result of years of work. Your escape was quite spectacular too. Of course you were lucky. You jumped in front of a Humvee. They could've shot you to pieces. And the only reason you managed to free yourself in the first place was that a car bomb exploded in front of your basement."

"Nah, I'm sorry. I gotta make some corrections here", I say. Hernandez looks surprised. "I've had enough time to think about it. The idea to use the bed as a tool to break down the door, that's something that occurred to me after I used the bed to make my first attempt to break out of the window. But this whole door-opening thing is something I could've tried months earlier. For instance in the middle of the night when Saad or Khassem weren't around. What I want to say here is this: I could've left my prison much earlier. I came up with the idea of breaking down the door only after there was a hole in the wall. It's pathetic."

Hernandez turns the computer mouse in his hands. He looks at me, pondering what I've just said as if I'd tried to explain something very complicated.

"You're very critical of yourself", he says. "You constantly wonder what you could have done better. I must say this is the only character trait I like about you so far."

Whoa. Did he say 'like'?

"My family and also my unit and especially Gillespie, they suffered a lot. You can imagine what they went through. I could've saved them a huge pile of misery if I'd escaped earlier." Maybe it helps to talk about my feelings of guilt. It would be nice if I could just unload my guilt somewhere, just like Jesse unloads horseshit onto a muck hill.

Hernandez looks skeptical. "Suppose you escaped after two or three months of captivity. Where would you have gone? Without the tablet or the smartphone, it would've been suicidal to just err around in Baghdad."

His last remark makes the hair on my neck stand on end. I've completely forgotten that I truthfully described searching Al Jazeera on Saad's tablet. I also told the interrogators that I called my mother. No one bothered asking what I did with these devices. Somehow each of my interviewers seemed to assume that I left all that stuff in Saad's shop.

Hernandez looks at me with alert brown eyes. "Why didn't you take these items when you left?"

I have a feeling that his voice has become gentler. He's the big bad wolf who's trying to sound like a nice grandmother. My hands feel cold and then suddenly very hot.

I clear my throat. "I was still completely ecstatic because I was free all of a sudden", I say. "There was total chaos in my head. I couldn't think straight. And I was bursting with energy. I just wanted to get out of there."

Hernandez nods. Apparently he expected this response from me. "What's with the laptop? The night before, you were watching this movie together, and your captor left it in your room."

"True", I say quickly. "But I didn't switch it on because I already knew from the night before that there was no internet access. It was so old it didn't have WiFi. That's why it didn't even occur to me to take it. As I said, I just wanted to get away."

The boss of my boss of my boss leans back in his leather chair. I resist the temptation to go back to the window. I'd love to look at the river and the urban landscape that is so alien to me. I feel the physical urge to get moving, but I don't do anything. I've spent the last two weeks sitting on my butt, and I will survive the next two minutes. It's clear that our conversation is coming to an end.

Hernandez gets up and walks around the table. He stops in front of me. He puts his hands into the pockets of his expensive suit and looks down at me.

"The day after you left Iraq, Captain Gillespie handed in a tablet computer and a smartphone. The MPs seized the items. They belonged to a certain Marvin Abadi, who was injured in the blast and then disappeared off the face of the earth. We're still analyzing the data but there's as yet no reason to believe that Abadi was in touch with extremists or other insurgents."

There's no more air in my lungs. There's no air in this room.

Saad is alive.

Gillespie betrayed me.

My interrogators knew I was lying all the time.

Hernandez takes his hands out of his pockets and leans against the table, posing like a male Armani model. He's got the casual posture and the self-confident expression that you need if you're a model. I'm expecting the deathblow now.

"You're an excellent liar. I'm impressed. Manipulating other people seems to be your number one talent. But bullying an officer of the U.S. Army is a bit much. For once you may have overestimated your skills."

Hernandez is waiting a little with the deathblow. He's probably enjoying himself.

"But the way I see it, you're not going to make that mistake twice."

I get up and see how Hernandez' body tenses at once. I'm dangerously close to invading his personal space.

"Maybe I should just go home and fix cars again", I suggest.

And that's the second miracle for today: Hernandez laughs.

THERE IS A LIFE AFTER WAR

For reasons unknown to me, the deathblow doesn't come. I expect the worst every time I check our mailbox. But nothing happens.

I buy my car back and end up participating in a very strange film project. They hire me to get a group of amateur actors in shape. I decide to play the evil drill instructor that everyone knows from the movies. I teach those bums how to look good with a nineteenth century rifle. I invite Shelley to help me, the woman who sold me the lingerie in Denver. We'd kept in touch after my disastrous Rohrman experience and I must have exaggerated whenever I told her about my "interesting" life in the Air Force. It had the comical effect that Shelly eventually enlisted in the Army. Weirder things have happened.

Shelley stays with us for two weeks and enjoys her new life as aggressive instructor. She yells at the "recruits" until her voice stops working.

I tell her about my adventures in Baghdad. Even with her I get the impression that she doesn't believe me. If I told her right from the beginning that I was beaten and raped hundreds of times, I guess my story would be more credible.

I wasn't physically tortured during my captivity. But I went through hell anyway. At no point did it look as if I would ever leave my basement room alive. Although Saad (or Marvin) eventually began to make promises of letting me go, there was never a reason to believe that he would go through with it and drive me into the Green Zone. In the first weeks I nearly died of thirst, and the fear of a new dry spell accompanied me day and night throughout my captivity.

Fear is something you can't shake off easily. Even when the danger is gone. Fear is deeply ingrained in my body and soul, and it will remain there as long as it pleases. During the day I feel fantastic because I can do what I want. Things look different at night. I either toss and turn, or I wake up from a nightmare.

Most of my dreams have a recurring theme: the day I escaped. Very often I don't manage to break down the door. Out of sheer desperation I try my luck with the hole in the wall. More than once I get stuck in it and can neither move forward nor back. The man with the mangled leg is a permanent presence. I have no choice but to look at him because I'm stuck. Across the street I can see the burning car, but I always try to ignore the man inside. Normally I wake up after a while. But sometimes the nightmare is stronger. That's when I can no longer ignore the man who's burning to death.

Often I try to just stay awake after that. Whenever I watch TV or something on the Internet I try to avoid anything that reminds me of Baghdad. It's pretty easy to keep the war out of my thoughts. For the media, OIF is over and OEF is winding down.

It's strange that nobody here is talking about it. Several hundred service members died in the war last year. The mainstream media prefers to give us cat videos and the latest updates on celebrities getting arrested.

I get more picky over time. At least these days you can choose what you watch. I read milblogs and look up videos that were made by troops. My favorites are combat ops filmed by helmet cams. But I also enjoy the dance videos. A rifle-wielding Marine shaking his butt to Shakira, that's funny. It would have been great to find some footage of my old team at Bagram, with Robert and Kyle showing off their dance moves and still-intact David posing in front of the Hog. I guess no one came up with the idea.

The 'welcome home' videos are hard to watch. They show the homecoming of troops, but not in a traditional way. You see someone in cammies sneak up on his unsuspecting wife or children or parents. I watch the hysterical outburst of relief and joy with a mixture of dread and awe. I experienced it myself when I stood on the airfield of Lewiston and my father almost crushed me to death. Luckily no one was filming us. A sobbing bunch of Indians would look very uncool on the Internet. There was a TV crew present. We recorded a short interview that was aired on the local news. They showed me beaming at everyone, wiping a tear off my face and saying something about being grateful to God. This is the kind of stuff people want to hear.

David and I exchange cautious emails. I send him the TV footage of my arrival. He's still in Mannheim and won't be stateside anytime soon. He knows that I have a lot of free time at the moment, but he doesn't ask me to pay him a visit. Sometimes I don't think of him for days. Then something happens and completely throws me off the track. I hang out with a friend who is expecting her third child. While I have her firstborn on my lap I get overwhelmed by a memory that nearly takes my breath away. I remember how David and I were lying on his futon and we were visualizing what our children would be like. I have to hide in the bathroom for a while until I'm in control of my emotions.

My part in filming the Western comes to an end.

Shelley returns to Fort Benning.

I need to do something.

I decide to pay the traitor a visit.

MY BIGGEST FANBASE IS IN BOSTON

Gillespie is smart enough to protect his Facebook personality, but not smart enough to do this with his LinkedIn data. It's amazing how people can be so naive. Since I know his unit's location it doesn't take long until I can narrow down my search to four addresses that would make sense if he went to Boston University. That should be enough to find him. At least for me it shouldn't be a problem because I have something very valuable: time.

I drive to Boston in my beloved Polo, taking in the glorious landscapes of the U.S. of A. What a privilege to grow up here. I'm never going to say anything unpatriotic ever again. I'm not always in perfect sync with the traffic regulations though. 210 hp is no joke. I think it's good for the engine if I make it work a little harder once in a while. Luck is on my side. Not once do I get caught.

Address number three turns out to be the right one. At first I'd searched the affluent white suburbs. I'm surprised that the Captain and his family live in an apartment block close to downtown Boston.

It's not cheap to live in the city. There's a reception desk I cannot sneak past. The clerk calls upstairs, and while I'm waiting for the go-ahead I hope I've got the wrong Gillespie. All of a sudden I'm not sure what exactly I'm looking for here. Worse, I haven't prepared for what I'm going to tell him.

I guess it would be appropriate to yell some insults at him for a while and see how it goes.

I take a small lift and avoid looking in the mirror. I don't think I'm as determined as Lara Croft right now. The ninth floor has dark red carpeting. There are three apartments. My heartbeat is too loud. At the end of the corridor Gillespie rushes out the door and runs towards me.

"Holy shit", he says, crushing my upper body in a violent hug. "Holy shit!"

He allows me just a little bit of space so that I can breathe again, laying his hands on my shoulders and shaking me enthusiastically.

"What took you so long? I made it easy for you to find me!"

I'm too shocked to answer his question. He pulls me down the hall into the apartment. Two girls with long ginger hair and an impressive number of freckles are sitting on the couch.

Gillespie closes the door behind us. "Lissy, Drew: this is Marina Laroque, war hero."

The girls kill the TV sound, get up and come to meet me. They're both teenagers and shake my hand with the shyness of adolescents who don't feel comfortable in their own skin.

"These are Melissa and Drew, my red-haired stepchildren", Gillespie says, not without pride. "We've been living together for five years. We know each other inside out. And they know exactly what buttons to push to get what they want."

The girls are embarrassed by Gillespie's praise and take off into their rooms. Gillespie offers me orange juice, and we sit down on an elegant leather sofa that could easily accommodate five football pros. I sit down at the far end of it, but Gillespie has no intention to keep his distance. He makes himself comfortable right next to me. I had no idea he's such a cheeky asshole.

"Well, how have you been?" He's so cheerful it's irritating. "Did they take you completely apart in Quantico? And did you tell them about the bag and its contents?"

I drink all of the OJ at once. I can't believe this. Any normal person would start with small talk, but Gillespie immediately punches the hornet's nest with his fist.

"Come on, Marina", he says. "You're not here to hang out with me and talk about old times. We don't really have old times to talk about."

I put the glass on the table, leaning against the arm of the couch so that I can face him. It's a very comfortable piece of furniture.

"They didn't really ask me much about the stuff. For two weeks they pretended to know nothing of the two pieces of evidence that I kept secret from them. I could've said something of course. But I withheld that info. I really thought they had no idea."

"Wow", says Gillespie. "So you had two weeks to tell the truth. And now they know that you're a dedicated liar."

I nod. "They were testing me. They wanted to know how long I'd manage to conceal something that important. On the last day they told me."

"That's not good", says Gillespie, looking perplexed. "They know now that they can't trust you. What you've done is more than just a breach of duty."

"Yeah, no shit. If you'd just kept your promise I wouldn't be in this situation."

"You're absolutely right, Marina." Gillespie doesn't really look as if he had a guilty conscience. He doesn't seem to mind that I'm angry. "I got you into huge trouble."

"Right. You started talking about this. Let's get this conversation over with so that I can go home again. Why did you hand in the devices instead of smuggling them out of the country?"

Gillespie looks at me thoughtfully.

"Just tell me why you did it", I say. "You promised. I was totally relying on you."

Gillespie shakes his head, grinning. "That's not really what happened. You wanted me to smuggle the stuff for you. I never promised you jack shit. It's not good to lie to yourself."

I can't remember the last time I was so mad. I'd like to throw my empty glass at the TV. But Gillespie's home furnishings don't deserve my wrath because I'm actually angry at myself. I thought the Captain would follow my orders. In hindsight, I must have been delusional.

"Captain", I say, but he stops me.

"Marina, you know my name. I want to be addressed properly by you. Please."

"Fine", I say. "John, are you out now? You wanted to be a civilian again."

"Well, that's not so easy", he says and leans back. He has his eyes fixed on the TV. He picks up the remote from the coffee table and switches to a radio station. Monotonous Easy Listening music fills the room.

"Why is it difficult to turn your back to the military? That's what most people do."

John hesitates. He seems to deliberate how he can best explain his situation to me.

"Could be. But I don't have such great qualifications for the job market out there. My specialty is to blow things up and to lead men into battle. That's what I'm good at. Twelve-hour patrols in hundred-degree heat, without whining. Keeping eighteen-year-olds from accidentally shooting innocent people. Things like that."

"And that's not enough to get a job? Those are leadership skills, right?"

He laughs. "Sure I can lead men. But that's the only thing I'm good at. Probably because it's fun. Or because this was what I always wanted. If I try to find a job in corporate America, that's when the compromises start. I honestly don't know if I can do that to myself."

We sit in silence for a while. John is only a couple of years older than me.

"But the best time to get out is now", I say. "The older you get, the harder the transition is going to be. What does your wife say about this? I'm sure she wants you to get out, right?"

John looks at me and grins. "The problem is, I have the best wife in the world, and she says that it's my decision. Of course she would freak if I was sent into a war zone again, but that's unlikely. We're done with Iraq, and Afghanistan is turning into a playground for Special Forces."

I don't have anything to add to this.

Ambient music is wafting through the living room. It has a calming effect. I look around. I know I missed my chance to yell at Gillespie. I wanted to hurt his feelings by calling him a traitor. I decide to postpone this because I'm not able to be mad at him at the moment. The room has windows on three sides and is so large that it could accommodate half a tennis court. There's bright art on the wall we're facing. The paintings look as if someone had copied them from an old comic book. The furniture is modern and made from the kind of wood I don't know. But the most expensive thing about this apartment must be the location. It's safe to presume that only millionaires live in this neighborhood. There's no way an officer's salary can pay for all this.

"What does your wife do for a living?" I finally ask because our silence lasted a little too long.

John laughs. "You think she's the one footing the bill here? She works for a think tank in Washington, but I'm the one with the money. My family were big shots in the textile industry. In the nineteenth century, when this country was still producing stuff. Nowadays we all have clothes that were sewn by small children's hands in Asia."

The tried and true feeling of bewilderment and ignorance is back. I wish this wouldn't keep happening. I'm not on the same intellectual level as my conversation partner. I would love to say something cheeky to gloss over my inferiority complex but my head is empty.

"The next thing you have to ask me is how I ended up in the Army."

"True", I say and study the pattern of the carpet. It's almost the same color as my 50-dollar sneakers.

"I'm in the Army for the same reason as a lot of other folks. I wanted to serve my country. I had a sense of adventure. And adventure is what I got", he laughs, but he sounds strained. He can't only have fond memories of his time in the military.

I look up from my shoes and look him in the eye.

"Do you regret your time in the military?" I ask. "You could've spent those years in an Ivy League college instead of the sandbox."

"No, I regret nothing at all. I can't imagine what an undisciplined and weak person I'd be if I'd gone to Harvard Law."

"Why? The Harvard students gotta work hard to get their degree." I have to laugh about myself because it's absurd to defend elite students without knowing what I'm talking about. I've never seen a university from the inside.

"Yes, but the Harvard students don't know that you can go without sleep for thirty-six hours sometimes. That you can sleep on the cold desert sand at sub-zero temperatures – if you're just tired enough. That your mind eventually shuts down after you rolled past the hundredth roadside corpse, and you no longer register all the dead. That you can carry a two hundred pound man out of the kill zone even if you weigh less than the buddy you're carrying."

I contemplate what Gillespie is trying to tell me. "Sure, but perhaps the Harvard students don't even want to know."

"That's what my wife wants to change. After she met me she started taking an interest in military matters. And she came to the conclusion that there's too much of a disconnect between the military and the general population."

We're on unfamiliar territory again. I'd really like to say something about the state of our society. But I'm not so familiar with "normal" people. My friends outside the military are all Indians. We're pretty much the most exclusive minority in this country.

"I don't know much about the general population", I begin. "I can definitely confirm that there's a disconnect between me and the rest of the world. What I experienced is just too different from what I consider to be normal. Try to describe a place like Bagram. Or think of my strange relationship with the Arab man in general and in particular."

John laughs.

We hear someone unlock the door. We listen to the sounds of a key and a bag being dropped on a table.

A red-haired woman walks in. She stops next to the dining table, taking off a chic blue jacket and hanging it over a chair, without breaking eye contact. A huge smile spreads across her face.

"I know who you are", she says quietly. "You're Marina Laroque. Welcome to Boston."

They force me to stay for lunch. I get to witness a dispute that could not have taken place in my family: Melissa wants to go vegan, and her parents try to talk her out of it. A long discussion ensues about modern society's relationship with farm animals. About the importance of vitamin B12. And then on the political dimensions of the vegan movement. Lissy seems to have an encyclopedic knowledge of all the books that promote the vegan lifestyle. If I started this kind of discussion at home, my father would growl: "Idiotic hippie culture", and that would be it.

Drew tries to stay out of this. She's the elder of the two and looks pretty much like a college student. I ask her if she has graduated from school. She laughs and tells me that she's only fifteen.

I decide to keep my mouth shut. All I can do here is embarrass myself. Eventually the vegan discussion is over. It's Drew's turn to clear off the table. John brings dessert from the kitchen.

For the first time in my life, I eat ice cream made from chestnuts. It's not surprising that the upper class not only thinks differently, but also eats differently.

Welcome to the 1%, I think, and can't help giggling.

Margaret, John's wife, smiles at me. "Well, at least we're not too boring for you."

I shake my head. "I wasn't laughing about you guys. Just thinking of two former colleagues. They were both very funny. And I haven't seen them in like, forever."

"Maybe you should just go see them", Lissy suggests and blushes.

I nod. "I think that's what I'm going to do. I just need to first find out where they are now."

"How long are you staying in Boston", asks Margaret.

"I should get going. I came by car. Which means I'm going to have some stopovers until I'm home again."

Drew snorts, and there's a piece of ice cream that almost drops out of her mouth.

"You seriously believe they're going to let you go?"

I must look rather clueless. *What is she talking about?*

Margaret says: "I'm afraid Drew is right. You just got here. A couple of days is the least we can expect you to stay here. Come on. John says that you're enjoying a vacation of indefinite duration."

John nods in agreement. "You have no excuse for leaving right now. We have a guest room with a computer and a private bathroom. I'm sure Margaret will drag you all over Boston. She's very proud of her hometown."

I'm too astonished to fight back against this unexpected outbreak of hospitality. My plan was to make Gillespie regret that he betrayed me. Get some closure. Drive back to Idaho in anger. But my plans tend to completely transform into something else. So I resign myself to my fate.

In the afternoon Margaret and I take a guided city tour for tourists. She thinks this is the best way to get a feel for the city. We sit in a two-story open-air bus and get to see all the highlights. Then we go home and bake pizza together. We use strange things for the topping. The pizza looks horrible when we put in the oven, but tastes fantastic afterwards. Margaret and I have known each other only for a few hours, but we can chat as if we were old friends. The only other person with whom I had such an immediate connection was Tim. I push back that thought in the hope that it won't resurface too soon. There's a secret place for it in my brain. Everything I don't want to think of goes into exile right there.

It's just the three of us for dinner.

"The girls are at the movies", John says. "I hate it when they go out."

Margaret chuckles. "He's such a helicopter dad."

It occurs to me that today is Saturday. I can't remember the last time that I needed to know which day of the week it was. In my life, this is the kind of thing that's completely irrelevant. At least for the moment.

I have to reluctantly admit to myself that my hosts are adorable. I decide to entertain them with wild stories from my past. I'm not sure where to begin at first. If John and Margaret are to understand the plane hijacking, I have to tell them first about my Dan - Tim - Bagram past. Only then will they be able to grasp why I suffered an attack of paranoia during the flight.

It's not the first time that I talk about my three-way relationship at BAF. I've done it for Khassem. I also had to tell Johnson, carefully using the names "Danny" and "Troy", and then I had to tell the story to various people at Quantico. But it's something else to report to the Captain and his wife. It starts with the day I picked Tim off the street. John looks slightly embarrassed about my sexual exploits. Margaret grins.

"Sometimes I wonder what it's like to be young again", she sighs when I'm done with Bagram.

I leave out the normal life I had between my deployments and skip to my abduction. I sum it up in a few words. They don't ask questions. The critical part of my story starts with the helo flight and my reunion with Dan.

John is stunned.

"How unprofessional is that?" He scratches his head. "They send you an ex-lover to interrogate you? Even if he said that he's just your friend, I mean come on!"

I shrug. "In hindsight I guess it was a mistake. If they hadn't sent

Dan, I would've been picked up by agents I'd never seen before. I wouldn't have fallen into this insane panic mode. It was pure paranoia. I swear that for a moment, I was quite sure that these two wanted to throw me into the Atlantic Ocean."

Unsurprisingly John is more than appalled by the hijacking while his wife can no longer suppress her admiration for me.

"You thought you were James Bond for a moment", she says.

"But I was a pretty crazed James Bond", I correct her. "The real Bond wouldn't have had such a misunderstanding."

John looks at me dumbfounded. "I still don't understand how you came up with the idea that these two would open the door in mid-flight and push you out."

I laugh. "You know what? When I thought about it later, it occurred to me that I saw this in a movie. Matt Damon was the bad guy, and someone was thrown out of a plane on his orders. It was really shocking."

After dinner I feel tired for the first time. I park the Polo next to John's Lexus in the garage, get my stuff out of the car and place it in a guest room that could rival any five-star hotel room. The computer is a huge iMac.

We sit on the couch. John is drinking water, Margaret whiskey, and I ask for a glass of Chardonnay so that I'd have the opportunity to pronounce the word "Chardonnay". When I order a few ice cubes, John laughs and lifts a warning finger.

"Don't do that in Europe."

"Thanks for the well-meant advice, you elitist one-percenter", I chuckle. "In Europe I drink beer."

We watch the news together. Later John switches back to music. We all agree on a jazz station.

"You know", I say to Margaret. "We had two KIA in Afghanistan today. I heard it on the radio. In the news they hardly bother mentioning that."

Margaret says, "There are too many, I'm afraid. If they wanted to make a background story on every fallen soldier on the evening news..."

Margaret can see that I'm not satisfied with their response.

"You talk like a politician", I say.

Margaret sighs and looks at her husband. "She wants the truth."

John nods. "I think you're right."

"Very well." Margaret puts down her glass. "All governments are the same everywhere. They try to sweep the bad news of war under the rug. Until about a couple of years ago, the media weren't even allowed to show the coffins of the fallen."

"What does that have to do with the evening news? TV stations are corporations. They're not run by the government. And they're certainly allowed to report on war casualties."

"What if they just don't feel like it?" John asks. "TV producers do a lot of research to give their audience just what they want. If they know that people would rather not hear bad news about our wars, then the news shows will act accordingly."

"Exactly", Margaret says. "People like to thank John for his service. But by now they all think we lost the war. It's something they prefer not to think about much. That would explain why the news shows don't dwell too much on the subject."

John nods. "Media coverage is bad for war anyway. Things have been going downhill since Vietnam. It was the first time the general public got to see footage of bad stuff. Little girls running away from a plane that just carpetbombed their village. So what happens these days is excessive flag waving all over the country when the war starts, but if it drags on too long, people turn their back to it."

I take a sip of my fancy white wine.

Margaret is on the same page with her husband. "Instant gratification, that's what people want. If we'd pulled out of Iraq after a couple of months, everyone would've billed this as a victory. But then there was this mission creep into occupation and nation building. It costs money, and more importantly, it costs lives. After a while, most people don't see the benefits of this huge war effort. And they get really sick and tired of it. This is the kind of thing that influences the outcome of elections."

"So you think just because society has changed and the media has changed we can't go to war anymore?" I ask.

Margaret hesitates. "We can always go to war. But it shouldn't last too long. A war shouldn't outlast an election cycle I guess."

John puts his hand up like a school kid. "I'd like to add that some of the more stupid strategic decisions came from people whose primary concern was winning the next election. Remember the stop-loss, Margaret? "

Margaret groans.

"What I'm trying to say here", John says, "if you want to be successful, you need to have the right number of troops, equipment, close air support, everything. But those decisions are taken in DC, far away from the battlefield. And if someone thinks he's going to lose the next election if he sends ten thousand more troops, then it's not gonna happen."

"Oh great." I can't hide my frustration. "So if the military is supposed to do its job well, that means we should simply abolish democracy. That way we no longer have to worry about the war-weariness of the voters."

John laughs. It occurs to me that he has a tendency to laugh about me. This reminds me of David, the other dude who used to find my rants amusing.

"I guess the cheapest wars are those where we just bomb the place from above, and that's it", John says. "We should definitely avoid full-blown invasions. They're just too expensive."

Margaret sighs. "And we could've made some useful investments in our own country with the trillions that we could have saved by not invading."

"No, I don't agree with you." For the first time today I have an original thought. "All the money we spent on the war – just imagine we could've bought a house with a pool for every single Iraqi and Afghan family. With Internet and satellite TV, in order to convince the locals of the advantages of the western world. And within a single generation, they would've become like us."

Margaret laughs. "I like that. You should go into politics. We urgently need people who think outside the box."

"Don't believe her, Marina", John warns me. "In politics, mavericks just get themselves into trouble."

"I think I would be their token Indian", I say and finish my wine. "I don't think it's possible to be taken seriously by these people at all. Politics is still an old boys' club."

"Ouch, that hurts." Margaret smiles. She seems to like my worldview.

I can't help yawning. "I guess I'm a bit tired."

"Yup, you might want to go to sleep now. Tomorrow is going to be exhausting", John says as he gets up to take our glasses into the kitchen.

Margaret giggles. "Tomorrow you'll get a lesson in American history, whether you like it or not."

"Oh God", I moan. "If only I'd stayed in Lapwai..."

The next day is tiring indeed. Lissy and Drew come along on our tour through the history of the War of Independence. It all started in Boston, and Margaret is very proud of that. Interestingly my hosts always want to know my "Indian" point of view. I have to do some very hard thinking. How do I feel about the fact that we kicked the Brits out a couple of hundred years ago?

Margaret doesn't forget to mention that just around here the first war between my ancestors and hers broke out.

"I have to admit the pilgrims didn't exactly behave like the good Christians they were supposed to be", she says ruefully. "This part of our history, no one is really proud of."

"Maybe", I say while we're eating overpriced muffins in a Starbucks. The two girls look at me attentively. "But the oppression that started back then, it never really stopped, you know? It went on and on, only the methods have changed. My grandmother grew up in the fifties. They took her out of her family and sent her to a Catholic boarding school. Trust me, you don't wanna know."

"And what's it like now?" Lissy looks genuinely interested. I must be her first Indian.

I shrug. "Depends on where you are. In Lapwai, for example, we have to fight the pollution of our waterways. Especially by the white farmers. And if you try to argue with them, then they say that we lost the war back then and we should just accept the way they do things."

"That's not quite right, is it?" John asks. "Your leaders were promised some kind of mutually beneficial agreement if they agreed to stop fighting."

"Exactly", I say. "So Chief Joseph signed some contracts, and those agreements were breached by the settlers and the central government. That happened everywhere. The Lakota are still trying to get their Black Hills back. It's probably better not to think too much about it."

Time to change the subject. I'm not sure how to make a transition to a new topic, but I want to because I'm uncomfortable in my role as a representative of Native America.

"What's the purpose of a think tank?" I ask Margaret.

"Oh God, no!" Not only John groans, even Lissy and Drew make faces as if I'd just mentioned something truly disgusting. "Please don't ask Margaret about her work, okay?"

Margaret laughs. "It's complicated, and I'll tell you over wine tonight."

That's fine with me, just as long as I've managed ι conversation away from Indian issues, especially King Phι. That war ended with the head of the Indian chief on a pike, admired by Margaret's and John's forefathers while it was rotι away for a couple of decades.

In the afternoon we visit the balcony from which the Declaration of Independence was first read. I take pictures for the folks back home. I wonder if I should send some to David as well. Once we get home we order Chinese food and decide to watch a movie. The girls disappear into their rooms while John searches an online video store for something suitable. We agree on the third Twilight movie. It's more than awesome. There are quite a few fight scenes. The girl in the center of all this has a complicated love triangle going on. To my surprise, real Indians are playing real Indians. They wear some strange body make-up, but it doesn't matter. Somehow the film is a good continuation of what we talked about today, and I go to bed with a feeling of satisfaction and harmony. For the first time in months I sleep through the whole night.

The next morning John takes me to a shooting range outside the city limits. I'm no competition for him. I wish I could practice more. The AR-15 is almost indistinguishable from my M4. But to spend a thousand dollars on an assault rifle wouldn't really make sense. If I was really paranoid and worried about the safety of my family, a small handgun would be quite sufficient for self-defense.

"I really enjoyed that", I say after we've fired our last shots. We clear our weapons and get ready to leave. "I was in a war zone for years and I never had to use my weapon. I always wondered what it's like."

I haven't really asked John anything. But he still hears the implied question.

"I used it more than once. The M4, I mean." John leads the way to the armory. "Once I shot off the face of a very young man."

ok at him in the hope that he's going to elaborate. We walk side
side, and I enjoy the last moments of feeling the weight of the
ıfle in my hands.

John continues: "It was, as I said, a very young man. No idea if he
was eighteen yet. I'm not saying that I'd feel guilty if he was
underage. He had his AK at the ready. It was either him or me. But I
can still see it. His face before the shot, and his face afterwards."

"Can you live with that?" I ask softly.

John nods. "Of course. But that doesn't mean that I tell others about
it. I don't believe in all this psychobabble bullshit we're getting these
days. You know, the people who think that you have to talk about
stuff like that again and again."

I'm not sure who is right - John or the shrinks he seems to despise,
but I'm glad he told me.

"That was great", I say to John as we turn in the guns. "Thank you."

"I would've liked to try the USP Heckler & Koch with you, but we
have to go back. Margaret wants to take you to Harvard after lunch."

He settles our bill at the exit. We make our way to the parking lot.

"Why are we going to Harvard?" I ask. "Is that where she got her
degree?"

My question seems to be somewhat unpleasant for John. He
fumbles for the car keys in his pocket. I'm waiting at the passenger
door.

"I'm afraid she has plans for you", John mutters as if he'd suddenly
found himself in a very awkward situation. We climb in and buckle
up.

"Plans?" I'm very curious now.

We pull out of the parking lot. John keeps his eyes on the road.
When we stop at a traffic light, he looks at me and says: "Marina, I
don't know how to say this. But Margaret is not going to let go of

this. Of you, I mean. We can't pretend that nothing happened. A she feels very strongly about this whole thing."

I'm confused. We had a good time so far. Margaret and I get along just fine. We couldn't be more different. She has two children, it's her second marriage, she's incredibly well educated and has a complicated job. And yet we were on the same page all the time. So what is there to let go of and what does she feel strongly about?

John sees how clueless I am. "This is what Margaret thinks: if it wasn't for you, I would've come home in a casket. And I think she's right."

"Yes, but if I hadn't been there at the time, someone else would have taken care of you", I say.

"True", says John. "But it was you and not someone else. And you did everything right. That's a fact. Margaret won't let you disappear out of our lives."

"What's she planning to do for me?" I ask.

"I think she'll suggest something in the field of education. Something that you otherwise couldn't afford."

John is not really enjoying this whole thing. I guess this is our first awkward moment since I came to Boston.

"John, you don't owe me anything at all. Neither you nor your family. It's called first aid. You would have done the same thing for me."

"I know, I know", John says. We pass a school bus and then we change lanes. The next exit leads to downtown Boston.

John signals to the right. "So I have to ask you a favor. I want you to go along with whatever she's come up with. It's extremely important to her. Believe me, she won't let this go. Redheads are so stubborn, and I honestly don't feel like going through a marital crisis in the near future. Do you think you could do that for me?"

He shoots me a quick glance while we turn right.

I feel blindsided. I keep my mouth shut until we're in the garage and John turns off the engine. I remain seated.

John is obviously waiting for some kind of acknowledgement, so I say: "Captain."

John groans. These last few days I always addressed him by his first name.

"Look. I don't need a rich sponsor to encourage me. Or empower me. Or whatever. I know your wife means well. But I don't need access to the privileges of our elites. I'm doing fine. If the Air Force kicks me out, my Dad will hire me right back."

John wants to argue, but he doesn't get a word in. "I'm not a little Indian girl who's got nothing to eat and who needs your generous support. Do you understand that?"

John's face has turned bright red. He's holding the steering wheel firmly with both hands. It's getting uncomfortably warm inside the car. I'd like to get out.

"I like both of you, and you have great kids. I came to Boston to scream at you, and instead I totally enjoyed the time I spent with you and your family. But we're going separate ways again, and I'm sure I can succeed in life. Without your help."

I think I made myself clear. I grasp the door handle because I want to get out. But one look at John tells me we're not done yet. He continues to look straight ahead. His profile suddenly looks hard. He still has his hands on the steering wheel and turns his face towards me. I see nothing but determination. John is in Commanding Officer mode.

"And yet, you're going to accept Margaret's offer", he hisses. "It's either that or I'll keep all the data."

And here we go again. I have no idea what the Captain is talking about. Maybe I am not the brightest crayon in the box.

"What data?" I ask.

"The data we pulled off the tablet and the smartphone." At last John lets go of the steering wheel. He puts his hands in his lap and looks at me, his cheeks blushing in a shade that I would label 'superangryred'. "Before I gave the devices to the MPs. Did you never wonder why I handed over the stuff only twenty-four hours later? What do you think I did in the meantime?"

At lunch I try to enjoy a T-bone steak while my thoughts are racing and doing some unpleasant loops and jumps inside my head. I'm glad Lissy is not around because she'd certainly turn up her nose seeing us stuff ourselves with dead animals. That would make me even more nervous. John is unusually silent and his cheeks are still a nice shade of red. I don't have any doubt that Margaret can feel the tension. She asks me about my education. I try to focus on my host and tell her that between my time as a mechanic and my new beginning as an agent, I attended a no-name college in California to get a degree in Arabic.

"That must have been so difficult. I only had Latin."

I tell Margaret about my private teachers from Morocco, Egypt and Iraq. I also mention that I almost gave up at some point. And that I'll never be as good as a native speaker. And that I only half understood the directions I got from the boy I met in the streets of Baghdad. It's not that I'm trying to downplay my skills, but I don't feel like I deserve anyone's admiration.

It doesn't work. The more I tell her about myself, the more Margaret is in awe of my out-of-this-world brilliance. We take off for Cambridge after lunch and take a guided tour of Harvard with a bunch of British tourists.

"It's always fun to behave like I'm not from around here", Margaret says cheerfully.

I try to pull myself together and listen to the tour guide. It's not easy because I keep thinking of the gift that John has for me. If I can see what was on Saad's (or Marvin's) smartphone, this opens up boundless possibilities. I can find out about Saad's contacts. His home address. Perhaps the names of his family members. And then I can find out if they went to Germany or not. And Khassem will appear somewhere in there. It might be a phone number or an email address. I could pay him a visit in Scotland and ask him if he's gay.

"I didn't know that was funny", Margaret says.

"Sorry. I wasn't listening. I just thought of something funny."

Margaret, my future benefactor, gives me a warm smile. I feel like pointing out the fact that she's not my mother. I do think I can take care of myself.

"That's okay, Marina. As long as we've got something to laugh about... Life is serious enough I guess."

In the evening I announce that I have to go home. My parents have started nagging.

Margaret understands. "But you have to come back at the latest at Thanksgiving. I won't take no for an answer. I'll introduce you to my whole family."

"Oh great", I moan. "You want to celebrate Thanksgiving with me? You're going to make me feel like Pocahontas."

In the morning John hands me a hard disk.

We're in the hallway. John's hand is on the doorknob, but he hesitates. I make no attempt to reach for my suitcase. I can't go yet. I have a question that needs to be answered.

"John. Why didn't you do what I asked you for? I'm not mad anymore, but I'd like to know."

John's eyes are as hard as yesterday when we were arguing in his car.

"It's very simple. I wanted them to hunt down these criminals. No one has the right to imprison you. I think it's very noble of you that you were actually worried about this scum and how they might end up getting tortured or whatever. But I want revenge. An eye for an eye, a tooth for a tooth."

"I'm sorry, John. I shouldn't have run away."

John takes my head in his hands and comes as close to me as never before. He kisses my forehead, and we keep standing together in the hallway for a long time.

HOW TO SEDUCE AN NCO IN 213 EASY STEPS

On the ground floor I get my car keys from the reception. For some reason John has made sure that the porter parks my car in front of the building. I thank the guy and give him five bucks, and I don't tell him that he should have left my car alone. I don't like the idea of other people behind the steering wheel of My Car Imported From Europe. The porter is beaming at me in what seems to be a state of total bliss as he hands me the keys. He wishes me a good trip and winks at me as I say goodbye. I'm afraid he may have taken a pill too many.

I walk through the revolving door and see a man casually leaning against the driver's door of the Polo.

He's wearing an eye patch, and I run out of air.

I let go of the suitcase handle.

There's white noise in my ears.

David catches me and pushes me against the car in an effort to stabilize me.

"Breathe, Marina! Come on!" He has to hold on to me, otherwise I would just slide to the ground. I focus on my breathing.

The noise disappears, but the dizziness remains. David somehow manages to drag me around the car. He opens the passenger door while an elderly lady with a dog is watching us. She seems to consider whether she should call 911. David manages to push me into the passenger seat. Then he closes the door.

I press a button to let down the window. The fresh morning air is the only thing that keeps me alive. The woman with the dog keeps watching us while David is stowing my suitcase away.

Eventually he makes himself comfortable on the driver's seat. He leans over to buckle me up.

"Marina, you're green in the face", he says. "That green looks good on you."

It's important to take long, deep breaths. The last thing I want to do today is throw up in my own car. David hasn't started the engine yet. He seems to wait for me to get better first.

"Asshole", I say eventually.

"Love you too, babe", is David's answer.

I'm too weak to slap him. I also would need more space to beat him up. I close my eyes and take a rest. I need to recover from David's sudden appearance.

We listen to the radio for a while. The woman with the dog has moved on. The chatter between the songs starts annoying me, so I turn off the radio and instead listen to the noise of city traffic that passes through my open window, ignoring David as if I was alone. Eventually he starts the engine and pulls into the rush hour traffic. I leave the window open until we hit the freeway. The silence in the car bothers me. I have absolutely no nerve to start some polite chitchat now, so I switch the radio back on. My driver doesn't seem to mind. He just keeps driving.

The sky keeps getting darker on our trip west. Heavy raindrops land on the windshield. I decide to make the most of my situation and adjust my seat. I make myself comfortable with my eyes closed, realizing that having a chauffeur is not that bad.

Late in the afternoon we eat lunch at a gas station. I'm sitting on a red bench and watch David biting into his burger. My stomach is contracting and hurts, a familiar feeling that I know from my time with Khassem and Saad. I only ordered fries, but I struggle. Even this small portion is almost too much. I'm too tense to eat. I wonder if I'm starting to develop an eating disorder.

"It's great to be stateside again", David says between bites. He points to my plate.

"If you don't eat up, I'm going to stuff those fries into your mouth."

"Are you threatening me now?"

David nods. "You have to eat more. I'm not into skinny girls. There's nothing sexy about a woman without curves."

I shake my head in disgust. Men only think about sex. I hope that at least Captain John Gillespie saw something other in me than a mere sex object.

"I'm getting a medal, I think", I say abruptly. "I kept someone alive while the bullets were flying. Keeping calm under duress and all that."

David grins. "I know. I got a Purple Heart. For standing in the wrong place during the mortar attack. Not quite as heroic as you."

"The stupid thing is, I still don't really remember exactly what happened. The whole day's been erased from my memory. It drives me crazy."

I try to finish the fries. I can't imagine that David would cram them down my throat. He likes me too much for that.

"It will come back sometime", David says. "The memory isn't deleted, it's just buried deep down. You're just traumatized."

"No I'm not", I disagree. "I don't have PTSD. Just some sleep issues."

David shrugs. "Good for you. I had panic attacks at the beginning. They came out of nowhere. Never found out what triggered them. It's just like the incoming that always came out of nowhere."

I imagine David shopping for groceries. He's standing at the cash register and suddenly suffers an anxiety attack. As he's quietly freaking out, unable to move, a woman behind him accidentally pushes her cart into his ankles. David takes off in panic and runs out of the store, leaving his groceries behind. After that he's too afraid to go back. From that day on he does his shopping in another supermarket.

As always, whenever I think of David's suffering, I'm drowning in compassion. I'd like to reach across the table and stroke his hair. David eats his lunch, unaware of my overflowing feelings of sympathy. After that he bullies me into sharing a slice of cherry pie with him.

I get right back into the passenger seat. I want to doze away with my full stomach. David's cozy style of driving gets me even more tired. Before I fall asleep I have to ask him something.

"David, did the panic attacks stop?"

David laughs. "Yes and no", he says as we take the ramp to I-480.

"What's that supposed to mean?" I'm trying to pick a CD and realize that I don't know David's taste in music. We were together for a night and a day only, definitely not enough time to get to know each other. I opt for "Best of Justin Timberlake."

On the highway we finally go a bit faster.

"So this thing with the panic attacks." David is looking straight ahead. "I had the whole thing under control pretty soon. I knew what kind of situations I should avoid in order to have peace of mind. And I was able to get off the meds. It was all good."

It starts raining again. I turn the volume down so I won't miss out of anything that David is saying.

"So it's all good?" I repeat.

"Well", he says. "As I said, I was doing fine, and then I made the mistake to track you down in Spang."

"What, and then the panic attacks came back?"

"No, of course not. We hooked up in Heidelberg and everything was great. And I thought to myself that I would get in touch after your return from Baghdad. And all that."

I'd like him to elaborate on his future plans and what role I should play in it. I think I know what David is going to say next.

"Then I sent you an email from time to time but there was no response. After a couple of months, I made some inquiries. Your boss in Spang told me what happened."

I close my eyes again. "Let me guess: You thought I was dead, you got scared again."

"It was a bit more complex", David mutters. I turn off the music. "No one knew what happened to you. That was driving me nuts. I don't even wanna know how your family and your friends were able to deal with that."

He keeps his eyes on the road. The windscreen wipers are making squeaking sounds. I'll need to replace them.

"I imagined the most horrible things. My head was like a fucking prison. I tried not to think of you. So I was fighting myself all the time. I thought I was going to lose my mind."

"Let's just forget about it", I suggest. "We could just pretend I had a totally normal deployment, without any abnormal incident."

"You can't be serious", he laughs.

"Yes, I am. I told my story a hundred times already. In Iraq, in Lapwai, at Quantico. In Boston. That's enough speech therapy for me. It's over. I need to move on, you know."

Even as I'm saying this, I realize that I'm not really honest to David. If I had really closed the Baghdad chapter, I wouldn't carry the hard drive in my suitcase. I would have asked John to delete the data.

"Marina, you don't have to tell me everything today. I can wait a few more days. Okay?"

David looks at me quizzically.

"Watch the road", I say. "Yeah, I guess someday I'll tell you everything. Now I have to take a well-deserved nap."

We make our first stopover late in the evening, in a small town in Ohio. David has chosen a hotel with a swimming pool in the basement. It's not a cheap place, but he doesn't want to tell me the price for a room, so I presume he's footing the bill.

"The basin is at least thirty feet long", he explains to me while he's pulling my rolling suitcase into the room. He throws his gym bag on the bed and starts rummaging for his trunks.

"You want to go swimming now?" I ask.

"Sure, I spent the whole day in your miniature car, and I need to move my limbs."

As soon as David leaves I slip under the covers, unshowered und without having even brushed my teeth. The bed is large, the air conditioner hums softly. I fall asleep almost immediately.

I don't hear David coming back. I see him coming out of the bathroom the next morning. I sit up yawning. He has the towel wrapped around the waist and is brushing her teeth. I recognize the burn marks from the time we spent in Mannheim. Nothing will change. He will have to live with his injuries until the day he dies. The eye patch will always accompany him, as will the prosthesis. Every morning when he dresses, he will be reminded of the mortar attack in Kandahar.

"What?" David looks grumpy today. "Are you pitying me again?"

"Not at all", I lie and jump out of bed.

We don't bother with an expensive breakfast at the hotel and get back on the road. I'm at the wheel and try to annoy David by demonstrating what the Polo is capable of. I have to stop after ten minutes because David's face takes on an overly unhealthy color.

"The shade looks good on you. It's kind of yellowish", I say as I take my foot off the gas and the speedo needle goes down to seventy.

"Yellow? Not green?" David asks, sounding a bit weak.

"Green at about eighty, but when I floored it, your face was getting more yellowish."

"I see."

We listen to the radio for a while. The sun comes out. In the afternoon we are in the flight path of a regional airport, and David is looking out the side window. He watches a small Boeing on its final approach.

"Why are we driving all the way to Lapwai?" he asks.

I grin. "Why the hell not?"

"We're crossing a continent, Marina. Just saying. We'd be about ten times faster if we went by plane."

"I have time", I say. "What about you?"

"Eleven days", sighs David. "Three of which are already gone."

We drive through an industrial area and see the airport disappear behind us. I pull over and unbuckle. David looks surprised when I lean over to him and press a very gentle kiss on his closed mouth. I support myself with one hand on the handbrake and tenderly bite his bottom lip.

"Ouch", says David.

"Stop whining", I say sternly. "Tonight at the hotel you're going to have to endure much more."

David laughs. "Oh yeah? Maybe I've got a headache tonight and won't be able to perform."

I let my teeth graze his upper lip for a change. It's his own fault if he doesn't open his mouth. "You don't have to do anything at all, David. You just lie on the bed and don't worry about anything at all."

I put on my seat belt and get going. I also turn up the music before David can begin a discussion about whether, how and why we should be sexually active again. I'm aware of the fact that he is insecure about his appearance, his disabilities and maybe some other things. It's better not to talk about it.

The last time we had sex, he was relaxed because we'd previously spent an exciting night in the forests of the Neckar valley. But even then it occurred to me that he was hiding his wounded leg under the blanket. When he put on the prosthesis he put on long slacks and socks so that his artificial foot was not to be seen.

Last night he was probably alone in the swimming pool because it was almost midnight. It's pretty obvious that he wants to protect himself from other people's curiosity. Whenever we go out to eat together, he tends to choose a corner table or at least a table next to a wall instead of in the middle of the restaurant. His injuries are not new, but I'm under the impression that he can't live with them very well.

I have also noticed that we've been together for over twenty-four hours now. So far there has been no attempt from his side to touch me. Maybe David needs a little time to warm up to me again.

Tonight's the night, I think, trying to encourage myself.

If all else fails, I'll fill you up with booze until you're too drunk to be inhibited.

While I'm driving at almost-legal speed, I have to tell David about Quantico. I mention the two pieces of evidence I tried to make disappear. David is stunned.

"How old are you, Marina? Twenty-eight, right?" He shakes his head in disbelief. "You can't be that naive."

I prefer to keep my mouth shut. My own stupidity has been bothering me for a long time, but what am I supposed to do about it? As long as there is no drug that can make my IQ skyrocket, I guess I'll have to live with my idiocy. Maybe I should get used to the idea that I will always be a victim of incredibly poor judgment. I haven't even told him about my eventful flight back to Lapwai. Not yet. Because when I do, David is going to lose it.

"You're just too crazy. You can completely forget about your career. You'll never get any kind of leadership position. Because they can't trust you." He keeps shaking his head.

"And besides, you keep committing this mortal sin for someone who's in the military: you break rules, with full intent. It's almost like you feel magically drawn to everything that's prohibited. I noticed that in Bagram."

I overtake a truck. David has finally stopped shaking his head. "You're a fucking trouble magnet. There are reasons why I called you a punk back then."

As I struggle not to fall asleep behind the wheel, I take a decision. It's not necessary to tell David about my surprisingly early landing in Lewiston. I don't need to tell him that I was supposed to spend a few days at Quantico first. And that I broke the nose of a federal agent. And I don't really need to report all the other events that made my flight home so memorable.

"Where are we staying tonight?" I ask in an attempt to change the subject.

"Lemme see", David mutters and studies his cell phone. "Lincoln, Nebraska would be good."

He chooses a hotel and reserves a room. I wonder if he will once again pay the bill.

"Why don't we stay in motels?" David doesn't look up. He's still studying his smartphone. "I mean, to save time."

"I don't like motels."

It's that simple. We can only do things that David likes. I hope he still likes sex or else we're in trouble. I feel the urge to touch the little hairs on his left arm. It would be nice to move my fingers up and down his strong arm. There's a sexy song by Marvin Gaye on the radio, in sync with my erotic thoughts. I let my imagination do what it wants for a while, but I concentrate on the rush-hour traffic at the same time. In the end I come up with a plan: we'll go for a run first. David will find a decent jogging route on his phone. The run will relax him. And then we'll take a shower. There I will relax him even more.

"What are you thinking right now?" he asks. "Must be something very nice."

I laugh. "Maybe I'm just thinking of your belly button. That's what I like best."

David actually blushes.

I keep my mouth shut until we get to Lincoln, Nebraska.

The hotel is located downtown in a quiet side street. We drop off the luggage in our room, and I reluctantly accompany David to a fancy restaurant where the food is served with candied walnuts, wild artichokes and other complicated things. It tastes great, but I would have preferred eating a quick sandwich at the hotel bar - due to time constraints. I'm still planning to seduce him tonight. The excellent dinner fills up our bellies. There is a danger that we might just be too lazy for sex by the time we get back.

I refuse dessert and watch David slowly drinking his espresso.

"Why do they serve Norwegian salmon here? That's a fish you can still catch in our rivers", I say.

David shrugs.

"You know what?" I feel like bitching about this restaurant that is stealing our valuable time. "It's probably salmon from around here, and they pretend it's from Norway."

David doesn't even notice I'm trying to provoke him. As always he pays the bill.

"Ever since you picked me up in Boston, I didn't spend a cent of my own money", I say as we leave the restaurant and step into the cool evening air.

I'd like to go for a run. "Did you bring some PT gear?"

David shakes his head. "Just the swim trunks. I didn't want to pack too much, but now I regret it. It would be great to get some kind of workout after I've been sitting on my ass all day."

I take a good look at his butt. "Well, I must say, your ass looks like it's in perfect shape. No need to worry."

David ignores my remark. I think I'm making him nervous. I wonder if I'll manage to get him going tonight.

Back at the hotel, David disappears into the bathroom. I have no desire to humiliate myself by waiting for him in bed.

The hotel has a small gym. I work out like crazy for half an hour in the hope that David doesn't fall asleep while watching TV. In Denver he always went to sleep immediately to prevent me from starting something. If he uses this trick here I won't be able to do much about it.

David is in the hot tub when I enter the bathroom. I take off my sweaty workout clothes and join him. He has dimmed down the lights. It's almost as romantic as candlelight. David smiles at me and doesn't look tense at all, so we just chill in the warm bubbles. We've done enough talking today.

The hot water makes me tired. I decide to wait for him in bed.

It doesn't take long until David comes out of the bathroom, dressed in an old T-shirt and boxer shorts. He smells good.

"Did you use a body lotion?" I ask, trying to sound very casual.

"Who is Tim Rodriguez?"

I feel like asking him to get into bed. But it's better not to pressure him. David has an ultra short haircut. He looks sharp and a bit dangerous.

"Who?" I ask.

"I found his letter", says David. "I was going through your stuff when you were at the gym."

I close my eyes. For days I've hardly ever thought of Tim's suicide note. I didn't even know his last name was Rodriguez. So far I have not taken the trouble to read his letter. I was just too busy enjoying my new freedom in Lapwai, visiting Boston, and then with my transcontinental car trip in the company of my beloved. There simply was no place for Tim in my thoughts.

"I suppose it's a very sad story", David continues. "But you're going to tell me, right?"

I nod. "Honestly, I didn't dare to read the letter. Not yet. I don't seem to have the courage it takes."

David gets into bed. He waits. He folds his arms behind his head and looks at the ceiling. I find the light switch and dim the light. We're sitting next to each other in semi-darkness, and I start telling him about Tim and Dan. First the Bagram love triangle, then the reunion with Dan in the helo. Finally I get to the part where Dan tells me about Tim's suicide.

At first David laughs about the fun stuff I did at Bagram. I wonder how much about it he already knew back then. And how much spying he did himself. By the time I talk about my last conversation with Dan in the jet, his face turns more serious.

"Marina, you should just read the damn letter", he finally says.

"I really don't feel like it", I reply. "I want to be happy with you. Right here, right now. By the way, it's not okay to go through my stuff. That's not how you build trust in a relationship."

David laughs. "Where did you get that from? Oprah? I didn't even know we had a relationship."

"Of course we have a relationship", I say, not bothering to conceal my frustration. "You've spent several hundred dollars on me these last few days. Plus the flight from Europe. And you're investing your annual leave in driving me across the country as if you had nothing else to do."

David rearranges the pillows behind his back. "I think I should just read you the letter, then it's done."

I argue for a while, but David wins in the end. He reads me the note and holds me for a long time after that. Now and then he hands me a fresh tissue.

In the early hours of the morning we go to sleep.

Salt Lake City is beautiful. The mountain range looks a little like the Hindu Kush. Which reminds me of Tim's letter, so I have to suppress that thought immediately. I'm trying to persuade David that this time I'm the one paying the hotel bill, but he laughs at me. He claims that the bill has already been debited from his credit card, which I find hard to believe. But I don't feel like arguing.

We manage to go for a run after David purchased running shoes. We jog through Liberty Park at dusk, two young, dynamic, active service members. A good-looking couple. A match made in heaven. I'm so happy to be with David I have to stop myself from giggling during our run. As we enter the hotel lobby drenched in sweat, I realize that we've been running across town for almost two hours. We eat sandwiches in our room, and after the shower go straight to bed and just pass out.

I wake up from the cold night air coming in through the open window. I get up to close it and feel some of the muscles in my legs.

I don't manage to fall asleep after that. Eventually, I get up and brush my teeth because I don't know what else to do.

I slip back under the covers. From the window there is a little light coming in. I can see that David isn't sleeping either. He's lying on his back with his arms crossed behind his head. I gently pull the blanket away and kiss his belly button. No response.

I straddle him and pull the top of my pajama off. David doesn't seem to be in a hurry to touch me. I gently pull his arms out under his head, stretching them wide. My hands squeeze his wrists against the mattress while I lower myself down slowly and kiss his neck. This is going to take a bit longer. Better not to rush things. I make myself comfortable on him, stretching out my legs and pressing my hips gently against his. I kiss his shoulder. His collarbone. Then I move back up to his neck.

David seems to like what I'm doing. I can feel him against my pubic bone. His breath seems to be heavier. I kiss his hair. It's still a little damp from the shower. The question is whether now is the right moment to go for his mouth.

Before I can decide on where to kiss him next, David takes over. Suddenly he shakes my hands off his arms, presses one of his legs against my pelvis and throws me on the back. He starts kissing me. Now his breathing is really heavy.

"Marina", he gasps. "You still have no hand-to-hand combat skills."

I think of Dan and Johnson and how I got them under my control.

"Don't worry about me", I say generously with both my hands on his butt. It feels too good to ever let him go again. David keeps gently pushing against me while we're making out. We're almost too breathless to take off our underwear. Finally we are naked and free and together.

We get up too late and leave Salt Lake City much later than planned. I call home to tell my parents that we won't be in Lapwai before tomorrow. My mother's disappointment is unmistakable. I start feeling guilty again. After what they've been through, they're simply entitled to be with me every day. I have absolutely no right to make them wait any longer.

I let David drive. I read the letter in the hope that it's less depressing at daytime. But Tim's reasoning is as brutal as a punch in the face. It would have been disastrous if Tim's father had read this letter out loud at the funeral.

I feel the urge to call Dan and to comfort him somehow, but I have no idea how I can reach him. After lunch I take the wheel. As usual I can't always respect the speed limit and David has to talk me into slowing down. He takes over on the last stretch. I take out my flashlight and read Tim's letter for the second time.

This is what I want on my headstone: he spent too much time in Afghanistan.

They say Afghanistan's future is of grave importance to America.

No, it's not.

They say that this is where we will either win or lose the war on terror.

That's a lie.

They say that failed states like Afghanistan are a safe haven for terrorists.

No, that's Pakistan. That's the enemy we should be fighting.

Instead we've been throwing money at people who despise us. We nurture and protect drug lords, warlords, rapists. My brothers risked their lives driving criminals around, training recruits who were high as a kite, and pulling security for meetings of government officials whose sole reason for being is to take bribes from organized crime.

The Afghans hate us. Did you know that?

You will say they have their reasons. Sure as fuck they do.

They have religious reasons for torturing dogs. They have cultural reasons for finding themselves eight-year old sex partners. Historical reasons for being illiterate. Geographical reasons for rampant drug use. Some other reasons for running as soon as we get into a firefight.

Reasons, reasons, reasons.

I wanted to be badass, hanging out of helicopters and going on night raids. I wanted to capture high value targets. What I got instead: dropping off clueless goat herders at the kind of facilities they wouldn't leave alive, facilitating drug deals, providing the spooks with targets they could send their drones into.

You want to know who's responsible for a dozen dead civilians at a wedding in Herat? Me. Just doing my job. Maybe one of the wedding guests was a terrorist plotting to blow up the White House. I guess we'll never know.

You don't know abject poverty unless you've seen the countryside of Afghanistan. People live here the way their forefathers did two thousand years ago. Even Jesus Christ would be amazed by how little people need to survive. We met a family who had lost their entire livestock and two babies after a cold winter. We gave them some cash because we simply felt sorry for them. These survival artists would deserve a government that works for them. Instead, our tax dollars are going straight into the pockets of thugs posing as politicians. Let's raise our glasses to another thousand years of misery, paid for and supported by NATO and all the other do-gooders.

We all left girlfriends and wives behind in the States. We left our families and friends and a life of comfort because we wanted to do something worthy. The moment you put on a uniform, you become part of something bigger. We signed up for this, all of us.

After more than a decade of service to my country, I know that I sacrificed my youth for an idea cooked up in DC, West Point, or Tampa. I don't care if it's called GWOT or COIN as long as we're getting results: protecting America from her enemies.

Well, you all know how that turned out.

It's time for me to go. Forgive me.

"Jesus Christ", I whisper.

David sighs. "Yup."

I carefully put the letter back in my wallet.

"You know, it's weird that he would write his name on the other side of the paper. It's not like he actually signed the letter."

David agrees with me. "There's something else that's strange about this. I'm not an expert on suicide notes, obviously. I don't know what kind of stuff people write before they put an end to their lives. But he's giving political reasons for his death. That's just weird."

I need to think about this for a while. We cruise along the freeway at a very boring speed. Sometimes I miss the Autobahn.

David says: "People kill themselves because they have PTSD. Nightmares. Or a traumatic brain injury. They can't live with the fact that they lost someone in their unit to an IED. That kind of thing. But this guy says that everything we did over there was wrong. It's not that I don't understand him. It's just weird for a suicide note."

I take out the letter again. The flashlight illuminates Tim's last words. I read it again.

"You're right, David. It doesn't sound like he's saying farewell to his loved ones. It sounds more like he wanted this to be published somewhere."

This time we spend the night in a motel. We drink whiskey in bed. It's the first time we're drinking alcohol together since Denzel's barbeque in Denver.

"David, what was Denzel's real name again?"

David chuckles. "Michael."

"Right."

The booze makes me feel so tired that I lie down and pull the cover over my head. David switches off the light after he's finished his drink. We start making out again. But we had too much whisky. Before I know it, David is snoring into my ear, and I catch myself thinking that even his snoring is kind of adorable.

I wake up at dawn. David must be standing outside. I can hear him yell at someone. I jump out of bed and open the door.

He's standing on the parking lot, screaming obscenities into his phone. I look closer and notice it's actually my phone he's using, not that I mind. I just wonder who he's yelling at.

"She was scared, and she freaked. She had no reason to trust you fuckers. There was nothing reassuring about the way you picked her up at the FOB. She had every reason in the world to be terrified."

He paces back and forth like a lion in a cage while he listens to whoever the other person is. I don't think I've ever seen him that angry.

"Gimme a fucking break. You just tried to take revenge. There's no fucking tactical thinking on your side. You just wanted to get back at her, you son of a bitch."

The other person gets a word in or two, and then David explodes again. "She's smarter than you and your retarded co-worker. She's more determined. She's faster. She knocked both of you out, and you know why? Because you underestimated her. I don't feel sorry for you idiots. You're just average, Dan. Fuck you and your operator friends. As soon as you feel superior, you start underestimating the enemy. I hope your career is over, asshole."

He gets off the phone and storms past me into the room. He takes my wallet out of my travel bag. He holds Tim's letter in his hand and says: "Your ex is alive and well. He didn't kill himself, Marina."

I sit down on an old armchair. "What?"

David is holding on to the piece of paper while he's pacing up and down. He's way too agitated to talk. It's safe to say that if Dan was here, David would be beating the crap out of him right now.

"You called Dan and asked him about Tim? Is that it? And then he told you Tim didn't go through with killing himself?"

"No", David yells. "Tim Rodriguez never had the slightest intention to end his life. This", he waves the letter in my face, "this is a draft suicide note from that fruitcake you like so much. Dan Navalny, the guy who likes to mess with people's heads."

I'm speechless.

David picks up the wallet from our unmade bed and puts the letter back in. He sits down.

"Are you okay?" I ask.

David buries his head in his hands. He looks vulnerable. He also looks like he'd rather be back in Mannheim right now.

"I called that dickhead in the middle of the night because I knew there was something fishy about that suicide note. It was piss-easy to find out his number, by the way. So I asked him, and he admitted that your operator friend Tim lives in Georgia with his girlfriend and their baby, and he's fine."

I feel a wave of relief crashing down on me, and I can't help smiling.

"David, don't be mad at me, but this is great news."

"Sweetie, I'm not mad at you. I'm mad at your insane stalker, the guy who had no reason in the world to come pick you up in Baghdad. He walked straight back into your life and then he tried to fuck you up. Unbelievable. Not only he lied to you. He never came back to you to tell you the truth."

"I still don't understand what exactly happened. Where did that note come from?"

David gets up. "I don't give a shit, Marina. If I ever meet him, I'm gonna fucking kill him. He's a psychopath, that's what he is."

He locks himself up in the bathroom. I can hear him brush his teeth. Then he gets in the shower. My phone is lying on a crumpled pillow. I walk over to the bed and pick it up. I dial the last number that David used, and as I hear Dan's voice, I lie down.

"What", he says. "Is there anything else I can do for you?"

He thinks it's David calling him again. "Dan, it's me. Can you tell me what's going on?"

Silence.

"Dan?"

Dan sighs. "Hi. Nice to hear your voice again. I'm sorry, okay? What do you want me to say. I was mad at you. You behaved like a fucking lunatic on that jet. You made me and Johnson look like complete idiots. Yeah, so I was mad, and I took revenge."

"Okay", is all I can say for the moment.

"This note I gave you is something I've been carrying around for a while. I'm the one who wrote it. I was fucked up when I came back from my last deployment, and things just got worse and worse stateside. So I was playing with the thought, you know? But I didn't put an end to my life. You know why?"

I cover myself with the blanket, holding the phone to my ear and hoping for a solid explanation. This better be good.

"One day I looked up the meds they gave me so that I can sleep. One of the side effects is suicidal thoughts. Awesome. Then I had an idea. I looked up everything else I'd been swallowing for the last ten years. For instance the pills against malaria, the ones that give you nightmares during your deployment. Turns out they don't just drive you crazy, they can cause permanent damage to your mental health. Psychosis. Depression. Violent behavior against others and yourself. That kind of thing. For the rest of your life, if you're unlucky."

I remember the vivid dreams I had at Bagram. Not all of them were nightmares, but they were stronger and weirder than anything I'd ever dreamed before.

"So that's what happened. I found out that it was the meds that made me miserable. I stopped taking them, I stopped seeing doctors and shrinks and therapists. I went sailing with my brother. I helped my dad renovate his house. I got better. I got a new job."

It sounds like a happy ending, but Dan doesn't sound happy.

"I kept that draft suicide note, though. To remind myself of how close I was to the brink. To make sure I'd never forget to question everything that's considered 'normal' or 'reasonable'. You can't sleep, you get a prescription for Ambien. You go to Afghanistan, you take Mefloquine. Everybody does it, so it's gotta be okay, right?"

He sounds angry.

"Dan, if you're so mad, you should've beaten up your doctors."

"I'm sorry. I was just really pissed off at you. It was a last-minute idea. Tim's name was on my letter because I wanted him to get it. So when we were on our way to Idaho and you asked me about him, I decided to tell you he was dead. It's stupid, in hindsight. I know. What am I supposed to say?"

The water in the bathroom stops running. David has finished his shower.

"Jesus, Dan. It was almost three months ago. You could've called me. All you had to do was tell me about the lie and that's it."

David unlocks the door and walks through the room with a towel wrapped around his waist. I wonder if an *Infidel* ink would look good on him.

"To be honest, Marina, I'm still mad at you. Our destination was DC, not Lewiston. You should spend the rest of your life in jail for what you did."

Technically, he's right. But I don't care.

"I was in love with Tim. And after he was gone, I missed him. You had no right to do that to me."

"Yeah well, we're even. I wish you well. Just try not to cross my path in this lifetime."

He hangs up on me.

My parents and my grandmother are more than happy to see me again. I don't make a big fuss out of taking David into my bedroom. I'm old enough. David employs his old East Coast Sunny Boy routine to wrap everyone around his finger. He even charms Jesse into taking us on a trail ride. I don't trust horses. I hate sitting on something that moves and has its own free will. After a three-hour ordeal, I hop off my horse and secretly vow to never, ever do this again.

Grandma teaches David a few sentences in Nimipuu and shrieks with joy when he gets it all wrong. He makes the mistake of asking if there's a barber in Lewiston. After a vivid discussion, he ends up getting his hair cut by Mum while Grandma stands next to her to make sure she does it right. Basically everyone is competing for David's attention. But for some reason unknown to me, they never manage to say anything embarrassing. Even Dad, who's an expert in weird remarks, doesn't provide us with any awkward moments. I would hate it if they asked David what his intentions are and whether his future plans involve me in any way.

David and I don't talk about the future. We just enjoy the time we have left.

I drive him to Seattle, where we spend another night in a hotel. I try not to cry at the airport, and I almost succeed.

We stay in touch.

I get summoned to Texas. I get a new assignment in Arizona.

Life goes on.

One day I get an email from Kyle. He's heard of my miraculous return to the free world and sends me a number where I can reach him.

I call him, and he's genuinely pleased to hear from me.

"Bitch, where've you been? Can you try to stay out of trouble in the future? I didn't even know you went AWOL in Iraq. Robert told me one day that you went missing and then you came back. Did they turn you like in *Homeland*?"

"No, they didn't turn me, and by the way, I didn't go AWOL. It was a bit more complicated than that."

I try to explain my Baghdad experience in not too many words. I leave out most of the crazy stuff, but I don't forget to mention the hard disk I have with Saad's (or Marvin's) personal data. If there's anyone who can help me, it's Kyle.

Kyle cuts me off right away.

"Do me a favor, honey, don't talk about this on the phone. Come see me in San Francisco and bring the thing you just mentioned."

I spend a wonderful Labor Day weekend in San Francisco. Kyle and I have a lot of catching up to do. He works for a small tech company and drives an electric car. He tells me that Robert has found the love of his life and lives in New Jersey with his wife and their offspring.

"They're very productive", Kyle says. "Last time I checked, they had three kids and another one on the way."

We look at Saad's data. Text messages from his phone, emails, personal messages via social networks, but no credit card information. I'd read everything as soon as I had the time to go through the files, but none of the information will help me find out where he lives now. If he's still alive.

Kyle tries to help me, but his expertise doesn't make a big difference. It's easy to read the data. The problem is getting the intel behind the data.

"First of all, you need to realize that our government had experts going through all this as soon as they got hold of the tablet and the phone. All the friends and relatives you can find here have most certainly been identified. And questioned. Unlike you, the guys who were trying to hunt him down were able to do their research in Baghdad. I guess it's safe to say you'll never see that place again."

"Right." We're sitting on the terrace of a vegan restaurant, surrounded by skinny people in expensive clothes. "Not that I would want to go back there. On the other hand, it would be an interesting experience."

Kyle laughs. "I admire you. I think I'm your greatest fan. Cause you're crazy. San Francisco is your kinda town. You should move here after you left the Feds."

"No, why? It's perfectly okay to be crazy in Idaho. Or anywhere else, for that matter."

"I guess Denver would be nice, too", Kyle says. "And then you and Rohrman can get hitched and start the perfect biracial family."

We don't talk for a while, just enjoying the sunset and the relaxed atmosphere created by people who don't have to work on weekends.

"Do you think they found him?" Kyle asks.

"Frankly, I don't know but somehow I can imagine he was smart enough to change his name. He's a very intelligent dude. You can't imagine the English he spoke. It was unbelievable. My guess is he managed to get out of Iraq with his family. I don't think he'd be stupid enough to immigrate to Europe under the name of Marvin Abadi."

Kyle orders a raspberry sorbet for me without asking. He gets something that's orange and looks too sophisticated to actually taste good. I let the sorbet melt on my tongue. It's delicious. If I ever invited friends over, I would serve them this kind of dessert. I start imagining the dinner parties I would throw in Denver in my new life as Ms Rohrman, but Kyle interrupts my thoughts.

"Where does an Arab who never left his country learn to speak perfect English?"

"He was in Ireland as an exchange student."

Kyle finishes his dessert. He lets his gaze wander to the very desirable waitress who is serving the customers at the table next to ours.

"Interesting", he muses. "We didn't find any foreign friends or contacts of any kind, did we? There wasn't anything Irish there. Not as far as I can remember."

"True", I say. "He was there during a soccer world cup year. I could look it up, but my guess is that it was several years before I met him. I think that he didn't really keep in touch with the people he met in Ireland."

The cute waitress disappears inside the restaurant. I wonder if Kyle has a girlfriend in the City Of Love. Before I can ask him about his love life, he gets up to use the bathroom.

I pour myself some more of the overpriced mineral water. It sparkles in the evening sun. I wonder what refugees do when they get to Europe. They have to find people who can help them, give them advice on what to do, where to go to get housing and jobs. In Saad's case, presuming they made it to Germany, that would mean he and his family tried to find other expats from Iraq. But would they even want to socialize with Muslims? Wouldn't they prefer to find other Assyrians? Or maybe Coptic Egyptians. They might simply knock on the door of the nearest church and try to find like-minded people there.

Kyle comes back. As he sits down, he asks: "When you were debriefed in Quantico, did you tell them about this Ireland thing?"

I try to remember. It was more than a year ago.

"No", I finally say. "Definitely not. It just never came up."

Kyle grins. "You know what that means, right? You know something that the FBI or whoever is looking for him doesn't know."

I shrug. "That's great, but even if we find someone in Ireland who knew him back then, it doesn't mean we'll find out where he is now. If he made it out of the country, I'm sure he and his family went to Germany."

Kyle sighs. "Okay."

He plays with his empty glass and observes the waitress. "Yeah but look. He didn't stay in touch with the people he met in Ireland because he thought he'd never see them again. But if he managed to escape to Europe... Why wouldn't he rekindle old friendships? Go see some old acquaintances. Remember how Robert and I were travelling through all of Europe? Flying was cheap. They called people like us the *EasyJet Trash*."

"Cork. He was in Cork. I would need to find out which college he was in, who else was there."

"Exactly!" Kyle looks excited all of a sudden. "You see, that's the difference between you and whoever else tried to find him. You have the same data on that hard disk, but unlike the others, you know what to look for. If there's really no person from Ireland in his contacts, maybe you should have a look at his browsing history."

As if this wasn't good enough, Kyle manages to have a chat with the waitress while I go to the bathroom, and he succeeds in getting her digits.

"What an incredibly successful evening", I say as I close the door of Kyle's futuristic car.

"That's you, baby", Kyle says as he switches on the car. "You brought me luck. I should keep you right here by my side."

But I have to get back to work. I try not to rush things. Before I dive back into the data ocean that Saad has left behind, I make a list of things I want to find out, of presumptions connected with Saad's time in Ireland, and of options that may have been explored by others before me.

I don't find any traces of Saad's Irish acquaintances among his contacts. It's a huge setback at first, and it takes a while until I start going through his bookmarks and his browsing history. I find the college he went to while he was in Cork. And I find a church he seems to like.

It's not much. I decide to use an ancient technique of communication, in the hope that I can find a human being who might want to help me. I use the phone. I call up the church that Saad is likely to have gone to, and I call the college he must have been enrolled in. I talk to quite a few secretaries, a priest and a very cheerful nun. Nobody remembers Marvin Abadi.

Christmas comes and goes. I call Kyle to let him know of my failures. He tells me to try harder. He's still dating his waitress and has celebrated Hanukah with her family. I feel like a born loser. I'm doing great at my job, but there's no one in my life that I would want to introduce to my family. David doesn't count, he's a fixture in my life, but I won't see him again before April, when he gets redeployed. I can't wait for him to get back stateside, but I'm not sure I'm his official girlfriend.

I spend too much time on the Internet. I find a book that might be interesting. It's about the long history of Christians living in Arab countries. Before I click the "buy" button, I read some reviews written by customers who bought the book. They're mostly positive. One review is more critical than others. It's written by someone who identifies himself as Murad. He describes his childhood in Iraq as a lost paradise. He criticizes the fact that the author of the book forgets to mention that the US President spoke of a crusade at the beginning of the Iraq war. And he blames the Americans for the hate and persecution that Iraqi Christians had to deal with ever since.

I click on the other reviews this guy has written. He dismisses Tom Clancy novels as "American hate propaganda" and deplores the ignorance of the West. Just as I'm about to decide to leave the page with Murad's reviews, I come across a comment he wrote about a book on vintage BMWs: "My father had a BMW that he drove until it fell to pieces. The car had to deal with potholes in the streets of Baghdad, it survived sandstorms and mechanics who didn't treat it with the respect it deserved. It was practically indestructible. If my father had known back then that one day it would be seen as a vintage car, he would have taken it to Europe with him."

My heart is pounding in my chest.

I click on Murad's profile. There's a picture of a young man wearing Ray-Bans, standing in front of a Gothic church. He's slim and he has black hair. The profile doesn't say much. He studies engineering at an institution called HTW. He likes cars and all the latest music trends.

I google HTW. It stands for "Hochschule für Technik und Wirtschaft", those are technical colleges. I find one in Berlin, in Munich, in Dresden. Other cities too. They all have a lot of old churches. At three AM, I find the church that Murad used as a background for his profile picture.

I call David. He doesn't pick up on his landline. It's noon in Germany. I call him on his cell. He doesn't take the call.

I spend a sleepless night thinking of SaadMarvinMurad. I keep looking at his picture. He smiles. He's wearing a bright orange T-shirt. He looks happy.

My phone vibrates. It's David.

"Hey babe. You have trouble sleeping?"

I laugh. "Yeah, definitely. I'm wide awake. D'you want to know why?"

"Yes, please. I've got a lunch break of twenty minutes."

"I found him, David. I found Saad."

Silence.

"He lives in a town called Saarbrücken. It's not that far from Mannheim."

"Are you sure?" David sounds very calm. "How did you find him?"

I try to trace back the steps I made on the Internet, but my excitement gets in the way. David spends his lunch break trying to calm me down. He promises to call me after work.

"We'll figure something out, Marina. Together. You're not going to do anything right now, okay? Promise?"

I promise.

It takes a couple of months until I manage to get ten days off work. In the meantime, David finds out Murad's last name and his whereabouts. Apparently he graduated recently and is now a Peugeot employee, which is a bit ironic if you dream of BMWs. We drive to Saarbrücken in pouring rain, and I try to test the limits of his truck.

"What do you need a truck for in Germany?" I complain.

"If you keep criticizing the consumer choices I make, I'm not going to marry you, that's for sure", David mumbles in response while checking his phone.

"What makes you think I want you? You're an engineer. That's boring. I want a pilot. Pilots are cool."

We check into a vacation home, a one-bedroom apartment in a quiet suburb. Spring has come, and if it wasn't raining, the air would be filled with the scent of blossoms and flowers. We go for a run in one of the many forests that are surrounding the city. We spend a very romantic night whispering sweet things to each other.

Before we can confront the enemy, we need to agree on our strategy. I made it clear from the start that I won't hand over Murad to the authorities. He's clearly off to a fresh start, and it's very unlikely that he will lock up other people in his basement in the future. If he gets caught, it's not only his life that's ruined, but also the happiness of his family. They went through some really hard times together. I don't know what his family is like, but my guess is they deserve to live together in peace.

"Then why go there at all?" David asked when we discussed this on the phone for the first time, David calling me from an Internet café in Mannheim in the hope that nobody was listening in, and me using a public phone in Sierra Vista. "Murad's going to have a heart attack when you show up. Maybe he's going to panic, and run away, and get hit by a truck."

I giggled. "That's wishful thinking on your part. I don't think he's going to panic. I just need to talk to him one last time. And I want to know what happened to Khassem."

David wasn't happy at all. "It feels wrong, you know? We didn't notify anyone. What we're doing is not just unofficial. We can't even carry here. If he attacks us, I can't even pull a gun. If anything happens, we're going to have a hard time explaining this to Hernandez or anyone else."

"David, everything you say is right", I answered. "But notifying anyone of Murad's whereabouts would be so wrong. I don't care what Gillespie says about this eye-for-an-eye shit. Taking this kind of revenge would make me miserable. I don't want to be miserable."

And that settled it. Now we're sitting at the kitchen table of our vacation home. Our running gear is in the washing machine, including our muddy sneakers, and the rain is splattering against the kitchen window.

"We could get hold of him on his way to work. Either when he gets out of the house or when he arrives at Peugeot", David suggests.

"Yeah, let's do this at the earliest opportunity. The moment he comes out of his house, we step up to him."

David nods. "Good. Get this over with. Go home. Forget this whole thing and move on."

I wonder if he's really planning to marry me. He should have asked me first. I wouldn't say no. Every time we meet, my heart beats so fast I feel like a teenager who has a huge crush on someone. But I'm too old to have a crush on David. This must be the real thing.

"Are you worried?" he asks.

"Yes. Every time I think of Saad — erm, I mean Murad, well, I get this heavy feeling in my stomach. Last time I felt like this, I was in second grade and I was scared of being bullied by the bigger kids."

"Well, you've got me now. I'm going to protect you."

David finishes his coffee and gets up. The washing machine is integrated in the kitchen, and he stands in front of it, watching our PT gear spinning around. I look at his strong back.

I wish I could discern the precise moment when our relationship turned serious. It may have been after our Heidelberg adventure, when we were lying in bed imagining what our offspring would be like. But I'm not sure he was serious back then. He knew my deployment date, and he'd made sure that we would only meet three days before I boarded my plane to Iraq. He wasted precious time; probably because he still couldn't make up his mind whether he liked me or not.

It's our road trip to Idaho that really brought us together. The way he held me in his arms when I was inconsolable about Tim. And the way he charmed my family. He was irresistible in Lapwai. Everyone he met asked him to come back some day.

"David, did you send me that email at Bagram?"

David is still waiting for the laundry to finish. He turns around.

"What email?"

"The *slow the fuck down*-email", I say.

"Oh, that. Yeah, I'm afraid that was me."

Out comes the Sunny Boy Grin. He turns around and tries to open the hatch of the washing machine, but it's still blocked.

"That was totally immature", I say. "You know that, right? And you knew it back then. Turn around, David."

He obeys. He's stopped grinning.

"Marina, I wanted to protect you at Bagram. And you were doing all the things that were dangerous. Getting involved in a rape case. Threatening a soldier. Spending entire nights in some dude's B-hut. That was reckless, and I was seriously worried about your personal safety."

"You could have talked to me."

"True", David admits. "The problem was, I also had this thing for you, so I tried to keep as much distance as possible. But I'm seven years older now. I guess these days I would handle this situation differently."

The laundry is done. We distribute it onto the heaters and turn them up. The apartment starts smelling of detergent. It's the first time we have a household together, and we turn our evening into perfect domestic bliss by watching a Game of Thrones episode in German synchronisation. Daenerys frees the slaves in an unusually girly voice.

Saad's neighborhood is not very nice. The buildings are a mixture of old and new, most of them about five stories high with no elevators. Satellite dishes of all sizes are scattered all over balconies. Some people use the extra space of the balconies to keep all kinds of stuff there. The building we're looking for has a green façade, the lower part of which is turning dark grey from the exhausts of traffic. There's a lot of cars and tramways because the road is the main shopping street of this part of town. I looked it up; on the Internet they call this neighborhood a "traditional working class district".

The names at the entrance are mostly foreign; it seems that the German population has moved away. Maybe the local working class lives in the quieter side streets. I feel like ringing Saad's bell. Or I could wait for someone to come out of the building, and then storm in, taking two stairs at a time, and knock on his apartment door. But I don't think David would let me. He shows me Saad's family name next to his doorbell, then he pulls me towards the car. We have parked it just a few yards away from the entrance.

People are on their way to work. Children are on their way to school. There's a tramway stop in the middle of the road. The trams are modern and I read somewhere that they go all the way to France.

I want to talk about something just to ease the tension. We don't know how long we're going to have to wait. David has done some recon two weeks ago. He noticed that Saad doesn't always leave the house at the same time. Sometimes he leaves as early as seven, sometimes he comes out much later. We presume that his entire family lives there. David has been inside the building and believes that the apartment has at least two bedrooms.

The door opens. Crazy fear rushes through my veins. A teenager comes out and crosses the street to the tram stop.

It takes a while until my blood pressure comes down.

I can't think of anything to talk about. David is always quiet in the morning; he doesn't really come alive before lunchtime. I know quite a few things about my future husband. I feel like asking him if we can have our honeymoon in Paris, but this isn't the right time.

The door opens again. A young woman is cautiously leaving the building on crutches while someone inside is holding the door open for her. She stops on the pavement and waits for Saad, who is carrying her backpack. The door closes behind them as Saad opens the passenger door of his car. He takes the girl's crutches and helps her into the car.

We don't speak. David turns the key in the ignition.

Saad throws the girl's bag into the back of the car and gets in. Our engine is running. I look at David's profile as he is trying to see past the van that's parked between us and Saad. It's blocking the view, and David almost misses the moment that Saad's vehicle pulls into the street.

We follow them to a school, where the woman gets out, again helped by Saad. He gently helps her shoulder the backpack. Now that I have more time to look at her face, I'm pretty sure she's his sister.

She walks into the schoolyard.

"Marina". David is whispering. There's no need to whisper in the car.

I know we should get out now. I watch Saad get back into the car and pull out of the parking lot. He drives away.

We sit there for a while.

"I'm sorry." I smile at David. "I just don't feel like talking to the fucker."

"No need to apologize. We agreed right from the beginning that it's your call. I'm just pulling security."

I sigh. "I've been preparing myself mentally for two months now. But whenever I was visualizing Saad coming out of the building, I thought he would be alone."

"That must be his sister. Did he ever mention a sister?"

I shake my head.

"So what do we do now? I'm awaiting your orders."

"Can we break into his apartment?"

David laughs. "No. We don't have the tools. And, more importantly, we don't know who else is in there. My guess is that his parents live there too."

"You think they might be home?"

David shrugs. "Let's find out. This whole thing isn't going according to plan anyway. Why am I not surprised?"

We park the car at the exact same spot as before.

"So what now?" David wants to know. "We ring the bell, and if someone lets us in, we just walk in?"

"Yup. It's as simple as it gets."

"Fine. You do the talking. I pull security."

"You're repeating yourself", I giggle as David locks the car. I let him ring the bell.

Two seconds later, we hear the door buzz. I push it open, and now I'm taking two steps at a time. I know it's the apartment on the top floor, on the left side. The hallway hasn't been painted in a long time, but it's not dirty. I see a man standing in the door of the apartment, and I instinctively take David's hand. We walk towards the man hand in hand.

He must be Saad's father. His hair is grey, the face is not the same, but his eyes remind me of Saad, except that there's no Cold Fish Stare. Instead, Mr. Al-Bayati looks friendly and curious and absolutely open-minded.

Before I can even say "Hi", he waves us into his living room. We sit down on a large red IKEA sofa, and Al-Bayati disappears in the kitchen. There are two bookshelves and a mid-sized flatscreen. Many small frames are hanging on the wall behind us, displaying pictures of what must be family members, some of them black and white, some Polaroids, and some seem to be printouts of digital images. The other walls are bare.

The floor throughout the apartment is old and wooden; it creaks underneath the steps of Al-Bayati as he walks in with two mugs filled with black tea.

No Arab drinks tea like that. It seems that this family is trying to assimilate to their new surroundings.

We get up and introduce ourselves. Actually, it's David who is doing the talking. I'm a bit overwhelmed at the moment.

Al-Bayati smiles. "My English is horrible. *Aber mein Deutsch ist sehr gut.*"

I answer in Arabic. I suggest we speak his mother language, and if need be, I'll translate for David.

He nods and we sit down with the mugs in our hand.

Al-Bayati makes himself comfortable in an armchair.

"I know who you are", he says to me. I translate this for David, who doesn't look too surprised. I decide that I'm going to translate every single word of our conversation.

"I'm the reason why you're free", he continues. "My son wanted to kill you, but after you spoke to him in his language, he was confused. He ran to the clinic where I was working, and he told me about you. He said that he wasn't able to kill you, and that it would be better to sell you. I made him understand that we're not barbarians who sell other human beings. I made him get his act together."

Al-Bayati looks as if he still couldn't believe his son wanted to sell me. He shakes his head while I'm translating for David.

"How did you get out of the country?" I ask.

Al-Bayati laughs. "That was simple. I exchanged the house that my grandfather built for four passports with brand new names. You see, Iraq is a very corrupt place. And there's a bureaucrat in Baghdad now who owns a nice house in the Adel neighborhood."

He doesn't sound bitter.

David says: "Ask him why they never turned you in to the authorities."

Al-Bayati keeps smiling. "Until Marvin came running to me for advice, I didn't know you were still his prisoner. But we were in the middle of our very illegal passport deal, and the last thing we needed was the attention of the Americans. So I told him to wait."

I take a sip of my tea. It's much too strong and tastes bitter. Al-Bayati is not drinking anything, just sitting there with his hands in his lap and the same friendly look on his face.

"The car bomb almost killed him. I got him out of the hospital and he stayed with a relative until he got better and we got the passports. It was unbelievable when the plane touched down in Frankfurt. I wanted to kiss the ground like the Pope always used to do."

"And did you?" I ask.

"No", he laughs. "No such luck. We walked through a gateway. I really would have liked to kiss the tarmac."

"Where's your wife?"

"At work. She's learning to be a nurse because her medical degree is not sufficient here. It's hard because she's still struggling with the German language. But she will be a great nurse."

I don't have any doubts about that. This family is obviously doing okay.

"Do you know where Khassem is?"

Al-Bayati's smile freezes. It disappears completely as he clears his throat.

"He was going to Scotland with his family. But they never arrived there. We have been trying to find out what happened. But nobody heard from them after they left Baghdad."

I translate for David. He shrugs.

"I don't care about this dude and his family", he says, and I'm sure that Al-Bayati understands this much English.

"Thank you for inviting us in", I say and finish my tea. It tastes better now that I get to the sugary part. I put the mug on the coffee table and get up. David does the same.

Al-Bayati gets up too.

So what now? Shake hands? Hug? We stand there and stare at each other.

Finally, David puts his hand on my shoulder and says to Al-Bayati: "Thank you for the tea. All the best for you and your family."

Saad's father smiles and watches us leave.

We find a different forest for our run. In the evening, David cooks a great paleo meal. We ruin the health effects of the food by drinking beer afterwards.

"How did he graduate so fast?" I ask after we've binge-watched more GoT. "I should've asked his dad, but I forgot. I just wanted to get out of there."

"Yeah, I noticed that. We were in there for like, two minutes." David switches off the TV. "There's some English-language courses here. Maybe he was able to pass his tests in English."

"He's off to a nice start, right?" I yawn. "A diploma in engineering from a German university. Not bad. I wonder what his sister does. Damn. I should've asked his dad."

"We can go back there tomorrow", David suggests. "Or we ask Murad. Or we talk to his sister."

"Definitely not", I say. "I don't want to see any of those people ever again. Not even his mum, even though her cooking was excellent. I think I'm done here."

"Case closed", David says. "That's great. Let's do some more sightseeing tomorrow. Pretend we're tourists. And then go back home."

I watch him stretch his limbs. We've been watching way too much TV lately.

"David, do you remember how you pinned me against the wall at Bagram?"

"Jesus. You're ruining a perfect evening, Marina." David's grimacing as if he'd just bitten into a lemon. "I get disgusted with myself whenever I think of that. But I almost managed to forget about it. It was ages ago. Why d'you have to bring it up?"

"Don't know. It's just weird to think we were enemies and now..."

Now we're what? That's the question hanging in the air.

David shakes his head. "We were never enemies. I was in charge of you and I had no idea how to handle you. I hope I'm better at managing my people now."

"Your underlings", I say.

"My minions."

I'd like to know more about his work, but David changes the subject by starting a fight on the sofa. I'm still no good at MMA. I end up lying underneath him because of my lack of skills. And because he's stronger. And because I like it when he crushes me. The little noises he makes will be ingrained in my memory forever, even if we never get married and never have a honeymoon in Paris.

You have to live for the moment.

You have to be happy now.

"I love you", I whisper.

"I love you too, Marina. You have to promise me one thing, though." David's blue eyes are boring into mine.

"What's that?" I don't feel too confident about making promises and keeping them, too.

"You just stay out of trouble in the future. That's all I'm asking for."

I don't know, I think. *I guess I could try.*

THE END

If you'd like to know whether Marina is able to keep her promise, you'll have to read "Queen of Estonia".

58134429R00187

Made in the USA
Lexington, KY
03 December 2016